ALSO BY KAT & STONE BASTION

THE TRAVELER: Initiate Years
Veil of Realms · Secrets of Alexandria · Panther Rising
Stones of Power · Highland Magick

Highland Legends Series
Forged in Dreams and Magick · Bound by Wish and Mistletoe
Born of Mist and Legend · Found in Flame and Moonlight

Unbreakable Series
Heartbreaker · Rule Breaker · Lawbreaker
Forthcoming: *Ball Breaker · Icebreaker*

No Weddings Series
No Weddings · One Funeral
Two Bar Mitzvahs · Three Christmases
For Valentine's

Standalone Novels · Novelettes · Collections
Brand New Year · The Espionage Effect
Braving Soteria: The Quantanauts Collection

Romantic Poetry for Charity
Utterly Loved

AWARDS & PRAISE FOR KAT BASTION

Forged in Dreams and Magick

First Place – Unpublished Beacon Award
Best Paranormal Romance

First Place – Hold Me, Thrill Me Award
Best Paranormal Romance

Chosen by FreshFiction.com as their
Fresh Pick for October 22, 2013

"A beautifully woven tale about love, choices, courage
and destiny, *Forged in Dreams and Magick* is one of the
best time-traveling novels. Fans of Gabaldon's *Outlander*
will love it."

— *BOOKISH TEMPTATIONS*

"I was gripping my iPad like a crazy woman and fanning
myself from the smoldering romance. Lawdy!"

— *THE FLIRTY READER*

"Bastion's debut is pure perfection, a combination of
romance, magic, emotion, adventure and surprising
twists and turns. This is a truly unique romance that
should not be missed!"

— *THEBOOKQUEEN*

"HOLY HELL!!! I am so… um… wow! FABULOUSNESS. *Forged in Dreams and Magick* definitely makes my BEST OF list for 2013…"

— *THAT'S WHAT I'M TALKING ABOUT*

"A story guaranteed to enthrall with lushly detailed travels into times long gone by. Woven with love, passion, magic and legend, the story had me hooked from the very first chapter."

— *READ-LOVE-BLOG*

"Kat Bastion's wonderful debut brings a new voice to the fore. Her voice is strong and unhesitating, very human and real, sometimes young and delicious in her treatment of intimacy and relationship development."

— *FANGS WANDS & FAIRYDUST*

"OMG, Bastion hits all cylinders in this supernatural tale. The layers in the book were fascinating, and I devoured the fun, adventuresome read."

— *LITERATI LITERATURE LOVERS*

Bound by Wish and Mistletoe

"I LOVED it! *Bound by Wish and Mistletoe* is, to my mind, a perfect entry in the historical / paranormal fiction genre and has quite a bit to offer."

— *FAB FANTASY FICTION*

"Kat Bastion has done it again! … Excellent holiday novella, perfect for a cup of cocoa and snuggling under a blanket in front of the fireplace this holiday season."

— THAT'S WHAT I'M TALKING ABOUT

"Move over, Julia Quinn and Sabrina Jeffries! Kat Bastion is an absolutely gifted author and deserves to be recognized for her talent."

— LOVESHISTORICAL BOOK REVIEWS

"*Heartbreaker* is a phenomenal story."

"I loved it…wonderfully compelling, a story that touched my heart in so many ways and characters I will remember for a long time to come."

No Weddings and
THE NO WEDDINGS SERIES

"One of the best romantic comedies of the year!"

"The No Weddings series is one of the best I have read that follows one couple. Cade and Hannah are both lovable characters, the storyline is real and entertaining, and the banter is fun and witty."

"I loved it, and I mean REALLY loved it!"

"This is an exceptional series… You find yourself fully engrossed in their world and can't put the book down."

"The No Weddings series has a group of such amazing characters; you can't help but relate to them and feel the emotion in every situation they encounter. It has been a long time since a story has made me feel that way let alone an entire series!"

"The story of Cade & Hannah's relationship is realistic, heart-warming, and filled with real-world connections that shook me in a way that few titles I've read this year have managed...I have loved every minute of the No Weddings series."

BORN OF MIST AND LEGEND

BORN OF MIST AND LEGEND

KAT BASTION

First Publication, April 2020

First Printing, March 2021

ISBN: 9780998232997

❦ Created with Vellum

To the different, perfect just the way we are . . .

CHAPTER 1

*T*he very fabric of time...*shifted*.

Skorpius arrived during that split second in Earth-realm when all that had happened, everything which currently was, and infinite events preordained to pass began a monumental cascade of restructuring.

From the shadowy coolness of an ancient forest, the powerful angel arched his black wings and drew in a slow breath as he concentrated on identifying the destructive anomaly.

The timeline-quake rippled forth on a subatomic level, detectable to only a rare few: those uniquely attuned to elemental forces. As the curious disturbance rumbled on, hair-line cracks shattered outward through the ether, a bending and bucking that began to liquefy the foundation of the manifested world.

And an ever-increasing energy pulsed from its epicenter.

Faster than the blink of a human eye, he materialized his sword and burst into a haze of light and speed as he ghosted through old-growth trees in his path.

His blade—made of bluish otherworldly metal and forged

from the imaginings of his winged race—arced around and regained full solid form as he arrived at ground zero. But at the last instant, he jerked up, just shy of delivering a deadly blow.

"Brigid?" he mouthed the female's name as recognition struck. A person he knew, barely, by association.

A mere mortal.

Impossible.

A flinty gaze stared up at him from pale gray eyes. That sparked silver—*with magick.*

Then the physical world *stretched.* Instead of the startling human standing her ground scant inches from the edge of his sword, she flashed into nothingness, then back into existence hundreds of yards away, bow in hand, arrow nocked back.

An instant later, her loosed arrow raced through the air. Tendrils of mist curled in its wake, carved by a goose-feather fletching. The faint whistle of its flight hushed the birdsong of a pending dawn.

The arrow's iron tip came within a hairsbreadth of piercing the pupil of his eye before he shifted into fine mist once again. But a chilling draft of molecules brushed over his senses as they fogged through his being.

Hot fury pulsed through his veins as his cells surged back into solid form.

The female narrowed those silvery eyes. "*Doona* follow me!" she bit out on a whisper. A slight breeze lifted the outer ringlets of her long copper hair—that glinted, from no apparent light source. Her very essence charged, unable to contain all the magnificent energy she embodied.

"*Not* following." The preternatural bass of his voice vibrated the dense forest floor. *Hunting,* he silently corrected as he dematerialized his sword. No need for bloodshed. *Yet.*

With his own flash, he vanished, then reappeared inches away, towering over the tall female.

Her cool gaze tracked along the upper curve of a wing as he

arched them over his shoulders. Every feather ruffled, taut in irritation.

Unafraid, the reckless female lifted her chin, hardened her jaw, and huffed out a low snort. An unforgiving expression blasted his way. *Liar!* Her thought, charged with aggression, echoed toward him on the mental plane.

"*Not* by choice," he growled in retort.

Obligation, he further reasoned to himself. Mandated by some sudden potential cataclysm. Because nothing else explained why *superhuman* powers emanated from her, and why he'd blinked onto the scene the moment they had.

And why *wasn't I briefed on the situation?* Even when dire, there'd always been time.

With an indignant snort, his aggressor whirled around, then stalked away. She disappeared through a leafy curtain of saplings. And the power signature she'd been blasting moments ago dimmed to a faint echo.

Toward his left, a slight rustling of scrub announced someone's clumsy entrance before a second, more familiar, female arrived. Familiar, but just as irritating.

In generous respect, he dipped a curt nod toward Isobel. "*Traveler.*" The prophesied Traveler, a recent immortal, originated from the twenty-first century, when she'd been human; but through the time travel that had transformed her, had since developed roots and a home nearly a millennium prior, in medieval Scotland.

"*Sunshine*," she mimicked, attempting his deeper tone. The corners of her lips twitched, exposing her self-amusement as she reveled in a favorite derogatory nickname for him.

Not in a mood to indulge in humor, he ignored the jibe.

Of greater import? Time had begun to waver.

After a brief systems check, he consulted his inborn chronometer to verify the time and place he had materialized into rang true, that the two females remained in their common-home time by the human Julian Calendar. They did: the Scottish Highlands, 1297 CE, the twenty-fifth of August. Then he catalogued the energy signatures of their surroundings, because if he hadn't been officially assigned the task at hand—and the unorthodox lack of intel suggested as much—some other elemental force had compelled his presence.

"What brings you to our neck of the woods?" Isobel's gaze tracked a yellow-and-black swallowtail butterfly as it flitted nearby on an air current.

Good question. "Business. You?"

"Same."

Interesting. "You're not here because of Brigid?" He stared off into a dark void between the trees, the invisible pull at his core growing stronger the farther his quarry traveled.

"I am." She shrugged. "Bridge invited me hunting. But I bailed on having any sporting fun the second I got out here. Something feels...*off.*"

"*Beyond* off." No doubt about it.

"Okay, good. You feel it too." Isobel also glanced toward the direction where her friend had disappeared. Then she pressed the heel of her hand to her chest and rubbed. Her face scrunched, then she frowned with a heavy sigh. "Tell me it's not Brigid."

With narrowed eyes, Skorpius continued to stare into the dark recesses of the forest as he considered the ever-increasing tug to the same area of his chest.

Isobel stared at him.

He remained silent. No point in confirming the obvious.

They both clearly sensed the growing danger.

Two keepers of time—one born of ancient power, the other a fledgling coming into her own—had been summoned to rectify a developing situation.

The fact that he'd had no forewarning, no details of the impending event as per custom, didn't faze him. It invigorated him. Nothing beat the challenge of a mystery, especially after eons of predictability and habit.

A flock of birds erupted into the sky from the tree canopy at the same instant a deeper vibration resonated through the air.

"Holy shit." Isobel blinked, then tore off at a sprint after the source—toward Brigid.

He strode behind at a slower pace, not in any hurry to step into the path of another arrow. "One way to put it." In the modern vernacular Isobel clung tightly to. "Definitely more and more interesting." The source-power from the epicenter had magnified. And generated infinitesimal rifts in time. Again.

A sunny wide clearing opened up, and Isobel slowed as she approached Brigid who stood at the far end. Beyond them toward the west—across a rocky chasm and another swath of verdant forest—stretched Brodie Castle's one-of-a-kind curtain wall, its corners anchored with magick stones quarried from Skorpius's world. Faint sounds of swordplay carried on the wind, into preternatural ears able to hear far beyond the capabilities of any human.

Skorpius eased into the dark shadows that fueled his unique magick, maintaining a greater distance from his apparent target and her nascent time-bending powers. He needed to test Brigid's sensing ability while he masked his presence.

By the wild gesticulating and animated postures, it appeared the two females were engaged in heated conversation, expressions tense, breaths shortened. But Brigid failed to react to his distant presence.

And the threatening power surge? Had faded to a low hum. *For now.*

With his obscured vantage point, and the distraction between the two of them, he'd gained the space to observe. He took rapid mental note of everything, the mundane and special. Including that neither wore the period's feminine daytime garb of flowing dresses in muted colors. Instead, the two wore custom-made animal hides—that didn't hide a thing. Coming from rebel Isobel, the discrepancy didn't surprise him. But the scandalous outfit on Brigid, one born into the clan's ruling family? Noteworthy.

Then again, of the handful of times that he'd visited to monitor Isobel's progress, he'd never noticed Brigid doing any normal female task. He didn't recall noticing much about her at all.

"I'm noticing now," he murmured.

As if to punctuate her defiance, Brigid paced away from Isobel, nocked another arrow and aimed midstride, drew back, then released. Before the arrow sank into the truck of a slender tree, she rapidly loosed a second arrow. Then a third. The tip of each subsequent arrow shaved bits of feather from the prior one's fletching before piercing the bark in tight formation.

Well done. Brigid exhibited skill that nearly defied the laws of physics. And probability.

The imperceptible background noise of swordplay from the castle ceased. And the moment it did, Isobel tilted her head, as if she'd detected the difference. But Brigid also tilted her head, narrowing her eyes to the slightest degree. *Ah, you noticed the change as well.*

Evidence continued to mount: Brigid no longer remained *just* human.

"What have you become, Highlander?" he murmured. "And how. *And…why?"*

The reasons had to be virtuous. Brigid's life depended on it.

Until Skorpius judged the matter, life everywhere *in every time* hung in the balance.

Isobel stepped into the line of fire as Brigid nocked a fourth arrow. Brigid moved to the side a few degrees—like a normal human—then took aim once again. Isobel shook her head, then began to gesticulate at Brigid again.

Skorpius rolled his shoulders and stretched the arches of his wings up as he concentrated on their discussion.

"Regardless of the amazing skill you've shown, Bridge"—Isobel gave a nod toward the impressive display in the tree trunk—"I still disapprove...in every way."

Brigid loosed the arrow, then leveled a heavy stare at Isobel. "You canna speak a word of this to Iain."

Skorpius recalled what he knew of Iain, Isobel's husband, Brigid's brother, and their laird. The man was fair and wise. Committed to the protection his clan. The courageous leader had nearly sacrificed his life once to protect them. Skorpius had every confidence the valiant man would do the same again for them, one and all. For Brigid to want—or need—to hide something from her brother, meant she sought to circumvent all Iain stood for.

"You promised." The expert archer loosed two more arrows. Each sank into its target with the same precision. When Isobel failed to respond, Brigid huffed out a lungful of air and stared off at some point above her archery target. Tension drained from her shoulders and her voice. "You *know* what drives a woman to go to battle for her man."

"That was different," Isobel countered, tone also tempering as she propped her hands on her hips. "I had nothing to lose. And I knew where Iain was. You have no idea where Fingall is. Or if he's...even..."

Brigid shot a hardened stare at Isobel, daring her to speak the worst.

Oh.

Fingall.

The disappeared *Viking.*

Skorpius clenched his jaw. But only for a moment. "Couldn't be helped," he muttered, still unapologetic for his maneuvering act to bring the Traveler forth. When Isobel had come into her own destiny, the timeline had demanded the pivotal action. For her, and for countless others.

Brigid strode toward her target, then yanked out her arrows one by one, every movement filled with quiet aggression. Isobel trailed after. Once the last arrow had been stowed in Brigid's quiver, Isobel placed a gentle hand on her friend's shoulder.

Additional tension eased from Brigid's stance. She angled her face to catch Isobel's gaze. "You doona choose my path, no more than I choose yours." She turned and stared off into the distance once again.

Long seconds of silence followed.

A low hum of energy crackled into the air; Brigid summoned some amount of low-voltage substance from the ether.

"Summer's fadin'," she continued, with near-indecipherable inflection that hinted at deception. "Months have passed, but no one searches for Finn. Iain's done more than abandon the huntin' parties; he refuses to hear even a word from me. I've been needin' to tell him what my dreams showed me, what my wakin' mind couldna see. But Iain? *Och!* He'll hear none of my 'nonsense.'"

"Her dreams," Skorpius murmured. *A vision?*

And what portion of Brigid's plea to her friend rang false, concealed some hidden truth?

More important, *why lie?*

Isobel sighed and shifted around Brigid, then gave her a consoling hug. "Iain has our clan to protect. That includes us. Our borders are becoming more dangerous than ever; he's decided to settle things with our neighbors, one way or another, through treaty or battle. No one can blame him for taking strict protective measures. Not even you. *Especially* not you."

Brigid turned to face his way again and gave Isobel a weak smile before she frowned. "Iain's my brother. You're my friend.

But your loyalty should remain with him as your husband and Laird before all...even before me."

Isobel scoffed and folded her arms. "Fat chance. You're *both* family to me. Have I voiced strong objections? Yeah. But you are your own woman. You're strong. Independent. Capable. And no matter what you do, I will *always* support you."

Brigid's expression brightened a little. "You'll keep my secret, then?"

"I won't lie. But unless Iain directly asks, I'm not your keeper. And he never forbade me to train you in the weaponry of men."

Traveler, you are a handful of trouble for your husband.

To back up the evidence of her weapons training, Isobel turned and, with lightning speed, arced a short sword up toward Brigid's throat.

Brigid materialized twin daggers and thrust them outward to deflect the sneak attack. The piercing screech of blade scoring blade rang out until both weapons slid to a safe resting point. Isobel tipped a respectful nod toward her opponent.

Brigid gave a clipped nod in reply, then stepped back and sheathed her daggers in fluid motion. Then she manifested a short sword of her own.

From where? His eyes narrowed in suspicion as the pair of warrior females parried and thrust, without pause. The hum of slight baseline magick remained, but hadn't flared. And if Brigid had done something surprising to Isobel, the Traveler hadn't made any sign of notice.

Have you learned to mask your ability from your friend?

The energy subtleties Skorpius detected came from innate ability and millennia of experience. But for Brigid to exhibit them, a newcomer to magick? Defied explanation.

Without any ready answers, he observed their actual sword-play. Which was impressive. The females were equally matched. Great skill drove every action.

For the moment, whatever magick Brigid had harnessed earlier, had dissipated back into the ether.

Yet with a brief glance within, Skorpius determined the timeline rift still remained. However, upon further examination, he discovered that something else lay at the heart of the incessant pull tethering him to the human.

Or rather, *two somethings.*

A sudden coolness fogged over his bare back accompanied by the faint scent of vanilla. "Enjoying yourself brother?" teased a low, lyrical voice.

"Hello, Cass." The rare visit from his favorite sister surprised him, but thawed a small part of his icy heart. "Sure. Angel-to-human stakeouts keep me riveted."

"Oh, don't sound so glum. You know it makes me have to work harder to cheer you up." Her pure white feathers brushed against his inky black wing in a nudge of warm affection. Her head tilted a fraction as she gazed out in the same direction, toward the two human females. "Reconnaissance, then."

"Of a sort." He glanced over and cast a brief smile at the composed guardian angel. All beings from his realm adored Cass. The snowy beauty had an arresting charm and unyielding brightness. He arched a brow at her. "What brings you from your guard post? Lose your soul?"

"Hardly." She ruffled her pristine feathers, as if dislodging the ridiculous notion. "I'd been released. My latest wayward soul chose a moral path fairly quickly. Lately, the human race has been embracing hope with only a gentle shove from me. How goes the time-bandit business?"

"You make it sound as if *I'm* stealing time. Humans waste plenty, but their idiocy has nothing to do with my influence."

She leaned in and whispered conspiratorially, "So those two female warriors you're eavesdropping on. They're in some way tied to your mission? Are we gathering intelligence?"

He hedged her question with a more important one. "Cass, have you ever been tethered to a human without orders?"

Pale blond hair shimmered across his shoulder as she cocked her head in thought. The heavy pause got his attention, but he waited for her input. He trusted Cass more than any soul on any plane, besides their brother Orion. Else they would not have been conversing at all.

"No," she finally verified.

And Cass's experience matched the information he'd come to understand in his. He'd never compared notes with another, never asked...never needed to.

"Specific instructions *always* come with human-guardian assignments." Her tone softened. "I know it's been a long time, Skorpius, but surely you remember..."

Remembering had been devastating for so long. And Cass knew the suffering he'd endured. She knew why his heart had iced over.

"I remember." The words came out flattened, devoid of all emotion. Survival had forced him to strip his soul bare. Only one thing remained. *The protocol.* His purpose. The rest no longer mattered. "Something unusual has come to my attention, but I'm getting to the bottom of it." He cast her an unyielding look. "Do not worry over my affairs. I'll solve the mystery soon enough."

"Well, good." Cass straightened to her full height of seven feet, a good half-foot shorter than the rest of angelkind. A great sculptural beauty in appearance, his sister was a deadly warrior, as were they all. Their species had been crafted from the start into hardened perfection.

Skorpius rolled his neck, then stretched his wings overhead with a final glance toward his unusual and unexpected project.

A sheen of perspiration beaded across Brigid's brow as a steady breeze blew her hair back. Bright sunlight illuminated her coppery locks, which appeared to set the very wind on fire.

The incessant dual tug within his chest twanged as he resisted its pull, planned to leave.

But if his suspicion rang true, the aching pain that anchored him to the human would be dull and tolerable. For now. The second connection—the timeline tether that had been triggered by the power-induced quake—had quieted to a low hum as well.

Both directives still remained, however. Clear and strong. Opposite and undeniably vying for his attention.

"Brigid, what are you up to? And *why in the worlds* does it concern me?"

THE MOMENT the angel's fiery energy vanished, Brigid straightened.

"He's departed." Better to focus on the frustration about the unwanted angel than on the uncomfortable guilt from the lie she'd been forced to tell her dear friend and sister. *One wee lie, atop so many half-truths. 'Tis the pilin' up that makes the next all the easier.*

Isobel narrowed bright-green eyes at her, then glanced toward the forest's edge near where the creature had hovered in the shadows, watchin'. "You *feel* Cupcake? The...angel?"

"Aye." There'd been no need to identify "Cupcake" as the angel; they'd talked of him before. But that had been Isobel's tale, of fightin' for Clan Brodie. When the two warriors, Isobel and the angel, had saved her brother Iain. Brigid had never mentioned any personal encounter with the warrior-angel. "But...different, this time."

Isobel blinked at her in surprise. "There've been other times? When? Where?"

"Aye. Everra night, for a fortnight. In my bedchamber. A flash of male *other* energy. But when I awaken, 'tis only air snappin' and cracklin'. The dark angel's no longer there."

Isobel frowned. "He doesn't strike me as the peeping-Tom type." Then her eyes narrowed. "Different *how?*"

Brigid concentrated, but shook her head. "I canna place why." Even so, she made an attempt. "Today, his power burned hot. Sharp-edged. Strong and ancient. Carryin' the scent of a...spice."

"Cinnamon." Isobel nodded. "Cupcake smells like snicker-doodles."

"*Snickerdoodles,*" Brigid repeated, speakin' in slow rhythm as she learned another of her friend's foreign words.

Amusement sparkled in Isobel's eyes. "A sweet cookie. Like a crumbly tart but without fruit." Her expression grew thoughtful, then her brow furrowed. "And the other times?"

No need to think hard to relive them. The cold presence in her bedchamber had flowed forth in an unclear haze, like milky fog at gloamin'. A metallic flavor rolled over her tongue. The power churned heavily of raw emotion: anger.

But only one word made it past tight lips on a hoarse whisper. "*Terrifyin'.*"

CHAPTER 2

"*R*idiculous." Skorpius folded his arms and focused more intently on the animated map.

Beside him, Orion ruffled his white wings and canted his head. "Unprecedented."

Two brothers, insomuch as any could be of angelkind, stood side by side within the cool iridescent mist of the archives, deep within the heart of their world. The domain of angels existed in a vast utopian realm beyond the material world of Earth, yet right alongside it; only a thin veil shimmered between. Humans had named the angelic realm Heaven. His brethren called it home.

Every other *angel did, anyway.*

For the last half dozen centuries or so, Skorpius crashed there. Sometimes.

Recharged. More often.

And reconnoitered, when an assignment required more details.

Within the archival map they interacted with, vital information from infinite alternate realities floated in an energy cloud. Countless time stamps for events existed in each reality, catalogued only once a directive had been issued from those viewing. Awareness drew the pertinent item to the surface, from the depths of every possibility.

Each mission mandated that Skorpius tug on delicate threads once they'd begun to unravel due to imbalance. By design, his sensitive intuition got him most of the way there. But he believed in supplementing instinct with knowledge. Therefore, the archives had to be accessed. The clues within their immeasurable collection of information had never failed to fill in the blanks.

Until now.

The day's distinctive mission drew one absolute blank. And a *massive* amount of disruption. "Still no idea?" Why he'd been sent. *And* tied to a human.

Pushing the time and distance limits of the tether that bound him to his charge, he'd spent the rest of the day, and well into the night, seeking answers. First, on his own. Then, with the added opinion of one of the rare few he trusted.

"None." Orion stepped closer to the unique map, examining the details and nuances revealed therein. For the last handful of minutes, they'd analyzed everything that had begun to change on Earth, what had begun to restructure within time itself. "But I've never seen a disruption like this. The difference is striking."

All were cogent descriptions he'd heard before, long ago. About himself. After his fall from grace. *Different. Unprecedented.*

Orion glanced at him.

Swirling platinum eyes met his. White hair flowed around a near-identical face. Alabaster skin radiated with glimmering brightness. Even a pure untainted heart beat in his brother's chest.

Whereas his own beat heavier, darker. And everything else matched from the inside out. *Burnished. Marked. Black as sin.*

A burst of motion within the map captured Skorpius's attention. He zeroed in on the new development. "There's another."

Together, the warriors viewed an interactive aerial of Scotland, as events unfolded in real time, at the pinpoint marker of the anomaly *and* that which tethered Skorpius to the human female.

Once-human. He couldn't be certain Brigid remained fully human any longer.

Skorpius gave a nod toward a fresh image that had begun to take shape, blurred at its edges, crisping in the middle, which signified an emerging event, one that hadn't previously occurred in that specific time. Details sharpened and expanded in response to his concentration on it.

Better to focus on hard evidence, that which he could see and control.

The rest? *Being tied to a human for the first time since...*

He forced the quandary from his mind. The catastrophic time-rift took precedence. The rest would resolve itself one way or another.

The aerial view continued to stream like a giant three-dimensional board game. Unchanged markers shone crystal clear: the significant castles of Stirling and Edinburgh along with their unique Brodie Castle, key events and locations of William Wallace and Robert the Bruce, strategic movements in the beginnings of the Scottish War of Independence. However, the time-rifts were another matter. Places or events that had once been, were increasingly delineated by ragged edges and ever-blurring centers, as if being sucked out of existence down a massive whirlpool. New events materialized with vivid detail at their core, outer borders blurred, stretching the very landscape itself as each burgeoning incident tore through the fabric of time.

Three Viking ships materialized off Britain's eastern shores, out of nowhere—centuries after they'd begun to ignore Scotland.

Scores of Knights Templar advanced with stealth into dense

Highland forests, out of time and place. While a much smaller number of their brethren were rounded up and arrested in France—a full decade early.

Extinct Pleistocene mammals sprouted into existence, woolly rhinoceros, mammoth, and the massive Irish elk. And they appeared not only into their former Scottish roaming grounds, but into other parts of the globe as well.

And in Asia, Marco Polo still remained with a very alive Kublai Khan. Which doomed the famous *The Travels of Marco Polo* by Marco's fellow inmate Rustichello—penned during an imprisonment that had suddenly ceased to exist—to absolute nothingness.

"How much do any of us know?" Orion continued to puzzle on all things unprecedented as they witnessed history rewrite event after event, with accelerating speed.

"Some more than others." Skorpius remained the first and only of angelkind to guard time itself. Knowledge served as a base requirement, which Orion well knew. The black void of the unknown? *Unsettling.* "However, I've never been completely blind." Never without a compass, never aimless regarding a mission.

Orion let out a resigned sigh before he landed a heavy stare at him. "Then surrender to it. Focus on the present moment, the task at hand, whatever its requirements dictate, nothing more."

Surrender. What humans did.

He locked gazes with his brother. They both knew Skorpius had done that once before. Surrendered. Accepted. Rolled with events.

And then, in a bizarre twist of fate, he'd become human.

Trapped as a tormented mortal, in a prison of his own making, Skorpius had down-spiraled. Eventually, like all doomed mortals, he'd died.

Then, he'd become something entirely *other.*

Angelkind had accepted him back into the flock—to a point.

And as eternal penance for sins against both races, he'd accepted the cold role of outcast. Rebel. The one marked by blackness, different among all kind.

"Surrender," he murmured. "Of course. Why not?" Only in the last months had things gotten interesting around the realms anyway. The arrival of the long-prophesied Traveler had ignited his brethren with an infusion of fresh energy.

Why not test his own limits, face his own demons?

Guard another human? *Protect time* from *said human*, he reminded himself.

"Surrender," Skorpius repeated louder, forcing conviction into his tone. His continued existence required a stretch of imagination. Even his own. Then he released all doubt, any reservations. He accepted that he'd never had a choice in the matter anyway. No point in fighting the inevitable.

With a sudden rippling wave, molecules of energy excited around them. The nature of the disruption washed over his senses as foreign, youthful, exuberant.

The Traveler. *Think of the smart-mouthed devil.*

"Well, *hellooooo*, boys." Isobel gusted out a dramatic sigh from behind them.

Silence followed. After several odd seconds of no-commentary, he and Orion turned.

A smitten expression softened her face. Tightly clasped hands clutched over her heart. "So poignant, you two. Dark Knight and Snow White."

A low growl rumbled from his throat. *"Runt."*

Orion merely arched a disdainful brow. "Ms. MacInnes."

"Really? Not *Mrs. Brodie*? Still with the whole MacInnes thing?"

Skorpius fought an amused tug at the corners of his mouth. "Does it bother you?"

"Yes."

"Then, yes," Skorpius ribbed.

And yet, a smile brightened the Traveler's face. Plump cheeks were pinked. Wavy blond hair appeared rumpled. Settling into marriage and embracing happiness suited her. The ivory linen of a night shift peeked below the hem of her black wool cloak. Interrupted sleep, then.

"Nice map." The female strode between the two towering angels and stared at the morphing depictions.

"My work here is done." Orion vanished.

"Hardly," he grumbled at his escaped brother's energy-stream wake. Then he sighed in resignation, no closer to any answers.

Isobel quirked up a brow. "What's got your panties in a wad?"

He ignored the jibe. Still not in the mood.

"Wow." Her full attention diverted back toward the ever-evolving map. "Your map puts every known cartographer to shame."

"Not our map." The Authority's. But close enough.

Isobel stared hard at an empty spot on the lower-left edge. Script began to appear at her mental command; she'd learned well how their world operated, how her clear focus created matter. *"Here there be dragons..."* As she spoke aloud, the words took shape. Then she waved the fingers of both hands beside her eyes, but toward him. *"Ooo-ooo-oooooo..."* Her higher octave rose and fell in ghost-story mockery.

If you only knew. He dared not envision actual dragons. The stray thought risked the actual magickal creatures bursting into the chaotic mix.

"Whoa!" Isobel quick-stepped backward. The map stretched down as her gaze tracked toward its lower edge, spilling out onto the mist under her feet, images crisping in detail as it floated atop the iridescent backdrop.

But her attention wandered back upward. She eased closer to the map, zeroed in on a spot, then pointed at a northern thickly forested region. "Aurochs." Large wild cattle. "European brown bears. *Polar* bears." She shook her head. "Impossible. They've gone extinct in Scotland by now."

"'Now' is relative." Skorpius scanned over countless developing anomalies. "And anything is 'possible.'" Proven by her friend's recent power disruption. "At least the realms themselves haven't been breached," he muttered as the realization hit him. *Yet.*

If Isobel heard any of his remarks, she offered no indication. Instead, she swished her hand through the misty colored particles of the map. Back. Forth. Back again.

The image shimmered with each wave, then coalesced into a static form once again. When Isobel focused her gaze on a new area. The reactive map responded to her, zooming then crisping its summoned details in response.

She batted her hand through the translucent image again.

Like a child with a shiny new toy.

Irritation rumbled up and he growled again. Louder. "What do you want? I'm busy."

"Quit *growling* at me. I thought you appeared anytime I wanted."

He snorted. "You *need*, I support. Wants never concern me, *Ms. MacInnes.*"

"Skorpius." A rare event, her speaking his official name as she landed a serious stare at him. "When are you gonna call me by my actual name? *Eeee-sooo-bellll…*"

"The moment *irritating you* stops *amusing me.*" So never. Of course, she'd garnered his respect for her hard-earned position as Traveler. But the needling banter? That was their thing.

With a melodramatic huff, she brushed past him, ruffling his feathers.

Skorpius stifled the urge to tense his wing.

"Fine." Isobel spun toward him once she reached the edge of the map. At their combined inattention, the map fuzzed into the background, its details obscuring into a blur of muted colors. "I *need* to talk to you." She smiled with crafty sweetness and batted her eyelashes. *"Pleeeease…"*

Some aberrant soft spot in his heart caved. He leveled an unforgiving look at her, while endeavoring to harden over that tiny weakness. "Not here. I don't do idle chat in the archives."

She smiled broadly, like she'd won a jousting match.

He didn't care enough to correct her misassumption.

Inclined toward rapid commencement of her requested consultation, in pursuit of an even swifter conclusion, he stepped close, lifted his hand near the wool cloak covering her shoulder, then paused and cast her an inquiring glance.

After a slight brow furrow, she dropped a slow nod: permission granted.

Skorpius gripped her shoulder with a gentle touch. Energy burst from his heart's center, fusing their essences together, then flashed them as one into the Scottish Highlands of her new home-time. They materialized on a favorite outcropping, the weathered top of a rock spire, a granite sentry perched high upon the nearest mountain range that overlooked Brodie Castle, which was asleep under a blanket of fog.

"Holy *hell!*" Isobel clutched his arm as her knees gave way. Shaken, she wobbled down onto her ass on the gray stone.

He swung down and seated himself beside her, settled his wings back, and dangled his boots into the open air. And even though Isobel had shifted into nascent immortality, he pressed a shoulder against hers to radiate his warmth amid the subfreezing temperatures; snow-covered Highland peaks at night exceeded the human tolerance of wind chill.

"Warn a girl next time! I've got plenty to battle with morning si—" Gaze tracking beyond him, her eyes widened as she absorbed the unsurpassed view of an expansive starry night over the silhouetted mountains. Her lips wordlessly parted, expression softening.

Silence. Blessed *silence.* And all it took was a change of scenery.

Skorpius gestured a sweeping hand along the far horizon line. "Welcome to my office."

"What was *that* back there, in Mist-Land." She pointed a finger toward the sky, her only—mistaken—concept of where they'd been with the map.

"A briefing." Not quite. But as far as she needed to know.

"Care to brief me?" She angled an arched brow at him.

"No."

"Aren't I one of you?"

Hardly. "You are *not* one of us."

Neither was he, technically. But Isobel didn't need to know that. No one did.

Her expression hardened into a scowl.

Which had no effect on him. Leniency didn't belong in her new limitless world. "You're a mere fledgling. Add a few millennia. Then we'll talk."

She heaved out a long-suffering sigh.

"You chose," he reminded her. "You knew there was a price."

That straightened her spine. "I did." She gave a firm nod. "For good reason. You know that." Her determined gaze swept over the moonlit mists that blanketed those she'd vowed to protect, as well as the man she loved, and her voice softened. "And I understood there would be consequences."

Skorpius let her self-realization settle with her for a moment.

After a stretch of silence, he relented. "On with it, *Runt.* Tell me what you need, so I can watch over the world in peace." And resume his intriguing mission.

He stared down over the obscured ancient forests below. Somewhere under that Highland mist, his new charge stirred up trouble. On a monumental scale.

"First"—her brows shot up, tone deepening into a command

—"explain why you're visiting Brigid's room in the middle of the night."

Fury shot through his system as he shifted; he towered over the neophyte, muscles tensed, eyes narrowed, irritation radiating outward. "I will ignore joking nicknames, but I *will not* suffer insolence."

Isobel winced. A rarity for her.

Good. You're learning.

Skorpius granted her a slow nod, satisfied she recognized the danger of crossing the thin—but distinct—line between them. That she respected his rank above her. Which was how they needed to function.

As to an explanation of appearing in Brigid's room? He settled back, centered on his granite perch. "Not. *Gonna.* Happen," he replied in her vernacular, soft but clear. And although he didn't owe anyone an accounting of his whereabouts, he added, "But not what you think."

Because *he* didn't have any recollection of it. No point in Isobel theorizing.

More silence stretched.

A rare restlessness took hold within him. He had things to do. Missions to decipher. Another hell-bent female warrior to guard. Or rein in. After a measured inhalation, he tempered his mood. "Next?"

Isobel's jaw firmed. A slow nod signaled that she'd relinquished her friend's battle. "Iain forbade me to fight. Or time travel. His bairns"—she scratched quotes into the air and deepened her voice a couple octaves—"his rules."

Skorpius glanced over with arched brows, pleased he wasn't the only one giving Her Feistiness grief. "And your feelings regarding your ruler's decree?"

She rolled her eyes, then huffed out a soft laugh. "Typical Iain. Issuing orders. But there's love behind his protectiveness. And common sense." She smoothed a hand over her still-flat belly. "I don't want anything to happen to the twins either. I'm stepping down as Traveler. You'll have to find someone else."

Sudden laughter boomed from his throat so hard, its echoes bounced off the granite walls and down into the jagged chasm below. "Doesn't work that way, *Princess*. You don't decide. Your vocation has been chosen for you and accepted by you. There's no 'givesies-backsies.'" The bold hilarity of her suggestion tempted him to use her modern human slang.

Impervious to his teasing, she crossed her arms, expression defiant. "No way am I fighting."

Skorpius had to give her credit. The female held her own in an argument or an actual fight. He admired the quality of temerity in others, most especially in humans.

Ah, yes, but you're no longer human.

He shook his head, reminding himself she'd only crossed that mortality barrier mere months ago. As had her husband. Both still thought like humans, their once-limited minds adapting in slow stages. They hadn't yet fully comprehended that she and the babes couldn't be harmed. *Mostly.* At the thought, a sudden streak of generosity broke through that weak spot in his heart.

Irritated at all his sudden compassion, he rolled his eyes. "Fine. I'll grant you maternity leave, like your human tradition. As long as no catastrophe develops. The worlds can function without you for a while."

The worlds had survived for eons before her.

And the developing situation with Brigid?

All mine.

Isobel gaped at him, speechless.

Skorpius touched a finger to the tip of her chin and closed her mouth. "What?" he asked as her wide-eyed stare persisted.

"Seriously? You can just decide my welfare like that?" She snapped her fingers beside her narrowing eyes. "You have that authority?"

"Not that your welfare is my concern, but yes. The Authority gave me the authority," he replied. "And if you feel no undeniable inner pull toward a task, then yours is to rest. Even with responsibilities, everything requires balance."

Relief washed over her face. "What will you do with no dire time-wrinkles to iron out? Without harassing me?"

As if Isobel's vacation meant everyone's lives ground to a halt.

The rest of angelkind would guard all that existed, carry out their missions as directed.

And with his two opposing threads to attend to, he'd be the busiest one of all.

For Brigid's power-event had transcended dire, registered as far more than a "time-wrinkle." But the greatest incessant pull he'd ever felt—*to Brigid's person* and her place in time—marked the task as his sole responsibility.

"I'll find a way to manage." In fact, he looked forward to the unique purpose, a greater challenge. Threats were meant to be dealt with, one way or another.

A heavy furrow marred her brow while she scanned through the nighttime darkness, as if she surveyed the expansive rugged terrain below. "It's dangerous out there. Armies building. The War of Independence."

Skorpius knew the purported historical records. English defending their recent occupation of Scottish castles. The proud Scots uprising in rebellion to seize their territory back.

If the historic war still remained on course to happen in the new magick-reorganized reality.

Aside from all the reintroduced great predators.

Assuming it all ended there. Cataclysmic events induced by magick rarely did.

"It *is* dangerous," he agreed. For someone like Brigid. For so many reasons more.

Silent seconds dragged by.

Another long-suffering sigh gusted out from her. "If you *are* stalking Brigid."

"I am *not*." His tone darkened, final.

"Will you check in on her, maybe? Make sure she's safe?"

He intended much more than that. "She'll be watched over." Safe? He couldn't promise. Not if Brigid herself proved to be the worst danger.

The slow relaxing of her shoulders and a drowsy nod marked the end of Isobel's concern. She yawned loudly, eyelids drooping.

Consultation? Over. Both of Isobel's queries had been addressed.

And that ever-present dual tether—to his new charge and the time-rift—burned hotter in his chest. He had important issues to resolve; they would no longer wait.

"Back to bed with you." On her slow nod, he touched her shoulder, then flashed her under the linen covers, cloak and all, beside her slumbering man.

Skorpius dematerialized, returning back into the ether to charge his reserves from the icy cold of utter darkness. Instinct suggested his journey ahead would be long. Premonition flared, warning him that he'd need all the energy he could gather.

When he returned to the granite perch he'd occupied mere hours before, gloaming dusted the misty landscape in hues of purplish gray. And the undeniable ache in his chest from his dual mission escalated as he stared down through the mist, toward an awakening Earth-realm. The first rays of sunlight began to splash over a landscape that had developed unparalleled time anomalies. And within it, Skorpius faced an unrivaled challenge: Save the female *and* end her. With a complete absence of guidelines—and no strategy.

His interrupted discussion with Orion trickled back into his mind, what Orion had advised: *Then surrender to it.*

As the mists swirled through the tree tops, he forced a slow exhalation, resigned to his fate. "Accept what you cannot change," he muttered to himself. Fighting against the stupidity of flying blind into an unorthodox mission would do him no good.

"Determine the issues, assess their parameters, seek to rectify," he murmured, aligning himself with his only course of action.

On his next breath, the burning vibration behind his sternum snapped so hard, he gasped from the intense pain. His leeway for reconnaissance had run out. He'd held fast against the inevitable for as long as he dared. Until he could no longer resist the dual tethers that bound them together, that obligated him to end her if need be.

As Skorpius stood from his perch, he wondered how Brigid had come into her extraordinary power. And the fierce soul behind those penetrating silvery eyes flickered into his mind. He scanned over the aerial view of the Highlands, knowing she was down there, somewhere. All he needed to do was let go of his reservations and allow the dual tethers to lead him.

Who are you, Brigid? And what have you been up to in my absence?

Eager to solve the mystery, he dove into the wind, and…let go. After a long exhalation, he snapped open his wings.

When a strong updraft caught him, he released all resistance to the path, to his course.

But I refuse to surrender.

CHAPTER 3

Clan Brodie lived a lie.

Nay, 'twas not the whole of it.

With a heavy headshake and her eyes pinched shut, Brigid gripped the chestnut mane of her thunderin' mare and swallowed past a cramp in her throat.

'Twas not merely her brother and kinfolk who'd gone adrift through life: endless days tendin' to food and shelter, births and deaths, festivals when lasses collected bonnie ribbons, battles where warriors fought with deadly weapons. Aye, those within their castle's curtain wall had long been protected from the outside world. Fast asleep.

But all the folk beyond their clan's sheltered existence? Lived in a blindin' fog as well.

Everyone based their worlds, their verra lives, on solid objects, on matter. But none of what her fellow Scots believed to be real held any true import.

Matter no longer...*mattered.*

Somethin' greater did.

And she'd happened upon that shockin' truth by accident.

Weel, in truth, Brodie Castle's sparklin' magickal wall had

always held her fascination, since she'd been a wee one. Ripplin' like the surface of a loch when awakened, still as a midnight sky while asleep, its pinpricks of glowin' light mesmerized. Knowledge of their great wall's purpose had been handed down from generation to generation. Only the rulin' laird was entrusted with its most powerful secrets and instructed on how to wield its power. Along with a second, an apprentice in kind, one dependable who'd step in should Laird be away or incapable.

And on one harrowing day, she'd become that second through a strange twist of fate.

Tasked at once with savin' her clan from attack, she'd leapt to action, pressin' her hand to the wall. The next thing she knew, she'd *stumbled through* its shimmerin' surface—and awoke...

...within another world...

...awash in the vast knowledge of the ancients...

...imbued with the secrets of the mysteries...

The whole of it had filled her nigh to burstin'. Then, with each rapid beat of her heart, the flooding tide of information had begun to recede from the forefront of her mind.

Yet nothin' remained the same as she'd once known it.

Not the world, upon her return. Nor her.

For as she passed through her days since the encounter, the verra elements had sparked, alive. They'd glittered and flashed behind her, alongside, above, and all around, like a million stars dancin' in the dark of night. And she'd become their new sun, pullin' them toward the horizon.

In the blink of an eye, her entire existence had altered.

One mere taste. The smallest *glimpse.*

"Aye. 'Twas only the crack of a door," she whispered. But through that crack, she'd stumbled from harsh darkness into unimaginable light. Her mind *still* grappled with the enormity of that brief flash. "'Twas only a wee peek...but enough to know."

Enough to crave more. Be immersed in its glow, a tranquil floatin' through the warm shallows of a clear summer pond.

The rest of the world still existed, but only as a journey—no longer as an end unto itself. "For none holds truth in purpose."

Such vivid...*life*...existed beyond the realm of her kinfolk, of Scotland, of earth and sky.

Furthermore, upon Brigid's return to her castle and homeland from the realm beyond the wall, another vibrant new awareness awoke within her: the ability to sense energy, power.

"*Magick*," she murmured. She believed that to be the reason. For her accidental taste of otherworldly magick had not merely enabled her to discover the same exquisite form of energy hidden all around them. She'd developed the ability to sense her own. *And another's.*

Frightful nights had startled her awake in her bedchamber, sensin' that strange *other* energy. The occurrences had heightened the urgency of her takin' the leap—clarified that she had no other choice but to escape the confines of Brodie Castle, the only home she'd ever known.

For after she'd burst from the keep one midnight hour to gain some fresh air, the endless night sky had banished the smotherin' energy of the unwelcome creature. Repeat departures had confirmed the same. She'd still sometimes detect its immense power, but less so, and only on the edge of her awareness. Then upon each return to the keep, she'd discovered that the ominous presence had since vanished.

Escape had been her only course.

Darkness hunts me. The clear threat nipped at her heels.

Which was why she'd left the castle in such haste. Exposin' herself to the powerful magick had brought forth a heavy burden. *'Twill be mine alone to bear.* She'd not be puttin' her clan in harm's way. Especially not her brothers, Iain and Gawain, and not her new friend Isobel. All who'd already fought plenty for her, risked their lives for her and their clan.

"*Nay.*" The new power sizzled under her skin. "'Tis *my* path that stretches forth." She tightened her grip on the reins until the leather bit into her fingers. *Mine alone.*

Even though none of her clan would see it that way.

Alone. What she'd always been, even in her home, amidst her clan. Fate had made hers a way of solitude. *Journeyin' on my own, 'twill be no different.* They'd have to accept what she'd done, the solitary path she'd chosen.

A lance of fear spiked through her for the hundredth time.

But as with each bout of unease before, she drew in a deep breath and closed her eyes, focused on the heavy thump of her heart, then struck the false emotion from her mind.

Warriors doona question duty.

And warrior she'd become. A woman warrior? Uncommon, to be certain. But true, all the same.

"'Tis too late to stop me." Her clan had protected her from danger for her whole life. "'Tis *my turn* to protect you," she vowed on a fierce whisper.

She'd given chase to her own destiny, drawin' the dark *other* magick to follow.

And as she ducked under a low branch, then broke into an open meadow, the menacin' presence prickled right behind her like an icy winter's wind breathin' down on her neck.

Verra weel. She'd face whatever power stalked her, on her terms. *When I choose.*

Feelin' the magick spark all around as it called out to her, Brigid smoothed her upper body over the muscular neck of her steed and grounded herself with the strength of the beast beneath her. As she did so, she opened her mind and heart, breathin' in the vital essence of nature itself.

Warm energy hummed through her body.

Tingles sparked under her skin.

Alive like never before, her spirit soared.

"I'm followin' my true course," she whispered to the wind, knowin' the rightness of it to her bones.

All of a sudden, her mount bucked, planted its hooves, then reared.

Brigid leapt from the startled mare's back while it pranced sideways in agitation. When the horse tossed its head, Brigid freed her packed satchel with the tug of two slip knots, released the reins, then pushed outward with her mind on a strong and silent wish for the mare to find safety.

With amazin' obedience, the horse charged off, back the way they'd come.

Did you hear my plea? But she had no time to puzzle over the oddity of talkin' to beasts.

Dried twigs snapped far off to her left.

Thick bramble jostled through the forest ahead.

Muffled angry shouts echoed from the dark woods.

A short blur raced by, then another, and a third. Children, she sensed. She caught only a glimpse of drab colors, no details of form or shape, but one hadn't been taller than her chin, the others, smaller by nigh half. None were older than ten summers.

Babes.

Instinct rushed in with her thunderin' pulse. And on a deep inhale, she somehow gathered the sparkin' magick around her.

Then time seemed to slow, draggin' by at a snail's pace over the next handful of seconds.

Tiny shimmers of light floated up from ground to sky, winkin' brilliant hues as they swirled, like the verra air had caught fire in a turbulent rainbow. And while a heavy warmth radiated from deep within her body, the cool, wispy, color-drenched particles brushed over her skin with a wintry kiss.

Till time exploded back with a burst of activity.

Rough lookin' men broke into view from the denser scrub,

some on foot, a larger man on horseback. Sunlight glinted off the chainmail that the lone rider wore. *Soldiers.*

"C'mon out, yo' bloody chits," a foot soldier taunted. He stabbed his broadsword into blackberry bramble off to her left.

"Criminy, Albert. Don't kill 'em li'l buggers."

English soldiers.

But not one of the men detected her, even though she stood at the edge of the glade.

Leashed wolfhounds bounded into view, eager hunters whose muscular legs and diggin' claws strained the hold of their keeper.

Without thought, she stepped back. And a twig snapped.

She held her breath.

But none noticed the loud sound. Not even the hounds.

"'Tis as if...*I'm not here,*" she whispered, loud as she dared.

Yet none reacted.

The group of a dozen men and three dogs were well-nigh upon her. She stood directly in front of them, yet no gaze angled her way. The magick she'd gathered appeared to work like a cloak, concealin' the whole of her from detection.

Amazin'! But she decided to be brave, and find out for certain.

"*Och!*" she shouted. Breath held as her voice echoed forth, she pinched her eyes shut.

No response came.

Somehow, she'd been spared.

But the wee ones? Remained in harm's way.

Grippin' the marvelous magick around her like the cloak she imagined it to be, she spun and ran, searchin' for them.

As she ran, she fanned out her awareness, probin' outward with her mind.

Cold terror! She sensed the frightened emotion; it originated from twenty paces forward, from behind a large fallen tree. Stretched along the length of the trunk's decayin' bark, a delicate patchwork of wavy mushroom caps and bright-green moss crouched under a lacy canopy of fern fronds.

But the growth did not hide all, for as she approached, wheezin' breaths exposed the wee ones' position.

"Loose the dogs!" the rider bellowed, from not far behind.

Barks erupted as the beasts lurched free.

Then the world broke apart into rapid-fire images.

Dried leaves trampled underfoot.

Wet dirt kicked loose.

Mold spores exploded.

A bitter wind gusted.

Terror gripped her heart. She snapped her magick out, taut and wide, panicked for the wee ones. She had no idea how far she'd cast the curtain of energy, only hoped its magick protected more than just her.

When the gallopin' wolfhounds bolted on either side of the fallen tree, then kept on runnin', she pinched her eyes shut and exhaled in relief.

But she didn't release her hold on the camouflage. Because the dozen soldiers scoured the terrain ahead and to the immediate sides of the fallen tree. And the dogs had circled around and searched vigorously behind them. She and the wee ones were trapped between.

Tense seconds crawled by while she endeavored to hold her protective magick curtain in place.

The warm rush of energy that radiated from within...grew hot.

Hotter.

Beads of perspiration sheened over her brow. Open hands at her sides curled into fists. Jaw clenched, she swallowed past a hard lump in her throat. Shallowed breaths soon lapsed into ragged gasps. And every tightened muscle began to fatigue, till she trembled with the pressure of the unusual exertion.

She bit her lower lip, fightin' harder, afraid that the tiniest weakness in her rigid stance would cause their magick camouflage to fail.

A low whimper escaped her throat when the strain burned through every fiber of her being.

All of a sudden, a blissful coolness rushed over and through her. The tension eased at once. A pulse of energy invigorated her from head to toe.

Surprised by the sudden change, she blinked her eyes open.

But her shimmerin' rainbow curtain remained intact.

Her brow furrowed. "I dinna..." Then at once, she understood why. She sensed...*Skorpius*.

The dark angel's unimaginable power flared from behind her, close, but not threatenin'. At least, not at that moment. Whatever his reason, Skorpius had come to their rescue, bolstered her magick with his.

Yet, regardless of his timely aid, she refused to let her guard down, would not release her tether on the magick she'd drawn forth.

And the shimmerin' protective cloak held stable, her energy its primary source, but its strength clearly bolstered with the angel's added power. For the first time in painful endless seconds, she drew in a deeper breath, relaxed her muscles enough to alleviate the burn.

Had Skorpius suspected she'd been close to collapsin'?

How'd you known where *I'd be at all?*

Low sounds began to infiltrate the hazy muted bubble of her cloak. Nearby twigs snapped. Male voices grumbled. Sniffin' wolfhounds wandered into the glade once again, well-nigh bumpin' into her. The soldiers circled back into her peripheral view. And the bramble-stabber resumed his deadly assault of brush, a methodical elimination of hidin' places. His fellow Englishmen unsheathed their weapons and joined him, skewerin' leafy hidey-holes as they spread outward into a wider and wider perimeter.

Rapid quieted breaths from the hidden wee ones scraped over her ears. A frail whimper started, then muffled.

A hot flash of anger flamed through her. That her kinfolk—innocents at that—had been reduced to lowly prey.

By invaders.

Outrage roiled deep in her gut, firin' up greater heat. The tiny shimmers within their magick cloak spun faster, flared brighter.

Particles of decayin' plant matter began to lift from the forest floor within her translucent shield—leaf bits, moss filaments, fern spores—all risin', vibratin'. The lower branches of the firs nearest them, well outside her protective cloak, started to tremble, bowin' outward, upward.

Immense power discharged from the cells of her body, ripplin' forth in ever-greater waves.

Both dogs and soldiers alike started to glance around. With widened eyes and swivelin' heads, they scanned about the glade, clear panic in their rigid frames, down to the last beast and man. None focused on her. All cowered in sudden fear.

Till their leader, the lone man on horseback, narrowed his eyes. He cocked his head, as if listenin'. Then he leaned forward in his saddle and stared with intensity—directly toward her.

But then a foreign pulse of energy burst out from somewhere behind her. A translucent energy shot through the forest, cracklin' leaves as it flew past. It angled toward her far left, then raced toward the horizon, like a sideways lightnin' bolt. Dried leaves rustled and branches snapped in its rapidly vanishin' wake.

The dogs and men alerted toward the sudden new sounds.

Then the beasts tore off, eagerness in their expressions, invigorated once again by the hunt. The soldiers on foot glanced at one another, then up toward their leader. With his clipped nod, they chased off after the hounds.

Brigid's pulse hammered a hard beat against her eardrum as

the keen rider turned back, facing her. A ruthless stare landed directly at her, before his brows twitched down in confusion.

But after a brief headshake, he disregarded gut instinct over his more reliable senses and abandoned his suspicion. With a snort, he turned his horse, then negotiated back through the thick brush to chase after the rest of his group.

However, even with their departure, she held fast. She harbored a great distrust of everythin': beast, man, newfound magick and, *above all*, the angel at her back, so close, the heat of his presence burned like a summer's midday sun.

The children had no such patience. After a first few seconds of silence—apart from the returnin' sounds of birdsong and insect trills—the wee ones flushed themselves from their refuge, their aggressive hunters none the wiser.

A boy, the eldest, stared at her. His eyes widened as they sidestepped around at a safe distance, but within the perimeter of their magick cloak. The two smaller ones clung to his waist, tuggin' at his tunic to urge the lot toward safety, back toward the direction they'd run from.

Within a half dozen steps, the huddled children breached through the far side of the shimmerin' curtain that had obscured them. And each one paused, half-in, half-out, as if caught for an instant marvelin' about the extraordinary net. Thin chests expanded and eyes grew ever wider in wonder as they each spun in turn and stared at her.

And as the wee ones crossed through the curtain of her magick, a startlin' chill shivered through her. The crisp bite gripped her, seizin' her breath, till they passed all the way through to stand wholly on the other side.

Then the elder boy's jaw dropped open. He gave a heavy blink in her direction, but his gaze grew unfocused. The magick cloak now obscured her alone. *And him*—the angel.

Another energy pulse flared from behind her, but slower than before, warm and tinglin', flowin' out toward the children.

The energy's essence tasted calm and protective. As the softer wave passed through her curtain, its force splashed tiny glitterin' fragments of both magicks over the children. Faces alightin' with a flash of joy, they inhaled deeply, then darted off into the darkness of the forest.

The danger had passed.

But still, Brigid struggled to let go.

Even through total exhaustion, she remained motionless, clutchin' the unusual gathered magick around her. Breaths short, muscles cramped, mind frayed from emotions runnin' hot with anger and fear, she began to fret that she dinna know *how* to let go.

"*Exhale.*" The soft command rumbled low, as if echoed from afar. "To the count of five."

Closin' her eyes, body tremblin' from fatigue, she did as Skorpius urged. A comfortin' warmth spread through her, then eased away, like the cool shade of cloud cover had drifted overhead. Relief sagged her shoulders. Locked knees nigh gave way. Shaky breaths began to lengthen, growin' steady.

But then, her mind snapped taut.

She gasped when a different kind of heat—richer, darker, edged with seductive danger—danced across her skin, raced up the curve of her neck, and sizzled over the shell of her ear.

Och! His *slow exhalation.*

A slow, cool draft followed, chillin' back down her neck, then paused directly over her shoulder. *A deep inhalation.* Like some primal beast, the ultimate hunter, had breathed in...*her.*

A disconcertin' ache flared from that closest point of exposure near her collarbone, downward. A sudden awareness of her whole body peaked; the deerskin material of her newly made huntin' clothes rasped across tender nipples, the fitted cut between her legs clung where a pleasurable pulse began to throb.

Did his *magick bewitch* me?

She frowned. *Remember who you are! Focus on why you're here.*

On a slower breath in, to another count of five *at her own direction*, she straightened her frame, hardened her jaw, and tensed her muscles. The powerful male needed to know she wouldn't be stalked, couldn't be dissuaded, and refused to bow down to the will of any other.

I alone *decide.*

More of his charged air feathered over her skin. On the last bit, light huffs and a low chuckle vibrated. *Of course, you do*, boomed the male's words—*inside* her head.

She jumped, startled, and her loosened satchel tumbled from her grasp, spillin' its contents onto the ground. Her breath caught, chest frozen in place. And her vexin' body ached in response to the primal *maleness* of him once again.

On a low growl, she blew out a frustrated breath through clenched teeth. Night after night, power had saturated her bedchamber. *Alone!* she boomed back. He dinna get to follow.

"*Without you.*" The last echoed aloud, powered by a fiery burst of her magick.

Anger wellin' up, she lifted her chin, then turned and faced her pursuer.

CHAPTER 4

ithout me? Skorpius stifled a laugh.

"Not an option."

If the female had any inkling of the true meaning of his presence, especially of the duality—his obligation to *and* against her—she'd cower in fear.

Most mortals exhibited the wise instinct to be afraid anyway.

His very essence screamed apex predator.

Brigid? Simply straightened her lean frame and glared at him. The astonishing female steeled her spine in the face of danger.

Nevertheless, she had charged down her precarious path of her own volition.

And he, created as a warrior to battle a cause far greater than either of them, had no choice in the matter. On both counts, he'd been bonded to the female for the duration: until some unforeseen event released his guardianship of her, and once the time-rift—the disruption that had nearly cost her a very beautiful head—had been repaired.

"Nice trick." His gaze lingered on the inert air that had quivered with magick mere seconds ago, while her provocative scent imprinted on him. *"Impressive,* even," he murmured. Even if her ability to hold such immense power had faltered.

Skorpius had never witnessed anyone obscure with glamour. *Besides angelkind.*

Of course, other humans through time immortal had been documented to achieve a similar feat, but only after years of training, under a master of the secrets.

Never without elaborate ritual preparation.

Not unaided, in an instant…on instinct.

The female warrior had wielded elemental forces as if they'd been inborn, until fatigue had set in. Rudimentary laws of experience trumped a beginner's aptitude. Even Olympians, whose innate skills had awed humans through the ages, had to practice for years to attain excellence.

"Nay." Her tone deepened, loaded with power—again.

In slow progression, she resumed her rigid stance: muscles tightening, breaths shallowing, brows lowering, nostrils flaring. And those elemental forces she'd just lost her grip on began to vibrate again, as if she summoned them on a subconscious level. And they *would* serve her, if she commanded them completely.

Calculating silver eyes narrowed at him. *"I'll not be havin' you on my journey."*

But the magick particles she incited never fully coalesced; she failed to complete the circuit. Either through lack of knowledge, exhaustion, or by choice.

Skorpius needed to test which. "My mission says otherwise."

"What mission?"

"Above your paygrade."

She cocked her head. And the power buildup began to subside, quelled for the moment. "You and Isobel…and your strange words."

Technically not his and Isobel's words, but modern vernacular nonetheless. Even so, Brigid intuited far more than she let on. "You know what it means."

"Aye." She gave a slight nod. "Yet, as you doona wish to share your secrets, I'll be keepin' mine."

"Understood." Not that it mattered. Brigid's secrets would be revealed, one way or another.

Her eyes brightened. "Aye, so you'll leave, then?"

"No." He folded his arms.

Her current of energy snapped alive again, instantly agitating around her. The molecules vibrated with staggering acceleration, till they trembled at peak tolerance, a threshold dangerously close to combustion. "*I'll* not *go with you.*"

"You will." Skorpius sensed she inherently knew it, even though she balked at the notion. Everyone realized the inevitable things on some level. He understood theirs was the same journey by his very presence there. That, and the dual tethers pulsating their urgent message at his core. "Your decision—the only one you have in the matter—is whether you'll *accept* my company with you, or not."

Brigid glared at him, lips tight, stance rigid as ever.

Shifting tactics, he tilted his head down a fraction. "*Hmmm…*" He softened his voice. Decided to work the bonding angle. A little. "*Surrender* to our path."

Orion may have had a point with the outrageous suggestion. Perhaps young Brigid would prove more amenable than a stubborn ancient angel. *Who knows? If you yield to the inescapable first, I might be more inclined to.*

"*Nay.* I'll *never* surrender." Defiance glinted in those mercurial silver eyes. "And 'tis not *our* path."

"*It is* our path, like it or not." Yet with her immediate refusal to submit with almost the same vehemence as he, Skorpius began to like the idea of their being stuck together quite a bit more. "But fine." He gave a half shrug. "From afar it is."

She frowned. "What do you mean 'from afar'?"

He arched his brows. "Exactly how it sounds. With you, but not *with* you."

"Spyin' on me?" The volatile energy crackled with her anger.

"Guarding over you."

"To protect me." Suspicion riddled her tone.

"Among other things." *Above your paygrade.*

Her power flared another notch higher, without discharging. Somehow, she'd learned to brew her magick toward a massive excitation, building layer upon layer of pressurized power. "I doona trust 'other things.'"

The vibrating molecules began to change their behavior, flowing toward her as they spun hotter. Additional electrons manifested from their invisible cloud into existence, becoming a part of the material world. And the field of sparking unseen magick that had surrounded her became visible, ebbing and flowing, golden in its essence.

Excellent. Now *we're getting somewhere.*

Skorpius decided to test a theory. After drawing a deep breath, he exhaled while centering on a calm wave from within. Then he burst out a torrent of power, glacial as the Arctic, dark as a starless midnight.

Brigid's magick?

Extinguished at once under the onslaught of his.

She gave a heavy blink of surprise, then furrowed her brow and glanced around with a stark expression of disbelief; her comfort blanket had vanished.

Novice, then. Learning and developing at lightning speed, but still unable to control or understand. Clearly inexperienced. She'd probably never encountered another being with magick.

In the next instant, she burst into motion. Copper hair rippling behind her, sleekly toned arms arcing around, silvery eyes sparking with fury, she lunged toward him with a fierce war cry. The echoing ring of her dagger blades slashing apart rent the air.

Until she froze. Or rather, his magick immobilized her forward momentum, her controllable muscles, all but her autonomic nervous system. He didn't want to kill her. *Not yet.*

Seconds ticked by.

Defiant beats powered a strong heart.

Furious breaths expanded healthy lungs.

A hard swallow contracted her slender throat.

But nothing more. No jaw clench. No narrowed eyes. *Oh, but you* want *to.* He sensed how she strained, the effort she made. Hot anger radiated from every cell of her body.

Her shining copper hair glinted in the sunlight, as the wind moved what she could no longer.

To further demonstrate his absolute control—and to illustrate the breadth of his power over the toe-dip she'd ventured on her own—he began to release her, one miniscule muscle at a time, softening their rigidity, relaxing each in linear fashion. While he still supported her where needed—so she didn't crumple to the ground.

Well, there's a novel thought.

Her eyes widened as he then released her in an accelerating cascade, racing from shoulders to fingertips, quickening through to her hips, whipping down to her toes.

Suddenly freed arms flailed wildly for balance that never came. She toppled backward and landed flat on her ass. Gravity remained king.

From her dumped position, deerskin-clad legs bent, arms braced wide and back on the ground, her *now-freed* eyes glared at him, unspent rage burning in their silvery depths. A low growl reverberated. *"Doona* play with me." Small fisted hands tightened on the hilts of her daggers, their blades rendered useless as they lay prone on the moldy forest floor.

"Wouldn't dream of it." Nothing transpired by half measure, all held purpose. His unusual assignment demanded that he vet her threat level. And he'd do so in any fashion he pleased. "Instead of play, let's do this for real."

With a forceful mental shove to her backside, he "helped" her up.

She stumbled forward a few steps to gain balance, then shot him a caustic glare.

Aside from beginner's-luck, which had combusted her energy into view, magick typically remained invisible to the naked eye, to her kind and his. However, if the wielder focused on the alchemy taking place, echoes of pure energy could be detected as it reacted within the material realm. Traces born by personal perspective, when colored into the world, bathed anyone paying attention—of those able to see—in the afterglow.

Lesson time. For both of us.

To add power to his demonstration, he infused the formidable magick stoked from his core with his fiery essence, which glowed a blackish blue. Then he gathered the paltry remaining sparks of magick Brigid had brandished, which flashed a bright gold, and wove them with his. When her light bonded with his dark, the fibers cooled into her dusting of silvery gold sparkling at the edges of his midnight hue.

Once fully merged, he exploded their blended magick outward, toward her.

A layered energy field snapped into place, into a glittering dome that surrounded her. The sphere spanned seven feet in diameter. Plenty of room for her to move. *Within it.*

Her shrewd gaze scanned three-sixty along the ground, flicking up and over as she spun. Then she landed a hard stare at him. "What trickery is this?"

"Rudimentary magick. Yours with mine. The first recognizes you. The other tests you."

She glared with ferocity at him, breaths slowing, anger sparking hot under her skin. Then she diverted her attention toward the magick field that imprisoned her. After a moment's consideration, she extended the tip of a dagger toward the nearest perimeter.

"I wouldn't advise it. Metal is a great conductor of energy." Moreover, a newbie mistake—one that fried her into unconsciousness—would reveal nothing about the extent her ability. "Unless you like to catch lightning bolts."

Her chest expanded on a measured breath, then she shot him an exasperated expression. Gaze locked tight with his, she spun the blades on her palms before sheathing the weapons into the leather scabbards at her hips.

Then she turned from him and examined the magick shield more closely. She lifted an open hand and floated steady fingertips over the luminescent barrier. A small pulse of energy flared out from her core and floated over her fingertips. Not much magick coated her vulnerable skin, but enough. Enough to protect her from a mortal wound.

On a slow exhale, she drifted her eyelids closed and pressed her fingers forward.

A loud crackle sounded. A spark flashed.

"Och!" She pressed the zapped fingertips to her lips and shot another scathing glare at him.

"My magick is greater than yours," he murmured.

Which puzzled him. Only threats great enough to disrupt entire timelines, destroy whole worlds, demanded his attention. What was so special about the harmless creature before him? *Perhaps a chain of events yet to occur. Maybe several.*

"For now." She stared at him a moment longer, aggressive expression cooling. Then in slow motion, she lowered into a cross-legged seated position and folded her arms over her chest.

So defiant, this one. "Ah. Then, you know what's to come?"

"Mayhap." No deception colored her tone. Only solid truth. At least, how she perceived it.

Foresight? He wouldn't rule out the rare attribute.

"Well, aren't you a bundle of surprises," he murmured. But if Brigid had tapped into the mysteries of power creation, her mere belief would be enough to fuel the reality.

"*Hmmm…*" A meditative calm settled over her. She withdrew into some distant inner realm.

He took full advantage of her distracted state and extended subtle probing waves from their woven-magick sphere in toward her, assessing her technique.

Surprises, indeed. His brows lifted as he observed her unique power exchange.

You're good. Too *good.* Her burgeoning talent at manipulating energy defied explanation. "Tell me how you've learned to harness energy."

If she'd heard his demand, she ignored it. For a full inhale, slow exhale, then another inhale, her expression remained serene. Toward the middle of the second exhalation, her lips parted. "*Nay.*" The soft-spoken word fell with heavy finality.

"Not on your own," he worked aloud. No one could've mastered frequency on that level alone. Not with any speed. Her power bursts would have hit his radar long before now if any significant time had passed. Magick wielding, rare as it was, had a distinct learning curve. "Who's been teaching you?" Not that he expected a forthright answer from the hellion. But the idea of brutal interrogation soured his stomach. Complicated his endeavor as well.

"*I'll* not *be helpin' you.*"

And yet, *he'd* been tasked to "help" her.

And stop her.

He stifled a laugh at the ridiculous irony.

"So, do I end you now?" He hadn't decided. The dual threads of his mission, their urgent constant vibration, remained equal.

One protected her. The other condemned her. Neither spiked as priority over the other.

"Set me free and find out." Spoken so low, only his preternatural hearing detected the words.

"Tsk-tsk. Threatening your judge and jury never ends well."

"'Tis no threat." Her statement registered louder, near conversational. "Imprisonin' me is no way to decide."

"It's not?"

"Nay. Watch and see."

Oh, he was watching. The female piqued his curiosity.

"I've got all the time in the worlds." He folded his arms and cast a cool glance her way. No point in revealing exactly how interested he'd become.

Long seconds dragged by. A minute. Then a few. Nothing happened.

Brigid simply sat there, motionless.

Yet with the patience born of thousands of human lifetimes, he waited, ready for anything.

Midday approached, marking well over an hour since she'd last spoken.

Plenty of interesting activity happened outside the peaceful sphere. Attracted to the energy field, various fauna wandered or flew close by: a deer, a mountain hare, rodents, curious birds, insects. But each creature sensed only the vibrant golden essence delineated by Brigid's magick. Not one detected Skorpius's presence, aside from their woven magick field. Because to conserve energy, he'd mostly dematerialized, become part of the forest itself.

Tiny sparks periodically flashed and crackled at the energy threshold; kamikaze winged insects torpedoed straight into their magick's fire, igniting on impact.

All of a sudden, without a sound, Brigid drew a slower, deeper breath.

Muscles languid, expression serene, she rose from her seated position with grace. Golden luminescence began to radiate from her skin until its bright aura surrounded her. The copper spirals of hair floated into a rippling halo around her face. Irises, already a pale shade of gray sparkling with magick, glowed brighter, brilliant with energy.

Then her arresting silvery gaze held his, soft and accepting.

Already a raw beauty, she now exuded something pure and elemental, pristine.

Angelic, even.

The moment the resemblance crossed his mind, she moved.

Padding with graceful steps on leather-booted feet across a leaf-strewn forest floor, she approached their magick barrier. The white-gold magick that fringed his midnight blue, flared and licked toward her in recognition, in deadly invitation.

His breath caught.

Yet a hairsbreadth away from making singeing contact, her form faded. And she passed through.

"Incorporeal." The stunned murmur escaped tightened lips as he unfolded his arms and straightened to attention. He'd never once, in all the millennia of his existence, witnessed a human accomplish the feat inborn to angelkind.

And as her ethereal form whispered through the barrier, the magick field flared. Her golden and his blue vibrated hotter, brighter. Until all at once, in a flash of brilliant light, the energy burst outward into millions of spinning particles. Their fused magick, which hung in suspension for a split second, then imploded straight into her chest.

Residual energy sizzled and snapped through her golden aura.

Those silvery eyes sparkled with more unearthly vibrancy.

The halo of copper hair rippled from the force.

"What are you?" he murmured under his breath.

Angelic? Perhaps. *But more.* Much *more.*

Dangerous to time? Without doubt.

Any being as powerful as Brigid had become could tear a rift through time at will. Become supreme ruler of not just one plane, but multiple *realms*. And the fact that she obviously was still learning, still *evolving*, portended grave implications.

Yet regardless of the risks, the situation didn't automatically sentence Brigid to death. Not in his mind. Not *all* power corrupted. He failed to pinpoint any specific example, but his gut warned him to stay her execution. For now.

She pegged him with a hard stare, chin lifting a fraction. "I'm no *wee lass* to be trifled with."

"Clearly."

"So, *let's do this for real*." As she murmured his words back at him, she infused them with power.

Atoms throughout the glade charged.

The dense forest beyond quieted, as if waiting on baited breath.

A clear sky above misted over, water molecules crystalizing before hanging in suspension.

With a preternatural lunge, Brigid blinked out of existence, then began to materialize right before him as she spun around like the twisting tip of a tornado. When she slowed into the lower frequency of solid form, twin razor-sharp blades skimmed up his chest until the dagger edges pressed against either side of his throat.

Fierceness blazed in her eyes.

Cool metal bit into his flesh over each jugular.

You've been well *trained.* Magick didn't grant that kind of talent.

Skorpius didn't flinch, remained in solid form. With a slow exhale, he arched his wings up.

Brigid glared up at him.

He held his ground, staring down into eyes that swirled and glittered a rich dark silver.

They stood in the solitary clearing, dark outcast angel

towering over a fair human maiden. The soft ends of those coppery curls brushed against a chest battle-honed into sleek muscle. Scant inches remained between their beating hearts.

But human maidens don't have swirling glittering *silver eyes, do they?*

He suspected Brigid had no idea. That she'd begun to transform. That she was becoming something...*other*.

Seconds ticked by.

A minute.

Longer.

Their great standoff took unspoken form.

To advance matters, he inhaled a slow breath, then exhaled and leaned against the edges of her blades. "What a warm welcome," he taunted. A daring smirk tugged at the corner of his mouth.

"You're *not* welcome," she replied, gaze still locked with his.

Razor edges sliced into skin.

The fearless vixen stood her ground.

So quick to behead me? "Have care," he warned in a soft tone. Toward the both of them. Because few things could end him permanently, but losing his head was one. And neither of them understood the limits of Brigid's new power. More important, if she pushed her luck too hard, he'd force those blades to sever *her* neck before she'd manage a blink. "I'm not here by will," he admitted.

The slightest twitch furrowed her brow.

"Have you ever taken a life before, Brigid?"

"I *came into the world* takin' life." The fierce whisper escaped tightened lips.

Interesting. He stared hard into the depths of silvery eyes churning with raw emotion. However, he had no desire to delve into psychoanalysis. He also refused to relent. Instead, he pressed harder on the struck nerve. "And *now*? Could you take a life now, watch the lifeblood drain from another whose fragile heart beats…until it beats no more?"

Brigid's face paled at the crude description. But her gaze sharpened. Those soft shoulders squared from her spine of steel. She leaned her weight into the sharp blades threatening him. "Aye," she whispered, confidence booming in the barely spoken word.

Fair enough.

The time had come to appeal to more reason, less emotion. "Brigid, please lower your weapons. They are ineffective on me." As far as he knew. "Besides, you are treating your assigned protector like an enemy."

His polite request was answered with a cutting slice as she withdrew the blades with a cross-handed release. Warm twin rivulets of blood streamed down, joined at the base of his throat, then ran down the center depression of his chest.

He chuckled. "*Only* necktie that will *ever* touch this body."

Brigid took a step back. She gripped the blades comfortably at her sides, aiming at his mid-section. The woman remained at the ready to disembowel him, if so inclined.

"You *are* my enemy." Venom laced every word. Hard eyes stared him down.

Skorpius tilted his head, watching her carefully. Accusations of nighttime visits—that he had no recollection of—were a concern, but he didn't broach that topic yet. Better to keep her on the offensive; she'd be more likely to drop inadvertent clues regarding the mystery of her sudden magick. "Why do you consider me your enemy?"

Brigid stared up at him, eyes shifting back and forth while she took his measure. He almost heard the cogs turning in her head as she weighed his question with the merits of her answer. Those assessing silvery eyes narrowed. "You're *not* my friend. You disturb *everra* good dream I've ever had. You're the first person to approach me on my journey. If you're here to stop me, you're mistaken."

His brows arched. "Quite a list for having just met." He crossed his arms, ignoring the tips of her blades as they tracked his movements. "Let's see if I can address your claims, in no particular order."

She gave no reaction to his humorous tone. Simply stared at him with a cold expression.

He continued, as if she hung on every word with rapt interest. "I've *never* had a good dream. If I've somehow interrupted *all* of yours, I deeply apologize." He paused, letting the sarcasm drip to its full effect.

"I've not made a new friend in a *long* time. Therefore, your assessment of our relationship status is correct: *not* friends." He gave a slow nod. "But that does not make me your enemy.

"As far as stopping you on your journey, I'd have to know what quest you're on and why, before deciding whether I'd stop you, or not."

That did the trick: her brows furrowed.

Confusion caused by sound reasoning. He bit back the laugh that lodged into his throat and unconsciously brushed his fingers across the dried blood there.

Brigid gasped, eyes growing wide.

Ahhh…the wound healing.

"You're…" She shook her head in disbelief, her delicate brows furrowing again. "I doona understand. I…I…cut you."

"Really? I stand taller than any male you've encountered, eyes swirling blue-and-green, black wings arching up from my back like a monster hatched from your darkest nightmare, and *that's* what you focus on? That my wound—that *you* inflicted— healed before your eyes?"

She glared anew at all his obviousness. Then she lowered her weapons and turned her back on him.

Great. He snorted. *I've been relegated to* absolutely-no-threat *status.*

Brigid shrugged as she stooped to gather a handful of belongings strewn across the ground beside an open satchel. "Isobel warned me of you."

"Oh, she did, did she?" The runt even antagonized him by proxy. Yet his interest piqued. "What did that...*sweet*...girl have to say about me?"

The corners of Brigid's lips twitched as she fought a smile. "I doona remember *everra* detail."

Translation: Females hold all girl-talk jokes sacred.

"'Twas a wee bit like 'barkin' with no bitin',' that you'll be 'comin' in handy' when she'll be 'needin' some muscle,' and..."

Brigid paused as she turned toward him with her small stack of belongings in her hands. She pursed her lips as if trying to control a great flood of amusement that threatened to break free.

Skorpius forced a steadying breath, mentally grumbling a too-distant-to-receive message at the Traveler. *You little* runt *of a troublemaker.* Isobel wasn't even present and *still* she annoyed him. *Paybacks, Ms. MacInnes. They'll be painful. And character-building.*

To Brigid, he raised expectant let's-have-it brows.

"Isobel claimed she called you by 'nicknames.' And you liked it. She said, although she liked to call you Sunshine, her favorite was...Cupcake."

Slow breaths.

Deep, slow breaths.

He managed to stop the low growl instinctually forming in his throat. Then he coughed out a laugh and shook his head. No one held true power to torment him by proxy, not even Isobel.

And Brigid bravely stood up to him in the here and now. Only she earned the right to provoke him at present. And he alone decided on whether or not he'd be provoked. He waved a disinterested hand in the air. "Call me what you wish. It matters not to me."

Brigid gave a satisfied nod, then strode away with her stack, toward the edge of the glade. But she paused, then veered back toward him, until she stopped a few feet away. She regarded him with cool assessment. "What's your real name? She dinna tell me."

In rare form, he considered his answer. He typically replied to that question with sarcasm—as he'd done with Isobel—because angelkind never uttered given names, theirs sung in a frequency so high its vibration would shatter glass, and human eardrums.

But Brigid had asked in a context altogether different. She wanted to understand what he preferred to be called.

Whether or not she realized it, her request was a tentative olive branch.

He relaxed his wings and chose to respect the subtle gesture. "My name is Skorpius."

With a thoughtful nod, she uttered his name in three slow syllables, as if rolling the flavor over her tongue to savor its taste for the first time. Then she repeated it with fluid grace. "Skorpius."

When she turned with her stack, plucked her satchel from the ground with two fingers, then strode away toward thicker forest edging the glade, he followed.

"Do you even know what a cupcake is?" An olive branch back. Conversational. One step toward camaraderie. Helpful if they remained together for any length of time. Crucial to gain her trust.

From the shadows of the trees ahead, light laughter tinkled like breeze-rustled wind chimes. "I dinna know, at first. Isobel said 'tis a wee sweet cake for children. And yours, she said, 'tis 'frosted' in pink. With somethin' called *sprinkles*?"

"Of course," he grumbled.

But as Brigid relaxed further and paused beside a large oak to pack her belongings back into her satchel, his attention diverted to one item in particular. A split-second glimpse was all he managed before she stowed the object: a weathered black book, leather-bound with distinctive strips at the middle of each cover's edge, which wound around to secure it closed.

His breath caught. *That can't possibly be…*

CHAPTER 5

*S*korpius arrowed an icy stare at her.

His blue-green eyes swirled, tiny sparks of silver flashin'.

And then, those unearthly eyes narrowed further.

Brigid had plunged from friend to foe in a heartbeat.

Which served her well. 'Twas a healthy reminder that the creature not only possessed greater power than she, but also held more knowledge of her newly acquired strange magick. It dinna matter the value of learnin' from someone wiser of how to wield it. His incredible energy set her on edge, prickled the hairs on the back of her neck. Continued acquaintance with the angel posed a risk not worth takin'.

She shot a colder glare back toward him, then resumed her journey. She angled off in the direction she'd been headed. Before the skirmish with the English soldiers. Before the wee ones. And the magick. *Before the angel.*

"I'll *still* be travelin' on my own."

A heavy sigh gusted behind her. "We're at an impasse, then."

"Aye. *I'll* be stayin' here on dry shore. *You're*"—she hiked a chin toward a jagged peak on the horizon that pierced the sky, then scanned the glassy stretch of blue at its feet—"welcome to stand knee-deep in muck, on the *other* side of a freezin' loch."

When pure silence followed, she glanced back to find him starin' her down, jaw twitchin'. The bare-chested angel forced a deep breath into his lungs.

Brigid disregarded the male's state of undress, likenin' him to any of her clan's guardsmen that trained at Brodie Castle. Pleased with how she strained his patience, she arched a brow.

After a handful of seconds, he loosened his rigid jaw with a side-to-side motion. "So it would seem," he conceded with a short nod.

Yet he made no indication to move.

Brigid unsheathed a dagger, aimed it at him, then flicked the point toward that distant peak. "'Tis where I prefer you."

"Understood." He turned and strode away, in the opposite direction she'd been headed.

Tension in her achin' shoulders began to relax for what felt like the first time all day. She resheathed her dagger and resumed down her path.

"But it doesn't have to be that way." His soft-spoken words somehow sounded loud and clear in her head.

"Nay?" She half-turned, amused at how their finished conversation continued to linger.

Skorpius still faced away from her, but had stopped. His chiseled jaw and the corner of his eye angled toward her, over his shoulder. "No."

With a sweep of his chin, he completed his turn, stance widenin'. His gaze caught hers. "Although, getting cold...*and wet*...does have its merits."

Brigid gasped as a sudden frisson of heat sizzled through her, sparking tiny embers of pleasure in unmentionable places. *From his carnal tone.* Because *none* of that sounded appealin'.

Her eyes narrowed. *More trickery?*

And the way he stared at her, with the knowin' of a thousand human lifetimes—down into the verra heart of her—warmed her further. He dipped his head a fraction, but never broke their locked gazes.

He waited.

His expression grew…predatory.

And in an odd fashion, some once-idle part of her began to awaken with interest, desired to bargain with him.

The magick? Had her new ability responded to him?

If so, she'd need to learn exactly how much control she had. "What're you proposin'?"

"We should work together."

"*Och!* In what way?" No warrior in Scotland would agree to work with a lass. The verra idea made her cough out a disbelievin' laugh.

"You've discovered how to tap into great power." The meltin' heat in his expression cooled. "But you don't understand how to use it."

She scoffed and crossed her arms.

But as Skorpius's words settled with her, her thoughts drifted over his earlier accusation: that she'd learned to summon her magick from someone. Mayhap, she'd take advantage of his false assumption. "I'm doin' fine. On my own." On the last words, her tightened fingers drummed once on the hilt of the dagger that she'd sheathed moments ago.

His gaze flicked down at her pointed movement. He gave a short nod, then tilted his head, glancin' back up at her. "Acknowledged. You excel in combat skills. You *have* done well with your magick. But could you do better? Everyone needs guidance, on occasion."

While she slowed her breaths to clear her mind—and calm her body—she considered his reasonable offer. In truth, she'd only achieved what she'd learned thus far through the instruction and counsel of others. Even if they'd been a trusted and select few. Even if they'd only trained her in traditional warrior skills. Even if none had even a wee notion of her newfound ability.

But can you *be trusted?* She pinned him with a hard stare, judgin' his character.

Skorpius remained calm and motionless.

But after a few seconds, his expression softened. Then he drew in a deep breath and exhaled, brows liftin' a wee bit. As if to yield, to submit. Which, from such a powerful creature, appeared to take great effort.

She tilted her head, sensin' no falsehood in his demeanor. Trust could be earned. And her suspicion would remain high till she knew for certain. *Even then, far beyond. For good measure.*

After another few seconds of his extended patience, she granted him a short nod. "Mayhap."

"*Good.*" He relaxed his wings down a fraction, then strode toward her with confident grace. "Some degree of cooperation will make the guarding part easier."

And I've got a strong feeling, his low voice boomed, *'some' will be all I'll be able to manage from the hellion. Fine by me. Your fight? Makes my mission that much more enjoyable.*

Startled, her gaze shot up toward the grim set of his *closed* lips, the tight clench of his jaw. Even as the last of his unspoken words filtered into her head.

"Och! I *heard* that!"

He paused midstride, starin' at her with widened eyes. Then he gave a heavy blink and shook his head. "*Of course*, you did."

"You'll be stayin' outta my head."

"*I* didn't trespass into *your* mind." He tilted a curious glance her way. "*You* eavesdropped into *mine.*"

"Oh." Mayhap, she needed more guidance with her magick than she'd realized.

"Unprecedented, by the way," he grumbled.

"*Good.*" She shot his retort back at him, satisfied in causin' him dismay.

Skorpius stared at her with that penetratin' gaze for a few seconds, then scanned along the tops of the trees, from one end of the horizon across to the other. "Which way are we heading?"

Brigid turned without reply and strode down the game trail she'd begun to navigate. By the sun's track, she could've determined their direction and answered him, but chose to cut their conversation short, preferred to maintain some safe amount of distance.

The clear action spoke for her. All he needed to know. "If you're guardin'—not interferin'—you'll follow," she murmured. *I'll allow the intrusion. For now.*

No argument boomed from him, aloud or in her head. Blessed silence settled there.

Nimble steps wound her along the narrow shadowed path. An intuitive tug, some new sense she'd developed, led her toward where she needed to go.

When a chill crisped the air, she hastened into a light-footed trot through open straightaway sections to warm the blood pulsin' through her arms and legs. As she ran, the trail grew barely visible. Lacy ferns lashed across the fronts of her thighs. Thick spongy moss bounced underfoot.

But even when the path grew difficult, her progress slowin' to skirt thorny bramble overgrowth or overreachin' bracken, she recovered then raced on in an unmistakable direction, as if a tempest river beneath the ground itself had scooped her up and swept her along.

After some distance, lungs burnin' and pulse thumpin', she perceived a flare in the sizzlin' energy of the one sent to guard her. Then she slowed to a walk, surprised that she noticed the angel at all. Upon greater concentration, she stretched her mind outward and collected even more information: his presence raced alongside the trail she used, but a dozen paces back and a half-dozen paces aside, beyond a dense growth of trees.

And yet...not one sound resonated from his rapid movement.

Well-trained as Brigid was by the most skilled trackers within her clan, even she rustled a wayward branch, broke an occasional dried twig underfoot.

Curiosity drew her more focused attention toward Skorpius's position, no matter how intently she tried to ignore him.

When she homed in on his well-defined energy, she caught sight of him, a blur of motion. After a heavy blink, her lips parted on a gasp, mouth fallin' wide open.

Och! You're not travelin' through the woods, you're passin' through the trees.

A good ten feet above the ground, wings spread, but fixed as a soarin' hawks, his prone body floated on a swift current, vanishin' then reappearin', as insubstantial as Highland mist.

When Skorpius gave a slow shrug, then cast a glance her way, she realized she'd projected her shocked exclamation into his mind. Again.

But his small movement did nothin' to mar his smooth flight as he raced past her. A rich, low voice echoed into her mind. *Less energy is expended when I go incorporeal. And stay to the shadows.*

"Like a ghost," she whispered aloud, then stared with wide eyes at the unbelievable sight again. Her mind struggled to accept the strange feat. *Mistin' through trees!*

Seconds passed till Brigid blinked back into awareness. She found herself alone, then chased after him. As she alighted down her path, she soon sighted his misty shape again.

His deep voice resonated into her mind, softer, reflective. *In some ways.*

Another stretch of silence passed while she negotiated rougher boulder-strewn terrain. Once on flatter ground, she eased into a comfortable trot, grateful for the respite while she enjoyed the wild beauty of a rollin' moor swathed in bright purple heather.

The angel remained quiet, maintainin' some amount of distance between them. She still sensed the faint warmth of his power out there, somewhere. But for a time, she traveled with great joy alone, while her guard remained out of sight.

Yet before she reached the shelter of more shadowy forest ahead, her once-easy pace grew strenuous—with no explanation. In a trice, each next step demanded immense effort. Leg muscles that had ached in a pleasant way, began to burn, then twitched in spasm.

Before she stumbled on a protrudin' root or rock that undulated through the earthen path, she slowed to a walk. A lone tree beckoned off left, and she staggered over, swayed a bit, then leaned against the rough bark of its solid trunk.

Weariness fogged her brain, and she loosed a loud yawn.

"I'll be restin' here a bit," she murmured, dimly aware that her guard's energy had drawn near, growin' warmer.

The great shadow of his form loomed above.

Then her world plunged into darkness, cold and absolute.

THE METAL BLADE whistled past Brigid's ear.

A split second later, a low thump followed.

She startled awake, seated and leanin' against the wide base of a tree. Then she blinked and glance up at the carved hilt of one of her daggers, sunk into the bark above her shoulder. Confusion fogged her brain, as she'd only just paused to lean against the large tree.

When had she sat down? Or fallen asleep?

The dark angel stood a dozen paces away, starin' intently at her. He balanced her other dagger upon his fingertips, as if he considered hurlin' the second one at her as well.

She forced herself *not* to think of how he'd stolen them both from her person.

"Lesson one." Skorpius pointed the gleamin' blade at her. "Never let your guard down."

"Aye." She reached over her head, yanked the first dagger from the soft bark, then stood. *"Angels* canna be trusted."

"Not me." He shook his head. "Wild animals. Other humans. Worse, any other being who yields magick. One who might want yours."

"Och! Someone can steal my magick?" *Her* magick. The soothin' warm essence—energy that protected, yet whispered of endless possibilities—had already become a vital part of her.

"Someone might think so. And likely kill you simply to find out."

Her breath caught, pulse spikin' at the absurd notion. "Is that why you're wishin' to kill me?" Because she sensed Skorpius held some critical truth back. And even though he meant no harm at the moment, deadly menace radiated from him. She took cautious steps to the side, circlin' into the sunny moor of heather.

"No." The black feathers on his massive wings ruffled as he rotated to follow her movement. A flash of amusement sparked in his eyes, as if he already possessed all the power he needed, wouldn't be bothered to think of wantin' more. But his lethal gaze never wavered, and he dinna deny her accusation. *"Some* will believe to kill you will release your magick, in the hope of absorbing its energy as their own, increase their power within your realm. And beyond it."

Heaviness clenched deep in her gut at the notion of some thief killin' her to drain her dry. *"Och!"* she murmured, horrified. "Is that possible?"

Those unyieldin' blue-green sparklin' eyes bored into the depths of her soul as he unfolded his hand to display the weapon he'd lifted when she'd been unconscious. *"Anything* is possible."

*Lesson one...*his earlier words echoed into her mind. Her grip tightened on the hilt of the first dagger. "Doona let my guard down."

The shaggy ends of his wild black hair rustled at his faint nod. "And trust no one."

She almost laughed. "I'm trustin' you." But as the statement tumbled from her lips, she felt the rightness under its tone, firm and true. Because the uneven ground beneath her feet tilted a bit. Or was that unsteady legs? Uncertain how long she'd dozed, or why everythin' seemed a wee bit altered, she widened her stance, not trustin' her senses. Or her knees.

"Different matter altogether. And necessary." He pointed the dagger tip at her again. "Apprentice." Then he hooked his thumb and jerked it backward, toward his bare chest. "Master." Teasin' wickedness gleamed in his eyes.

At his boldness, she parted her lips, but the sharp retort that formed there died on her tongue. For the idea of callin' him "cupcake"? Some sweet treat? *Nay.* Her mind reeled at connectin' the fierce angel with a food that made her mouth water. After a hard swallow, heat sparkin' under her skin, she drew a deep breath, then narrowed her eyes.

"Go on, *angel.*" The truth of the matter, a safe "nickname." And she'd grant him his amusement. For a moment.

"Trust only me. No one else." His formidable gaze kept tight hold of hers. "Some might see killing you as only *one* option to gain your power."

"There are other ways?" A sickenin' weight churned in the pit of her stomach. As if, down deep, her magick knew, sensed the danger.

"Worse ways."

Unbidden images crowded into her mind. *From Skorpius? Her magick?* A cruel nightmare of creepin' shadows stretched through a pitch-dark tight space. Bitter cold. Never-endin' loneliness. Time stretched eternal.

"*Captive*," she breathed the repulsive conclusion on the scarcest whisper. *To be prisoner?* On a shudder, she exhaled and scraped the word and vision from her psyche, in solid fear of her manifestin' the nightmare from her immense well of magick. Some inner protective impulse warned her to tread with care.

"Yes. Or as a puppet."

"Puppet?" Her gaze drifted down. Her belly felt as if it had plummeted through the ground. The heather's wee purple blooms and green needle leaves fuzzed and spun, dancin' and weavin' like she'd drunk too much of Iain's stout mead.

"Evil works in any conceivable way." Skorpius's voice twisted, from wide and thin to dense and tight, then exploded outward to boom rich and echo long, as if they'd entered a great cave. "Like water," he continued in his twisty boomin' voice, "malevolence seeps into every void until it breaks through on a rush or a trickle. Some might try to control your mind. Perhaps you'd be aware of it, but unable to do anything. Or, maybe...you won't be aware at all."

Once-effortless breaths grew shallow as she gulped for air that failed to reach starvin' lungs. After a hard swallow, she ran her tongue over her teeth, then along her lips, to moisten a mouth gone bone dry. Twirlin' specks floated up, all around them. Sparklin' gold dusted the odd particles. With wide eyes, she reached out to touch one.

"You're not even aware of what your mind's doing now. That's dirt you are raising up. Layer by layer, the particles around you are coming to life, honoring your silent wishes."

She frowned, then winced, as incredible pain lanced through her temples, then remained to throb as a tortuous drumbeat behind her eyes. *Why would I pull dirt into the air?*

Wrong question.

His deep and extraordinarily soothin' voice resonated into her mind again.

And the excruciatin' pain ebbed at once.

Awash in his comfortin' essence, she inhaled its vital energy and took a step toward him. Entranced into a dreamy pliant state, a childlike trust took hold. She sought to wrap herself in the warmth and protection that the steely undertones of the angel's voice promised.

"What's the right one?" she murmured. Exhaustion tugged at every fiber of her being, unravelin' her from the inside out.

In an instant, the compassion in the angel's gaze hardened to ice.

"How to stop *your own magick* from killing you now."

CHAPTER 6

*G*lassy silver eyes stared up at him, trusting.

Too trusting.

The perfect heady cocktail of temptation. Unimaginable power and pure innocence.

Numerous potential threats would rise against Brigid. And *from* her.

Pulled under by an intoxicating surge of power, she'd fallen under its spell. Even more telling, without full awareness of her actions, she'd drawn perilously close to him.

A clouded gaze swept under the length of his nearest wing. Longing softened her expression, and she reached out, fingers outstretched.

"*Brigid.*" His tone charged low, riddled with warning.

The *last* thing she needed was more sensation. Nor did he trust himself to provide it.

Of all the dangers against her, facing them all, one slip of his hard-earned control would prove cataclysmic.

She blinked hard, breath catching. Her foggy gaze cleared. "*Och!* I…"—she stumbled back, out of his reach, shaking her head—"'Tis strange. I doona understand what's befallen me."

"You're crashing. The magick you summoned to save the children consumed energy. The challenge you faced to overcome my magick spent more. You're having a cascading meltdown."

Her brow twitched down as she took another retreating step. Her eyes widened, then narrowed. Already shallow breaths devolved into tense panting.

"You've got brain fog," he muttered. Which meant she likely had difficulty understanding his logical explanation. Or she was hallucinating. *No telling.*

But Skorpius refused to force her obedience. And if she melted down from lack of knowledge, he'd have to end her right then and there.

Easy. However, he also refused to destroy such a beautiful creature from lack of instruction. Not from something as elementary as the balance of energy.

"Your body and soul are starving for fuel to such a degree, you're summoning magick to feed your need, which expends more energy than it replaces. You need to replenish that energy."

Her delicate fist clenched tight under her ribs, between her heart and her stomach. "I *ache.*"

"When was the last time you ate?"

An indignant snort followed. She gave a slight headshake. Either she didn't believe the reason could be that simple or she'd tumbled down so far, the idea of stomaching food repulsed her. Yet food would stave off the worst of it, the beginnings. They'd deal with the rest later.

But first, he had to get her on board. Fast. *But how?*

Brigid took another quick retreating step, a frightened deer ready to bolt.

Distract.

Particles continued to float, vibrating, animated by her magick. All glistened with her golden energy, from larger twigs and rocks to miniscule pollen and clay dust.

Before Skorpius engaged her further, he checked their internal bonds, the two distinct invisible threads that connected them. The cord leashing him to her at all costs remained taut, tugged him toward her. Paradoxically, the one meant to have him fix the time-rift Brigid herself had caused, even if it meant ending her, also held fast.

Both strong as ever. Even in her drained state.

Interesting.

"North." Tone matter-of-fact, she sheathed her dagger, then straightened her shoulders.

"What?" The sudden out-of-context word threw him. Along with her redoubled force of will. As if she forged on, despite her exhaustion. Which, he knew from experience, would only last so long.

"North." She darted a glance toward the forest beyond the moor, down their original course. And she acted oblivious to his confusion and her inexplicable behavior.

Maybe she was. Maybe in her brain-fog state, she'd distracted herself. Then again, with all the magick humming around them, maybe he had manifested his desired outcome. Through her.

Then he realized she'd finally answered his *Which way are we heading?* question.

Okay. I'll bite. Not much to work with, nothing to lose. "Anything else?"

An assessing stare landed on him. She inhaled slowly, exhaled slower. Those silver eyes narrowed, sparking with wariness, and no small amount of magick.

"In truth?" she asked.

"Usually how it's done."

Brigid walked toward him again, palm outstretched, gaze fixed on the remaining dagger he'd absconded with. But a tiny crease furrowed between slender brows. "You speak like Isobel."

Great. "How so?"

He spun the dagger with the flick of a finger and dipped it toward her, hilt-first.

When she grasped the weapon, he shifted his hold, enabling their skin to touch for an instant.

The brief contact sparked on an infinitesimal level. That electrical impulse gave him a wealth of information on the condition of her health. And at the rate she drained her adrenals by magickally manipulating elements around her, she careened toward another crash any second.

Oblivious to his check of her vital-signs, she sheathed her weapon and continued, "As if you're teasin', but not quite. Or you're speakin' one word, yet meanin' another."

"Ah, sarcasm." Excellent distraction tool. Easy to knock an opponent off-balance when their brain is busy wrestling with word puzzles.

With his impassive tone, and lack of explanation, she shot him a deadpan.

"It's a form of humor. Meant to disarm, to put at ease." *Plenty of what's needed now.*

One of her slender brows arched. "And mock."

"A little. Not to dishonor. To build rapport. Gain trust." Insomuch as the two of them ever could. "You share a truth. I share a truth."

Brigid's inscrutable gaze held his for a few seconds. Then she turned and resumed her course down the trail she'd been navigating, albeit at a much slower pace.

Without further comment, he followed. But he noticed every teetering bob and subtle sway, how her body reacted to its growing need for energy. Of particular note was her perseverance, in spite of those undeniable demands.

Yet with no real threat, his role remained the same. Support only, on the one thread. Swift eradication, on the other. Monitor in the meantime. Until either forced decisive action.

Mandate required Skorpius's assistance for his charge, but not force-fed. She had to be receptive to guidance. And her stubbornness had quarantined him to an unhelpful distance.

With slower strides, she trekked another fifty yards. And as she placed each trudging step, her gaze darted back and forth; she scanned along dirt-exposed parts of the trail and examined the extended ends of tree branches and other overgrowth.

You're tracking something. He considered the most logical possibilities. *Your horse.* Because no matter how powerful Brigid had become in so short a time, no Highlander in their right mind—nor even a determined female some might label insane— would leave on a long journey without a reliable mount. And with the last of her magick all but snuffed out, hurting as she had to be, it shocked him that she pressed on.

By sheer will. A mighty *force to be reckoned with.*

Brigid paused at a fork in the trail. On a slow inhale, she closed her eyes and reached out with a brush of magick so faint, he suspected she had no idea she'd wielded it. But her depleted body knew. She swayed a little, then chose the right-hand path.

"*In truth*, my most pressin' need..." She stretched out the syllables and took a few more measured steps. Then she turned to face him. "'Tis retrievin' my horse." Her tone dropped, flat.

"Well done."

A tiny wrinkle furrowed between those slender brows. "Weel done, what?"

"Sarcasm. Not a bad attempt. But you'll need to work on your subject matter. Obvious statements of fact are good. But a dry tone when you say one thing yet mean the exact opposite? Better."

"*Och!*" She shook her head, threw her arms halfway up, then dropped the tired limbs as she propped her hands on her hips. "You'll be drivin' me mad before long."

Who says you're not already there? Internal sarcasm. Which he wisely kept to himself. What he needed more than anything was for Brigid to let her guard down. Not armor it up.

So instead, he said nothing and stared at her.

But in spite of his control, or maybe because that weak part of his heart continued to hairline fracture, he freed a hint of mirth: the minor crinkles bracketing his eyes, a slight lift at the corners of his mouth.

Brigid twitched her lips, fighting a return smile.

But then she sighed, shoulders relaxing down. "I'm *huntin' my horse* because I doona wish to march across all of Scotland." She flung those fatigued arms wide to emphasize the enormity of it all. Or in case he'd forgotten on what ground the two of them stood.

Her stomach growled. "*And* I'm hungry." Deadweight arms dropped to her sides again. "Now, your truth."

Perfect timing. For her surrender, and the topic segue.

"I'll give you two. First, you're not just hungry. You're ravenous. You've used massive amounts of energy—you *still* are —and it's drained you to a near-unrecoverable level. If you don't eat soon, you'll lose consciousness again. At any moment."

Tenacious to her core, she scowled. "Nay. Tough blood flows through my veins."

Clearly. But that's beside the point.

"Yes, you will. Stone-cold pass out. Total face-plant." *Maybe some of Isobel's twenty-first century words will break through your stubbornness and brain fog.* Even so, he added a physical demonstration: raised a bent arm to chest level, rested his other elbow on those fingers, then, with a descending whistle, slow-toppled his arm to an explosive crash, complete with a puff of his cheeks when he slapped down that last inch. "Down. *Whether or not* you find a good landing place."

Brigid swallowed hard at his grim prognosis. Held her breath for a couple of absorbing seconds. Pegged him with a shrewd look.

Then, as if seeing through her mental haze for the first time, she scanned her surroundings, eyes widening as she noticed all the miniscule sparkling items she'd cast aloft with her magick. At once, every single thing dropped, leaving behind a dissipating cloud of glittering gold.

Without a word, she strode off trail.

Along the southern edge of a nearby grove of saplings, Brigid scooped raking hands over bobbing yellow dandelion blossoms, yanked the fluffy tops off their gangly stems, and popped one after another into her mouth. Even the plant's young tender leaves got stuffed in, chewed. Other broadleaf plants caught her eye, and she made quick work of harvesting, then devouring. For a solid five minutes, she plucked and ate, stuffing her cheeks, chewing nonstop, swallowing as fast as she could, to make room for more. Herbs, edible wildflowers, weeds, each was expertly identified by a Scot familiar with foraging. And what she consumed delivered a powerhouse of dense phytonutrients and protein.

Afterward, following some innate sense, she wandered out into the bright sunshine, face tilting upward, eyes drifting closed. She raised her bare arms toward the life-giving radiation and soaked up its pure energy.

Skorpius simply watched, pleased and impressed that she followed her intuition.

A visible calm had settled over her by the time she turned back toward him.

But through the further lens of a fine wave of his own magick, which filtered her brilliance with his smoky hue, he determined her reserves had already been topped off. Skin that had begun to turn pallid flushed a healthy pink once again. Clouded silvery eyes brightened, white and observant. Even her hair glowed with renewed radiance, her aura pulsing with fresh energy.

Then that astute mercurial gaze locked on to his. "And the second?"

Very well, truth. As promised. *But not everything.*

"I'm not sent to *merely* guard you." *Aside from guarding time itself...* "There's a caveat to my guardianship." Brigid needed to understand the parameters, would find out at some point regardless. "I cannot interfere in which path you take, you must decide. But I'm at your service to assist, when needed. Guardian angels are only able to guide."

The first sign of joy alighted in her gray eyes, turning them to quicksilver in the sunlight. "Escort and advise." She peeked over her shoulder, toward the bottom of her satchel.

His gaze tracked to its slight bulge, his thoughts turning toward what she'd stowed there.

"So, you're like a knight sent to protect me." She glanced back at him with a beaming smile. "Like Sir Galahad."

Skorpius coughed out a laugh. "No. *Not* a knight. *Not even a little* like Galahad." That unique leather journal—which she'd *somehow* acquired—had filled her head with romantic notions. Idealism had no place in her world. No place in *any* world he'd come to know.

She huffed out a light snort at his ready dismissal. "How will you protect me?"

"The same as I assisted you with your magick. Like I am *master*"—he arched a brow and dipped a pointed nod toward her —"and you are *apprentice*."

Brigid gave a heavy blink, then rolled her eyes at his not-so-subtle reminder.

Nice. In spite of their opposing roles, he began to like her. *A little.* Only enough for them to tolerate one another. Not enough to endanger the delicate situation they'd stumbled into.

Dread tripped through him. That damned weak spot in his heart.

Skorpius had sought to have Brigid bond with him, like him. Not the other way around.

He couldn't afford to like her. The risk for a misstep loomed too great.

So he redirected back to the task at hand. "*Only* after your horse?" He suspected more. Because she'd been tracking with great skill on ground-born signs. But she also darted an occasional glance skyward with a sharp inhalation, then panned along the hidden horizon line, searching. Or listening.

"Nay." But she didn't elaborate.

And he didn't need her to.

Magick itself, and whatever role she played with it—for or against time remaining whole—was leading her toward some unknown destination.

THEY WALKED ONWARD at a slower pace, side by side, in almost companionable silence.

Almost, Skorpius thought.

No daggers had been drawn or thrown, no verbal barbs had been flung, and no magick had been summoned, not even inadvertently. Plus, he'd graciously muzzled the sarcasm. So "almost" counted for a lot between two inharmonious companions.

He also noticed that Brigid had casually allowed him into her personal space. Noticed, but wisely chose not to comment on the recent development.

When the sun dipped another few inches closer to the horizon, his focus flashed inward, toward the two threads that bound him. The one tied to her guardianship vibrated a degree faster. Which meant some unseen force nearby threatened her person or mission. And although he couldn't interfere, at the very least he needed to offer guidance.

A quick mental inventory drew his attention toward where Brigid had come from...and when. He glanced over at her. "Iain will come after you." *If he isn't already on his way.*

Brigid's easygoing pace slowed a fraction. A slight frown tugged at her lips. Then she gave an imperceptible headshake. "Isobel will hold him off."

"From protecting his own sister?" He laughed. "Not even a remote chance."

"I'm safe." Brigid squared her shoulders, confident and relaxed. "She'll sway his opinion."

Something about her absolute faith in that gave him pause. *Denial? Or something more. Something powerful.* To conduct another subtle test of her status, he pulsed an undetectable wave of magick her way. A low hum of magick radiated from her core out into the ether, so slight in energy it seemed to be a baseline constant.

Could she have tapped into the unified field?

Would such a subtle low-level vibration be enough to disrupt or alter anything she wished? Even Iain?

Manifestation worked in mysterious ways.

But Skorpius doubted she'd mastered magick to that level. To become that proficient? Would require decades of practice to achieve that kind of pinpoint accuracy over such distance and time.

Which meant her brother's interference remained a factor that Isobel would be hard-pressed to circumvent. Therefore, they needed to address the issue in a real-world way.

Skorpius strode farther ahead, then turned and angled in, cutting into her path to gain her full attention. "Not regarding your safety, she won't." Iain was almost as stubborn as he.

Brigid continued with a few more steps, then stopped, inches away from him. Curiosity sparked in her pale eyes. "If I'll be askin' your assistance, you'd be duty bound to prevent Iain from stoppin' me?"

He leveled a hard stare down at her. "My duty to you only goes so far. No guardian can go to war for his charge. I cannot harm another who has virtuous intent to enable you to have your way. Fighting for you is not the same as protecting you."

Waging battle? Going to war? Those actions fell soundly into the realm of protecting time. So, he *would* fight, if the situation demanded it. Whether or not the act gained Brigid her wish.

"But I'm needin' to see this through." Her voice softened. Her gaze held a quiet plea.

"See *what* through?" *Here it is.* The big question and its elusive answer. The reason for his being there. And she'd relaxed her guard enough, finally trusted him enough, to confide in him.

After a few second's pause, she blinked, shook her head, then wandered beyond him. Under the canopy of a great tree whose leafy boughs stretched over the trail, she turned, then leaned against its trunk. Her slender brows twitched down before she relaxed back against the bark. Then she stared up into the giant's many branches.

The late afternoon sun dipped below the treetops behind them, and a slight breeze rustled through the leaves overhead. Varying patterns of leafy shadows played over her fair face.

But as a creature relegated to darkness—whose very essence charged from the chilling absence of light—he discerned each slight nuance, the parting of her peachy-pink lips, her breathy sigh. Then her skin began to illuminate, a faint golden light.

Recognition struck.

His brow furrowed. *Impossible.*

Yet, there she stood, impossible as ever.

I stand, as well. And many would utter the same of him.

Every little clue pointed toward the fact. But in all of millennia, it had never happened.

No. Not *supposition. Fact.*

Skorpius wiped the suspicion from his brain. Because he had to be sure.

Brigid's face tipped back down and a weary smile wobbled her lips as her gaze landed on him again. "It calls to me. 'Tis the greatest task." She clenched a fist over her heart, eyes drifting closed, chest expanding on a slow inhale. "But...*I* doona *know*," she whispered.

Well, great. That made two of them.

"And somethin'"—her eyes narrowed as she pulsed a probing wave of magick toward him, then gave a solid headshake —"some *other* presence with magick is tryin' to interfere."

Another clue. One he'd not given enough weight to before.

"Disturbing your dreams." Which she had earlier accused him of. Yet some differentiation had suddenly taken place. Her ability had evolved to a level where she sensed the distinction.

Brigid swallowed hard, then nodded. "Aye."

"Good?" Skorpius had to ask, needed her gut reaction.

Her stronger headshake tossed those long copper curls behind her shoulder. "*Nay.*"

"Of course." He frowned. *Not good.* On every level. For her. For the rest of the worlds.

She shoved off from the tree, expression grave. "Mayhap, 'tis the one who's huntin' my magick?"

"*One.* There could be others." Other entities, myriad potentialities. "When you use your magick, the energy signature echoes out, a beacon to anyone searching for power." He stared at her while he puzzled out all the clues. With no clear instructions of how they fit into the bigger picture, his two tethers were all he had to go on. And neither tugged with any great urgency.

Her hard gaze remained locked on him. "Those who'll be wishin' to kill me." *Besides you.*

Brigid's unsaid sentiment filtered into his brain, crystal clear. Vague as her thought was, whether or not she'd intentionally directed it toward him, her strong emotion cast it aloft. And bolstered with the special elixir of magick he suspected she had somehow acquired, telepathic communication had been added to her emerging abilities.

Yet with her innocent expression, she appeared unaware that her accusation had been broadcasted.

And Skorpius didn't acknowledge hearing it. Because his presence *was* a mortal threat to her. But dragging that morbid topic out into the open served no purpose and stood in direct conflict to his gaining her trust.

"Or take you captive," he redirected. Aloud.

Her assessing gaze held his. At the same time, a gentle golden magick probed at him as her chest rose and fell on steady deep breaths.

Skorpius allowed her slight energy access. A wave washed over and through him, warm, but subtle. So subtle, only a being attuned to magick would notice. No mere mortal could.

"Ask what you wish to know of me." With a spark of energy, he shook her nascent magick free of his system. "No need to probe for it."

Brigid's chin lifted. Defiance sparked in her eyes. "I'll be demandin' the same from you."

Ah, so you've sensed my magick testing you? he mentally asked. Time to strip away the pretense.

Aye, she mentally replied. "You've been searchin' for answers."

Answers like this, your action a clear admission that you'd known about your telepathy. "And other secrets even you may not be aware of."

Just discovered, now known, she countered. "And you'll only breach my mind when I give you permission." An unyielding gaze brooked no argument.

Skorpius dropped her a brief nod. "When I'm able to request it."

"And these 'others'?" she asked.

Besides who she'd sensed, disturbing her dreams. "Any being who dares. *They* won't ask. They'll take. With whatever means they see fit. Barbaric, not humane. The easiest way, for most."

A wounded expression flashed over her features. "But why?"

Even raised during times of war, Brigid remained innocent to the vicious greed of others. Human cruelty was the tip of the iceberg compared to entities in other realms. However, she had charged into the game of power with eyes wide open and a passion for some unknown cause blazing.

Her kingdom's bards spouted tales of mortal fragility, subject to the callous whims of wizards and gods. Better for Brigid to understand reality now than suffer by experience later. "To use you. Harness your power, your will."

"*Och!* I'd rather die."

"You might not have a choice."

Those astute eyes widened, then narrowed. "They'll be usin' trickery?"

Possibly. As he mentally sent the reply, a sudden suspicion had him burst out a wave of energy to ensure they weren't being monitored as they spoke. Yet at that moment, he detected no presence other than their own, along with the native flora and fauna.

Brigid winced. "Aloud, please. I doona like all the talkin' in my head."

"Enchant you." All he ventured.

Because he didn't like stating all the darker possibilities. Didn't want to even think them. With all the power sparking in both of them, they ran the very real risk of their magick amplifying words and thoughts into suggestions or demands, bringing them forth into the realm of matter. "And you need to practice mental communication. The skill needs to be second nature if you're under stress. And you'll be grateful for the talent, particularly if it's the *only* means of communication you have."

"Then I'll abandon the magick." With a hard exhalation, an invisible percussive wave blew out and down. The sounds of the forest distorted, then flattened. The drop of her magick happened so hard and quick, the energy blast briefly extinguished Skorpius's magick as well.

Well, that's a first, he commented to himself alone. Then he reignited his inner flame, and, for the moment, ignored the paradoxical implications of that unprecedented action. Especially given what he suspected about the origins of her magick.

"Too late." No being could fully douse such a powerful flame. "Whoever or whatever's hunting you has been doing so long enough to find you."

"'Tis never too late." She turned on her heel, then resumed her path along the trail.

"For this, it is." Because she'd been marked. Residue of magick remained, even if she never summoned one further molecule of energy again; the unmistakable scent of carrion to a vulture traveled vast distances through space and time.

No denial came, even though he knew she'd heard him.

She simply walked on, into the cooling environs of the forest.

"Besides, don't you first want to know *why* you have it?" Skorpius followed, but hung back a few paces, to give her room to process her predicament.

Because, in order to fight a hidden enemy who hovered on the outskirts of their awareness, they needed to find out why she'd obtained such unimaginable power in the first place. And Brigid remained too dangerous a tool for either of them to let it alone; she could be weaponized in half a heartbeat, without her consent. Even a god couldn't be omnipotent and omniscient all of the time. Every being had a weakness. Opportunists lay in wait, patient. Ready to exploit.

Why hadn't *he* detected any other magick signature though?

Had his presence kept the predators at bay? If so, they'd have to remedy that. Bait a trap. Flush the hunter.

"North, then," he continued their conversation with all that she'd revealed thus far and increased his strides to catch up with her.

"Aye." She initiated a light jog down their trail again as it narrowed into denser forest. Yet even with the treacherous path, darkened by shadow and riddled with gnarled roots, she pushed her pace.

The breadth of Skorpius's wings made it impossible for him to follow behind, so he shifted incorporeal again and ghosted through the forest beside her.

Within minutes, glowing tendrils of energy trailed her like disturbed mist.

"You're leaking magick again."

And even he, sworn guardian that he was, felt drawn to her seductive rare energy.

He sighed. *Might as well erect a giant neon blinking arrow. Send out engraved invitations.* "Permission to speak freely into your mind?"

The trailing tendrils vanished the moment her soft presence penetrated into his thoughts. *Permission granted.*

Their telepathic communication held minimal risk, as the power came from a latent human ability and bore a different kind of undetectable energy.

Any other clues? Why north? Away from the borderlands with England.

North, for now. And…I doona know.

Her horse had apparently known. Maybe Brigid had sent the suggestion to its mind. Maybe she'd bound herself to her mount in the same way Skorpius had been tethered to her as guardian. Because for the distance they'd traveled, she couldn't be that skilled a tracker.

He also sensed there was more to the story. A faint undercurrent in her tone led him to believe she kept something important hidden.

There's smoke. Her brow furrowed. *A horrible pungent scent.* She snorted as if clearing her nostrils of the stench. Then she paused, as if searching her memories of a dream, or a vision. *There's ocean, and...*

The forest ahead abruptly ended.

A well-traveled road crossed their path.

And by the immediate blur of movement and boisterous sounds, a large group occupied the road at that very moment.

Brigid darted off-trail, through the screening cover of ferns and vines.

Skorpius materialized beside her.

The traveling party caravanned past their hiding spot without detecting their presence. English, by the looks of it. Soldiers on foot and on heavy mounts. But wealthy riders also rode astride finer steeds. And teams of horses led adorned carriages. Behind the apparent nobility, followed their entire retinue, wagons laden with linens and housewares, trains of horses, and servants who ambled alongside.

They watched in silence from the shadows. The scant layer of foliage was enough to obscure them from sight; no need to waste energy with magick.

The travelers meandered up the road, heading toward a castle that appeared to float on mist in the near foothills.

You were saying? Where's *ocean?* he wondered toward Brigid, hoping she'd expand on the recent disclosure. The mental exchange also helped pass the time of their forced wait while she exercised her telepathic skills. *Nowhere nearby*, he added. *A good day's ride on horseback away, if we abandon our northerly course and hook west.* They would need to skirt all the activity to go unnoticed. *And elucidate the "and..."?* For she'd been about to reveal more, before they were interrupted.

I doona know. She gusted out a frustrated breath. *A place where the air tastes of salt. Where waves crash with a thunderin' roar. And we'll be needin' to go into that castle. Tonight.*

Of course, they would. *Why?* To risk exposure, the reason would have to be great enough.

*'Tis where the pull leads. And I've never been here before—*she gave a nod toward the stone towers and battlements floating above the mist—*but I've* seen *that castle.*

Well, okay. A great enough reason. And the perfect place to test his theory, since she'd just inadvertently volunteered to bait his trap.

Then I've got a plan.

The mere mention of it contradicted Skorpius's counsel-only guardian code.

But when one wanders into uncharted territory? The wise improvise.

You wanted no interference? He glanced toward Brigid. *You're about to get your wish.*

CHAPTER 7

*G*loamin' dimmed the midsummer's sky in darkenin' shades of gray.

A crisp Highland breeze chilled the air, rustlin' the leaves of the giant chestnut tree.

With stealth, and a wee bit of magick, she and Skorpius had snuck unseen through the forest, away from the bustlin' crowd of travelers that wound toward the castle's drawbridge. And they'd spirited high above, up into their secret hidin' spot that overlooked them all.

"English soldiers have occupied every inch of that place." Skorpius dipped a nod toward foothills that met an undulatin' stone curtain wall, then beyond, up toward the forbiddin' castle that rose from a thin layer of mist.

Brigid dropped her gaze beyond the curtain wall, scannin' the castle's bailey. The open courtyard teemed with the enemy, conquerors to her native lands. A goodly amount were dressed in finery and walked in groups up toward the keep, to join those who'd begun to flow through the main entrance. Some grand celebration was about to transpire.

"Aye," Brigid acknowledged his comment, and understood the risks.

For the angel's plan? Once she was sighted, she'd be alone.

Yet, she'd been no fool. The journey itself brought danger. And to see her quest through to the end, she'd no choice but to go forward. Even if it meant bravin' the insolent invaders.

Not all were English, though. Between small thatched cottages that speckled the bailey, she spotted others who had to be Scots: men who wore basic tunics and trews and stood taller and broader in the shoulders, the smithy and a few lads from the stables who tended to the incomin' animals, a handful of hardy women who carried baskets of various foods.

"And you're determined to go there."

"Aye."

"On a hunch."

"'Tis greater than a hunch. Some power has developed there."

Skorpius arched a dark brow, stared at her with those blue-green sparklin' eyes. His wild black mane of hair ruffled in the breeze. "Some power has developed *here*."

Developin'.

In truth, she'd only tasted the energy. Had no real knowledge of how to summon it forth. Nor hold on to the magnificence of it for verra long.

"Only to vanish," she admitted. She'd lost hold of her magick seconds ago. No longer sensed its cracklin' energy, her connection with all…seen and unseen.

Amusement sparked in his fiery gaze. "How do you plan to get down from here?"

The giant tree they'd landed in. At the edge of the forest, when the magick had coursed through her on solid ground, she'd but saw the high vantage of the ancient tree, wished herself within its heavenly boughs, then appeared within.

Brigid glanced down. Her breath caught when nothin' but

thick gnarled branches angled together as far as she could see through the moonlit shadows. But she swallowed hard, found her inborn Brodie resolve to quell the flash of fear.

Ever since she'd toddled as a wee one, she'd secretly trained in all manner of weaponry. In recent weeks, she'd further mastered short swords, become adept at archery. But escapin' trees had somehow been overlooked.

"Climb down." Brodie lads had only their God-given abilities, and those striplings climbed trees. Therefore, so could she. Determined to continue her quest, she grabbed the nearest side branch, then stepped off the one she and the angel both stood upon.

Once her weight shifted, the upward bounce of the branch jostled Skorpius, and his glorious black wings arched and spread. But all the while, his watchful gaze tracked her every move.

Shadows and moon glow danced from the tree's quiverin' leaves as she tried to get a clear view of the best path below her. With each next step, she placed the toe of her leather boot with care to gain a solid foothold. Then she bent her knees, reached down, and grasped another sturdy branch with both hands.

"We're over a hundred feet up," his low voice purred from above.

"Doona remind me," she grumbled, hands chafin' as she clamped tight fingers around rough bark.

And yet, as much as the old tree scraped on the surface, its essence embraced Brigid. A part of her connected with the life force of the great chestnut, akin to belongin' to the same clan. And the giant's warm radiance engulfed her with a soothin' sense of peace.

Without one *drop of magick in my grasp.*

Mayhap, 'twas their shared circumstance.

For within the massive chestnut's limbs, the gnarled bends

and scarred curves bore witness to the years of hardship it had quietly endured. It had persevered in spite of harsh environs.

And from Brigid's first gaspin' breath, through death and heartache, she'd also angled toward the light in her world, coveted the heat of the sun, the nourishment of vibrant plants, the rich land beneath her feet. Yet although she'd shied away from darkness, she'd also stood in the path of cold indifference without complaint, and had grown stronger for endurin' the pain. Even so, she'd known from the verra start that she existed for a purpose greater than mere survival.

We are the same, gentle one.

A male shout echoed from the bailey below.

Alarmed, Brigid's attention shot out toward the sound.

And her foot slipped.

Cool air whooshed over her skin as the thinner branch in her grasp snapped from the sudden weight. Rough bark abraded her arms and sliced her fingers as she fell while scramblin' to grasp another handhold.

In the next heartbeat, warmth enveloped her. Skorpius surrounded her in a cushion of safety—while they hung in midair. Muscular arms flexed outward. Large hands spread wide. Dark wings curved around. And still a hairsbreadth of space existed between them.

His magick.

Jesu! Immense power snapped from the angel. Pure raw heat licked at her senses, invitin'. Not at all dangerous. Or dark.

Yet at the same time, *so verra* dangerous and dark.

Brigid swallowed hard. Overcome by sensations, she drew in a steadyin' breath.

Till an echoin' thump reverberated within her chest. The persistent tug that had ruled her thoughts and governed her dreams. A second thumped, then vibrated, distractin' her attention away from the angel and back toward her course.

At the same instant, commotion sounded at the drawbridge.

A half dozen guardsmen on horseback cantered into the bailey. Two teams of horses followed, drawin' a grand carriage.

And all within the castle, English and Scot alike, swung their attention toward the sudden excitement. Then the crowd flowin' toward the keep picked up their pace, emptyin' the bailey's outskirts.

Urgency quickened Brigid's pulse. She glanced toward where they needed to be: hidden in the shadows between the thatched cottages. *Inside* the curtain wall.

An instant later, solid ground pressed underfoot. The night breeze blew through the wee bit of air space between her and the angel. And they both stood exactly where she'd imagined. Without even a spark of magick. Of her own.

Skorpius glanced ahead, then arched a dark brow at her. "Well?"

"We'll be goin' in."

"Of course, we will."

But first, Brigid eyed his attire. Or lack thereof. "You'll be needin' to…" Her gaze trailed from his bared chest to land on his enormous velvet wings.

"Blend?"

"Aye."

"Not a problem." Skorpius's appearance shimmered.

In the span of a blink, a tattered black cloak covered his face and unearthly eyes. Those odd boots he wore, with their longs strings and shiny metal, had disappeared. So had the wings.

When Brigid focused into the shadowed space under his hood, his hardened expression stared back at her.

His gaze tracked her from head to toe. "You'll need to blend too."

"*Aye*…" Her voice drifted as she scanned across the courtyard. Women no longer tarried nearby, all were enterin' the keep or had already disappeared.

"Summon your magick," he prodded.

Uncertain she'd be able to do so on command, she let her eyes drift shut and stretched her senses down into the earth beneath her feet and out through the sweet night breeze swirlin' all around. No reply came. Not even a recognizable tingle. She let out a frustrated sigh. "I canna."

"Inhale, deeply." His tone gentled. "*Feel* the chill of the air drawn into your lungs, *become* the vibration within each particle."

On instinct devoid of any thought, Brigid did as he instructed. And was richly rewarded. Thousands of tiny brushes of warmth flowed into her, like the gentle kiss of a springtime sun. When she reopened her eyes, the darkness around her had illuminated like a dim torch, sparkles shimmerin' on invisible currents of air.

The magick had returned. And felt...*invigoratin'*.

Skorpius gave her a short nod, expression intense. "Now."

An image of a favorite sapphire gown came to mind. In the next instant, her deerskins had been replaced by the fine fabric, her trail-dusted skin glowed with freshness, and her wind-blown hair had tamed alongside one breast in loose shiny spirals. A glance over her shoulder confirmed her satchel, along with her bow and quiver of arrows, had vanished. So had the sheathed daggers at her hips. *To where?*

Skorpius inhaled a sudden breath. Under his dark hood, his eyes flashed...*with heat?*

Nay. His reaction was but the simplest explanation: surprise at her quick ability.

Skorpius tilted his head, then gave it a hard shake. Those sparklin' eyes pinched closed for a moment. When they opened again, the fire within had banked.

His cooled gaze flicked down over her garb. "Not quite." He drummed idle fingers once along his side, against the dark material of his cloak. "This suits you more."

A ticklin' warmth brushed over her skin. With a swirl of

fabric, the blue dress spun into emerald green. The once-tight bodice flexed with her next inhalation. When cool air traveled up her leg, she pointed a toe outward in curiosity. The angle revealed a slit in the fabric that rose halfway up her thigh, where one of her daggers was fastened, beneath the silken material. A matching kiss of coolness and slight press of weight suggested her other dagger rode her opposite thigh. A darker green cloak shadowed into place as gradual weight tugged onto her shoulders: her satchel, bow, and quiver of arrows inventively placed. And when she raised an arm, the fabric of the cloak even parted with her movement.

"*Och...*" Skorpius's vision topped her own. "I…"

His dark brows lifted. "Approve?"

"*Aye.*" She could *fight* in the gown he'd gifted her. Her heart warmed at his thoughtfulness.

"Good." He glanced toward the castle, then narrowed his eyes at the dwindlin' crowd. "You don't have much time to arrive and still blend. And discover your purpose here."

Her purpose. How would she know?

You'll know. His voice boomed into her mind again, unbidden.

"Cease that," she whispered with a harsh glare. She then strode ahead of him, unsettled by the sensation of his occupyin' her mind.

"You need to exercise the ability." Skorpius appeared by her side as they approached the entrance to the keep.

"I'll *not* be usin' it."

"Perhaps not yet. But you will."

She scoffed and shook her head. *Nay. I'll be the one decidin' what magick I use. You'll be stayin' out of it. And my head.* At first, she'd directed the firm conviction to herself. With an afterthought, she wondered if she'd aimed the entire rebuke at him.

But the growin' number of others within earshot ended the debate.

A group of English soldiers stood outside the open wooden doors. Before them, men and women alike pressed forward in a slow but steady flow, like a river curvin' around a bend.

In more extravagant garb fashioned from stripes of bright silk, a herald barked out the introductions of each person gainin' entrance. One by one, announcements were made, without exception.

A nervous spike lanced through her. She glanced toward Skorpius who stood an arm's length away.

Skorpius boomed no words into her head. Only gave a firm nod forward that spoke volumes: Proceed without a care.

And so, Brigid squared her shoulders, lifted her chin, and strode forward with confidence, as if she'd been born amongst them.

As she passed through, not one person, not English soldier nor Scottish clansmen, paid her any heed, whatsoever. All appeared to be bewitched, in truth, for not even the herald took note of her presence. Though she felt no heat of magick cloakin' her, she'd become invisible to one and all.

Skorpius appeared to be naught but a shadow as well. For even in drab attire meant to blend, the angel stood a good foot taller than even the brawny Scotsmen, taller and broader for certain than all the Englishmen. But even to those whose shoulders brushed against his side, to the entry guards and the herald, 'twas as if the towerin' creature in their midst simply dinna exist.

And then, by prearranged agreement, Skorpius *truly* dinna exist. As he'd vowed.

"Alone. *With the soul and strength of a warrior,*" she whispered.

But alert with watchful eyes and attentive ears, she found everythin' had altered by wee degrees. Sounds had muted; conversations could be heard, but the words only discerned with great focus. Colors had dulled, as if overcast by storm clouds. Even movement appeared to have slowed, both of those around her and her own, like each step forward slogged through the thick water of an icy loch.

Not till she'd traversed the long stone entryway and entered the great hall, did the world resume back to normal sound, sight, and speed. And when a spark of magick tingled over her skin, she hurriedly cast her cloak and possessions off, willin' them to stow away with the other travelers'.

At once, someone addressed her. "Ale, M'Lady?"

A wizened man raised a tray that held a silver tankard of fragrant amber brew. His graveled voice held a rich low timbre with a heavy Scottish brogue. Wavy grayin' hair covered the man's head but turned a wiry white the closer it grew toward his chin. Charcoal eyes sparkled at her, bracketed by deep creases as he smiled.

"Nay." She turned away from the old man, not wishin' to dull her senses.

And her senses...*had come alive.*

Sounds had amplified, without overwhelmin': A trio of lasses whispered beside the stairway, twitterin' bawdy gossip about their clan's newly unseated laird. Her vision sharpened: A water droplet clung to a clerestory windowpane; the reflection within a candle's flame crisped then flickered.

And, och! The scents!

Rain gathered in clouds she somehow knew hovered *nowhere* near, yet their mineral fragrance washed over her. While she focused on the distant storm, a faraway rumble of thunder replied, ticklin' her breastbone as it reverberated through her. And although servants rushed in carryin' trenchers of bread filled with stewed meat, her mouth watered as she inhaled the aroma of sugared berry tarts she again somehow knew bubbled in the oven.

Over a hundred men and women filled the cavernous room,

many dressed in opulent fabrics displayin' their wealth. Most stood and mingled, smilin' and laughin'. To her surprise, a number were from the Scottish clan who'd surrendered the castle but a short time ago, to the verra English who hosted the night's feast.

Her fellow countrymen smiled and laughed right along with their hosts.

Spyin', most likely. No proud Scot would sleep well with foreigners on their rightful lands.

Trestle tables had been laden with a sumptuous feast, from succulent pig with root vegetables to roasted goose with apple stuffin', from fragrant crusty breads to bubblin' meat pies.

Brigid's traitorous stomach grumbled.

But a far greater vibration within drove her to be patient, to search, to wait. For along with her heightened senses, her magick had returned—in force. The growin' power of her energy illuminated fine particles of air, warmed her skin.

She drew in a shudderin' breath as she struggled to control the power of it.

Calm. She recalled Skorpius's instructions that had guided her release of it once before.

Exhale. His method allowed her to maintain a fine thread with the elements of the magick, without drawin' it fully within her.

In the span of the few seconds it took to learn her boundaries and practice her skill, a familiar maleness licked across her keen senses, oily and dark.

From her dreams! Cause of her nightmares.

Such incredible power.

But *far* different than Skorpius's. Brigid knew that now. Her angel's tasted spicy and dark, snappin' with ancient energy that teemed with the fire of life. And death.

The foreign male's magick tainted the air with some kind of *wrong*ness. Life, yes. Death, as well. But it reeked of decay, as if it had closed in on itself and fermented into sufferin' and want. Yet beneath it all, substantial power roiled, cold and brutal, destructive.

The malignant magick's source flickered somewhere verra close.

Frantic to identify the cause of the disturbance, Brigid searched the room, lookin' for... *What?* She hadn't any notion.

No one stared back at her.

Against her own stubborn will, her mind flashed to her guardian angel. But Skorpius no longer remained with her, to protect or advise. If he *had* been beside her, those amazin' blue-green eyes would've narrowed and his nostrils would've flared. They'd have been kin, together in sensin' the change in the magick currents.

But as quickly as the foreign snappin' power had infused the hall, it suddenly abated.

A quick scan around the crowded great hall yielded no answers. As before, in the entrance hall, no one paid her any heed. Pretty young lasses twittered nonsense and batted eyelashes at eligible young men. Battle-scarred soldiers drank and boasted of their conquests. Musicians began to play. Guests proceeded to eat.

Uncertain of how to continue, Brigid edged toward a roarin' fire where a group of men had been gathered in hushed and focused conversation. The three nearest, includin' one she recognized as a priest, were garbed in brown. The others were cloaked in black. Aside from the priest, all wore short hair and long beards. None appeared Scottish. Nor for that matter, English.

A blond man in the group glanced up at her. His eyes widened and chest expanded, while his gaze held hers.

In recognition? Or her magick? *Nay.* But she glanced down to be certain. And a faint golden illumination did exist, the same as that mornin' in the glade with the soldiers and wee ones. But visible to only her, not others. Or so she'd thought.

But by the time she glanced up again, the blond man gave a stern headshake while he stared down at the rush-strewn floor, then lowered his face from sight. And the rest of his group huddled even closer together.

None of their secretive discussion filtered into her ears. But she was disinclined to waste magick to amplify their words.

Her gaze tracked across the great hall again.

Below woven tapestries mounted on stone walls, dozens of intimate groups talked and laughed. Benches at the trestle tables were all occupied with those who feasted. The center floor had come alive with twirlin' dancers.

All seemed to have a purpose. *All but her.*

On a weary sigh, she closed her eyes, feelin' a wee bit lost.

Alone. Well and truly alone. The experience dinna transpire like she'd thought it would. Strangers surrounded her. Foreigners occupied her homelands.

At Brodie Castle, aye, she'd been alone amidst her own kin. But their well-meanin' gestures—while all had known who she was…what she'd done—had at least included her.

She'd never ventured outside her clan before. Dinna know where to begin in minglin' with those who were unknown to her. And some sense, down deep, warned her not to make the attempt.

"Ale, M'Lady?"

A shiver ran up her spine. The same offer. That unique accent. Yet the old man's voice had clarified, freed from coarseness. And somehow she suspected, before fully turnin', that the man had altered himself. When she turned, her eyes beheld the proof: dark hair without a stitch of gray, younger frame broadened with defined muscles, a handsome face unmarred by time. But identical charcoal eyes held her attention.

"Nay." On instinct, Brigid still declined whatever the stranger offered.

"Perchance, information, then?"

"*Aye*," she whispered. The agreement tumbled from her lips, unbidden. *From my magick?*

His dark sinister eyes twinkled.

Then a hot pulse of magick unfurled from within her. The energy radiated outward into an invisible protective aura just beyond her skin, hoverin' from head to toe.

The man's inky eyes widened, then narrowed. He glanced left and right, then leaned a wee bit closer. But he stopped an arm's length away. "Ye'r in grave danger, M'Lady." The fierce whisper camouflaged the baritone of his voice.

"Aye." *From you?*

Brigid realized the stranger hadn't stopped at that distance by choice; her newfound magick held him at bay. And when she focused closer on her protective boundary, she detected a similar shield beyond hers, one that surrounded the charlatan. But the two shields were nothin' alike. Hers spun and vibrated, refractin' tones of golden light. His churned and roiled, shadowed, *oily*.

Anger welled forth. Whatever creature hovered beside her, no matter the guise he donned, his essence had been trespassin' into her bedchamber—into her verra dreams.

Nay! She cast the violent fury out of her head, funneled the power instead into her magick. The stranger had not created her dreams. She had. Combined with some other energized force. One opposed to his.

The knowledge of the origins of their magick flowed into her heart with the verra next beat.

Which was the information she needed.

Her purpose hadn't yet been clarified. But its foundation had been.

Whatever she sought to accomplish, the one beside her opposed.

The power he churned also wanted somethin' from her, his cold greedy hunger a burn against her warmth, her light.

The disguised man drew in a slow breath, desire firin' in the bottomless depths of his eyes. "We'd make a great alliance."

Repulsed at the thought, she stared him down, flarin' her power against his. "*Nay.*"

An instant snarl scarred over his visage. The handsome illusion flickered into sallow wrinkled skin for an instant before it snapped back into the firm mask of youth.

Then his entire form darkened and thinned, a shadow that began to swirl as it lost substance. While reedy transparent lips pressed into a tight line, a low multiple-voiced whisper emanated from his whirlpool center, "*A traitor lurks amongst us...*"

Mimickin' whispers rippled through the crowd, volume increasin' as dark magick washed over each successive guest and they joined in the eerie rhythmic chant. "*A traitor lurks amongst us. Cloaked in black.*"

Everyone in the great hall, to the last man and beast, scanned the room and searched for the threat, for their target. The whispers multiplied and grew louder again. "*A traitor lurks amongst us. Cloaked in black. Darkest knight. Soul off-track.*"

The magick-backed words gained strength, transformed into a boomin' herald. Englishmen, Scots, men and women, all with eyes glazed over, had become enchanted.

You must leave! A hot cinnamon fragrance filled her next breath as Skorpius's powerful presence flashed in, invisible, but vibratin' with clear urgency. *We haven't much time.*

Aye! She vowed never again to argue with his advice and fully embraced speakin' in their heads. Chilled air swirled in his wake as he vanished yet again.

She leapt forward, then began to weave through the incited

crowd, away from the trestle tables. Her empty stomach grumbled in protest once more, and a wave of exhaustion washed over her—magick demandin' its toll. But too many maddened people stood in her way. And the innocent revelers hadn't only fallen under a toxic spell, they'd begun to arm themselves with forks and daggers swept up from the tables.

Yet in much the same manner as she'd adorned herself in a gown, she visualized provisions for easy travel. In the next instant, her invisible satchel manifested itself, weighted heavier against her side.

And when she rushed from the great hall into a darkened larder, her dark-green cloak reappeared before her in midair. She strode through the swirlin' fabric, and it settled around her shoulders—while her bow and quiver of arrows settled beneath it—then magickly tied itself around her neck.

As she made her way toward the far end of the darkened room, the outer door sprang open and humid night air fogged in.

To her surprise, the door was held open by a stranger with short blond hair and dark blue eyes. A torch flickered light over his face. "This way, M'Lady."

Recognition struck as she strode out. *One of the mysterious men huddled by the fire.*

Wary of trickery afoot, she dug her heels into the soft earth, then darted glances left and right. But she detected no other, sensed no ambush. "And...you are...?"

"A friend."

One with an English accent. Nevertheless, his eyes dinna appear glazed, no aggression sparked from him. Only kindness, a lightness of being.

Even so...

"*Weeeel*, I'll be the judge of that." Upon command, magick burst from her. The energy saturated the immediate space, from the open larder door, up the towerin' stone wall of the keep, then out in a larger sphere to the edges of the surroundin' forest, well beyond the castle's curtain wall.

Within that wave of power—that she'd imbued with a deep sense of probin'—she detected no danger, no foreign presence of energy. Not the old man. Not even Skorpius.

She narrowed her eyes at the newcomer, suspicious on an entirely different level. Not all danger came coated in the obvious. "How did you—"

"Know?" The man closed the larder door, then moved a safe distance alongside her, his black cloak swishin' as he paused.

Brigid arched a questionin' brow.

"That you needed aid?" He furrowed his bushy blond ones. "I'm not certain."

Intuition, then. She'd grown up guided by the gut awareness her whole life. Long before the magick had taken hold. In truth, magick had become an extension of what she'd always experienced. Mayhap, why she'd grown skilled at wieldin' her newfound energy so quickly.

"And what 'aid' are you offerin'?" Brigid glanced at the closed wooden larder door. To offer aid herself, she visualized three of the large oak barrels that had been stacked in a corner to materialize just inside the door instead, to block the way of any enchanted pursuers.

Then she scanned behind the large man and searched for any sign of the official one sent to aid her—and thus far, the *only* being she trusted: Skorpius.

As far as trust will ever be granted.

With magick, she reached out into the ether. Yet she sensed nothin' but emptiness—absolute silence. *Some guardian angel.*

"Safe escort," the stranger continued, oblivious to her magickal actions. "Refuge and defense, if warranted." The man, who held all the bearin' of a knight, yet flew no colors, patted a gloved hand on the hilt of the broadsword that was sheathed in a leather scabbard at his hip.

Brigid scanned his garb. Found no signs or symbols. *A knight who boasts no clear allegiance?* His shorn hair and long, but trimmed, beard struck her as foreign. And he'd been conspirin' with similar men. And a priest. "Who sent you?"

"No one, M'Lady." He cast a worried glance toward the front of the castle when the cries of alarm erupted outside. "Pray, make haste. 'Tis safe no longer. Danger abounds."

Aye. But from who? Instinct suggested the man harbored no ill will.

Yet she'd been mercilessly trained by Iain, Isobel, her clansmen, and most recently Skorpius to employ caution in all circumstances. Trust, when needed. And even then, to the least degree. "How do you know?"

The man's gaze remained steady and calm. As if a lifetime of instruction to accept and trust, combined with a wealth of knowledge, lay hidden in their depths. "'Tis been foretold." He bowed his head toward her. "All that I'm at liberty to share."

"All?" She arched a brow.

"And that we are here, at this moment, to serve you."

Weel, then.

Before she had a chance to ask about his use of "we," the knight nodded toward a far corner of the curtain wall, then strode ahead, quick steps leadin' the way.

And on gut instinct, Brigid followed right behind him.

A dozen paces before the corner tower, the man pulled aside thick bramble to reveal a circular shadow: the mouth of a narrow tunnel. An iron grate but a wee bit wider than the breadth of her shoulders had been removed.

Beyond the shadowy depths within, the orange glow of flickerin' light beckoned her, toward where fresh night air flowed again. Then an additional flame split from the first: torches held by more than one who awaited her arrival on the other end.

"Brothers, mine." The knight dipped a nod toward his men

as their whispers echoed through the dank stone tunnel. "'Tis the same for them. We're here to serve, one and all."

She'd been sent a guardian angel *and* knights? "For my journey?"

"For this hour," her escort clarified. Then gestured an arm toward the inner darkness.

For a moment, she thought to test the rest of his men with a tendril of magick, but instinct reined in her temptation to overuse her power. She dinna yet understand the limits, nor the consequences. And for the duration of the verra long day, whenever she'd used her magick, another, more experienced than she, had appeared.

Onward, then. She ducked down into the tunnel, tugged her cloak tight about her body, and stooped as she shuffled forward. When her shoulders brushed the moldy stonework, she wondered how the large knight behind her, who'd have to more than double over, would make it through. When she dinna sense movement behind her, she glanced over her shoulder.

A metallic screech scraped across her eardrums as he fitted the iron grate back into place, from the outside. *Not followin' at all, then.*

"Your name?" she called to the mysterious knight.

"Wilhelm." The faint echo muffled, from behind bramble that rustled back over the grate.

On a determined exhale, she turned and forged ahead through the darkness, drawn toward the light. Exactly as she'd begun her journey. *Into the unknown.*

CHAPTER 8

Skorpius stood deep within the shadows of the forest and watched with fascination.

Coincidences didn't happen in the mortal world. Divine plans did. Regardless of what humans theorized about the subject.

Therefore, to believe that a dozen knights from the Templar order had miraculously arrived on scene, their sole aim to aid Brigid? *Not a chance.*

Nevertheless, Brigid appeared to have accepted their assistance.

At least her expression had evidenced some skepticism. And a healthy dose of wariness.

Good. That self-preservation will serve you well.

Brigid may have thought he'd abandoned her right at a critical moment: Her unhidden dismay and indignant glances shot outward and upward since she'd fled the castle grounds left nothing to his imagination.

But Skorpius had done exactly what the situation required.

The *unprecedented* situation. With the unknown factor embodied by her. With unidentified others attracted to her uniqueness. So he'd been forced to alter course, into the unconventional.

Intuition fully guided him for the first time. Which had led to the conclusion that to guard Brigid *and* time effectively, he'd needed to fade back, observe from the periphery, and intervene only if he deemed one or the other gravely threatened.

And in that observational role, if a conflict arose? Time took priority over Brigid's welfare. *Even if the one required the sacrifice of the other.*

Even if he'd begun to dislike the mandate. *Greatly.*

Because, against his rigid code, he'd begun to like the fierce and beautiful Highlander.

Templars. Skorpius narrowed his eyes at them.

Snuffed torches did nothing to hide the noble warriors from his detection. Two scouting ahead, one escorting alongside, and two trailing behind, along with teams of two strategically flanking at key points within the surrounding forest, spirited Brigid away from the castle toward the relative safety of adjoining clan lands.

Brigid and...

Templars. In unusual numbers for such a rugged northerly neck of the woods. And not garbed in white with their supposed red cross to proudly identify, but in black, to move covertly in the shadows. But as he'd witnessed with Orion in their archival map and time's rapidly appearing anomalies, only a drop in the bucket of the goodly number of Templars that had begun to move through.

On the pre-altered Julian Calendar timeline, under the cover of a new name, only a handful of Templars had fled into Scotland to avoid capture by the French. But not for another decade. The Scottish holdings that their predecessors had been granted in the century and a half prior? Were located in eastern counties near Edinburgh, a great distance from their current location.

And as irrefutable evidence unfolded before his eyes, the Templars' altered timeline event? Seemed tied to Brigid.

Are you *attracting the anomalies?* The lure of Brigid's power? Or the desire to protect it?

Time would tell.

Skorpius tracked their company while incorporeal, ghosting through the forest on higher ground. After a fair distance, he relaxed his muting camouflage enough to allow Brigid to feel his energy presence, let her know he still kept silent watch.

In reply, a half-relieved half-miffed emotion pinged back from the ether. The fiery gold-dusted essence of it? Unmistakably Brigid.

Once her disguised knightly escorts successfully guided her across the boundary line, Brigid and the Templars parted company.

And yet, Skorpius waited.

Through the darkness, along a game trail, she continued on.

Once she traveled far beyond the watchful gaze of the last Templar, Skorpius materialized by her side.

Brigid shot him an irritated glance. "Where were you?"

Wild amusement had him fighting a smile. In eight hours' time, they'd advanced from her wanting him "knee-deep in muck, on the *other* side of a freezin' loch" to her indignation that he hadn't been hand-holding her through her first day of school.

"With you."

In a way. Without trace of an energy signature, but still tethered to her. No matter what he did or where he went, he'd remain tethered to her until the issue had been resolved, one way or another. But the fact that she hadn't detected even a hint of their connection proved her powers still lingered in their infancy, her ability to gather and control magick still developing.

"In the keep?"

"Thereabouts." He owed no one an accounting. Especially not her.

"Weel, then. You saw the old man."

"*What* old man?"

"Nay?" She shot him a haughty look. "What about the *young* man?"

Neither. Skorpius had transformed into a stealth presence, not part of their material world, yet a part of its undetectable background energy. In that elusive form, he didn't *see* anything. He sensed. And the only subtleties that registered through to him when he became part of the ether were fluctuations in energy signatures.

And he'd perceived nothing out of the ordinary. Until the unmistakable yank of his tethers had demanded he protect Brigid *and time* from impending harm.

"Tell me what you saw. What you felt." Her intuition mattered more than anything. Because escalating events, small and large, appeared to be gravitating toward her.

And Skorpius may have missed witnessing her encounter because he'd dampened his magic. But the encounter had likely happened *only because* he'd removed his powerful presence from the equation.

Motionless, she stared at him with an inscrutable expression for several seconds. Then she gave a barely discernable nod, turned, and tugged her satchel from her shoulder, began to remove her weapons. "The old man *became* the young man. 'Twas the aggressive male *other* from my bedchamber, the one I'd first thought had been you. But tonight, his magick was...*different.*"

"Dangerous?" She'd know. If she could now discern between their power signatures—and any nuanced changes in her hunter's—she'd grown to identify the makeup of energy signatures on an elemental level.

"Aye." Her low tone held no fear. She dug into her belongings, withdrew a thick plaid woven in Clan Brodie's green-and-black pattern, then unfurled it onto a drier patch of ground under tree cover.

"Threatening?" What he'd sensed amid the chaos in the keep. But he needed her take on it.

"*Aye.*" After taking a seat and another few seconds of digging in her satchel, she pulled out a crusty roll and a wedge of cheese. She took a large bite of each, then continued with her mouth half full. "To me...or you. I haven't decided."

Fair enough. Sides were being taken. Lines drawn. Power did that: seduced, invited, lured. Until core values were stripped bare, held in place by fragile unraveling threads.

I haven't decided either, he thought to himself. *Which side* I'm *taking. With you...or against.* "And the Templars?"

Brigid yawned. Then her brow gradually furrowed. "Templars?" Weariness tugged her shoulders forward. Heavy eyelids dropped halfway closed.

And Skorpius was struck by her.

For the innocent beauty of the female warrior shone brightest when she let her guard down.

"The *soldiers,*" he murmured in a soothing tone, coaxing her to rest. She'd depleted a good amount of her reserves already. And bread and cheese served as poor substitutes for the vital nourishment of phytonutrients and pure sunlight.

Skorpius needed to work on instructing her to use a broader imagination when manifesting.

But there hadn't been time. And his gut screamed they were quickly running out of it.

Succumbing to the drowsy pull, Brigid curled onto her side and closed her eyes. "Aye. Wilhelm." Her breathing slowed. "And his *brothers...*" Her voice trailed off before another deep inhale. "They're my kin, in truth," she murmured on a final exhale before drifting off to sleep.

Skorpius stared in wonderment at her vulnerable sleeping form.

Your…kin.

Astonishing.

And yet Brigid's own stark half-aware confession solidified his suspicion.

Who…and *what*…she'd become? No longer remained a mystery.

The *how* it had come to pass? Bewildering.

Yet whatever Brigid's role in the unfolding reality, irrespective of his grasp of the situation—which was tenuous at best—some chain of events had triggered her appearance, here and now. And with her thunderous power signature, of course the Templars had been drawn to her. As had the dangerous "old-young" man.

Others will come. And soon.

Only the Templars had her interests at heart. Because hers aligned with their own. For now.

Skorpius stared at the remarkable slumbering beauty for long moments.

Blissfully unaware of who she'd become, his apprentice had fallen into a deep restorative state. A faint golden glow shimmered over her form in the darkness, the protective warmth of a magick blanket that she'd unconsciously wrapped around herself.

Since that foreign presence had visited Brigid's bedchamber nightly in the past, it meant either she hadn't before developed that protective blanket, or she had, but it had routinely slipped. In either scenario, while her guard remained down, her golden energy transformed into a bright beacon of succulent nectar. And through the ages, dark forces were irresistibly drawn to a nubile flower just beginning to bloom.

Guardian of Time. Skorpius sighed at the needed reminder. It meant he couldn't forsake his role. Nothing he wanted—even that he'd begun to like her—mattered. And even if he willfully disregarded his mandate, he still couldn't interfere. Brigid had to choose her path. For the vast consequences were determined by her choice. Hers. Not his.

But he could protect *her*. Even in his absence. Up to the fine line that the action didn't interfere. Therefore, to be certain her protective blanket held for a while, he gathered additional elements, suffused them with his own magick, and floated his darker bluish layer over her own.

As his essence hailed from the elements of shadow, none of her energy could be detected from the outside now. Not even to those who hunted magick. Because he needed to keep her safely tucked from harm while he ran an important errand. One that ensured that no hunter of a certain breed came looking for her.

"Sleep, *apprentice*. We've much to do upon my return."

In the meantime, Skorpius had a fearsome Scot to face—and convince.

CHAPTER 9

*S*ilvery moonlight beamed down from a peaceful night sky, blanketin' the inhabitants of the Highlands in a translucent bridal veil.

One chosen Scot, by birthright and destiny, slumbered on the eve of a strange weddin' night.

No dowry would pass, other than her own worldly sacrifice.

No groom would take her hand, aside from one who surrendered his life.

No home would shelter her body, for she belonged to the mountains and to the verra wind.

Cold. So…cold.

Nocturnal animals howled and hooted.

Insects trilled their matin' songs.

"Ye'r not alone." A deep male voice caressed her ear, bathed her in warmth, even as the darkness increased. *"Come to me."* Power-laced quiet words, seductive, entrancin'.

"Aye," she murmured in eager reply. How could she not?

Greater warmth radiated across her face, over her breast. Golden light drew her forward. Soundless, featureless, an undeniable peace flooded her being.

Colder. Darker. Freezin' bolts of ice stabbed forth. *"Everra…thing! Any…thing!"* boomed the voice, a solemn vow, shot through with desperation.

Urgent tension crackled into existence, sparkin' and dischargin' energy from earth to sky.

The melodic night hushed in awestruck silence.

Dark clashed light.

But no Earth-bound being could see the electrical storm.

The beautiful woman still slumbered.

"Brigid," the deep voice implored, calmness injected into unhurried tones. *"Trust me. Join me."* Heavier warmth flamed over her skin. A thick plaid tightened, bindin' her arms and legs. Tapestries whipped taut from corner to corner, blockin' the windows. An iron bolt scraped, barrin' the door. And in the center of the cavernous room, a wicked fire blazed, ravenously consumin' every last molecule of oxygen.

Nay!

Warmth. Knowledge. Security. All rang hollow, false.

Escape. Away from all she knew, chase the darkness into the light.

Breathe. Inhaled deep from within, fresher-than-air filled her lungs.

Freedom. Beyond all walls, grounded by that which gives more than takes.

A wild rush buffeted her awareness.

Within.

Throughout.

Bitter cold battled scorchin' heat.

A whirlin' inferno tossed the world.

On a ragged gasp for air, Brigid startled awake, tremblin'. Curled onto her side in a tight ball, muscles clenched and achin', she tentatively unfolded herself. When no ill consequences transpired, she stretched open a hand over dewy blades of grass, then pushed herself upright.

In the middle of a glade on a crisp cloudless night, she sat alone. Claspin' her cloak about her, she took stock of her condition. Even though her heart still raced, she forced her shallow breaths to deepen. Soon her pulse began to calm. And after stretchin' her muscles, they no longer ached. In truth, they'd been warmed, as if she'd been chasin' butterflies in the summer sunshine.

Yet the faint memory of the harrowin' dream shimmered over her mind.

The sheer power that had swirled around her had been humblin'.

And the pull of temptation toward the unknown force? Nigh irresistible.

Which frightened her. Because its magick tasted familiar. *Ancient.*

But not like another's Brigid had only just begun to know. She ran shaky fingers over the bared skin at her neck. The slight residue of warmth there vibrated with traces of her angel's energy. As if Skorpius had covered her with a plaid of his magick.

But the absolute silence remained odd.

"Skorpius?" Brigid called out into the vastness of the night.

No reply came.

His powerful essence no longer existed there. Her guardian had abandoned her once again.

She blinked up at the glitterin' peaceful sky. Settled within, grateful for the respite, she closed her eyes.

But in the next instant, she gasped for air. Her eyes popped open, wide with alarm.

The wild rush buffeted her with greater force—within.

Unearthly howls echoed in her head, but none sounded aloud in the glade.

Searin' flames scorched her lungs, though the night sky remained crisp and calm.

Solid ground beneath her trembled, then calmed. Trembled, then calmed.

She exhaled a slow breath and her eyes drifted closed. Then she straightened her spine, tightened her core on a deep inhale, and gathered her energy.

Fate bore down on her.

I'm prepared. With her mind's eye focused on the still calm at the bottom of a deep internal loch, she centered herself.

Great clawed feet tore into soft turf. Snarlin'. Racin'.

On another measured breath, she drew in power from the elements.

Smoky fire blazed through pure air as enormous wings beat. Screeching. Quickenin'.

Cool as the clear night sky, calm as the solid earth, Brigid embraced the hidden whispers of magick from her world. Raw sparkin' energy suffused her verra being.

"You may not be here, Skorpius," she murmured. "But I remember." How to control the hot energy: a calm coolin' exhale. How to wrap herself in soothin' magick: a slow warmin' inhale.

Silence followed.

Insect chirps and buzzes from the surroundin' forest gradually filtered into her ears. The hoot of an owl sounded from somewhere off in the distance.

"'Tis but a dream," she murmured from the bottom of her loch of calm. *An* unsettlin' *dream.*

Thunder boomed.

The ground shook.

On a startled gasp, Brigid blinked her eyes open again.

"*Och!* 'Twas *no* dream."

She spun up from the ground, shrugged off her cloak, and unsheathed her daggers. The rasp of the razor-sharp edges over leather sobered her.

"'Tis real," she whispered as her senses prickled with keen awareness.

The dark clear sky split open on the near horizon. Brilliant orange light exploded into existence from nowhere, followed by roilin' storm clouds. Flashes of movement burst forth from the wide pitch-black hole, some arcin' upward, others spillin' downward.

Guttural snarls and growls echoed into her mind. *And* her ears.

Deafenin' screeches pierced the night, which flushed roostin' birds from their night perches.

"*Verra* real," she murmured.

Seconds later, the magnitude of what descended upon her grew crystal clear. Surrounded. Outnumbered. *Out-magicked.*

"*Nay!*" Brigid gave a hard headshake, refusin' to give form to even one negative thought.

Instead, she flooded her awareness outward, into the darkness. And as she focused her greater attention everywhere, her vision sharpened, turnin' predatory. Then she evolved even further, beyond all earthly possibility—into somethin' preternatural.

Myriad shapes bounded over tremblin' land and soared through a stormy sky. And their energy signatures tasted *otherworldly.*

Chargin' beasts broke into the glade in a semicircle, pallid wolf-like creatures with gruesome wrinkled muzzles and oversized curvin' teeth and claws. As one, the hounds paused, their ghastly faces orientin' toward her. A brightenin' red glow rimmed their nostrils as they flared, as if the beasts drew in her scent. Long metallic spines covered their hides from shoulders to haunches, barbs whose spiked tips gleamed their menace under the moonlight.

A larger hound arched its massive leathery neck up and bayed an unearthly howl. Its brethren followed, howlin' in reply. Then their heads dropped below their shoulders, muzzles aimed her way once again. All flashed now-glowin' red eyes, dug hind claws into the turf, then charged, clods of soil cloudin' up in their wake.

Great twisted birds swooped down in response to the beastly call, opened elongated reptilian snouts, then exhaled streams of fire that torched the far treetops before they banked and dove, flankin' her from the opposite side as the hounds.

On instinct, terror flashed through her. But then she blinked, shook off the fear, and took a cleansin' breath as she banished the destructive emotion.

She hadn't *fled* Brodie Castle. She'd drawn danger away from her people, those she loved.

She *raced toward* somethin' greater than herself, greater even than her clan.

And some menacin' force sought to stop her. In the dead of night. *While I sleep.*

Beasts charged her from one direction. Winged fury plummeted from the other. As if the creatures had plotted their attack, to guarantee no means of escape.

As if you expected I'd flee.

They'd hunted her, come for her.

Verra well. She gave a resigned nod. Because as apart as she'd kept her tender heart her entire life, as alone as she'd been for so many years, even with her brothers—even with Finn—she no longer remained apart, was no longer alone.

Clan duties and family obligations may have kept her struggles hidden to all but the most watchful eye. But steadfastness and loyalty hadn't been her only secret trainin'.

Every solitary afternoon of quiet reflection had grounded her.

Each moment amidst gardens and wildflowers had connected her.

And then came the magick. Which had set her free.

On a slow inhale, she glared back at those that dared hunt her.

Immense energy surged through her veins as she connected with the vast space around her, one with the verra elements, askin' for what she needed with steady focus. Warmth radiated from within, fueled in endless supply from the natural world.

A bright glow shimmered over her skin in a rollin' wave.

Her vision sharpened at the world awash in a magickal golden hue.

As a furious nightmare descended, she blew out a hard breath, eased her hold on her weapons, and bent her knees, balancin' on the balls of her feet.

Time ta prove I'm no easy prey.

CHAPTER 10

"'*B*out time you showed up." Isobel dropped Skorpius a deadpan look.

"It is?" A rhetorical reply. He governed time. The concept did not govern him.

Tension reigned within Iain's sizable map room, where parchment scrolls were stacked in honeycombed pockets carved from two stone walls and a roughhewn oak table commanded the center. On the corner opposite Skorpius, half of Iain's elite guard stood on either side of their laird as the men pored over a large vellum map, the corners of which were secured by obsidian paperweights. From atop stone perches in the walls, beeswax tapers flickered, dancing light and shadows over hardened expressions.

Robert, Iain's commander, angled a larger candle over the map as he pointed toward various positions while issuing clipped orders to his men.

A percussive boom sounded.

The walls shook.

Dust rained down, and Robert cupped a protective hand over the flame.

But no one seemed fazed by the quake, as if explosions had been rocking their castle long enough to numb the surprise out of them.

Skorpius tucked his wings tight to his back as a scout rushed by him. Another followed. Each relayed urgent information to the eager strategizing warriors: coordinates, numbers of enemy forces, strange beasts.

"Yeah," Isobel continued as she strode past the busy men. She went to the far wall and drummed short nails on its black surface. "Your magick wall is on the fritz."

Interesting.

He scanned the inert stone that spanned an entire side of the room. The portal wall, constructed as a living part of Brodie Castle, had been crafted by angelkind long ago. Its root purpose had been safeguarded from all, while it discreetly obscured the castle for generations of Brodie. But the wall had never once failed to serve its purpose, to protect Clan Brodie, home of the prophesied Traveler.

"Not *my* magick wall," Skorpius corrected. "The threshold between worlds protects your clan, belongs to your clan."

"Whatever." Isobel rolled her eyes. "The thing hasn't been working. Not only that, shit's hit the fan. I'm not totally spot on about every detail in history, and I know *this* particular Brodie Castle didn't exist in my prior twenty-first-century timeline—"

"*This* castle exists now, therefore has *always* existed. Your erudite historians were unaware of it. By design."

She shot him a *shut-up-you're-trying-my-patience* glare. "What I'm pretty sure *didn't* happen was thousands of English soldiers laying siege to one side of said 'secret' castle while several *united* Scottish clans attack the opposite flank of said 'secret' castle— even though we're supposed to be able to make said *'secret'* castle…" She leaned toward him, arching her brows.

"Secret." Skorpius finished, tone flat.

She snapped her fingers with a nod. "Bingo."

A third scout raced in and shouted an update, the arrival a new roaring beast: enormous, hairy, brown, tusked. At the keep's west flank, right in the midst of a large group of Brodie warriors, the creature flashed into existence facing the towering stone wall. Then, apparently enraged at having shouting men surrounding it and a solid wall in front of it, the hairy beast proceeded to ram its giant forehead against the stone.

Another boom reverberated. The walls shook. Dust fell.

Skorpius sighed. *Time mocks me.*

"*A woolly mammoth*," Isobel murmured then stared at Iain when he glanced up at her. They exchanged a flabbergasted look, supported by their combined twenty-first-century experience.

Then Isobel shot Skorpius a scathing *what-the-hell?!* gaze. "A whole *ten-thousand years* out of place. *Inside* the curtain wall?"

Iain growled and pegged Skorpius with a harried look. "We've not been able to go invisible."

Isobel folded her arms. "And since *when* are the English and Scottish clans battling here? At this time?"

"Never," Skorpius grumbled. "Until now." Because, by his own explanation of their unique Brodie Castle existing, so did everyone's faulty timeline. "Iain. I need a word. In private."

Iain held his gaze for a moment, gave a nod, then uttered a dire phrase to Robert in Gaelic regarding their ongoing bizarre battle. His commander issued final orders to their guard and gestured a quick plan over their map. Then all but Iain and Isobel vacated the map room.

Skorpius glanced at Iain first. Then he stared pointedly at Isobel as he broached the bound-to-be-inflammatory topic. "I bring information about a missing Brodie clansman."

Understanding gradually registered on Isobel's face. She averted her gaze, took a few steps away from her commanding husband, then hopped up to take a seat on a corner of the table.

Skorpius pegged her with a hard look. *Distance won't help*

you, Runt.

Iain arched hopeful brows at him. "Fingall? You know where Fingall is?"

Skorpius frowned, let out a slow breath, then stared up at the ceiling a beat.

I do, but that's beside the point.

Skorpius leveled an expectant stare at Isobel again. "No. Perhaps I should've said clans*woman*…"

The Traveler had two options. She could fess up to Iain, to foster the most civilized conversation conceivable between two men and an impossible situation, or she could remain silent and force her mentor to take the yoke.

Skorpius leaned back against the wall, propped up a casual foot, then waited with the patience of a granite mountain.

And as the awkward silence grew, the tension mounted further.

Iain moved forward and stood beside his wife. Then he stared down at her, puzzle pieces likely assembling into a whole that would inevitably uncover Isobel's imprudent deception.

Skorpius began to realize sometimes patience wasn't merely a virtue. On rare occasion, the quality he'd taken for granted could be thoroughly amusing.

Iain squinted back over toward him, with a ruler's assessing gaze.

Isobel glared at Skorpius, then softened her eyes and raised her brows. A silent plea.

Skorpius smirked. *With pleasure*, he drawled to her telepathically. *Oh, yes, Runt. This* will *cost you.*

Isobel heaved out a resigned sigh and gave a slight nod.

"Your *sister* is missing." Blunt. Efficient.

Isobel's jaw dropped at Skorpius's brusque candor.

"*What?*" Iain roared as he advanced a couple of steps toward him.

Skorpius raised his hands, arching his wings slightly. "Don't yell at the messenger. I've found her." *In a manner of speaking.* "Brigid is safe."

Iain spun around, his broad shoulders blocking out his wife. "Tell me you dinna lie to me."

Isobel softened her voice. "I didn't lie to you, Iain. I said Brigid was worried about Fingall and unable to break fast with us."

"Because she *isn't here.*" Iain stated the obvious.

"No," Isobel admitted.

"What do you know of her absence?" he demanded with a harsh tone.

"More than I've shared with you."

Iain slowly shook his head. "Woman, you continue to test my limits. You and I are gonna have a serious reckonin'."

Skorpius cleared his throat.

Iain spun back around.

Two unhappy people faced him. Experience suggested it was about to get worse.

But with attackers sieging their castle, serious consequences would have to wait. And Skorpius had a charge to watch over. And time to save. Blessedly, the lovers' spat would have to continue in private. Later.

"Brigid is safe, she refuses to be deterred from her mission"—no point in rectifying that said mission encompassed a task far greater than her hunt for a missing Viking—"and she is under my protection."

"What do you mean *she's under your protection?*" Iain's breaths shallowed as he rocketed from agitated to fully enraged. "Where the *fuck* is she?" Iain stomped toward him with measured steps. *One. Two.* But then Iain halted his aggressive approach.

Wise man.

Nevertheless, Iain's frame tensed, a coil readying to spring: thighs twitching, shoulders curving, fists clenching.

Skorpius slowly pushed off the wall with his bent foot and

eased closer to the man whose only intent in the unexpected mess was to protect his sister. "Brigid's gone north on a mission to rescue Fingall. I can attest firsthand to the fact that she's well trained to protect herself. I've been sent to guard her for reasons that have not yet been made clear to me."

Partial truth. But all he was willing to divulge.

Iain's body relaxed a degree as he processed the information. "I'll not let her run off into enemy territory without the protection of *my* guard."

"And do what? Bring her back and chain her somewhere? Keep her under constant guard? In the middle of your castle being under siege? Brigid is adamant. I suspect it will be impossible to dissuade her."

Total truth.

Iain's expression shifted from concern to contemplation. The man knew the truth of his sister's stubborn determination as well.

"She's out of her mind." Iain sighed. "Surely you can see that."

"I'm not there to judge her mental capacity." Which was remarkable, all things considered. "But I believe she has her full faculties. My presence as guardian by her side is not my choice. It's been mandated and cannot be altered. We all would be wise to let the events take their original course."

Iain glanced at Isobel, as if some answer lay with the one who'd become the most important person in his life. She gave him an imperceptible nod.

All of a sudden, Skorpius's tether to Brigid twanged with intensity. Then it yanked taut.

The guardian tie.

Only grave danger to Brigid's person would demand such urgent attention. Then a second twang snapped so hard, the inside of his sternum burned from its violent sting. "I have to go."

Iain gave him a weighted stare, filled with grave warning,

then waved a dismissive hand toward him. "Keep Brigid safe. You'll get no quarrel from me."

Skorpius gave Iain a nod. *As far as I'm able.*

But before he strode out to find a darkened space to dematerialize, he paused. He tilted his head in thought, then glanced at Isobel. "When did the wall go inert?"

"About the same time that Brigid left."

They're tied to one another.

That final elusive puzzle piece clicked into place. Evidence to his suspicion about Brigid. No wonder her ability to wield magick had advanced at such incredible speed.

The portal. How she'd gained access to angelkind's source magick in the first place. "*Exactly* when she left," he muttered.

Nothing to be done about it now. The connection had been made, the chain of events barreled forth. And they would continue to steam forward however the source energy—and the power players who tapped into its limitless possibilities —dictated.

Isobel hopped off the map table, then angled straight toward him as she fastened leather scabbards with custom-made short swords around her hips.

Skorpius snorted, amused at the fierceness in the fledgling's expression. "Where do you think you're going?" Moments ago, he'd vowed—more or less—to protect one woman in Iain's life. There wasn't enough leeway in Skorpius's mercy or mission to expect more—not from a *far* fallen angel.

But *of course*, in all the castles in all the realms, he *had* to align with the one where prehistoric creatures winked into existence and a laird pawned off his females to an outcast angel. Because Iain folded his arms and stared hard at his wife—the mother of his unborn babes—and issued his request to Skorpius the only way a Highland laird could: as a command. "Take Isa somewhere safe as well. I'll not be havin' her at risk here, if the wall canna protect us."

Great.

Isobel trotted over to her husband with a beaming smile and gave Iain a sound kiss. Then she returned and stood by Skorpius's side. "Ready, *my protector.*"

Skorpius let out a weary sigh. "Your *escort*," he clarified. Then he led her out into the hall. "I'm *not* protecting you. You're the Traveler, for Authority's sake. You can take care of yourself." Granted Isobel did so differently than Brigid, didn't mold magick to her every wish. Only wielded energy as needed for a specific mission. And the Traveler used the electromagnetic field as a personal highway through space and time. If Isobel ran into trouble, she blinked into any place in time, no portal required. She'd become her own portal.

At a bend in the hall, where the relative darkness and silence obscured their presence, Isobel extended a fist out and stared at him, issuing a mental decree: *Let's do this.*

Done. Skorpius closed a hand over her fist.

The next instant, they materialized at the fringe of the glade where he'd last left Brigid.

CHAOS ERUPTED around Skorpius and Isobel the instant they materialized.

Bloodcurdling snarls vibrated through the foggy glade.

Unearthly shrieks pierced stormy skies.

Thick mist burst outward into a wake of spouts spiraling into the night as a giant balled creature bowled past them, as if flung from a cannon. The moment the monstrosity stopped rolling, the snarling miscreation unfolded into a macabre lupine-like beast, dug massive metallic claws into rocky ground with earsplitting scrapes, then bolted by them again, charging in the direction from which it had been flung.

Another snarling ball whipped by on one side. A third

barreled past so close, Isobel jumped aside to avoid being steamrolled.

Once the last hound churned up turf and raced back for more punishment, Isobel stared after the creature, mouth agape, eyes wide. "*Ummm...* What the *hell* are those?"

"*No* idea." Not that Skorpius needed one. With how fast and strong magick had begun to bleed into the human world, any manifestation had become possible.

"They look like the *hounds of hell.*"

"Probably are." Skorpius materialized his sword and flexed his fingers around the hilt. Magick alone *might* work. But that depended on the beasts' source magick, where they derived their energy from—or who'd summoned them forth. But he'd learned long ago never to depend on one weapon. Better to dispatch unknown threats with everything in their arsenal.

On a smooth exhale, he radiated his magick outward. Cold blackish blue flame flowed from his hands and licked over his sword, infusing the blade with his ancestors' ancient power. With a stronger power flex, he burst a wave of low frequency through the entire glade. The obscuring fog fanned outward to reveal a raging battle taking place in the middle of the clearing.

Bright white light pulsed in a slow rhythm from its epicenter, spreading outward.

Myriad magickal creatures assailed the pulsing energy, some charging by land, others swooping down from the sky. A hundred-foot circular perimeter had been blasted of all attackers, hounds and avians shaking off their beatings.

When his magick wave washed through the beasts, all paused for an instant, then flung themselves inward with renewed ferocity, charging and plummeting toward their target.

Skorpius focused on the brilliant light at the epicenter.

Brigid stood within it.

No. She'd *become* the light. Glittering. Magnificent.

Unimaginable energy vibrated from within her, increasing

in degrees of power with each successive pulse, a blazing star about to go supernova.

But Brigid's newfound level of energy had already begun to flag. Flickering markers in her energy pulses signaled that she teetered perilously close to flameout.

Even so, a massive surge of blinding light exploded outward. Hurtling toward where he and Isobel stood.

Skorpius blasted out a burst of his own dark energy, shielding Isobel.

Several of the lupine creatures tumbled past them.

The stench of singed fur and scorched metal soured the air.

Isobel strode out from behind his defensive shield. And they stared at the fiery brilliance in stunned silence for brief seconds.

"Who? *What the…*" —a punching shove smacked into his shoulder as realization dawned— "*that's* our girl?"

Our girl. Skorpius supposed she was. He gave Isobel a nod. "Brigid. She's grown more powerful."

Unbelievably powerful.

"Since *when?*"

Since he'd been gone.

But based on Isobel's lack of commentary regarding oddities with Brigid—even since her *holy shit!* and clearly felt tug at the initial time-fracturing power surge—the Traveler had been inexplicably insulated from the development. Until now.

"Since she 'fritzed' your wall."

Isobel gasped. "*She* touched *it.*" She glanced at him with a wince. "Back when I screwed up trying to power the wall up, lost my balance, and fell against it. Because I'd failed, *she* had to…" Her voice dropped to a whisper. "*I* caused this. I bungled things so badly, Brigid had to step in to protect the clan, had to press her hand to the wall in my absence."

"She *more* than touched it."

Isobel blinked up at him, frowning. Then she turned to stare at her warrior friend who glowed like brilliant starlight. "She went *through* it."

"Apparently." And then some. Brigid had somehow become one with his world's magick. It remained the only explanation of where her extraordinary power originated from—why it resonated angelfire.

Isobel folded her arms, expression full of wonder. "And she's holding her own."

Better than holding her own.

Additional creatures began to charge into the clearing. However, based on their trajectory, they'd been summoned by Brigid. A polar bear thrice any normal size, reared up on hind legs, roared with ferociousness, then loped after one of the hounds. A gargantuan hart charged after another, its forty-prong rack of antlers angled forward to impale. And to his astonishment, a male African lion—a species never documented to roam Scottish soil, *the size of a bull elephant*—leapt from the crown of a hundred-foot pine. With the skillful swipe of massive paws, the feline snagged one of the screeching winged creatures from the sky.

Isobel gasped. "A giant lion?"

"You've shown her pictures?"

Bewildered, she dropped her chin in a nod. "Bedtime stories."

"All Brigid needs is an image."

"She *created* that thing?" Her brow furrowed with concern as unsheathed her short swords. "Is she okay out there?"

"For now." His guardian tether to her remained taut, but didn't twang with urgency any longer. Her life force vibrated through to him, still strong and vibrant.

One of the loping hounds barreled from behind them and charged toward the fray again, gaining speed as it sprinted downhill.

Isobel darted from the sidelines and planted herself directly in a second one's path.

Skorpius flashed between her and the unknown danger. His altered magick—the antithesis of Brigid's, tainted with darkness —stopped the beast in its tracks, only a few yards away. Then he glared at Isobel for foolishly stepping out from his protection again.

The dramatic Traveler flung her arms wide, swords glinting from Brigid's brilliance behind her, and stared Skorpius down. "The historian in me is *freaking out*." Without a care in the world, she skirted him and strolled right up to the otherworldly menace until it towered over her. "It's like a stegosaurus-porcupine and a Godzilla-werewolf had a baby."

Skorpius pinched his eyes shut and cast out a silent wish for the patience he'd never found lacking. "Do *not* regale me with the sick kind of orgies collegiate humans dream up."

"Hey, I did shrooms once." She gave a half shrug. "We all experiment."

The blocked creature vibrated an eerie growl from its armor-plated throat and lowered its head, boring a red-glowing gaze at her.

Skorpius flared out an additional pulse of protective energy, holding the creature at bay.

"*Sit*." Isobel stared into those glowing eyes that stared back at her with unhidden menace. "Roll over." With the tip of a sword, she twisted a wide horizontal corkscrew through the air. "How 'bout play...*dead*?"

A mane of thicker spikes draped its shoulders and Isobel experimentally tapped the tip of her sword on one. A metallic clink echoed. Sparks flew as she slid the blade from tip to base. A louder, deeper clank sounded out.

"The thing's hide is armored." She tapped twice more. "Yup. Pretty sure our weapons won't penetrate that tank."

She stared straight into the glowing eyes again.

The creature's blazing gaze narrowed at her. And its red-rimmed nostrils flared as the thing took an investigative sniff. A snort followed and a putrid brown-green cloud fogged out and engulfed Isobel before he could remove her from harm's way.

Hold your breath!

She dropped a sword, pinched her eyes shut, and smacked a hand over her nose and mouth. *Uck!* So *holding my breath!*

Smartass humor and the vibrational charge of still-strong vital signs told him Isobel wasn't in immediate danger. So he left her in the disgusting cloud.

Feels sticky. Tacky. Like stale hairspray.

A breeze dissipated the pollution. And a sickly green film coated every inch of her. When she gradually opened her eyes, the stickiness coated her lashes. "*Great.* I've been slimed."

The hound nudged Isobel with its wrinkly gray nose, nearly knocking her over.

"Hey!" She scowled at the thing and took a wary step back while plucking up her dropped sword.

One of its packmates squealed in pain. The beast's head snapped up in response. In a blur, it crouched, leapt high over them, then bounded back into the glade.

Isobel snorted. "Guess I wasn't worth fighting. Or eating."

Skorpius stared after the charging creature. "They're drawn to Brigid. Her magick is a beacon to them, to others."

She wrapped her fingers around the hilts of her swords. "I feel like I should charge in there."

The timeline tether vibrated in agitation at the suggestion and Skorpius gave her a headshake. "Not your fight. Just as you had your path to walk, so Brigid has hers."

"And only she can walk it."

"Precisely."

"Will she be okay?" Isobel asked again as the beast joined the ongoing fray. Then she glanced back at him, brows raising. "Don't *you* have some *guardian*ing to do?"

"When Brigid needs me, she knows to ask." And the guardian tether hadn't twanged since they'd arrived. "Her power has already transcended anything I've encountered before."

Isobel narrowed her eyes at him. "Haven't you lived hundreds of millions of years, Oh Ancient One?"

Very funny. "Not quite." Skorpius glanced down toward Brigid, a mighty warrior who wielded elemental energy like no other. Not even among angelkind. "But long enough."

"Okay, then." Isobel sheathed her swords and gave a firm nod. "She'll kick their asses twelve ways from Sunday."

"We shall see."

"Yeah, well." The Traveler pressed a finger to her forearm, then lifted. A grotesque sucking noise followed as part of the putrescent substance released and the slimy rest stretched between her skin's surfaces. "If Brigid's got this locked down, and you've got her back, *I've* got a date with the pristine desert Spa at Amangiri."

"Excellent idea." Skorpius needed the Traveler tucked safely out of the way.

Isobel shot a regretful glance toward the glade and squinted at the brilliance emanating from her friend. "You *will* take care of her, right?"

Skorpius sucked in a sharp breath as both threads snapped taut, threatening to break. Unbelievable pain seared through his chest.

Skorpius!

The alarm cried out through the ether. Brigid's life teetered on the brink. As did the timeline.

But he gave Isobel an unaffected nod. "I will," he ground with gritted teeth.

When Isobel flashed out of their time and safely into the future, Skorpius turned toward Brigid. He cast an implacable stare at his charge, his duty.

One way or another.

CHAPTER 11

*B*right glitterin' light swirled everywhere.

Highland mist enveloped the sun, sparklin' into a thousand silvery moonbeams.

Snarlin' armored beasts danced between the shadows, their gleamin' teeth the size of claymores snappin' at her face.

Screechin' birds swung low from blackened skies, razor talons swipin' at her shoulders.

Brigid connected with her cold, dark loch of nothin'ness and leaned aside, avoidin' contact.

Then she plummeted, weightless, and surrendered to the empty void.

Sinkin'…

Sinkin'…

After a time, her weary body settled on the bottom. She curved her arms around her legs, laid a cheek on her knee, and drifted her eyes shut.

No sound penetrated the deep.

No other existed there.

Only her. And vast black space.

Time ceased to be.

From the nothin'ness, in the center of utter darkness, a white spark flashed.

A silvery gold flame danced, flickerin' heat and light.

With childlike wonder and joy, she stared intently at the wee flame, then exhaled a steady breath through pursed lips to kindle its fire to greater life.

Brigid!

A muffled tone vibrated through dense blackness. Far away. Beyond her glitterin' light.

Who is this Brigid? She dinna know. Had no care.

Only peace and serenity existed. Only the here and now.

Only the flame mattered. Only protectin' her bonnie golden light.

Brigid!

Urgency. Need. A sudden tug pulled her off the bottom of her calm loch and reeled her in, away from the vast nothin'ness, up toward the surface.

In a growin' fog, she tried to reach for the disappearin' flame, but her arms sagged, limp.

When she tried to kick, to somehow propel forward, her legs remained motionless.

Then she simply let go, imagined pure joy, visualized her flame. And white-hot energy suffused her with warmth, sizzlin' and bright. And the silvery golden flame no longer flickered out of her reach.

I've become *the flame.*

"Brigid!"

Deep vibration quaked through her body.

Her eyes flew open.

A velvety sky stretched wide, dusted with countless stars that sparkled brighter than usual. In a glade, long blades of grass were bent, heavy with glitterin' droplets of dew that trembled. The echo of her shouted name chased on the periphery of her mind, frustration colorin' its tone.

Above her, Skorpius's face hovered, brows drawn low, worry etched into deep furrows across his forehead. A sheen of tears glittered over the sparklin' blue-green of his eyes. His black wings bore a film a fine white powder on the feathers that seemed to glint with their subtle movement in the starlight.

Warmth cradled her in a strong embrace. *His* embrace.

Brigid bolted upright, jostlin' out of his iron hold. "Wh... what happened?"

Everythin' in the glade appeared pristine, untouched. The pine trees towered, majestic and silent. The night breeze carried a crisp fresh scent, as if perfumed from spring's misty rain. Gentle chirps of insects sang into the sweet darkness.

Skorpius's hold tightened as he stood while she wobbled to her feet. "Where are the..." She gestured toward the low hill on the horizon, the rocky ground at the perimeter, where turf had been tilled from the massive claws of horrific beasts diggin' in.

"Gone," he croaked, voice rough.

"And the..." She pointed toward the starry skies in confusion, where only moments ago it had been obscured by countless bony wings and torrents of fire.

"Destroyed," the hoarse whisper rasped against her temple.

"But..."

"Later," he urged. His large warm palm slid over hers till he clasped her hand in a firm hold. "We must go." Tone stern, his expression shifted from concern to fierce determination. "They will return. And next time, they won't be holding back."

"Holdin' back?" She blinked in shock, that those creatures could possess any greater force.

But when Skorpius gave her hand an impatient tug, she gripped back and gave a nod. Unsteady on her feet, head spinnin' from her ordeal, heart beatin' like a trapped rabbit's, she welcomed the chance to let go for once: not think, simply follow. And Skorpius offered protection, nothin' else.

For now, I'll be takin' it.

Because she'd not woken *from* a nightmare an hour ago. She'd been thrown *into* one. And no amount of trainin' had mentally prepared her for the fight of her life.

"They were sent as a test," he muttered as he led her toward the outskirts of the glade. Pushin' on into dense forest, they picked their way over rocky terrain and wove through bracken, their steps muted by mossy groundcover.

"Test?"

Skorpius paused at a rise. A calculatin' gaze swept down, into, and across a ravine, up toward the next mountain peaks, then glanced back toward the forest whence they'd come. "Your horse is long gone. Would it be acceptable if I carry you?"

"Carry me?"

"If we fly." Those magnificent black wings arched, velvety feathers rufflin', as if he warmed them up in anticipation to stretch wide.

She blinked, searchin' for some denial through the fog in her brain. It failed to come.

"We need to find shelter." He glanced toward the eastern horizon where gloamin' had begun to lighten the sky into dusky purple. Then his eyes narrowed and his feathers stood on end.

Brigid's skin pebbled and a shiver rippled up her spine.

They both sensed roilin' storm clouds speedin' their way. No magick needed.

He cast an unyieldin' stare at her. "We don't have much time."

"Aye." She eased closer to him, ready to take his assistance, his protection.

"Do you have any magick left?"

With a quick search within, she detected no warmth, not even an ember. "Nay."

"Good." He blew out a hard breath, relief washin' over his features. "If you feel your magick return, if you're tempted to reach out to use even the slightest bit of power, reject the urge.

I'm not yet certain how they're tracking you. When you use your unique magick, its own energy could be leaving a residual tracer."

The verra idea of the strange energy coursin' through her turned her stomach, exhaustin' her. "Nay. I doona wish to."

Then she gave a firm headshake. And the world... *tilted.*

Heavy eyelids drifted closed, though she fought to stay awake.

Black specs dotted the edges of her vision.

Dizziness spun her head, then dropped through her stomach.

Her knees began to give way, but Skorpius vanished from in front of her and caught her in a loose hold from behind; strong forearms threaded under hers, elbows to wrists, tight against her ribs. In her next flutterin' heartbeat, he flexed his arms outward with hers, slid his hands over his opposite wrists, then twisted. His arms were locked together in a shieldin' embrace with hers restin' atop them.

"Lean on me." His gruff tone tempered, softenin' to a gentle command. "Grab hold in whatever way feels comfortable."

The heat of his bare skin against her fingertips, the raw strength of a body built for war wrappin' around her in undeniable protection, at once lulled and energized her senses. While her achin' muscles relaxed, her verra nerve endin's sparked to life.

And yet, Brigid did her best to quiet the rush of sensation, struggled to center her foggy mind, as she exhaled a calmin' breath. Because she welcomed the tactile warmth from him. In truth, she missed havin' someone express tender care for her welfare.

Therefore, she did as her guardian asked. And without worryin' about propriety, she shifted her hold and slid her hands under and around the outside of his granite biceps.

Those muscular upper arms tightened against her sides, his

forearms lowerin' under her ribcage. "Close your eyes. The wind will be cold, but I generate enough body heat to mitigate the worst of the chill. And I'll fly as slow as possible when I can, but we need to soar above the cloud layer to obscure our position. And you won't be able to see with your eyeballs frosting over. Flight might not be the most comfortable option, but it's the fastest way to evade any pursuers. And it's the best plan that enables me to mute my magick too."

As suggested, she finally let her heavy eyelids drift shut. "They'll be trackin' you too?" she wondered aloud.

"It's *you* they're after."

Not quite an answer, but her clouded mind forced her to let it go.

A slight dip served as Brigid's sole warnin' before an explosion of coiled energy surged upward. An icy gust lashed her front side and plastered the emerald gown he'd fashioned against her body. A ruthless windstorm crushed her up against his frame from the top of her weary head to the curled toes tucked into her boots. But after a few harrowin' seconds, she relaxed against him. Her chilled body basked in his fierce heat, a roarin' bonfire amidst a snowy blizzard.

"Why me?" On the surface of it, she understood. The magick. But in her fuzzy mental state, she still asked.

"Good question. Why you've been chosen still eludes my understanding. But…what you possess is…"—he took a deep breath and tightened his protective hold, as if fearin' she'd slip through his grasp—"without equal. They will use whatever means necessary to acquire something so valuable."

"Who is 'they'?" she asked, as infinitesimal ice crystals frosted her face. In spite of his amazin' heat over her backside, a shiver wracked through her.

"Another great question without answer." Skorpius curved his head down over her face to bear the brunt of the harsh conditions. His thick silken hair, somehow unaffected by the cloud moisture, blanketed her cheeks. "Yet."

Unconcerned by what most would find indecent, she snuggled her face into the warmth of his neck. "Without equal?" she murmured against rather soft skin.

His hard swallow preceded a long pause. Then he cleared his throat. But he did not retract his head, nor loosen his protective hold in the least. "Your magick is possibly something never before found or created. Raw power. But on an elemental scale. You *acquired* that incomparable energy out of nowhere, or so it would seem. And you haven't had to tap into dark forces to wield it."

Dark forces. The *oily* magick of those who hunted her, the feral beasts who'd attacked her. "How do you know?"

"Your energy signature. The golden light you emit has a...*unique*...essence. Its very core embodies virtuousness."

The silvery golden flame. Her mind's eye captured the image, mentally shared it with him.

Yes. His embrace tightened for the briefest moment.

Then Skorpius's hold hardened into an iron cage. He banked hard, then they arrowed into a downward arc.

Brigid quieted her thoughts as icy wind sprayed over her face. Her exhausted body grew limp in his comfortin' grasp. A breathy sigh escaped her lips as she enjoyed the fiery heat radiatin' against her backside, warmin' straight through to her front side.

"You doona need your magick to heat us? To fly?"

"No." A soft chuckle tickled across the shell of her ear. "I was created to fly. And angel metabolism fires hotter than any human's."

"*Och!* 'Tis so verra..." She gripped his biceps. "Look at all the green. And the windin' water!"

"Yes. It's breathtaking." He glanced down at her, confusion drawin' his brows. "You can see? Through the cold, the wind?"

"Aye." Somehow, her eyes had opened. And what she saw astounded her. Crisped into more vivid detail than she'd ever beheld.

Foothills undulated in verdant splendor, rollin' into countless fens and bogs. Upon them, succulent blades of grass arched downward, droplets of dew suspended from their weighted tips. The jagged top edges of a great glen rippled with purple heather set aflame by breakin' sunrise. And on mountains to the north, faceted ice crystals atop snowcapped peaks flashed their splendor in glitterin' rainbows.

Brigid gasped in wonder at the sheer beauty. "You see all *this* when you fly?"

"When I take the time to look down. Yes."

Skorpius tightened his hold and widened those glorious wings as rocky ground raced toward them from below. To her surprise, he swung her up as a strong arm lifted under her knees. When he gave a heavy flap of his wings, he cradled her against his body, and his feet touched down into a gentle trot over solid ground.

At some point, Skorpius must have released her.

And precious seconds of time had fallen away.

Because when her awareness returned, she leaned against the gnarled trunk of a great beech tree. Yet Skorpius's powerful heat pressed so close to her side, exhilaration sizzled through her. A cool breeze fluttered through yellowin' leaves that dangled from the thick boughs high above. And with eyes wide open, Brigid stood in awe of the bright golden sun as it hovered above the eastern peaks.

"You stare directly at it," he murmured, the warmth of his breath foggin' over the sensitive skin of her neck.

"*Aye*," she murmured, unable to tear her gaze away. And some distant memory lingered on the fringes of her mind: blindin' light seared across a newborn's openin' eyes.

CHAPTER 12

*D*awn bathed Brigid's serene face in golden brilliance. Silvery eyes drank in the vital life force of the sun.

Yet another clue, among a growing mountain of evidence, that signified what she'd become.

"Have you ever done so before?" Skorpius wondered if doses of sungazing had played a role in her rapid transformation.

For the first time in minutes, she broke her intense solar gaze and stared up at him instead. "Nay," she murmured with a firm headshake.

But she'd intuited enough to consume straight from greatest source.

And her *power.*

Awed by the enormity of what Brigid had done, who she'd become, he shifted from beside her and stepped backward in measured paces to take in her unbridled magnificence. Because after only a handful of minutes of refueling her depleted reserves, she'd somehow *amplified.* And the immense power her body absorbed—still somehow managed to contain—boggled his mind.

She glowed with it.

"You're leaking magick again," he muttered.

"I am?" She glanced down, expression innocent. *Priceless.*

"Sarcasm. Mine." He arched a brow at her. "Because *leaking* doesn't begin to describe the blinding beacon you've become."

"'Tis verra bad, then." A stoic gaze held his.

Skorpius stared back, amazed at her fortitude. "Hopeless."

"'Twill be inevitable."

He gave a nod. "They will come. And soon."

"Let them." Brigid exhaled and radiated a fine shimmer of golden light out into the ether.

It took everything Skorpius had not to beam at her with pride. "As you wish, *goddess.*" What Brigid had become. No point in denying the truth of it any longer. To himself or her. Whether she'd emerged as reincarnate...or original...mattered not.

Understanding dawned in her gaze. *"Truly."*

"Yes."

"No longer apprentice."

"Never your master."

"Aye." Brigid pushed off from the beech tree, then meandered the short distance through the rock-strewn ground between them. "But you remain my protector." Vulnerability shone in the depths of her silvery gaze. With trembling fingers, she hovered a hand over his beating heart and stared up at him. "My...guardian."

"Always." Fuck mandate. *To hell* with the tethers.

Gut instinct screamed that the threat to the timeline never had been Brigid in the first place. Not alone. Not as causality unto itself.

And as soon as Skorpius mentally voiced the rebellious impulse, both tethers stayed silent on the matter. Each were detectable. Yet neither rebuked his forsaking them.

Well, then. Even though the tethers remained, likely as a

checks-and-balances on him if he strayed, perhaps free will had become his. Or had been all along.

And as Skorpius stared down into the eyes of an innocent turned savior, to not only her world but countless others, he wondered what unforeseeable forces would gather to stop her, seek to steal her vibrant power away before she had a chance to share her truth, enable the worthy—alter the course of events in a permanent way. *Obliterate time.*

Of course. Stroll in the park.

"What happens now?" she whispered.

Resolve hardened through him. "We face the unknown. Together."

Relief washed over her expression, and she gave him a firm nod. "Aye." Then she glanced toward the vast untamed wilderness surrounding them. "And while we wait?"

Because they weren't hunting the hunters. No longer would they hide. Enough baiting traps.

"We discover who you are. Why you're here."

Moments ago, Skorpius had sensed Brigid's brief but turbulent flashback to her human beginnings; she'd unconsciously broadcasted the startling image on the mental plane.

But they needed more. For her to understand in order to kindle and strengthen whatever purpose she held. For him to learn to be able to adequately prepare and protect. Knowledge imbued power. And they needed all they could glean. *Now.*

Skorpius slipped his hand into hers. He blinked in surprise at the strong grip she returned. And to have a mighty force such as hers on his side, seeking his protection? A true honor.

Leading the way, he drew her back toward the cooling shadows of the great beech, opposite the rising sun. Then they scouted farther out, hand in hand, as he scanned the mountainous terrain above them. Before long, the dark slot of a cave beckoned, its entrance camouflaged amid rocky crags along a cliff face through thicker forest.

Soft laughter tinkled out as Brigid gave a quick to squeeze his hand, padding on light feet behind him as they began to climb. "Where are you leadin' me?"

"A place where I can recharge too." Without alternative, from the depths of shadows. Surrounded by the complete absence of light? Ideal.

"Why in such darkness?" she murmured as they strode forward into the dank cave, venturing farther from the dimming light.

"How I've been..." *punished*. Skorpius stopped short of relaying that admission, pivoting the explanation. "All creatures evolve, given enough time." No point on dwelling on the finer points of his transition.

Once they reached complete darkness, within a cleft deep in the mountain, Skorpius halted. He closed his eyes, ruffled his feathers, and inhaled the moist coolness. From the vast space around him, absent of light, a different kind of energy seeped into every fiber of his being.

"You've evolved faster than most," he murmured. *Possibly all.*

"Into a..." Her voice trailed off as her hold on his hand tightened.

"Goddess." He weighted his tone. No sarcasm. Pure bold truth.

When Brigid said nothing, thought nothing, he opened his eyes.

There in the utter darkness, in the bowels of the earth, she stared up at him, gazing deep into his eyes. An ethereal glow shimmered about her form, transparent and shifting, a silvery gold. But the translucent aura did nothing to impact the lack of illumination, in no way impeded his ability to refuel, to regain his strength.

"Aye." She gave a slight headshake. "'Tis at once impossible to believe and—"

"—makes perfect sense."

"Aye." The beginnings of a smile twitched at the corners of her mouth.

A beautiful peachy-pink lush bow of a mouth.

Skorpius blew out a harsh breath. *Focus,* he reprimanded himself. *Help her discover. Guide the* both *of you to understand.*

To increase their comfort in the tight quarters of the intimate chamber, Skorpius released her hand and paced two steps back toward the more open portion of the cave as he rifled through the clues.

"Have you sensed familiarity? Like you've been places before? Seen events previously?"

"Aye. The castle." What she'd stated while they'd been reconnoitering up in the chestnut tree. She wandered a few feet along the wall, then deposited her satchel and weapons beside a stone outcropping. "And my visions."

"As you've mentioned. But were those instances familiar because you'd merely 'seen' them before or had you actually *been there* before?"

Her brow furrowed, gaze drifting lower and growing unfocused as she pondered the matter. Then she glanced back up, expression confident. "'Twas as if I'd traveled there. Durin' another lifetime."

Not conclusive evidence. But close enough. "Then it's likely you've been reborn."

And she was still evolving into her ultimate form, stretching her wings, learning to fly.

It also meant that every creature, every being—all those connected to magick as well as those created from it—would sense her power. They'd be drawn to her like moths to an incomparable flame. And she'd extinguish them with the same indifferent fire as before. Because during the ferocious battle back in the glade, she'd...*erased*...all the badness, as if both those destructive and destroyed had never existed in the first place.

Brigid sighed. "My birth was not a joyous event." Her lips tugged into a deep frown.

Reborn, Skorpius reminded himself, snapping back to their investigation and her comment. *I'm not certain this is joyous either.*

But perhaps the two origin events were intertwined. And maybe a clue lay there, in her past.

Because the timeline thread had begun to vibrate again, with growing strength—despite his earlier rebuke. And he needed to root out the cause. For Brigid's sake, they both needed to discover the whole truth. And soon.

"Tell me about it." Together, they needed to sort out what had transpired. Ideas and theories were great. Evidence and tested proof? Better.

Amid the rejuvenating darkness of the cave, Brigid's aura dimmed as her expression clouded over. Her unfocused gaze dipped toward the dusty ground again. "Scraps of the tale were gossiped over the years, and I know the lasses meant well, but I—"

Skorpius closed the distance between them and caressed a hand over her cheek. When she glanced up at him, tears glittered in her eyes. The callousness of narrow-minded humans never ceased to amaze him. "Don't relive the pain. Emotions will only hurt, not help."

Brigid swallowed hard and pinched her eyes shut on a nod.

He brushed a thumb over her cheek, catching a falling tear. Even goddesses had vulnerabilities. "What truths are you able to differentiate from the tales?"

Brigid inhaled a cleansing breath and nodded once more. Then she opened her eyes and gazed up at him, sliding her hand over his while it still cupped her cheek. She eased it down, then clasped their hands together and squeezed his with a firm grip.

There's my fearless warrior.

Tenacity hardened her gaze, obliterating all other emotion.

"Aside from the lasses' gossip, all I've known is the wee bit my brothers chose to share. Most from Iain as I grew older and asked questions about my ma and da. Gawain, my other brother, refused to speak of it—to speak to me."

Skorpius recalled their earlier altercation, Brigid's daggers pressed to his throat with her fierce retort: *I came into the world takin' life.* And the enormity of her struggles began to make sense.

"Because of your mother's death." From Brigid's birth. A mother's sacrifice. However, a young boy would never see it that way, incapable of understanding why a loving mother had been ripped from his world.

"Aye." She swallowed hard and stared over his shoulder in thought. "The gossips whispered of the frightful day, but therein lay much of the truth. 'Twas a storm like none other, darkenin' the summer's day to a moonless winter night. Great bolts of lightnin' pierced a churnin' sky. Roarin' claps of thunder shook the keep's walls. Torrents of freezin' rain and pellets of ice lashed any brave soul who dared venture outside. Not many did."

"Quite the event."

"Aye." After a connected glance, she released his hand and stepped beyond him. She turned and leaned against the cave wall, hands pressed to the rough stone. She tipped her head back, staring up into the darkness. "'Twas as if nature itself suffered with the pains of her labor," she said, tone soft but steady. "Iain said she wailed in agony all through that day, late into the night."

In silence, Skorpius fully turned to face her.

Brigid glanced back down at his movement.

And when their gazes clashed, he blasted a surge of emotional support her way, in solidarity.

Her gaze sharpened from the effect. A slight smile almost reached her eyes, then she huffed out a flat laugh. "And then…*weel*…what Iain had said happened after…none of it made any sense."

"Most rare events do."

Brigid stared at him for a long calculating moment. "Iain said, based on sworn accounts of the maids present, that a jagged bolt of lightnin' flashed *inside* her bedchamber. All sound ceased for an eternity. The air scented fresh from a spring downpour."

"Ozone. If we're talking *actual* lightning, the electrical discharge split the atmospheric particles within the room into nitrogen and oxygen. The oxygen molecules recombined into threesomes would have created ozone: the sweet mineral scent from an electrical storm."

Brigid's blank stare after the science lesson? Followed by narrowed eyes, twitching lips, and her *you and Isobel and your strange words* accusatory stare? Worth it. Anything to knock her off-balance enough to lighten her mood.

"And then what happened?" he prodded, tone gentle.

"Accordin' to the maids? I sucked in my first lungful of air and wailed."

"Would you like to see what happened?"

Brigid's expression blanked again, before wrinkling into an adorable disapproving scowl. "You *canna* do such a thing," she whispered.

"I can."

"Weel…" Her brow furrowed and she gave an incredulous headshake. "You shouldna."

"And *you* shouldn't wander through magick walls."

Widening eyes met his unyielding stare.

Gotcha!

Brigid now knew that he'd puzzled out her secret indiscretion. "But we all walk the path we're destined." And the way forward for the two of them relied on her trusting him. Maybe not everything at once. But advancing together, step by step.

"Time is my domain. And I assure you, peripherally observing the event of your birth will cause no harm, to the past or present." Yet she'd revealed enough of her notorious past to warrant further investigation.

Skorpius's duty required him to gather the vital information, but he preferred to have her accompany him.

He blinked hard at the revelation.

Well, that's a first. In nearly a millennium.

His mind and gaze then drifted to the stolen journal in her satchel. But he shook his head.

First, a fieldtrip back to Brigid's origins.

There would be time enough to visit the ghosts of *his* past.

CHAPTER 13

*T*he chillin' darkness of the mountain's cave surrounded them, but for the wee bit of breathtakin' blue-green glow of her angel's eyes.

Her angel.

The shock of Brigid's transformed feelings about Skorpius in such a short time splashed cold upon her, then fluttered away like spent petals on a gentle breeze. For 'twas only two morns past that she'd fired a furious arrow at his unwelcome presence. Two adventuresome days later, she failed to imagine her guardian bein' anywhere else but by her side.

And within the place of darkest shadow, deep in the bowels of the earth, she—a child of trees and flowers and bright summer sunlight—found the surprise of an even greater comfort, an overwhelmin' peace. In truth, cool calm air, dense stone walls, and the dusty preserved earth, embraced her like a second home.

Filled with a childlike curiosity about the strange comfort, she hovered a hand, fingers splayed wide, over the cold, dry surface of the massive stone wall. Vibration purred back through her skin, in recognition and…invitation. Hummin' the low tones of a tune that oddly seemed at once foreign and familiar, she pressed her cheek to the surface.

And the wall vanished.

Beyond where solid stone had been an instant before, bursts of bright starlight danced, ancient knowledge flowed, unseen souls sang with incredible joy.

Brigid gave a heavy blink, then stared in wonder through a gateway that led into a dazzlin' otherworld.

Yet none of the brightness she witnessed past the gateway breached into the serenity of their cave. Absolute darkness remained where they stood.

"You're evolving at an accelerating pace," Skorpius murmured from right behind her, his warm breath dancin' over her ear.

"Aye." Tingles shimmered within her, under her skin, itchin' to break free. A newborn butterfly anxious to take flight. "Do you see?" The brilliance of *all* the energy, at her fingertips.

"Yes. The birth of a goddess." Protective soft wings curved around her. But not in any cage. Solely in support.

With another slow blink, the otherworld vanished. Still there, somewhere, but hidden from the human world. Ready to be explored, she sensed. Secrets lay in wait there. To be shared through her to a chosen few. But when and to whom she chose.

But how? she wondered, to herself.

From the center darkness of the bowels of the cave, Skorpius extended his hand out to her. "Ready?"

To discover her present, she needed to uncover her past.

Brigid exhaled a clearin' breath.

"Aye." Confident her path lay there, she manifested her satchel and weapons onto her person once more, slid her hand over his palm, and gave a brief nod.

The next turbulent seconds stole her breath away.

Utter darkness…

Freezin' cold…
Pleasurable sparks whippin'…
Fiery hot…
Tense and achin'…
Blissful rollin' thunder quakin', down into her verra core…

But through the startlin' fall, Skorpius's hand held hers, tight and reassurin'.

Then Brigid blinked awake. Hale and whole.

The solid strength of Skorpius's hand still clasped hers.

A different cold stone pressed against their backs. Fragrant lavender rushes carpeted the floor at their feet. But their presence lay hidden in the shadows in a far corner of a room. In truth, they'd become a part of the shadows themselves. Real, but insubstantial. Visible, yet ethereal.

Another span of darkness surrounded them, save for the flickerin' light of beeswax tapers in an iron stand. And instead of the gentle brush of coolness to the air, cloyin' heat choked the room, magnified by tapestries that blocked the narrow windows.

Two ladies' maids wrung their hands at the foot of a large bed piled high with linens. The young lasses flanked an elder third who squatted upon a low stool.

"One more, M'Lady," the elder midwife urged. "Wee feet've popped out. But I need ya ta give 'er a harder push."

Atop the beddin', ghostly white fists gripped sweat-soaked sheets. Pantin' breaths preceded a low moan. A copper curlin' nest of hair tumbled loose as the exhausted form attempted to curve forward. The two maids, fierce pride in their steely gazes each took up a position behind a shoulder, bolsterin' the efforts, loyal servants determined to see their cause through to the verra end.

A low growl vibrated out, then escalated into a rasped empty scream.

One last silent gasp escaped.

A pained expression twisted further into stark agony.

Then a harsh exhale, moanin' grunt, and pale face flushin' beet red marked the final push.

The woman collapsed back onto the bed, spiraled hair fanned across a mountain of pillows. Limp. Unmovin'.

With quick work, the three hovered over a wee glistenin' red-and-white form. Wet linens were swiped head to foot, blood cleansed away. Tense hands swaddled the soundless bundle.

Hopeful faces stared down.

Seconds dragged by.

Grim frowns began to form.

In the hot room gone deathly quiet, the dyin' mother reached out an arm and pointed her fingers toward her newborn bairn. "To the verra Heavens we traveled. Star-dusted honey we gathered from the wings of angels. With all the strength of your namesake goddess." A fat tear fell from her eye, then splashed onto the floor. "I proclaim thee *Brigid*."

Time appeared to slow, stretchin' eternal.

Skorpius tightened his grip on her hand, eyes widenin'.

Your mother. She *traveled through the wall.*

Aye. With me in her womb.

Astonished, Brigid gazed into the hopeful eyes of a mother she'd never known. Red hair like hers spilled onto a pillow. Similar dimples marked her flushed cheeks as the lass gave a slight smile and a slow exhale. 'Twas amazin' to finally see a face she'd only imagined, so verra much like her own.

An instant after the maternal proclamation, a thunderous boom sounded and a thick bolt of energy flashed from the heart of the mother into the breast of the babe.

The newborn sucked in a ragged breath.

Then she wailed out her existence with ragin' fury.

Angelic magick scorched your mother's dying wish into your blood. Where it has lain dormant. Waiting.

Brigid stared in shock at the wailin' bairn. At her own wee self, eighteen long summers ago. An innocent.

Till I traveled through the wall. Again.

So it would seem.

As the midwife attempted to soothe the unsettled bairn, the two maids returned to find a lifeless form on the bed. After several distraught attempts to find life in her, mournful faces grew wet with tears.

In a thrice, Brigid yanked on Skorpius's hand, rushin' to the bedside to judge for herself. Yet as she'd already known, no breath lifted her chest, no pulsin' blood colored her cheeks.

Unprepared to face a mother who'd sacrificed her life to bring forth her babe, Brigid tasted the salty fall of tears. She exhaled heartfelt gratitude in wordless eulogy to the sweet bonnie lass that in all her life she'd never dreamed she'd have the chance to meet.

A fresh linen sheet snapped in front of her face. Then it settled onto the whole of the bed.

Pitch-black flashed again, Skorpius's hand firm within hers.

Another heavy blink, and they stood in a familiar room, Iain's map room. However...

Nay. 'Tis not Iain's *map room.*

Brigid's knees went weak.

Skorpius gave her hand a gentle squeeze of support.

"*Da?*" Her father. Laird of Clan Brodie, before Iain. A man Brigid had never met. For he'd fallen into such grave heartache in the fortnight followin' her ma's death, he'd faded into the afterlife to be with her. Yet there the man stood at the room's wooden map table, larger than life. Larger even than Iain.

Two wee lads, standin' near the base of their castle's magick wall, turned their way at her unexpected murmur. Both of the lads' gazes locked with hers, their darkened eyes widenin'. The youngest walked right up to her, a flat hand hoverin' over her emerald gown, as if to touch. "Look, Iain," the wee lad whispered. "'Tis an angel."

"*Nay, Gawain.*" Seriousness washed over the elder lad's expression as he took his brother's hand—an instant before the two divergent energies, one from the future dropped into the lads' present, collided. "Angels come to take lives, but t'night's about bringin' us one."

They see us? At her birth, Iain would've been four summers. Gawain barely two.

Yes. Innocents often do.

"*Bah,*" Laird scoffed without glancin' their way. His attention remained riveted on a leather tome he pored over by candlelight. "Naught but yer wild imaginin's be there."

Wee Iain's eyes narrowed at her. Then the lad's shrewd gaze fixed upon Skorpius. "Aye, Da. Somethin's there. But they're no angels. 'Tis our guardians. Keepers of our castle."

One of many names I've been called, Skorpius clarified. *Guardian of Time. Keeper of the Castle.*

Tears began to roll down the younger lad's cherub cheeks.

Mayhap, Gawain knows.

Sensed his mother's fate? Possible.

Without botherin' to ask, Brigid bent down toward the wee one, a brother whom she'd struggled to connect with due to the frightful night they now bravely shared, one that, to her, had become a rare treasured moment. "Aye, wee Gawain."

The lad's eyes blinked clear of tears upon hearin' his name.

"T'night we're angels *an'* guardians," she explained. "Death and life, 'tis but a thin veil betwixt the two. Cherish those ye still have, whilst ye have them. Hold them dear. And love yer wee sister. For she already loves you dearly." Tears welled in her own eyes as a cramp choked the base of her throat.

The lad frowned. "A *sister!*" Gawain gave a fierce headshake. "Lasses *smell* bad. All flowery an' sweet."

She bit her lip to suppress a smile. "This lass will smell bad as well. For a while. But forgive your wee sister. No matter how many summers it takes, brave Gawain. Love her, when you can."

Because, she'd understood. With life and death, overcomin' heartache took time. And through the trials of growin' up in a clan who'd known what terrible pain her birth had caused— Gawain mayhap payin' the highest price of all—she'd had faith that her youngest brother would love her.

In time, he had. *You still do.*

Her tremblin' hand reached for his still-wet cheek. She dinna touch. But she hovered radiant energy over his face, bathin' both lads in her newfound golden light. *And I love you too.*

Brigid shifted her gaze toward the stronger, wiser Iain. Fierce kindness glinted back at her. Always the rock-steady one, he'd immediately accepted her. Loved her. Been fair and noble when he could've hated her even more. But the ferocious night of her birth heralded his transition from carefree child into a lad who would become Laird in a fortnight. She gave young Iain a solemn nod. And a wink.

The lads spun around and ran off, excitement snappin' hot through their veins. Each holdin' a monumental vision of a fiery goddess and guardian angel to hold dear, meager solace for the hours to come.

One final glance landed on her da. Upon further examination, the tome he refused to stray his attention from made sense: a clandestine hand-scribed English copy of the *Vulgate Bible.* "Peace be with you, dear Da," she murmured to a man she hoped had found what he searched for.

Rest assured, goddess. Your father finds immeasurable peace.

Still hand in hand with Skorpius, and grateful for the solid cornerstone, she gave a gentle nod.

A familiar energy licked across her senses. *Teasin'. Temptin'.*

The wall!

Brigid stared at the massive unbroken span of stone that stretched from corner to corner, floor to ceilin'. Nigh black, but for a wee sparkle of darkest blue—akin to the inky hue of Skorpius's magick—the wall's surface hummed with power.

Before, she'd thought *her* lone action had instigated the chain of events, caused her magick. *I'd been through before. As an unborn bairn.* By her mother's own admission. *Take me back.* She tugged on Skorpius's hand, wishin' to travel back in time a wee bit farther. *I'd like to see when and* why *she'd done so.*

Skorpius gave a firm tug back. *No. We cannot risk another visit with your mother.*

Bound tight to his hand, Brigid angled closer to the gateway that had led her to the source magick. And in response, the sentient wall reacted to her proximity.

Only in a way far different than before.

When Isobel had activated the wall to protect their clan, pinpoints of light had brightened. Pulsin' and twinklin' like so many stars sprinkled over a black midnight sky, they'd flared to blindin', brilliant as the sun. But because Isobel had lost her balance and disappeared before the castle went invisible, Brigid had stepped in as her second, pressed her hand upon it, and stepped *right through it.* To the most amazin' place.

But the bright twinklin' lights were absent on the wall before her. And its vibration of magick greater, more seductive. As she watched, the surface shimmered into a translucent veil, a bluish black sparklin' shadow, a sheer dark curtain into the otherworld.

When she reached out her free hand to touch, Skorpius gripped her hand tighter, yanked her back, and energized her body with his protective shield, surroundin' her with his own bluish black magick.

Skorpius's powerful time-travelin' magick pulsed into her at their point of contact, as if he attempted to take her back, remove her from the map room, from her past.

With a keening cry of anguish, Brigid burst forth a surge of her own golden magick and lunged for the wall.

That point of groundin' contact with Skorpius? Broke.

And her whole world tumbled into icy darkness.

CHAPTER 14

Brigid!

Skorpius dove after her. Into the vast reaches of space *between* time.

Through a maelstrom of dark matter.

Where *nothing* existed.

No mortal body could survive even a split second in the tempestuous nonmatter realm. And no being untrained in the nuances of time travel would have any basis to be able to gain their bearings.

Were it not for his internal tether to the rebellious female, and her resilient—though nascent and still fragile—immortal state, she'd have been forever lost.

Skorpius! A panicked cry for help.

Her essence hovered nearby, but still beyond his reach.

Find your calm. Spoken to her. To himself. *Radiate that spectacular golden magick of yours.* All that stood between her and utter destruction. *Become more energy, less matter.*

Akin to my peace within your magick sphere?

Yes. Skorpius gritted his teeth against unimaginable forces that scoured the shell of his essence. The shaking vibration on her tether broadcast the similar strain she bore. For glacial dark-matter vortexes buffeted them both. Tightly coiled bottoms of infinite black holes swirled and scraped at the fringes of their souls, hungry to steal the vital essence from any unlucky energy caught in its unforgiving web.

The vicious realm of antimatter destroyed substance. Obliterated form.

Few beings in existence had the talent and navigational skill to use the support structure between worlds to leap through time. Skorpius did. And the Traveler.

Brigid had the makings. And power. Which would've been enough—if she'd had any training and experience.

If only he'd warned her before she'd broken contact.

No. Skorpius redirected his thoughts. *Focus on the now.*

And more, he called out to her. *Like in the glade.* On a subconscious level, she could tap into that immense energy again. To save herself from deadly forces—this time brewed from the depths of the universe itself.

Aye. Brigid's mental voice felt thready, stretched with exhaustion. *Burst…forth*, she continued. *Bright…starlight.* Whispered over his senses, her words had begun to slur.

Yes. Exactly *like that. Fight hard, Brigid. Be brilliant.*

Although she'd had no conscious recollection of battle details from the glade, her magick knew. And her fierce magick protected her now, any way it could. Yet fragile and new, without guidance, her physical body *would* succumb. Her brilliant light? Snuffed out, an inconsequential flame to the mighty storm of primordial forces.

As it was, only a precious few seconds remained before that inevitable fate would befall her anyway.

Time-rift problem solved. By her own hand.

Not on my guard.

Not her. *Not now. Not…yet.*

Focus. The realm of nonmatter existed as a causeway, to be instantly traversed, not endured. Consciousness, and the physical body that followed it, snapped from one point of time and place to the next, a slingshot moment. For good reason.

A violent yank on the other end of Brigid's tether, then another, signaled the strength of her calm force weakening, her body being tossed about by the lethal elements.

On a steady exhale, Skorpius relaxed and let go, allowed the tether to reel him toward her. And on the way, he blasted as much of his magick to propel him as he dared.

There! Through the swirling bitter darkness, Skorpius spotted her distant position in the never-ending nothingness: a pinpoint of fading light.

Talk to me, he urged. Almost there, but he needed her strong and in one piece.

Verrrrra…ccc…cccold.

Near flameout himself, Skorpius stoked his inner core, coated his form with every ounce of magick he had remaining, and plummeted toward her.

On instinct, he tapped into his internal chronometer, calculated speed and trajectory, gauged a sufficient distance of travel beyond her, then locked on to a safe exit point.

A slight shiver coursed along their tether. Then nothing.

The taut bond…snapped.

A split-second haunting image seared into his mind. Brigid's perished form, weightless without gravity, hovering on the brink of combustion back to its base elements. Motionless. Breathless. Pulseless. Slack arms and legs floating wide, splayed copper hair and dress, drifting backward. Unseeing silver eyes. Luminous titanium skin.

Fractal light manifested on every surface molecule, each infinite pinprick brightening toward blinding.

But before Brigid's limp body began to break apart, his rocketing fireball ensnared her. *Don't you die on me now.* They'd come so far in such a short time. With no threat to time surfacing. Not from her.

The heat of his magick swept her into his hold.

Arms wrapping, head angling down, wings enfolding into a protective cocoon, he curled around her as they pierced through the veil, traversing from the substrate of time back into the realm of matter.

From a bright blue sky, they shot like a missile, manifesting from utter nothingness into a targeted time and place. They hurtled in a low arc over the Highlands, a fiery comet in broad daylight.

And as Skorpius's magick sputtered on dwindling reserves, he shot a final burst of energy along his end of their dangling tether. The powerful charge seared across its length, snapped the tether rigid, and fired its pulse into her breast.

System shocked, Brigid seized with a heavy thump of a restarted heart and a loud gasp of air surging into deflated lungs.

Their bond rippled to life again.

Weak, but holding.

As they plummeted toward earth, Skorpius did the best he could to cant open his wings, lift their trajectory, soften their landing. But his strength flagged at the critical moment.

Instead of struggling with spent wings to gain more lift, he wrapped them tight around her.

And as the softer needled tops of the forested tree line raced toward their bodies, he pulsed the last of his life-giving magick essence into her. "Hang on, *apprentice*," he teased.

Through fading awareness, Skorpius sensed a slight tremble from her, a hint of mirth that tingled along their restored bond. Then firm fingers wrapped around his biceps. And a slight flare of warmth radiated outward—from her.

Exhausted, Skorpius exhaled in relief. Softer new-growth

boughs lashed at his arms, the arches of his wings, the top of his head. With a twist and roll, he angled toward the biggest pine crown, hoping it might serve as a makeshift net to break their fall.

Even so... *This might hurt a bit.*

Aye. Another tickle of humor along their thread.

Black dots edged into his awareness. A darkened shadow floated across his mind.

And as Skorpius drifted out of consciousness, a jolt jerked them off course.

They tumbled away from the treetops, into another direction altogether.

Straight down.

Kindness smiled down upon Skorpius.

Silky raven hair.

Gentle blue eyes.

Beauty incarnate.

Familiar, yet distant. A human face. Someone he had once known. Love long ago lost. Sacrificed for the greater good. Cast unto the ravages of Earth time.

I'm dreaming.

Yet angels did not dream. Humans *did.*

"*Let go, Skorpius.*" *Laughter tinkled out, its faint echo drifting off in the vivid dream world.* "*Forsake duty,*" *the raven beauty implored.* "*Be with me.*"

Which he'd done, once upon a *long* time ago. *Not* a dream, then. A memory.

Yeah. He didn't do memories either. No regrets. No dwelling on the past. No suffering. Mistakes? Best forgotten.

Merciless bitter-cold wind buffeted exposed skin.

But a soft porcelain cheek brushed against his own.

"Embrace life," the low feminine voice murmured. "Love me. As I love you."

Love. Pure weakness. Human emotion.

An illusion. *Great.* He'd catapulted from memory stalking to straight-up hallucinating.

Pain seared along raw nerve endings.

Heat saturated his body. A familiar soothing warmth filled his being.

"Fight, my angel."

Awareness wrestled to break through the hallucination.

Hot agony twisted in his chest. My angel. *Millions of razorblades scraped feathers from battered wings. Fiery ash singed into burning lungs. Raging lava coursed through throbbing veins.*

Parched lips split as they parted. "My angel," *he rasped out, confused.*

The raven-haired beauty had never known him as such. Only in guise, as trusted knight in a fabled kingdom. Then, at her seductive plea, he'd become fully human, someone for a doomed woman to love. To become newly mortal had been a fool's risk, a fool willing to try to be loved.

"Aye." The apparition shimmered, shifting color. "Mine."

Heavy eyes cracked open to blinding brightness.

Raven hair vanished, replaced by copper. Porcelain skin burnished golden. Fawn freckles dusted across a pert nose, spread toward rosy-peach cheeks. Silvery eyes that sparkled with the glow of magick gazed upon him, dancing with joy.

"*Och!*" she breathed in fierce whisper. A warm smile curved her lips. "*There* you are."

"Brigid?"

"Aye."

Skorpius lifted his head from her lap, attempted to take in the landscape beyond her. Busted tree limbs lay scattered about an open grassy field. Divots of freshly churned soil lay on either side of a strip that led to their position. Pain fired through every fiber of his being at the physical effort, so he pinched his eyes shut and dropped his head back down. "We crashed."

"Sarcasm." Amusement lightened her tone.

"Yeah." All he mustered through a raw throat.

"You caused me great worry."

Then we're even. The horrific image of her floating lifeless body flashed across his mind. But Skorpius banished the thought. Instead, he sought her hand, wove his fingers into hers, then squeezed. And he kept strong hold of her, even through the tremendous ache firing into each joint, every muscle and sinew.

"Guess I should have mentioned"—he swallowed hard past a cramp in his throat—"we needed to maintain contact."

Brigid's scorching glare would've flayed a mere mortal. A slender brow arched. "I've been told 'obvious statements of fact are good.'"

Ah. More sarcasm. Well done. His lips twitched. An almost smile.

Increasing warmth bathed him. And with it, the pain ebbed further with every next beat of his heart.

After a dozen more beats, Skorpius was able to fully open his eyes. When he lifted his head once again, stretched tight wings, then pushed himself upright, no further pain remained.

"What happened?"

"You skipped over the earth like a stone across a loch."

Skorpius frowned, scanning over her flawless face and seemingly unmarred body. "Are you injured?"

"Nay." Brigid glanced around at ratty tufts of black feathers that clung to grasses and heather all around them. Then her hard gaze pegged him. "But you were."

Apparently.

She stroked a hand over his left wing. A golden hue of

magick floated between her fingers and perfect new feathers. "Your wing. 'Twas badly broken."

"As opposed to goodly broken."

"Ha." A glint of humor flashed in her eyes as her gaze snagged his. "Your skin…"

Skorpius flexed a stiff hand. The tightness of new skin stretched over his knuckles. "Got shredded." Educated guess.

"Aye." Brigid's attention roved across his body, then paused over the now-unblemished black leather covering his legs. "I let magick and my memory guide me. Your body did the rest."

He blinked in surprise. "You healed me?"

"In a way."

Only one explanation existed where his immortal body would fail to heal itself. Death. But if he'd hovered on the brink of it, or had been too badly injured, it would take a long time for his body to heal.

"How long have we been here?"

Brigid glanced up at the bright sun overhead. "Less than an hour."

"*Impossible*," he breathed. Not without darkness. Sunlight sapped his magick. More than half a dozen centuries had passed since the last time solar energy had been able to restore him.

A knowing gaze stared at him. "*Verra* possible."

"But…" Skorpius tried to wrap his mind around the unique incident. Failed. "How?"

"*I'll* share the secret of how I healed you." Silver eyes stared at him, penetrating. "If *you* share what happened with me and the otherworldly creatures in the glade, what I did—all of it."

So it's like that, then? We're now bartering for disclosures?

Aye.

"Very well." Skorpius tried not to laugh. But damn, he was proud of her. Of her determination and her tactics.

A strange expression washed over her features, then her brow furrowed.

"First, there's a task we're needin' to see to."

Alarm tripped through him. That Brigid sensed some hidden danger he failed to detect. "What task?"

Skorpius scanned farther out. Then he realized a giant dome of golden magick stretched over the glade. Trillions of its glittering particles absorbed the sunlight, then refracted it toward a convex lens over them. The lens, faceted with a honeycombed surface, magnified the sun's power down toward the earth.

But before the magnified light reached where Skorpius lay prone on the ground, the energy filtered through a second, smoky lens, transmuting the lighter golden energy into a denser force. Cooler, darker, purer energy than any Skorpius had ever sourced radiated throughout his body. Had healed him. *Still* strengthened him on an elemental level.

"*Nice trick.*" The astonishing female continued to dazzle with them.

Brigid glanced up as if affected by some exterior force again. "A foreign magick has been tryin' to break through. Mayhap"— eyes narrowed, she gazed up and scanned along the surface of her protective sphere—"*many* magicks."

Skorpius huffed out a conflicted sigh. Strong as he'd become again—repaired and in top fighting condition—he still could've used more time. Good old-fashioned rest healed even the mightiest immortals.

However, if answers lay on the other end of those magick knocks at her door? They needed to find them. Ready or not.

The dual internal tethers were silent on the matter.

Except a fine golden filament had developed and glistened along the repaired guardian line. Like scar tissue. Or some new enhancement they had no time to explore. But they would. He added the anomaly to the growing investigation list.

"Well…" Skorpius dragged himself up from the ground, but he concealed a slight sway with a flare of his wings as he gained his balance. Immortal did not mean instant. And the greater the injury, the deeper the repair needed. Whatever Brigid had done —and they *would* have a discussion about exactly what, when appropriate—had worked miracles, even from angelic perspective.

Skorpius drew in a slow breath, then gave a slow nod. "Perhaps we should let them in."

CHAPTER 15

Skorpius held Brigid's intense gaze as she slowly stood. She was drenched in layers of magick.

Fire sparked in those silvery eyes.

Copper coils of hair rustled in a breeze made of pure energy.

A luminescent aura shimmered around her body, radiating outward.

And at some point during his lights-out crash, she'd shed her unique emerald dress. From the reaches of her imaginative mind, she had fashioned herself a golden diaphanous gown. Each gauzy layer floated with her every subtle movement, shielding enough for modesty, yet revealing a hint of feminine curves over the female warrior's sleek muscular form.

The stunning effect made her appear ethereal.

Yet the substantive energy that crackled beneath her glowing skin warned otherwise.

Eyes narrowing, Brigid cocked her head a fraction and swept a critical gaze over him from head to toe. The healer deciding her patient's fitness.

Even now, Skorpius felt her restorative energy sizzle

through him, further tightening newly formed fascia, weaving together cells between skin and feather, sinew and bone.

And something else swirled in those spectacular observant eyes: a deep…*knowing.*

Uncomfortable for the first time in ages, Skorpius raised his brows.

Battle with an unknown foe? Bring it.

Analysis of a broken angel? *Not in this immortal's lifetime.*

"Well, Doc?" Skorpius crossed his arms, feigning amusement to distract from the scrutiny. "What's the verdict? Will I live?"

Brigid granted him a sign-off with a curt nod. "Hale and whole…*enough.*"

He gave a respectful nod back. Message received. Not *enough* for him to engage in battle, although he'd measure up to the task. *Enough* for her to be okay with it, after recovering from the fright of nearly losing him.

On a calm exhale, Brigid dissolved the dome of her magick shield into a shower of glittering particles.

The heat of a midday sun followed, radiating down on them.

But an instant later, a black hole swirled into existence in the sky directly above them, then stretched down in an expanding shadowy sphere.

The surrounding verdant glade stretched tall and wide— then vanished.

Until a different glade appeared, with a darker, more ancient forest bordering its perimeter.

And for the first time ever, Skorpius's inner chronometer went haywire.

"*Multiple* times, *multiple* spaces, all at once," he murmured, astounded at the feat.

Upon closer inspection, he discovered details of the trees surrounding them blurred thicker, as if each trunk represented the same tree at various stages, new to old-growth. Branches and leaves, as well as ground foliage, appeared as a smoky haze.

Each image existed at some point, but not all together in the same time-space reality.

Therefore, whatever beings had summoned them—and it had to be *multiple* beings as well with the unbelievably powerful achievement—worked in concert. And possessed untold power, individually. Magnified as a collective. For each had somehow aligned, then superimposed their respective time-window to allow the wielder to remain on his or her home turf. While enabling the collective to assemble in one gathering place. *A multidimensional proving ground.*

Their vast energy vibrated just beyond Skorpius's visibility, from deep within a cold darkness, the utter blackness along the fringes of this one-of-a-kind layered reality.

Until the first mighty being appeared along the perimeter of the darkened glade.

Another came forth.

Followed by a third.

Then more arrived, one after another.

Druids. Clear from their energy signatures. Powerful masters of magick.

The sorcerers—the rare few tapped into source power, wielders of its genesis energy—revealed themselves into the shadowy alternate plane, materializing from the hazy depths of the forest. Their faces were concealed under hooded cloaks, the style and fabric unique to the time and place each hailed from. Staffs of all kinds extended from firm grasps: knotted wood, carved ivory, sparkling alloy, immobilized serpent.

Ancient magick saturated the air, tasting of elements far removed from Brigid's time. And realm.

Nice. A time-space summit.

In all, an even dozen appeared.

"How does it feel?" Skorpius asked her. Aloud. For two reasons: Brigid had been the one invited, and to gauge any of the druids' potential reactions.

"Like darkest danger," she murmured. "And powerful invitation."

Interesting. "Good or bad?" Powered down, he chose not to assess. Brigid's show, Brigid's lead.

"Nay." After a slight headshake, her eyes drifted shut. "'Tis neither. 'Tis the mountain. The brook. Meadow. Sky. Equal power exists in all; none register good *or* bad."

"Why?" The nuanced question served as education, guidance. How did Brigid interpret the magick-saturated assembly? Valuable information lay in the druids' energy signatures; their individual or combined frequencies could hide subtle messages, coded for her alone. If so, only she would have the ability to decipher any underlying meaning.

Did the druids wish to impart knowledge and power? Or had they gathered from the far corners of time and dimension to bear witness to her evolution? Worst case, their motives skewed darker—to steal, manipulate, consume.

Skorpius's role? To observe and assess not only the external forces, but also the resulting interplay of his dual tethers, both of which had begun to hum at a greater frequency with the power showdown.

And of course, to monitor Brigid.

Her root essence would determine the path she chose to negotiate through the rare challenge.

Because Skorpius knew history replayed in varying facets. Over the eons—with the natural ebb and flow of dominance and submission, through the rise and fall of civilizations that had veered one direction or the other—the moral compass of the one in power determined the course, channeled the flow of events from their influence outward.

"*Weel...*" Brigid's gaze lowered, growing unfocused as she gave thought to the matter. "The mountain simply is. The traveler curses the barrier as an obstacle. The hawk cherishes it as a huntin' ground."

"Perspective." Skorpius gave an understanding nod, grateful she'd grounded herself in analysis amid the strange chaos. "And if you became the mountain? Absorbed the power?"

Because that remained the two-fold crux of his mission: protect her, protect the worlds. And in his unprecedented challenge to intervene when necessary in a fluxing situation, he tugged on possibility threads, searching for an outcome where both could be achieved.

"*Och!*" Brigid's startled oath rasped out, albeit under her breath, as she scanned over the group.

But Skorpius had heard.

And felt.

Immense energy had begun to build from the visitors. Subatomic particles sizzled and sparked. They ascended from the ground in vibrational waves, then spiraled off into iridescent tendrils that kicked up forest detritus. A gathering cloud cover blotted out what remained of a filtered midday sun. The temperature plummeted twenty degrees. Thirty. And falling. Currents of mist flowed in from the surrounding forest, from some unseen torrent of energy that released power.

Skorpius manifested his sword and burst his blackish blue magick through it. He stepped closer to Brigid, then angled back to back with her, in a united front against the strangers. A clear warning. They stood together. And as her guardian, he would defend her.

His magick alone would defeat any foe under normal circumstances. But a dozen powerful druids would challenge any angel's abilities. And he had no way of knowing whether they'd witnessed his recent debilitating crash. Or her amazing powers of restoration.

However, the noteworthy gathering hadn't collectively distorted time-space to see if they could best the worst of the angels. The sorcerers had come together to test a newcomer's mettle.

Low intonation began from one of the druids. Tall and bony of form, he lifted his metal staff into the air. Lightning bolted from the ground through the staff and illuminated the dense fog into glittering brilliance. The lightshow ended abruptly when he stabbed the bottom of his staff onto the ground.

Another druid, across the circle from the first, joined with a lower tone, his incantation slower, deeper, pulsing with rhythm. He raised the immobilized snake which he gripped behind the head. The creature elongated to twice its length and snapped gleaming black fangs up at a wild sky churned blood red. Its ruby eyes flashed into the fog, highlighting a gothic landscape.

Druid after druid contributed their own distinctive toning. And the gathering of ancient powers roused the core elements of matter. Their vibrations altered the substances around them, transforming solid to liquid to gas to pure energy and back again. Once-solid objects within the eerie layered realm pulsed and floated between their various forms, as if awakened and stretched to their possibilities, brainless matter becoming near sentient. All brought to bear by druids whose power magnified as a collective, comprised of individuals who toned at a precise volume and octave to wield the vibrations of sound as their tool.

Tools make effective weapons, he thought as the ground beneath their feet—still solid—began to shake and heave.

Skorpius flexed then tightened his fingers around the hilt of his sword. And he punched a large amount of his magick outward and down. An angelfire-sourced energy field would protect them. For a time.

"How's it feel now?" he ground out. Because every last molecule vibrated *danger* to him.

"Unusual," Brigid murmured under her breath.

No time for riddles. "Unusual *how?*"

"Foreign. And friend. Their magick. And…mine."

"You feel the druids' magick as your own?"

"Aye. In a manner."

"What else?" Familiarity didn't mean safe. Nor did it mean the druids condoned a foreigner having access to what they deemed as theirs. Territory wars were fought fiercely in all realms, in every time.

A low whimper escaped her throat. "Pricks of pain."

Skorpius tensed, then glanced over his shoulder at her. "Where?"

"Into my center. My chest. My...heart."

"Okay." They could work with that. The druids were attacking her, but through a back door. Their toning to effect what her outer senses perceived, which was all she'd ever known till then? Pure distraction.

"Focus your attention inward, on your heart. And all the infinite dark space within. Make the dark space warm. Bright. Think of the most beautiful summer day you've ever had, bathed in sunlight, running through wildflowers." How he imagined Brigid happy. Free. They didn't have time to explore a quantum physics lesson; basic images on the fly would have to suffice.

The only reply Brigid gave was in her slowed breathing.

"Are you there?"

"*Aye.*"

Fissures in the earth cracked open beginning at the perimeter of his protective energy field, then splintered outward, widening, deepening. White steam and colored gases slow-spiraled upward in thickening streams. A putrid stench permeated the air.

We shouldn't be able to smell that. Not if his magick served as an impermeable barrier. "Burst that feeling out, Brigid. Toward the dark nothing-space beyond us." *Strengthen our shield. Before those egotistical ancients shatter it.*

But Brigid had already sensed the urgent need. A calming warmth radiated from behind before he'd completed the instruction. And a fresh sweet scent cleansed the air flowing into his lungs.

"Good. You've found it." Without needing further details, she'd solidified her heart's center, bulletproofing the source of her energy from the druids. And she'd protected both of them.

"Aye," she breathed out.

"Good. Keep hold of that feeling. Enhance it. Imagine the best you have ever felt, the strongest emotion, the happiest."

His impromptu coaching would have to work miracles.

Because Brigid hadn't had any time to exercise and learn the limits of her new ability; she'd only be able to harness and wield at a static level for so long. And even with Skorpius's heritage, and the unique magick cocktail that flowed through his veins due to his fall from grace, his energy would only protect them so far.

And it was her rare magick the druids had come for.

Further golden peace suffused Skorpius's being, warm and radiant. Brigid's pure *good* energy cascaded through him, then surged anew, outward toward the perimeter of his protective field, then fanning beyond.

The fractures in the earth continued to deepen as the druids continued their intonation. All twelve voices intertwined together, weaving individual threads of power into one incomparable supernatural force. And the magnitude of the concentrated energy electrified everything, in the glade and beyond.

Between the gassy fissures, large swells of earth began to bulge up. One, two, three, then several more, blooming in quick succession. With a deafening crack, an enormous slab of granite shot out from the first and largest bulge. Another crack, and a second tore free from its erupting mound. A third boomed its launch, shaking the ground outside of their protective field before hovering overhead with its forerunners.

But that last eruption quaked a tremor into their sphere of protection, its punching force vibrating up through their feet.

"They grow stronger," Brigid murmured. Her unconcerned tone bordered on serene.

Adrenaline fired hot through his veins.

The paradox of their evolving relationship made Skorpius smile grimly and shake his head. In the midst of a pending apocalypse, they no longer appeared to be apprentice and master.

More like monk goddess and mongrel angel.

Another boom, and another granite megalith catapulted loose to hover in the air. Then a fifth. And a sixth. Tension crackled through the atmosphere as Brigid's fresh and bright magick sparked against the druids' ancient and dark.

Clods of dirt and chunks of roots rained down from the sky from the massive floating rocks. Half of the shed material vanished as it dematerialized in a wash of magick, reappeared as a strange skeletal image, then vanished again.

The granite slabs themselves vibrated at such a high frequency, the stones had also become ghostly ephemeral images—part within the layered artificial plane and part fighting to return to their singular dimension.

"And you?" Skorpius fought to ground himself with his own inner peace, while still firing up his magick, readying for the fight of their lives.

Brigid exhaled, long and slow. "Stronger yet."

Good. Instinct screamed they would need every ounce of her secret brew.

In answer to his unspoken wish, Brigid's golden magick rippled outward in new dimension, not merely warm, but a tingling heat. Not only bright, but filled with healing essence.

But Skorpius knew Brigid would only flare at her hottest for a brief period. She remained a novice and those druids knew it, or they'd never have aligned themselves in such a risky manner. They'd flocked together and combined efforts because of the great energy beacon she'd become: nascent magick with the heady promise of a moldable—susceptible—greater power.

The giant slab of granite nearest them cracked again, snapping fully into solid form. Then the behemoth hurtled toward them, angled directly toward Brigid—at lightning speed.

In smooth reply, all her golden magick tightened in together, then detonated outward. Her energy wave crashed over the forward end of the rock—freezing the slab a scant few inches from her face—then shattered into a shower of platinum energy-snow that blanketed its entire surface. An instant later, the slab disintegrated into white-gold dust that sparkled brightly, then winked out of existence.

Heavy breathing marked Brigid's exertion.

Skorpius fired up his magick around them, to give her time to recover.

"*Nay,*" she breathed as a furnace of heat blazed from behind again. Wherever Brigid mined her resources from, they kept pouring forth, delivering everything she needed. "'Tis *my* fight."

"That it is." Without doubt. And she had held her own. From the first testing punch.

But it mattered little where Brigid found her reserves. Or how she tapped them.

Those druids were masters. The best of the best.

And they hadn't achieved that zenith without millennia of experience.

In comparison, Brigid crawled and cooed, a fragile babe before ancients.

They had learned. Had strategized. Had already determined what any given opponent would do in one set of circumstances. Then tested alternate hypotheses in the next.

Toss a giant granite slab at her? And Brigid, in natural reaction, attacked the slab.

They'd try something else next. Trial any number of other theories. Until they exhausted her. Then they'd strike a final and unrecoverable blow.

How wars had been waged. And won. Over eons.

However, no one had ever faced a goddess of her magnitude. Because none had existed.

Until Brigid.

Skorpius's thoughts flashed to her extraordinary evolution in the glade, with the beasts.

"If you've got any more tricks up your sleeve, *now* would be the time to wow them."

The smooth centering core within Brigid remained steady. But her magick continued to gather, growing in intensity. The warmth of its energy bathed him, from back to front, a soothing caress to someone unaware of its potential power.

And what would Brigid do with that immense power? That all depended on her character.

The dual tethers stretched equally taut. The one to protect her vibrated, hot and insistent. The other—time's mandate—vacillated, searing and fluid one moment, icing into rigidity the next.

The remaining floating slabs suddenly shifted in unison, angling up forty-five degrees while orienting toward her. A legion of stone threatened to entomb Brigid far below ground with tons of force and speed.

The undeterred pilots of those projectiles stared anonymously from beneath dark hoods. Their eerie toning gained a greater depth, voices doubling, tripling, into layers of echoes. Robed arms raised their varied staffs toward the sky as one, then struck the ground again.

A soundless, motionless second passed.

Massive energy pulsed into the nothingness.

Three distinct waves from different epicenters—the druids', Skorpius's, and Brigid's—exploded outward in a blinding flash of light.

Beyond their multidimensional glade, clear blue sky over all of Scotland—in every time and realm—echoed with the boom.

The earth trembled from westward ocean to eastward sea, from northern islands into bottomland England.

Naked silence followed.

Utter blackness blinded.

Eventually awareness trickled in, one slogging muted second after another. A rapid pulse thrummed through his veins. Shortened breaths rasped over his eardrums. Bright sunlight warmed his bare skin.

Skorpius opened his eyes, surprised to find himself...still standing.

He blinked and spun a quarter turn.

Brigid glanced at him. She stood, strong and beautiful, beside him.

And they both tracked heightened attention toward the semicircle of druids.

Not one robed figure remained standing. Or conscious. The powerful sorcerers lay prone, unmoving, and fanned out, like toppled bowling pins.

The massive granite slabs? Had shot end-first into the ground surrounding the fallen druids. Residual magick crackled a high voltage between the stones. Imprisoned by their own weapons.

Brigid shook her head, bewildered by the aftermath of her unleashed power. "I *doona* know..."

"I know." The event wasn't identical to the incident with the beasts in the glade, but it bore similar hallmarks. Somehow, she'd disarmed the combined power of the druids. Instead of defeating the stones, she'd conquered their masters.

"But are they..."

"Dead?" Skorpius probed a scan of magick over the group as a whole. Faint pulses. Shallow breaths. "No. But not down for long."

It amazed Skorpius that they were down at all. Lights out.

All the druids.

Sudden realization struck him. He walked closer to the assembled group. Examined the faces now exposed by fallen hoods.

"Not *all* the druids," Skorpius murmured. Countless had existed over the ages. The contingent who'd come after Brigid were unparalleled sorcerers.

However, one masterful druid remained conspicuously absent.

Skorpius's eyes narrowed with suspicion.

"Brigid? What do you feel? Does anything seem out of place to you?"

Because with all the residual magick from sources far and wide, Skorpius failed to distinguish among them. There hadn't ever been any need for subtleties regarding his missions. An angel guarding time didn't need the particulars of any magick that threatened the timeline, he only needed to eliminate it.

And angelkind distinguished only two kinds of magick: angelfire and everything else.

Brigid? Uniquely harbored both.

In fact, her special brew of extraordinary power, muted by their own shield of protection, echoed in faint vibrations through him. The heady cocktail buzzed through his system, jolting his cells into rapid excitation. And further advanced the repairs she'd made, by several levels.

"Aye. 'Tis somethin'… *other*." Brigid's gaze swept the outer perimeter of the fallen druids, scanned over the half-sunken slabs, then out into the shadows of the forest beyond. She squinted as she drew in a steadying breath. "Watchin' from afar."

Of course. For the universe existed in balance. Materialize a never-before-seen goddess? Match with an inaugural assembly of druid-puppets—with a greater master pulling their strings. "Describe the 'other.'"

"Cold. Metallic. Boilin' with anger." Brigid glanced at him. "And somethin'… *else*."

No need to detect on Brigid's level to finish discerning the 'else.'

Skorpius already knew.

Which meant the whole thing, from the very beginning, had been about her *and him.*

Lips firming, Skorpius cast a grim expression her way. *"Envy."*

CHAPTER 16

*S*korpius stared down at her, his blue-green eyes swirlin' with magick, expression grave.

Then an unidentified urgency spiked her pulse.

The druids' ancient power still hummed through the false glade, growin' in strength.

But a new vibration rumbled through her internal magick. They had mere seconds before a greater threat manifested into the strange layered space.

Skorpius narrowed his eyes. "That angry 'other' stalks us. We need to leave. Now." Those glossy black feathers ruffled on his archin' wings, and he extended his hand toward her.

"*Nay.*" Brigid shook her head and instead offered her hand out toward him. "'Tis *my* path. I'll be leadin' the way." *Through the cold, dark nothingness* behind *time. Back whence we've come.*

Surprise widened his eyes and arched his dark brows. "That didn't go well last time."

"Aye." Remorseful for what she'd caused, Brigid scanned his now-whole wings, the muscular strength of his body, and, with the aid of her magick, beneath his skin, to the fierce beat of his heart. She dropped her chin in a slow nod, satisfied that he'd endure an attempt with her leadin' them through. "But 'twill be different now."

Amusement sparked in his eyes. "Because…"

"We've no time to linger." Brigid grabbed his hand. "Let me prove my skill."

He clasped tight to her hold with a solid squeeze. "As you wish, goddess. Lead the way."

On a hard exhale and with a sudden burst of magick, Brigid vanished them away from the odd layered space.

The bitter-cold black nothin'ness scoured at the edge of her awareness. But with an idea of how to navigate its endless storm of fury, she dinna allow the darkness to overwhelm her.

Instead of bein' passive, Brigid concentrated her energy with a singular crisp thought and arrowed through the void, nimble of purpose, focused toward her target. She visualized their sunny glade. Where Skorpius had earlier crashed while protectin' her. When she'd discovered her additional ability to heal.

An instant later, they appeared there, feet alightin' into a gentle trot over solid ground. Returned hale and whole into her own time and place.

Och! The urgent vibrational warnin' dinna cease. *The one who hunts us attempts to follow.*

Upon her next heartbeat, she erected a glistenin' sphere of magick high above and all around them. And as she did so, she imagined the shield as a whole bubble of soap, extendin' it down and through the earth below, leavin' no chance for penetration from outside forces. Once complete, she energized a further layer onto the first, another more powerful coatin' of magick. Then she coated another greater shield, upon the initial two. Again and again, she layered more sophisticated coatin's, until she grew certain no "other" could detect the two of them within.

Skorpius whistled, eyes widenin' again as he scanned around, surveyin' her work. *"Nice."*

Breaths comin' fast and short from the incredible exertion of erectin' such a magnificent shield, Brigid tightened her grip on Skorpius's hand and glanced up to add one final important coat. Upon the inside layer, she brushed a darker cloakin', the same cave-like shadow she'd crafted to heal him, to strengthen his different sort of magick.

However, the moment her shadowed layer completed, allowin' the altered solar energy to radiate through to Skorpius, an electric spark sizzled up into her hand from the hot palm of his.

That intimate *male* pulse of power spun tendrils of thrillin' heat into unmentionable places.

Brigid gasped and broke contact, flattenin' her hand to her chest.

But her gaze clashed with his at the sound of *his* gasp.

The charge surprised him.

Excited him.

Taken aback by the growin' intimacy between them, she spun away and strode a dozen paces toward the perimeter of their protective shelter. A gnarled yew tree stood just within their boundary, and she stopped under its low canopy. To catch her breath. From so verra many things.

The heat of Skorpius's nearness pressed in from behind.

But she dinna turn. Nor did she flee.

"You like old-growth trees." Low tones soothed over her senses, slow and sweet, like warmed honey.

But greater than the sweet, Skorpius's bite of wild danger prickled through her, even more tantalizin'.

"Aye. The ancient ones call to me." Brigid hovered her hands over the trunk's rough bark. Then she leaned her weight against the mighty conifer, angled her head back, and stared up into curvin' boughs that sprouted the slender spears of its evergreen leaves. "Trees are our kin. Strong but quiet. Earth's silent guardians. They offer much. But take little."

On a deep inhale to bolster her courage, she turned to face him.

Skorpius stood an arm's length away. A respectful distance. But hot energy sparked in that gap between them. From him. From her. And it had naught at all to do with magick.

Deep comprehension shone in his otherworldly eyes. "A great example for all."

The trees. And more. Purpose and understandin' brightened within her. "Aye."

On a shaky inhale, she examined his unmarred body. "You wished me to share."

"How you healed me."

"Aye." Words failed to express how she'd spun the verra elements to life. How she'd known how to rebuild him from his tiniest roots, which she'd failed to see, outward to the glorious rest of him, muscles, wings, and...all. "'Twas the work of the magick."

Unrelentin' eyes narrowed at her. "*Not* magick."

"*More* than magick," she admitted. To herself. And to him.

In truth, she'd been overcome by the destruction of her magnificent angel. By her rash foolishness.

Heartbroken and angry at seein' him torn apart over the ground, hoverin' near death, Brigid had *willed* him back to life, into the glorious creature she knew.

Piercin' eyes searched hers as he lifted a hand to her cheek. "Strong emotion."

"Aye." Brigid sighed. Her brow furrowed at the frustration she felt.

But then, his brow furrowed as well. To her surprise, his conflicted expression mirrored her own.

"Mayhap, there's more to the tellin'." Her need to confess ran deep.

Skorpius's head tilted, confusion washin' over his face. "There is?"

"Aye." She drew in a steadyin' breath. "You dinna stitch back together with ease. Once I'd woven you back to where your heart beat and your lungs expanded, you *fought* me."

"Sounds about right."

"And you...*mistook* me...for another."

Skorpius's expression fell, darkenin'. "Ah. I see."

"You remember?"

"Some." He gusted out a heavy sigh. "That was...another lifetime ago."

Brigid gave a hesitant nod, then glanced over her shoulder at her satchel. Toward the bottom, where it bulged a wee bit. Where the leather-covered story of a man's journey had been chronicled. "A *human* lifetime."

When she glanced back up at him, he tore his gaze from the same bulge, from the knowin' of what lay within. "Yes. Before I'd gone dark. Before I'd become Guardian of Time."

"Before wings of black. Before feedin' from the shadows."

"Yes."

"You were a guardian then. *Her* guardian."

Skorpius gave a short nod, gaze holdin' fast to hers. A proud male, but honest, holdin' account for his actions. "In charge of her safety."

"For she needed your help. Escort to safe harbor." When he nodded again, she continued, well-versed in Arthurian legend from the bards, but also the private tellin' of it in the pages she'd spirited away. "And then you both...fell in love."

Skorpius's brows furrowed. Fierceness glinted in his eyes. "Against honor and code of angelkind and humankind. In betrayal of a king, a friend."

"But not her. You dinna betray... *Guinevere.*" The romantic queen had been a fable before. But the bards had regaled their clan with a tale far different than within the pages in that leather-bound book. "'Tis by *your* hand, the tale I've read." The knowin' of it rang true as she cast another glance at her satchel's bulge where it lay.

"My personal account of the events, yes."

When she glanced back at him, Skorpius's eyes searched hers. Not in judgment of her possessin' his book. Not upset of her knowin' his most intimate thoughts in a past life. Nor questionin' her ability to read at all, secreted from Clan Brodie's kind priest who'd shared a valuable skill with a lonely lass. But with unmistakable hope that shone bright in his eyes, that she'd understand. "From the framework of a Christian world, it served as penance for the sins of a tortured man. Chronicles of mortality's flaw: the fleeting joy of selfish love and its consequences, regret and pain."

"*Lancelot*," Brigid whispered, starin' him straight in the eyes. For the truth of it astounded.

"Once upon a time. Long, long ago. *All* of it."

The love. The heartache. The *human*ness. All had been written. Brigid had been profoundly touched by the depths of the sorrow that had bled onto those pages. *His* sorrow.

"And now?"

"I am no longer that man. No longer human. No longer capable of weakness."

"Love," she murmured, understandin' his admission: his limitation. The emotion had proved a weakness for her in the past as well. A yearnin' to be deeply connected to someone else. Even if that someone had...disappeared.

As Brigid hardened her heart anew, for both their sakes, his eyes softened.

One corner of his mouth curved up. "Perhaps. Not quite the human notion of love. But it appears"—he curved his hand and brushed the backs of his knuckles over her cheek—"I have a minor weakness I've recently been made aware of."

Hope sprang warm and bright in her chest, in spite of the armorin' of her heart. "Toward one who no longer remains mortal." Even she sensed the world as she'd once known it had been forever altered.

Velvety wings encircled her. Sparklin' eyes searched hers. His face lowered, hoverin' close. "Two immortals. No human rules."

"Mayhap, then, no weakness at all," she whispered over his mouth, so verra close.

"Precisely," he murmured.

The slightest brush of contact charged electric against her lips, then throughout her body. Warmth sizzled and sparked, a bonfire flarin' to hungry life.

And then, at once, 'twas gone. A cool breeze brushed into the space as he pulled away.

A hard gaze bored deep into hers. "Have care with this, Brigid. Be certain."

Head swirlin' from unbelievable events that had transpired in two days' time, heart achin' for an angelic male she'd known for but a moment, yet had come to understand better than any soul she'd known before, she sucked in a shaky breath. Weariness tugged at her. The kind from expendin' too much magick. And mayhap the kind from the quickened heartbeats of a lass who'd anticipated a breathtakin' kiss.

"*Aye.*" She exhaled to a forced count of five. For slowin' their romantic pace amidst all the wild adventure and danger seemed wise. "In truth, I'll be needin' to rest a wee bit."

"And eat. First."

Behind Skorpius, through a sparklin' shadowy mist, manifested the most sumptuous feast she'd ever laid eyes upon.

Scents of cooked meats and sweet desserts made her mouth water. "*Och!* Such a gift."

Skorpius gestured an arm and wing toward her flattened plaid, pinned on one corner by her satchel and the others by her quiver, bow, and daggers, somehow removed from her. "Your long-awaited supper, goddess."

A relieved exhale gusted from Brigid's lungs. And as the heated pressure of his nearness abated, the comfortin' glow of his protection replaced the erotic tension.

But when Skorpius's heated gaze traveled down the length of her body, she recalled the golden gossamer gown that had manifested unto its own when she'd been immersed in healin' magick to save him. She visualized a bolder color—a thicker *less scandalous* material—and wore the emerald gown once again, the verra one he'd fashioned and she'd grown to like.

But Skorpius frowned and gave a quick headshake. "I like the gold better. It suits you."

In a flash, she reversed the action, emboldened by his honest flattery.

While she folded her legs beneath her, then swiped a finger through a favorite of hot stewed cherries, the heated fire in his gaze smoldered down into warm embers.

Skorpius moved to the opposite corner of her plaid, but before he took a seat, he glanced up at her layered protective sphere. With a narrowed gaze, he magickally burned a section of the inner shadowy layer away to cast her section of the plaid into the warmth of sunlight. The altered effect concentrated solar rays onto her, but her alone.

Two sides of the same plaid, one hot and bright from the sun, the other cast in shadow, cool and dark. Day's energy for her, night's magick for him.

"Do you sense any force trying to break through?" His narrowed gaze searched the horizon.

"Nay." For the moment, their many-layered shield kept them hidden from detection.

For the next span of silent minutes, Skorpius appeared content to watch her while she consumed succulent roast pig, devoured varied soft cheeses, and sampled crusty herbed breads.

But after Brigid slowed, while she savored a spiced apple

tart, she cocked her head in question at his confused expression. "What plagues you?" The personal question felt strange after all that had happened, yet not so strange at all, since he appeared unfazed by their confessions.

"You did shockingly well with your first time-travel." He handed her a heavy wineskin.

"Leadin' us through." She took a few swallows of the bitter-sweet drink. "Aye."

"How did you know what to do?" His brow twitched down. The mystery truly puzzled him.

"I doona know." She licked a dusting of sugary cinnamon from her lower lip, then gave further thought on how to describe the gut feelin'. "When you'd swept me up the first time and flew toward the barrier, then through it, 'twas as if I saw an inked line on one of Iain's maps."

"*Impossible,*" he breathed. Then he shook his head. And a wee smile tugged at the corners of his mouth.

She huffed out a laugh. "Into the realm of verra possible, with me."

"Apparently. Because the only way you could've detected my line of travel would've been to have willed it yourself."

"Mayhap, I did."

"Describe what you thought when you led us through. Begin from the moment I took your hand."

A heated thrill had coursed through her at that innocent touch. "I imagined this glade. But I saw the glade at first large, like now"—she gestured an arm wide around them—"then as a wee green speck"—she drew in her hand and pinched a finger and thumb together to almost touch—"as if I'd peeked through the keyhole of our larder from across the great hall, then grasped your hand, and loosed an arrow of magick from my core through the glade's keyhole."

"Well done."

Growin' weary, Brigid reclined on her side and propped a

hand under her head to keep from fallin' asleep in their protected glade. Talkin' to Skorpius, being in the presence of one who safeguarded her, and cared enough about her to ask, caused an effect not unlike a full tankard of Iain's mead. "Is that not how you time travel?"

"Arrowing through a keyhole?" Amusement danced in his sparklin' blue-green eyes. "Perhaps that's how it would seem to a master archer. Although I do visualize where and when I want to go, with my internal chronometer, it's more precise. I lock in to the exact time and place I want before I go."

"How is that different?"

Skorpius gave a slight headshake, the ends of his black hair swayin'. "You aimed then *manifested* there, by magick alone."

"'Tis not typical?"

"*Time travel* is itself atypical. I'm the first, as Guardian of Time, and with an internal chronometer. Isobel is the prophesied Traveler. An apprentice of sorts to me. But she travels through time in a different way, connected to time rifts, events that need to be remedied."

"Only us three?"

"Without practicing and *mastering* the dark arts? Yes."

"Like the druids."

Skorpius nodded, expression grave. "Yes. Druids are masters of all magicks, natural and dark. Capable of time travel with enough gathered power and the motivation to expend it."

To steal mine.

He dinna reply. Simply stared at her.

Another thought struck, spikin' energy through her veins, racin' her pulse. "What of the other energy...whose presence tasted of 'envy'?" Skorpius had held a dire expression before they'd departed the battleground with the druids. "'Twas as if you recognized that angry foreign power..."

"I did." His wings flared as he stood. While scannin' the perimeter of their glade, he paced. Then he cast a glance at her with a resigned expression. "You met him as the young-old man at the castle. He goes by many guises."

She pushed upright, brows archin' in surprise. "You know of him?" The eerie presence who not only hunted her, but had been hauntin' her bedchamber.

"Yes." His face hardened into an unreadable mask. "I knew him as Merlin."

SPEAKING *THEIR* HUNTER'S NAME, revealing what Skorpius realized he'd suspected on some level all along, had a cathartic effect.

But Brigid cast no judgment. She had no reaction to the epiphany at all. In the silent seconds that followed, she only stared at him with stark intensity, as if seeing through to his very soul.

Silvery eyes sparking with golden fire, her penetrating look of *knowing*, stripped him bare. Laid waste with its raw power. Yet enveloped with soothing warmth. Magick hummed at its core, energy unlike any other. But woven throughout the rare scrutiny glittered her essence, good and pure. Inviting. Enriching.

Forgiving.

Accepting.

Without a word, she stood and crossed the plaid to her satchel. She stared down at that incriminating bulge at its bottom.

The material deflated, its contents vanishing.

At the same instant, the worn leather-bound book materialized in her hand.

"The same Merlin described in this journal?"

His journal. But she'd chosen to skip that detail.

A heavy feeling swelled in his chest, warm and somewhere

near that fracture in his heart. That the woman he'd been tied to, had begun to like, respect—and perhaps even a bit deeper—saw him only for the angel who stood before her. No more. No less. Separate from his past.

"The same." Honest. No point in holding back. She didn't stand in judgment of the tortured soul who'd penned those pages. And he had no need to color them with emotion. Hadn't for eons.

Brigid glanced at the journal in her hand then up toward her magick shield and the bright blue sky beyond. "'Twould seem more than happenstance."

"Yes. It would." What Skorpius had thought, after she'd leveled the druids, by the conspicuous absence of a particular one—the most powerful of all.

Her astute gaze landed back on him. "Mayhap my touchin' this book set our course."

"Perhaps." They'd never know for sure. Timelines had a trickiness to them where cause-and-effect blurred. And with Brigid's prophesy-charged birth, unfilled destiny had drawn her into fate's grasp, no matter the details.

"Do you have attachment to this?" Brigid tipped her head at the artifact.

"Not even a little." Strange that he didn't, yet had kept the object. A human construct, sentimentalism. Penance from a human time. But the past bore no imprint on his present.

"Verra weel." She stared at the book she held with a magick-heated glare. It combusted into golden dust, infinitesimal sparkling particles catching on a gentle breeze, then wafting away.

Skorpius watched the dust dissipate and felt…nothing. Aside from a sense of liberation in a second cathartic moment. "I wonder if that's how he's been tracking us." The mystery had been perplexing him.

As the last words left his mouth, Brigid swayed on her feet.

Skorpius lunged forward and caught her limp body as she collapsed.

Concerned, he bent his legs and lowered himself to the ground with her. While resting her head on his thigh, a quick check of her vitals and their internal tether verified she remained alive. Exhaustion had dragged her under, saving her from another all-systems shutdown.

"Ah, sweet girl," Skorpius murmured against her temple as he smoothed a hand over her wild copper curls. "You've expended too much magick again."

Brigid had gathered all the excess power she possessed to erect the magick shield to hide them from view. And she'd created a spectacular and unique form of energy architecture. The dome, perfect in its arching form and fueled by solar radiation, sustained itself. But because of its demanding self-feeding nature, only a negligible amount radiated down to reenergize her.

The problem he faced now? Due to Brigid's ingenious fabrication and laudable self-sacrifice, she alone held the key to unlock it. Skorpius was unable to alter the genetic makeup of the shield where it mattered for her benefit. Brilliant coding made its essence impenetrable from the outside, where most of the layers existed and were comprised of her golden magick. He'd only been able to burn away the dark of the inside earlier because it consisted of his energy.

"It's just as well. You need your rest." Still mending on the cellular level from his horrific crash landing, he needed some uninterrupted healing time as well.

Skorpius had given all he had for her.

Brigid had extended all she had for him.

"We are quite the pair." Rogue angel. Reborn goddess.

Trust came hard earned.

Loyalty even more so.

And whether or not they both realized it, they'd given each other those things. And more.

Skorpius settled beside her and draped a wing over her body. "Sleep deeply and well *and in*, goddess." No one would miss them come sunset in a few hours, nor at the sunrise yet again.

But all the worlds would need them at their strongest.

To face a demon from the past who'd clearly conquered time.

Whose power and influence had recruited the supreme among masters of magick.

One who, perhaps, had a grudge to settle.

Merlin.

CHAPTER 17

*E*nergizin' sunshine warmed Brigid's cheek.

    A reddish glow brightened behind heavy closed eyelids.

Soothin' firmness and heat radiated from under the rest of her face, her nose, her hand.

And a slow inhale ignited her senses with the strong spicy aroma of... *cinnamon...*

"*Snickerdoodles,*" she murmured. A smile tugged at her lips as an image shimmered forth in her drowsy state of the decadent male, and his scent of cinnamon.

The lazy stroke of firm fingers glided up her arm. "Have you tasted one?" Skorpius asked, tone low and calm.

Brigid pushed herself up, yawnin' as her mind tumbled over the puzzle of what she'd been asked. While she fully awakened to where she was—and with whom.

"Skorpius?" Disoriented, she blinked at the brightness of the day and glanced around, takin' in the glade, and tryin' to recall what'd happened before she'd deeply slept.

"The one and only." He also pushed upright to a seated position and stretched his magnificent glossy black wings up and out.

Then he held open a hand toward her. And upon his palm materialized a large copper-dusted *fragrant* flat cake.

Mouth instantly waterin', Brigid snatched up the baked tart the instant he lifted it toward her. When she took an eager bite, delightful tastes exploded over her tongue. Sweet. Spiced. "*Mmmm…*"

"An *actual* snickerdoodle." Merriment danced in his eyes. "The confection is called a cookie." He raised his brows, as if in expectation.

She then recalled Isobel had imparted the same definition mere days ago, when Brigid—and a well-aimed arrow—had officially introduced herself to Skorpius in the forest.

Brigid consumed another heavenly bite, then a third. With half the cookie packed into her cheeks, she answered his unspoken question. "'Tis beyond *any*thin' I've ever eaten."

"Well, good." Immense satisfaction shone in his eyes. Then he angled a nod toward her as the last bite disappeared into her mouth. "*That* is a snickerdoodle." His eyes narrowed, expression growin' fierce. "*I* am not."

Brigid fought a smile at his gruff tone. "Agreed."

Skorpius resemblin' a sweet cookie? *Nay.*

Gaze alightin' on dragonflies that soared overhead with their sticklike green bodies that glinted in the sunlight, she stood and stretched her stiff arms and legs with a frown. "How long've I been asleep?"

"*We've* slept forty-three straight hours." Skorpius stood and stretched his limbs as well.

"But…I doona…for that's—"

"—almost two days—"

"—*impossible*. 'Twas but a handful of minutes—"

"—possible, *needed*, and exactly two thousand five hundred and eighty minutes ago."

Eyes narrowin', Brigid stalked toward him. "How do you know *that?*"

Skorpius's eyes sparklin' with mirth, he tapped a finger to his temple. "Internal clock. Keeps time: year, month, day, hour, down to the precise millisecond. It also tells me my geographical location to the last inch."

"Weel, then." Brigid had no retort about the unusual and surprisin' skill.

Nor did she know how to react to Skorpius's sudden playfulness. His mood seemed lighter. "Sleep agrees with you."

Skorpius held her gaze a moment, then glanced up at the protective magick shield she'd erected. The dome still held fast. "Would you mind powering that down a few levels?"

"'Tis safe to do so?"

"It's time to do so. We can't hide forever. Power down, but perhaps also add another layer of that shadow-filter you created to heal me. Before we fully expose ourselves, it would be advisable for us to both be at full strength."

"Aye." Warmth bloomed in her chest, that her powerful angel wanted her assistance. With the brush of her mind, she peeled back the first of the interior layers.

A fine mist of golden dust showered down and Brigid offered him her hand.

When Skorpius made contact, a delicious spark ignited. Closin' her eyes, she focused upon it and kindled the flame of his essence with a surge of her own power. Then she burst his bluish black magick aloft. His darker energy sparkled forth and added another thick coatin' over the curtain of magick particles.

"Interesting," Skorpius murmured, watchin' with fascination as she wove their two magicks together.

"Not unlike your test, when you entwined our magicks that first time."

"Nice. You're a fast learner. And a master evolver."

"'Twas the only way I knew how to help you." Her brow furrowed at the image that burned into her mind that she couldna banish: of her beautiful guardian torn apart. "I doona understand. I thought you were immortal."

"I *am* immortal. Under most circumstances." Skorpius drifted his eyes closed, a peaceful expression washin' over his face as her shadow-magick bathed him with cool replenishment. "Had that only been an earthbound injury, it would've healed faster. Hours, maybe. But I'd flamed out before we'd broken through into your realm. Yet had I not succeeded in that, the scouring energy of the timeline would have dissolved me as well."

Anguished at the thought, she huffed out a scorchin' breath. "But you dinna perish."

"No." He opened his eyes and his piercin' gaze captured hers. "You saved me."

At the emotion blazin' in those sparklin' blue-green depths, romantic and sensual, a bold feelin' overcame her and Brigid stepped close behind him. She hovered tremblin' fingers over his silken black feathers.

"Be certain." He glanced over his shoulder at her with the repeated warnin', voice deepened into a wolfish growl.

Brigid flicked a glance at him, blew out a slow breath with a nod, then reached up into the arch of his glorious wing where it connected to his shoulders, to touch him. The same as she'd done after his crash. Only he hadn't been conscious then. Nor known that she'd used more than the sun's amplified power to heal him.

You asked me to heal you further, she mentally reminded him, fully aware that his seductive warnin' meant so much more.

At her gentle touch, Skorpius sucked in a deep breath.

But his shocked reaction dinna deter her.

Hummin' an ancient tune she somehow knew by instinct,

and with a gentle push from her heart's center, golden magick poured forth from her hand in a mist akin to faerie glow.

Skorpius's enchantin' eyes brightened with blue sparks as her fingers stroked the soft feathers, root to tip. Then her thumb glided over the softer down under-feathers along the edge.

Eyes driftin' closed, Skorpius turned and lowered his body under her potent touch. He took a knee and bowed his head, offerin' her full access to any part of his large body.

"*Aye*, I'm certain," she finally replied aloud. Certain of her actions. Certain of her heart.

Brigid's bold touchin' of a male would be deemed scandalous, were there any present to witness their exchange. She dinna care if anyone saw. However, in the first tender moments of connection she shared with a guardian she hadn't expected—with a soul so akin to hers—'twas as if the two of them had been ignited from the same flame. And she made certain their magick shield afforded them privacy.

Dippin' her head near his, Brigid pressed her lips to the heated skin at his temple.

A shiver quivered through his body, pebbled the bare skin down his back.

She smiled, pleased with the reaction her touch caused. Then she deepened the pressure of her strokes along his wing and infused the connection with the power of her healin' magick. "We'll borrow a bit of time for ourselves."

They needed that much. A gift unto themselves, for the moment.

Because in the first seconds of the aftermath of his devastatin' crash, Skorpius's pulse had fallen to a bare flutter. Brigid's heart had fully stopped beatin' in frightful despair.

Together, both hale and whole, they'd been given a blessed second chance. Brigid's heart now beat because of him. And she vowed not to squander the scant time remainin' before a battle that would test their limits. "'Twould seem your heart beats strong because of me as well," she murmured, feelin' their deep connection on an emotional level.

With a low moan, Skorpius turned toward her. He arrowed her with a fierce gaze before his focus lowered to her mouth. Then his soft lips brushed over hers. "Because of you. And *for* you."

A confession he dinna need to make.

Playful kisses danced light upon her lips, 'twas as if soft butterfly wings brushed over her, trailin' a warm afterglow of the sun through her mouth, flutterin' all the way down her throat, and fillin' her with a delightful wellspring of heated magick.

On a contented exhale, Brigid sighed in soft surrender, kissin' him back. Emboldened when he opened his mouth on a gasp, she suckled a wee bit at his full lower lip. "'Tis the same for me," she murmured. "A warm ache burns in my breast. For you."

With a low grunt, Skorpius tore his lips away.

A cool breeze chilled across her moistened lips, and she licked them, still tastin' his delicious spice on her skin.

He reclined down onto thick grasses. Mirth sparked in his gaze, tugged at the corners of his mouth. "*Only* in your breast?"

"*Nay.*"

Untried in the pleasures of her body, Brigid dinna have the words to describe the sensations.

Aye, she'd been kissed as a lass before, but by sweet love pecks from a human man, which bore no resemblance. But since she'd ceased bein' mortal, the whole world had changed regardless. 'Twas as if a pure spring rain had cleansed her new.

Skorpius's assessin' gaze pierced hers, right through to the verra heart of her. "Certain. Without doubt. No regret." The strong tone vibratin' beneath the words seemed like no question toward her, but a solemn vow from him.

"*Aye.*" Brigid affirmed with a confident nod. "Certain.

Without doubt. No regret," she vowed in reply. For in their private glade, under the shield of their entwined magick, they had only the present moment. The past no longer existed. For either of them.

The future? Remained to be seen.

CHAPTER 18

*W*ithin Skorpius warred the greatest conflict of his immortal life.

Brigid stood just out of reach.

Trusting silvery eyes stared straight at him, down to his blackened soul.

Sparks of potent magick flared in their depths.

Stark need and raw emotion brewed there too.

Yet something even more powerful in that bewitching gaze held him captive. As if the fierce warrior goddess *knew* him down to every last cell, and beyond, to the power that fueled them—energy she herself had infused there to keep him alive—and further still. *Into the very heart of a fallen angel.*

And that hardened heart—that fractured and clearly flawed heart—*ached*. For Brigid.

Fool! Stop this insanity. Because too much was at stake. For him. For all the worlds.

Take what you can. Because too little had been offered. To him. From any other soul.

She's too…young. A babe in the woods. Tempting a starving black wolf.

Only in human *years.* On the cusp of becoming a master. Alpha of all wolves.

Nevertheless, she's good *at her core.*

Immaterial. And not merely *good. Incorruptible.*

Incorrect. No *being is above being tainted by darkness.*

Enough! You're not that *dark.*

Selfishness won the inner argument. He sighed heavily.

Brigid's confidence and eager readiness aside, *he* needed to be certain. For *all* of their sakes. "We need to discuss what I've done."

Understanding washed over her expression. Sliding her hands down the front of her golden diaphanous gown, Brigid slowly sank to her knees before him. "'Tis of no consequence."

"You say that now."

"'Twill always be so."

"There are some things, certain *actions*, you may find unforgivable."

She searched his eyes for a deep breath, then replied in soft-spoken words. "No action is so."

When he opened his mouth to debate the point, she placed a firm finger over his lips.

He glared at the stubborn female.

"*Skorpius.*" Her tone brooked no argument as she leveled an unyielding look at him. "You're on a noble quest. I'm human...*weel*, I was. You were human once as well." On a hard swallow, her expression darkened, pensive. "Not every wee thing I've done would make my clan proud. I've lied to my family. To my friends. And I've broken more vows than I can count."

The corners of his lips twitched as he fought a smile. She spoke of the natural expressions of discovery and of independence in her short human life. "A little Brodie rebel? Lies *and* deceit?"

Those mercurial eyes narrowed. Then they widened, alighting with humor. "Sarcasm. You tease."

Skorpius arched his brows. "You've listed minor indiscretions."

"And yours is not." Statement of fact, seriousness weighting her tone.

All humor drained from him. He gave a slow headshake, gaze never wavering from hers. "My transgressions *far* exceed yours."

That adamant stare held his. Then she gave a nod. "I understand." Her gaze wandered along the length of his wing. "'Tis what made you midnight black, from snowfall white."

"From wings to heart." Skorpius blinked hard, shocked as her last word registered through. *White.* "How do you know I was once white?"

"I've been to your world. Remember?" She glanced at her now-empty hand then at the bottom of the satchel.

His journal. The only way she could've obtained it.

"You saw other angels?"

"Aye and...*somehow*...I saw you."

"Me?" Confusion clouded his mind. Because the journal hadn't existed when his wings had been white. Skorpius had never heard of a concussion among angelkind, but then, he'd also never heard of any other angel crashing to Earth from the dark matter of the timeline. "When?"

"After you'd saved me. When you clung to the barest thread of life. While I pushed all the magick I had into you to try to mend you, the world outside the shield slowly vanished. Then when I needed more and gathered healin' energy from the sun's rays, the glade around us within the shield also fell away. You were no longer there. Nor was I. Even so, I remained aware. And visions floated into my mind. I saw you. A past you. As you were."

"Describe it."

Her brow furrowed. "I'm not certain I can."

"*Try.*"

She gave him a clipped nod, then exhaled a heavy breath. "Heavenly mist floated about. Your hair was not raven, 'twas flaxen, whitish gold like the sun." Brigid's expression softened as she scanned his face. "Your eyes were not dark sapphire with deep emerald, sparkin' wildfire as they are now; they'd been pale blue, like the top of the sky with a midday sun. You shouted in a piercin' tone and tongue I dinna understand. Then you chased after a lad and lass who looked verra much like you.

"You unsheathed twin swords from a harness betwixt your wings and leapt high into the air to fly over the clouds after them. Cool wind bathed my face as I somehow flew with you. The lad conjured up a ball of blue fire then hurled it toward us. You threw up a golden shield and gusted a great wind his way, extinguishin' his fire. And you *laughed.* A deep and true joy. After a moment's pause, the lad and lass laughed with you."

Her eyes searched his. For confirmation.

Orion and Cass, close friends. When they'd all been mere fledglings. Fully fashioned, yet newly aware. That specific day, they'd begun sparring to gain further experience, get a feel for the vastness of their powers and the strength of their magick.

"*Impossible,*" he breathed. "You time traveled. On your own."

"Mayhap, not alone. I'm thinkin' your spirit, while our magicks intertwined and your broken body began to heal, led me there."

"To the past."

"To *your* past."

"Doesn't explain how you came to possess my journal. Which you had long before we crash landed."

"Aye. It does explain. You see, I dinna only see you when you were young."

"*Inexperienced.* Not young."

Brigid deadpanned him, took a deep breath, then continued.

"'Twas only a moment's time after the fire-play with your friends that everythin' faded away again. Only glitterin' mist remained for a time. White, silver, gold, and all the colors of the brightest Highland rainbows reflected in the tiny particles. After that, we traveled afar to...*Brittany*."

"Brittany." Northwestern France. Legend, fable, and fact. Where his transgression began. Brigid's emphasis on the locale drew almost as much attention as her expression. Almost.

Compassion shone in her silver-sparking eyes. She let out a slow exhale, then spun and took a seat beside him. A gentle hand rested on his forearm.

Compassion. The only way Brigid would view him. *Not pity.* Like so many others had done.

"You saw my mortal past." A subject dead to him. Until now.

Never before had he wanted anyone to know.

And Brigid had seen it without his knowledge. Yet on some level, deep in his fractured psyche while he'd been compromised and vulnerable—a time when the truest self is revealed—he'd invited her to his past. Two very different pasts.

In both instances, his magick, her magick, and codes wiring his very DNA, had given her the key. And Brigid had had the wherewithal and pluckiness to unlock the door.

"How much—" Skorpius closed his eyes. Not to keep past emotions at bay, those had died many centuries ago. But to keep a tight rein on his emotions now. Something he'd been struggling with for the last few days. For around Brigid, the world seemed to reset itself. His fractured heart included. "How much did you see?"

"Not verra much." She gave his arm a gentle squeeze. "You stood in an empty room. Stone walls. No bed. Only a desk. The journal. And a tall narrow window that looked out onto a snowy landscape."

"The monastery. Where I'd sequestered myself after..." He paused, refocusing on the present discussion and what she needed to know, nothing more. "After my plunge from grace. And it wasn't *always* stark and wintery."

"Nay. Another image materialized. You sittin' on a wooden barrel in an overgrown garden. Bees buzzed through the air, attendin' to all manner bright colored blossoms. An ancient tree stretched overhead. You seemed at peace under its great twistin' boughs."

"We have that in common."

"Aye." Brigid's voice softened. "A love for trees."

Skorpius closed his eyes and burrowed his face into her soft riot of copper curls. He inhaled the sweet wild scent of Brigid in the here-and-now, and forced himself not to imagine the stark scene she'd witnessed: a human life filled with the deep pain of sorrow, regret, and atonement for unforgivable selfish actions.

"Nature is where one retreats when nothing else in the world brings solace," he murmured.

"*Aye.*" Her heavy tone brought understanding. Commonality.

He turned toward her. "What I've done—"

A slender finger pressed to his lips again, begging his silence. "We need not speak of it."

Very well. For the best. For both their sakes. Neither side ever benefited from knowledge of past lovers.

The transgression, however? Another story. Critical for them to even consider a next step. Their connection, the outcome of their relationship no matter what came to pass, depended on it. Therefore, the fate of all the worlds depended on Skorpius and Brigid being on the same page.

"But you understand…what I went through. And why."

"*Aye.*" Unshed tears glittered in her eyes. "You'd given up your angelic world to become someone…somethin'…else. *For* someone you…cared about. 'Twas honorable."

Skorpius choked out a laugh. "We're talking about the same mortal sin, correct?"

A weak smile tugged at her lips. "A man in love." Boldly

stated, no more dancing around. "A woman who loved you. Who's to say that your sacrifice dinna heal her soul?"

"*I* say," he ground out. He wouldn't revisit the intimate details. But he wouldn't gloss over the facts of the matter either.

Undaunted, Brigid gave him a stern look. "I say *nay*." A patient breath filled her lungs. "Your paths crossed, then wound together. Whatever happened because of your actions? 'Tis not your fault. Mayhap much bloodshed was avoided because of your liaison."

Skorpius stared at her for long silent seconds. "You're an optimist?"

Gaze locked with his, her brow furrowed. "Op-ti-mist?"

"A dreamer." Heart softening further at the truth of her essence, he brushed a shining errant lock of hair from her face and tucked it behind her perfect ear.

"*Nay.*" She gave a dismissive headshake. Then she glared at him with a loaded look: Take her seriously or not at all. When he gave an imperceptible nod of cooperation, her expression softened and she cocked her head. "You were sent there?"

"Yes. On a mission."

"To guard her?"

"Yes." Skorpius clasped her hand, entwined their fingers, then gave a reassuring squeeze. Only one female mattered to him now.

Brigid held tight to his hand. "Did she know you were an angel?"

He huffed out a half laugh. "Yes. Angels make their powerful presence obvious. Part of our arsenal. Shock-and-awe. White wings and all."

"Aye." Her slow scan traveled from the black ends of his hair, then down the length of his wing. "I prefer your dark colors," she murmured. A tender gaze lifted to meet his. "And the deep jeweled tones of your eyes *now* pleases me most. If it matters."

"It does."

"Weel, then. *Listen to me*, angel. If what I think matters, then you must accept what was. Just as now, we must accept what is. Fightin' *what is* has never done anyone a bit of good."

"How old did you say you were?" *Far* wiser than her human years.

"I dinna." Brigid's eyes narrowed. "It matters?"

Unable to help himself, Skorpius smiled. "It does not." In the midst of a heavy topic, she managed to sprinkle golden light into the mood.

"Eighteen summers."

He pinched his eyes shut, sighed heavily, then dropped his chin to his chest.

Tight fingernails pricked his forearm. "You said it *dinna* matter!"

"And it doesn't." Not in any significant sense. Young and innocent of the flesh? Perhaps. But Brigid's ties to her former world and all its rules had begun to fray. One of only a rare few in all the realms, she'd transcended to a higher order, where the laws and morality of the material world held no sway. Skorpius gave her a serious look. "You are far older than your physical years. Were that not the case, we wouldn't be having this conversation."

Relief and confusion washed over her delicate features. Making her appear all the younger.

Goddess, Skorpius reminded himself. *Already more powerful than you*, he grudgingly admitted. "Besides, if we were talking about your former Earth world, eighteen summers is old enough by anyone's standards." And even then, Brigid had proved far wiser than her tender years.

With a gentle tug of the arm her fingers still gripped tight, he pulled her slight weight against him. Soft curves tempted under that diaphanous golden gown. But beneath her decadent packaging was the steel spine of a leader and the granite heart of a warrior.

When Skorpius began to turn his head, his lips a hairs-breadth from tasting her succulent mouth, a loose end snapped unbidden through his mind. He drew his head back and searched her joyful silvery eyes.

"But that *still* doesn't answer how you obtained my journal."

CHAPTER 19

*E*xcitement buzzed along Brigid's nerves, quickenin' her breaths.

Intoxicatin' heat flowed through her veins, flushin' up to warm her skin, sizzlin' down to burn other, more intimate, parts.

With her head fogged from the dizzyin' sensations, from Skorpius's nearness, from his incredible *male*ness, it took several heartbeats to realize he'd paused right when he was about to kiss her. And...he'd asked her a question.

Furrowin' her brow, Brigid sucked in a clearin' breath and straightened away from the delicious source of her body's loomin' thunderstorm.

"Nay." She gave a slight headshake. "I dinna fully explain how I came upon it."

Those sapphire-emerald eyes swirled. *"Enlighten* me." His voice deepened, commandin'.

And *Jesu!* that firm tone burst an electric pulse of heat through her body all over again.

Brigid narrowed her eyes at him and drew in another

calmin' breath. "If you keep *orderin'*, I'll be takin' my sweet time in the tellin'."

His glower intensified. *Master. Apprentice.*

But as his reminder boomed into her mind, a bit of wicked amusement sparked in his eyes.

Her skin flushed hotter. "*Cease* your teasin'."

"Then get on with the *tellin'*," he further taunted. As if he knew in full measure how his dominatin' continued to affect her.

"Aye." She blew out a slow breath and surrendered to their sensual quarrel. "I'll be tellin' the tale. And 'tis not a whole tale till you hear from first to last."

With the corners of his mouth twitchin' as he fought a smile, he stretched out and reclined back on a bent arm. "I promise not to interrupt."

"Weel, as I watched you—mortal Lancelot-you—in the garden, my gaze fell upon what had captured your focused attention. Quill in hand, head bent forward, you penned with great concentration onto a linen page. Now and then, your expression shifted from sorrowful to thoughtful. After a time, my gaze fell upon a stack of pages at your feet, weighted by a rock. Then my thoughts drifted to your journal.

"All of a sudden, Lancelot-you vanished along with the garden and the light of that day. Darkness surrounded me. Till pricks of light glittered before my eyes. Which illuminated another *me*.

"Somehow, I'd gone back in time to when I'd *first* touched the wall. Many months ago. I'd done so to save our clan, to make Brodie Castle disappear."

Brigid paused when he nodded his understandin', of their need to hide their castle and how the wall worked. 'Twould make sense that he'd know. Angelkind had gifted the castle and its many secrets to their clan generations ago.

"My human self dinna acknowledge my time-travel presence. She simply passed through the wall, as before. And I followed, stridin' through white mist behind her. Nigh at once, we appeared within a chamber of dense rock, made of a bluish black substance, much like the wall in Iain's map room that we'd passed through. It appeared to be a cave, but 'twas more. And so verra dark. No light penetrated."

Skorpius said nothing. But he watched her with rapt attention.

"'Twas your lair, was it not?"

He gave a nod. "For the beast I'd become."

"'Twas within that cave that your book...materialized. It hovered in the air like a smoky cloud in the darkest night. As an offerin' to my human self. And fascinated by the magickal world, and delighted by the unexpected gift, I...or rather *she*... accepted it without question."

Finished with her explanation, Brigid took a deep breath.

When Skorpius dinna respond, she gave a half smile. "You may now speak. Mayhap you'll have a better idea of how I'd come upon your journal than I."

His brows arched a wee bit. "A time paradox, actually."

Her brows furrowed.

"Your *goddess* presence, after you'd watched my human self in the garden, influenced your finding my 'lair' *and* the book."

When her mouth fell open, but no words came forth to express her confusion, he continued. "Whether or not your human self knew you'd appeared, your goddess presence carried a residual thought of what you'd just witnessed, my past. That residual image impacted you enough to remain with you when you time-jumped to *your* past. And as you followed yourself into the angelic realm, my world reacted by providing you with what you most desired."

"*Nay.*" Brigid blinked heavily. "'Tis *not* possible. I'd just materialized in the past. All these events transpired only because I'd gone through the wall. My goddess self wouldna... *couldna* have been there unless my human self had ventured there first. Alone."

"Ergo the time paradox."

Feelin' a bit lightheaded, she eased herself further to the ground and stretched onto her back beside him. She stared up at the glitterin' protective shield she'd erected, made of her unbelievable magick mixed with a touch of his dark energy. "I doona have any..." *words... thoughts...*

Makes perfect sense to me. The tone of his mental voice held a hint of amusement.

Bewildered, she glanced sideways at him.

"Time doesn't happen in a linear format. There is no 'past' or 'future.' *Now* is all that ever exists. And every *now* is folded upon itself. Happening all at once. So both of your selves, human and goddess, had been connected. Not one before the other, but both together. Your goddess self was always there with your past self, even the first time."

"My head *aches* tryin' to understand that nonsense."

Skorpius tugged her into his embrace and pressed a gentle kiss to her temple.

"Don't waste energy trying to figure out the chaos of life. We're far better surrendering to *what is*." The last, her stern words from moments ago, repeated in his own way.

Turnin' in his arms, she gazed at him. "True wisdom for the ages."

Skorpius coughed out a laugh. "Ages, all right. How long it's taken me."

"Surrenderin', you say?" Both stubborn and willful, they shared difficulty with the task.

"Apparently."

"What say you, mayhap we find a lesson there?"

"In surrendering?" His brow furrowed in confusion.

"Aye."

"Okay…" He kissed the tip of her nose. "I'll play along."

"Your lair." She had a suspicion. A leap from some feelin' she'd had while there.

"What…about…my…lair." His tone deepened with each slow-spoken word.

"A place wholly absent of light. Unlike any other, I'm guessin'. 'Tis *your* lair because only in that place are you able to fully regenerate. Its deepest darkness nourishes your body and soul." The unique place had a silky power to it. Cool and fresh, yet filled with an unusual kind of sizzlin' vibrational energy.

The adorable confusion on his face made her smile.

Then his expression darkened. A quick inhale preceded his entire body going rigid.

Skorpius's eyes closed. And for a brief moment, he seemed to drift far away, even though his body remained firmly wrapped around her.

Till he shook his head, as if to clear it from a daze.

Concerned, Brigid gripped his arm. "Where did you go?"

"Nowhere." He let out a heavy sigh. "Within."

Hands gently grippin' her shoulders, he straightened her away from him. Then he took her hand and heaved them both up from the ground. Expression grave, he stared deep into her eyes. "We need to have a talk."

"*Another* talk?" Brigid laughed and shook her head. "*Nay.* 'Tis not required. I'm settled with your past. With mine." A soft sigh escaped her lips at the vastness of emotion that filled her heart. Liftin' her other hand, she brushed aside a long lock of black hair that had blocked one of his bright jeweled eyes, then rested her palm over his cheekbone. "I'm settled about *us.*"

The sweet warmth of his larger hand covered hers.

But then he clasped on tight and drew her hand away. "Reserve how settled you are."

His expression hardened, eyes clouding over, mouth firming

into a grim line. He drew in a slow breath. "It's past time you know."

An electric frisson of unease rattled her nerves. "Know what?"

"The *other* reason I've been sent here."

CHAPTER 20

A burst of golden magick saturated Skorpius as Brigid shot trembling fingers to his lips. *"Cease!"*

And his lips hardened shut, immobilized by her sudden power-backed command.

Then a second, more powerful twang reverberated along the timeline thread, reinforcing the first that had startled him moments ago—what had prompted his decision for full disclosure. Because the timeline had come under greater threat again. Perhaps from his and Brigid's growing closer, since the sudden change coincided with their mutual desire to cross that intimacy line.

Yet her power-aggression had been unintentional, of that he had no doubt. She'd wanted him to stop talking with such force, her newfound magick obeyed and turned her wish into reality with the punch of manifestation energy.

You know that's not how it works, apprentice. *I don't need my lips to move to be able to communicate.*

Och! Brigid's eyes widened, and she pulled back her fingers to stare at his unmoving mouth. And a minute amount of probing magick shimmered through him as she surveyed what she'd done. Then another burst of warmth released her silencing command.

"*Please.*" Her eyes welled with tears. "Not here. Not now."

Skorpius tilted his head, surprised on multiple counts. She acted as if she already knew the bad news he'd been about to deliver. And that she suspected the consequence of him speaking it aloud would halt their actions.

Interesting. Yet since their entire circumstances remained in uncharted territory, Skorpius saw no harm in playing along. In fact, Brigid forcing the path they took influenced the outcome. Why not leave Brigid's fate in her own hands? "Then where? And when?"

With a drawn-out exhale, she stared hard at him. Another scan of her warming magick shimmered through him. "You've not yet fully healed."

"That takes time when I'm in your Earth-realm." Skorpius glanced up at the glaring afternoon sun. "More time in broad daylight. Less in the deep recesses of your caves." He pointed behind her, high up on the jagged cliff face where he'd flown them before.

But instead of glancing back toward the cave, Brigid scanned their protective shield. She focused on the portion darkened by his shadow-magick, then her gaze grew distant. "Time folds in on itself."

"So I've mentioned."

"And you have a lair." A slight smile curved her lips.

"More crash-pad than home, but yes." He failed to connect those two dots together.

"You said 'twould be good for you to be at full strength."

Brigid reached an open hand toward him.

Exactly as he'd done before with her, from within that cliff-side cave. When *he'd* offered to guide her into her past.

"*Brigiiid…*" Skorpius's tone hummed low in warning. Whatever Brigid planned, instinct told him she wasn't ready for. The timeline tether apparently didn't like it either, as the thread vibrated at an escalating frequency.

"*Nay*." Brigid shot him a nonnegotiable glare. "'Tis *my* life. To live or forfeit."

True. And with as powerful as Brigid had grown, immortal as well, as Guardian of Time, no matter his compromised state, he still had the ability, and duty, to end her.

"Trust me," she whispered.

He did. No matter what threat her magick posed to the timeline, he *knew* heart beat true.

"Very well." He'd grant her a measure of leeway.

Holding her gaze, he hovered a hand above her outstretched palm.

Then he made contact.

A flash of brightness blinded him for an instant. Until absolute darkness prevailed.

Thunderous shadow energy blasted into him. Cooling. Healing.

In an instant, he'd been made whole.

His hand still rested upon hers. And they stood within his…*lair*?

"Aye," she murmured in reply to his mental conclusion.

"But…*how*…"

"Your journal," she supplied.

Of course.

"I'd been here before." She grasped his other hand, slid both of her hands up his forearms, then tightened her fingers there. "And the marker for where your lair is located"—drawing a hand to her chest, she brushed her fingers over her heart—"has remained with me."

"But how did you make the jump. From Earth *straight* to here?" Not even Isobel could do that. *He* couldn't go directly there. Angelkind arrived into their realm through their entry portal's common field, the mist-filled place where no specificity

—object or location—existed until summoned forth. No one had ever *arrived* in his dark private domain.

"I chased after the *pull*." Her two fingers gave a slight tap to her sternum.

Skorpius sighed in frustration. Brigid had no words to describe whatever impulse she'd had. And angelkind had never been privy to the mechanisms of god powers.

The complete absence of light in his inner sanctum made him want to make her comfortable. "Do you need me to illuminate this space?" The unique blue of his prismatic eyes gave him alone the ability to see in his dark-matter space.

"Nay." The silver sparked in her eyes. "I'm able to see."

Well, then. His mind blanked at the ramifications of that. Or the reason.

Aside from himself, Brigid was the first.

He'd once tried to bring Orion to the place of his rebirth. Then later, Cass. Neither had been able to see within the absolute nothingness of his private space.

"What do you see?" Curiosity drove him to discover all he could.

"Bluish black sparkles. A wee bit like the magick wall in Iain's map room." She hovered a hand over the polished rock face. "Only here, the power is stronger. The energy vaster. Colder, mayhap."

"We believe it's ancient bedrock of my world. And as far as I've been able to investigate, this one pocket of mine is the only outcropping ever discovered within our realm. We only know about it because it's where I—" He paused, at a loss for words himself. How do you describe the unbelievable? *"Reawakened."*

Brigid turned to face him, understanding clear in her expression. "After your mortal death." Steady fingers stroked along the edge of his wing. "When you'd turned black as night."

"Yes." He swallowed hard when her easy touch charged an illicit thrill through him. "Exactly."

Those beautiful silvery eyes searched his. "Before we speak of the 'other' reason for your guardin' me, I wish to know what happened to me, in the glade, with the beasts." She removed her hands, turned, then sat on one of the flatter natural formations that jutted up from the floor.

The reminder of her actions in that battle caused him to draw a steadying breath. And had him perch on a rock pillar opposite her.

The explanation will take some...effort. He'd been astounded by what she'd done. And moved far beyond what he had thought his hardened heart had been capable of.

"Then 'tis good that I've brought you here, where you've become hale and whole. I'll also be wantin' to understand how I defeated the druids. If I'm your apprentice, then educate me, *master*." Her tone lowered to a gentle tease.

"Very well, *apprentice*."

The formal distance she'd initiated between them did not escape his notice.

And since they'd taken seats, slowed their intimacy down, the timeline thread had also calmed. Which posed as both an interesting barometer and a riddle unto itself.

Were they destined to become one? Had he merely been meant to educate her first?

Or did the timeline view their coupling as an intolerable threat?

Skorpius knew little of the breadth and depth of her powers, but he had discovered their source. For where he'd been reborn, so had Brigid. The walls around him had come alive with his presence, but they'd also electrified with her essence, bathing her in coolness, allowing her to see within its darkest womb. His "lair" nourished them both, but in different ways: recharging his power, aligning with hers.

And although he still had yet to understand what skills she possessed and the limits to her powers, if any, he had witnessed an impressive display of her power in battle. Not once. But twice.

"You are aware that those beasts that were attacking you hailed from another realm."

"Aye."

Their forms smacked of foul wizardry, one clue in a chain that had pointed to their cause. "And we now suspect they were summoned by Merlin."

"Aye." Brigid glanced around, scanned the floor, walls, ceiling, before landing her gaze back at him. "I'm thinkin' the events began here, but continued with your journal. Mayhap, my thoughts and my new magick manifested Merlin."

"His attention, for certain." Skorpius had come to the same circular conclusion. "Yet in the glade, while defending yourself, you also manifested newly created beasts of your own."

Her brow wrinkled at either the realization or the memory. "Aye."

"After that, when the pressure mounted and threatened your life, everything in the glade... froze. *Me* included."

"Froze?"

"Immobilized *and* iced."

"*Nay.*"

"Then you collapsed, unconscious."

She frowned. "I remained aware of myself within, but no longer of the glade."

"Your magick was aware. Even though your body no longer responded, your magick took over as an extension of your will. Within the frozen stasis, I sensed your golden warmth scan through me, watched it shimmer at once through everything, every particle, each lifeform. Somehow, your magick determined what belonged there in that glade and what didn't— which specific matter *should* exist in that specific realm."

Brigid's attentive gaze never left his. "Did I...hurt...you?"

"No." He gave a hard headshake. "And that's the astounding

part. The concern you had for each lifeform vibrated through from your magick. I *felt* your care in the filtering process."

"Filterin' process?"

"Yes. Because in an instant. You *unmade* everything that didn't belong."

"*Un*made." Her tone fell flat.

"All the foreign beasts—Merlin's and yours—winked out of existence."

"Winked." Another flattened tone. From shock, not misunderstanding.

He nodded, slow. "Then you *unmade the event*. To the last molecule, everything rewound to its condition before the fiery battle. The night sky was again fresh and clear, twinkling with stars. Every scorched treetop renewed to its former leafy green, swaying in the breeze. The clawed-up divots of earth replanted themselves. Each blade of crumpled grass stretched long, unbent."

"When I awoke, your feathers were coated in fine white powder. And you seemed... distressed."

"Because after everything had been restored, your magick then tried to unmake *me*. And you." Every last nerve had felt as if it had caught angelfire. "I blasted out a torrent of magick to break free and protect us both. And the magick 'ice' that had entombed me burst into a white dust that rained down."

"But I dinna have the powder on me."

"I covered your body with mine, infused my magick with yours. And I willed your deadly magick to see us as friend not foe, the same and belonging, not foreign to the realm."

Her steady gaze held his. "Why did that distress you?"

Distressed was an understatement. The whole event rocked him to the core. "Because the selfless act proved your true essence. Your magick carried out a basic instinct to protect."

"But not to protect myself." She gave a heavy blink. "Nor you."

"Exactly. You sought to protect all *from you*, if necessary."

Brigid's expression hardened. Her chin dipped in a slow nod. But she said nothing further.

The timeline thread, however, twanged with a vibration. A warning.

Whatever conclusion she had come to had tipped the odds once again. *Against* her.

After a deep breath, she straightened on her seat, drew her shoulders back, and lifted her head high. "I'll be hearin' the rest. Tell me how I survived the druids. And why *their* lives were spared."

CHAPTER 21

A sense of forebodin' shivered through Brigid as she waited for Skorpius's explanation.

The battle with the beasts had overcome her. Or her rather, her magick had.

But the confrontation with the druids remained crisp and vivid in her mind. And yet, she still dinna understand the whole of it.

Skorpius perched upon a rock steps away from her, more magnificent than ever in his own element. Fierceness hardened his gaze. Raw strength held his muscular body taut and ready.

And heaven help her, every part of her, body, heart, and soul, ached to touch him. For all that he'd done for her, who he'd become in spite of the horrible pain he'd endured, and that he dared risk his heart again, humbled her.

And yet, she had to be certain.

Silent moments dragged by as Skorpius stared hard at her. As if he awaited her command before sharin' unwelcome news.

Straightening her spine, Brigid drew her shoulders back and gave him a ready nod.

Never shiftin' his gaze, he dipped his chin. "Very well. You learned from the first battle. Evolved. And you wielded even more powerful magick. By magnitudes. Yet instead of the magick overwhelming you, it energized you. Yours did. *The druids'* did. Mine, as well. It's as if your unique energy aligns with and then masters any other energy."

"But I dinna collapse that time. I remember all of it."

"You maintained control. And you orchestrated the outcome. Only instead of 'freezing' all the granite slabs, you disintegrated only the one. In demonstration."

The memory clarified, as if 'twas her reflection in a glassy loch settlin' clear and true. "And the druids? Why dinna my magick *unmake* them?"

"I have a couple of theories. None of us belonged in that multidimensional realm, therefore your magick wouldn't have unmade them. But more than that, you maintained full awareness the second time. You knew they were testing you, no matter how real their threat was. You dealt them the blow of a valuable lesson instead of the finality of a death sentence."

Relief coursed through her. She valued life in all its forms, plant and animal. Although she'd had to destroy the beasts in order to protect herself, she'd also had the power to end the druids but had chosen not to. It soothed her to know that in the heat of battle, awash with magick, she'd been able to spare her opponent on instinct.

"You said my magick aligns?"

"It's doing so now. Do you feel the power of the rock walls around you?"

"Aye." Brigid closed her eyes and inhaled, stretchin' her senses outward. "'Tis like a cool spring rain. It refreshes. Energizes."

"Aside from me, you're the first. Angelkind are created within this realm. We're made of the elements from our world. And like detects like. But not here, not in the absolute darkness.

Two of my closest brethren have tried. Nothing registers for them here."

"Who are your closest brethren?"

"Cass and Orion." *The two white angels I'd chased and laughed with in your vision.* "The closest to a sister and brother that any of angelkind could have."

"I would like to meet them." Brigid stood. But she resisted the urge to approach him and walked to the nearest wall instead. She faced the bluish black surface so verra much like the wall within the castle she'd grown up in.

She hovered a hand over the stone. But she took care not to touch, for her single touch of Brodie Castle's wall had begun the entire chain of events. She respected the immense power the stone held.

Warm breath danced along her bare shoulder. His incredible heat radiated from behind.

Brigid turned to stare up into eyes of sparkin' blue-green fire.

Emotion shone in their depths as he smiled. "I would like you to meet Cass and Orion as well."

"In time, mayhap," she murmured.

All the magick in her stirred. It heated her from the inside out, beckonin' to give in to her desires, surrender to fiery lust and turbulent emotions.

So close. The temptation nigh won out over her great sense of responsibility.

But not just *yet.* Skorpius replied, vibratin' along her same energy wavelength.

"Aye." The time had come to talk about the 'other' reason he'd been sent to her.

Brigid stared into the depths of his eyes, willin' the outcome of their battle to be favorable.

All of a sudden, a sharp pain snapped tight in her chest.

"*Och!*" She winced, gaspin' at the unexpected shock and stumbled forward.

But as her knees gave way, Skorpius locked his hands around her forearms to steady her. "What is it?" Concern marred his brow.

"Another pull. Heavier. Harder. 'Tis like a towel snapped inside my breastbone."

Skorpius straightened her up a bit. Long seconds passed while she fought to calm her breath. All the while, his gaze intensified. "Has the pain eased?"

"Aye."

"Concentrate on where the sensation occurred, find the thread."

Her breath caught. "You want me to go back into the pain?"

"Yes."

When her mouth fell open to argue, he gave a slight headshake. "If it's what I suspect, then it's not dangerous. It's a communication line."

"Communication line," she murmured. She dinna understand, but did as he asked and searched within for the point of pain.

His mouth settled into a grim line. "I think your existence here created a tether."

"To what?" Closin' her eyes, she concentrated on the spaces between her heartbeats.

"We shall see."

"*Och!* I found it again," she whispered. However, the snappin' pain muted into a tolerable dull ache now, akin' to the twist of sun-reddened skin.

"Describe it." His low tone vibrated with urgency. Or excitement. Mayhap a wee bit of both.

Drawin' slow breaths to isolate the pain, she concentrated within. "A kind of energy glitters along the length. Rooted at my center, behind my heart, it extends out, then…disappears." She opened her eyes and stared down at the point between her breasts, as if to see another end protrude. But no mark showed. Nothin' revealed itself.

"More," Skorpius demanded.

To focus, she closed her eyes again. "The tug remains. A low vibration. Whatever that 'tether' is wants somethin' important from me. My attention to some task. Akin to a wee one tuggin' on its mother's skirts."

"What task?" he prodded.

"I *doona* know!" she bit out on a cuttin' whisper.

Then Brigid huffed out a breath to release her frustration, not at Skorpius, but at the difficulty of holdin' attention on an elusive energy thread that shimmered in and out of detection. However, at the exact moment she relaxed a wee bit, her ability to distinguish the tether and its properties strengthened, clarified.

So instead of forcin' herself to chase the energy thread any longer, she relaxed. And while she centered on peacefulness, she drifted her awareness into a broader spectrum, allowin' her attention to brush over the tether, without focusin' directly upon it.

"I've found it. The vibration appears to have slowed. The rhythm has altered as well."

"How so?" he coaxed, tone softened.

"'Tis no longer a painful pull, no longer a needle tuggin' a thread hard through my breast. The effect has gentled; 'tis now a tap on my shoulder. Someone wishin'…to gain an audience."

"Friend or foe?"

"*Hmmm…*" She focused to analyze the character of the energy, the essence of the vibration. "The thread has a goodly quality. Friend."

No further proddin' followed.

When she opened her eyes, his glittered down at her, energized with amusement.

"What?" she whispered.

"I…" Uncertainty washed over his expression. 'Twas as if hesitation stopped him.

Understandin' dawned upon her and she gave a heavy blink. "*You* felt the tug."

Those intense eyes narrowed a fraction. "I have, in a manner of speaking."

"In *all the manners* I described?"

Skorpius straightened, shoulders pullin' back a wee bit. "Yes."

"*Och!*"

Frustrated on a whole other level *at* him, she struggled to free her forearms from his grasp.

Skorpius only tightened his grip.

So she burst forward all her physical energy and shoved him. Hard.

Leviathan that Skorpius was to her slighter frame, he passively let her meager force stumble him backward. But he jerked her forward with him, and she tumbled headlong into his embrace.

Fists trapped between their bodies, she pounded on his solid chest. "You were *teasin'* me."

He arched a regal brow. "I was *teaching* you, as requested."

She narrowed her eyes at him. "*Doona* play my words back at me."

On impulse, she fought to free herself from the intimate hold. But his arms remained, bands of iron forged around her. And a pleasurable surge of warmth sizzled through her body. She pushed and fought harder against him. Yet the greater she struggled, the hotter the current pulsed into all kinds of sensitive places, tantalizin'—*erotic*.

With a shudderin' exhale, Brigid finally relaxed in his hold.

Then a different kind of warmth suffused through her being. *His* warmth. Akin to love. Carin', for certain. Protective. From his heart.

And Brigid found she no longer wanted to leave his embrace. She sighed, closed her eyes, and placed her cheek over his beatin' heart. To be held, to be wanted—*for her*, exactly as she was, as she'd turned out to be—felt amazin'. Made her feel almost...*human*...again.

A sudden thought skipped through her mind. She glanced up at him. "But you dinna know somethin' about the thread. When you began to ask, I sensed your surprise."

"Ah, yes." Skorpius gave a slow nod. "The surprise wasn't *what* you'd felt, or from whom. My shock? *That you'd felt the tether at all.*" His expression shifted into renewed puzzlement.

"Why?"

"Only *angelkind* has ever communicated through energy tethers alone."

One more connection to his world, to her origins. "Mayhap, my bein' here, when I'd found your journal, sourced angelic magick into me?"

"All evidence is leading that direction."

"Weel, then. You're sayin' you know the 'from whom'?"

"Yes." Skorpius gave her a light squeeze, then broke their comfortin' embrace.

He offered a hand toward her.

But when she hovered hers over his, a spark of energy flared to life within the slight space between their palms.

And he began to rotate his sideways.

Delighted with the new power surge, she mirrored his motion, palms hoverin' together as they rotated to maintain their energized connection. Till hers rested directly below his.

"You wanted to meet Orion and Cass? That time appears to be now, for they've detected your arrival. Your presence is requested in the courtyard."

Brigid glanced up from the sparkin' energy between their palms and stared into his blue-green swirlin' eyes. "The courtyard?"

"Our public space. Where others' presence will be there to witness the monumental event."

"Monumental event." She couldna help repeatin' his heavy words. They sounded verra dire.

"The first time a goddess has graced our realm." He tipped his head toward their hands, and the energy between their palms sparked brighter.

Then she realized Skorpius had positioned their hands in such a way with intention, for her to take the lead. She glanced back up toward him, and he gave her a gentle nod. *Follow the thread.*

A sudden nervousness buzzed through her. But then she banished the worrisome feelin'.

She'd conquered magickal beasts and masterful druids.

What was there to fear from a court of angels?

Instead, she centered her awareness on the vibratin' tether within her, then surged magick along the line, from the root outward. And once the energy surge traveled the point where the tether vanished at her breastbone, she clapped her palm up onto his to clasp his hand tightly.

The boomin' tone of his voice echoed through her head as they vanished from the darkness. *My family would like to meet you.*

CHAPTER 22

Skorpius drew no conclusions about the growing list of unprecedented events concerning Brigid.

That he'd initially been tasked to handle the remarkable situation mattered little.

In deeper than he'd ever imagined possible, he vowed to remain with Brigid for the duration.

Regardless of the dual tethers.

No matter the ultimate outcome.

Yet a frisson of trepidation tripped through him at her unorthodox summons.

Although he'd teased Brigid—had led her to believe he'd felt her same summoning tether—he'd actually felt nothing at all. Nothing aside from his two mission-related leashes that continued to vibrate in one degree or another, depending on the threat level.

Not one part of his makeup harbored guilt over the omission: the deceit was slight, he learned much from her sharp observations, she learned the most from the exercise. Sometimes masters employed sleight of hand to tutor their apprentices.

Divulgence or not of trivial details, the real mystery lay not in the fact that Brigid had felt it. The greater enigma? The creation of an angelic tether connecting to her at all.

Skorpius suspected its manifestation had been rooted by something more than her renewed presence in the angelic realm: that she'd appeared without aid in his solitary and inaccessible corner of it.

But how had Cass and Orion detected Brigid if she'd transported the two of them directly *within* his refuge—where his sister and brother could detect nothing at all?

Paramount to that, *how in the worlds* did Cass and Orion create *their own* tether of communication. And why *to Brigid*?

POINT OF ORIGIN mattered not when any angel reentered their realm, nor did a last departure point influence the location of rearrival; return into their home realm always, without exception, filtered through their mist-laden entryway. Skorpius's unique darker nature allowed him to leave any other world from his personal self-made portal, but unseen gatekeepers ensured no one arrived into their domain unannounced.

As always, the cool, bright, near-sentient iridescence avoided his darker nature like water danced around oil. But not so with his traveling companion.

The glittering frostiness surrounded Brigid, gilding her in a shining opalescence.

She closed her eyes and smiled wide, reacting to the air-current caress with a deep inhalation as she threw her arms wide with unbridled joy.

And Skorpius found his joy in staring at her, unable to look away.

When she opened her eyes, they grew wide with wonder as

she looked beyond him to take in the nuances of their ethereal realm.

Beautiful, isn't it? He'd taken the phenomenon for granted when he'd been untarnished, when he'd still been a part of the fabric of his world. *From a darker lens, splendor exists in the light.*

The iridescence glittered with energy at the subatomic level. Nearly imperceptible sparks fired as molecules vanished while infinitesimal puffs burst forth, reigniting their existence. The process ebbed and flowed ad infinitum, a microscopic lightshow within billowing mist.

"*Och!*" She gave his hand a firm squeeze. "'Tis as if bright moonlight set our Highland mists afire with life. 'Tis no longer a mystery why you've been frequentin' our castle."

Not following, he furrowed his brows. "Why? Does our current location explain something to you?" She'd admitted that she'd first arrived directly within his refuge—without deception.

But when she bit her lip and looked down, guilt tightened her expression.

It hit him that she hadn't been surprised at all by the unusual mist of the rest of their realm. Nor had she greeted the animated element as anything other than a welcomed friend. "You've been *here* before. *Outside* of my 'lair.'"

"Aye," she admitted freely. Still staring down through the glittering particles, she ran a hand back and forth through the mist, creating swirling eddies. But her other hand continued to hold his, grip firm and trusting.

The pure male part of him, primal and possessive, liked her hand clasped around his. However, his ashen heart and burned soul—strengthened by his hardened warrior mind—obliterated the absurd romantic notion.

"But how?" He ignored the fact that she'd been able to deceive him and puzzled out the logistics. His journal had connected her two essences through time, which unbelievably explained her path from her castle's wall to find his mortal-life's chronicle. The same location, where after his mortal death, he'd been miraculously deposited with whatever energy had remained of his essence...to be resurrected into the darkest angel.

Brigid's face rose slowly. Her gaze met his right as the most obvious answer struck him. *"The wall,"* they concluded in unison.

The magick wall in Iain's map room served as a protection device for his castle and was made of the same darkened material as in his lair, as was the cornerstones of their castle's curtain wall, the support beams in their keep's great hall, and a special box that held the secrets and powers of angelkind. But the wall alone also served as a portal into the same misty arrival hall they stood within, if used correctly. And clearly Brigid held the key to do so.

But because no physical doorway existed from his dark refuge to the rest of the angelic realm, and Brigid had only recently learned how to time-space jump, she only had the option of returning to Brodie Castle. But then she had reentered the angelic realm, a separate time.

"Only the *one* other time?" Each exposure may have suffused her with an additional surge of genesis magick. Even their present visit likely energized her even further.

"Aye." She gave a definitive nod, no deception in her tone.

Additional thoughts assaulted his mind.

Brigid had sensed his arrival at their first encounter—with her aggressive flying-arrow welcome—not only because she'd traveled into his world, but because she'd already begun to absorb their powerful source magick. Which had awakened her latent spelled-at-birth magick and had immediately begun to transform her into something *other* than human.

That Skorpius had been tethered to Brigid without assignment details, and that she'd had a connection to him through the timeline all along, shed light on one possibility he had not yet considered: Perhaps he hadn't been sent to guard her after all, maybe the protective bond spontaneously arose for a different reason altogether. One that explained his lack of information. A causality that arose more...*organic*.

But before he further interpreted the relevant clues, the obscuring mist dissolved.

Without my direction.

The mist continuously shrouded the entirety of their world. Only when an empowered thought sprang forth did an object, person, or location manifest.

Yet he had not envisioned their destination.

Which meant, Brigid had.

Therefore, she'd not only entered their misted world on her second visit. She'd instinctually connected deeper, into angelkind's shielded existence within it.

Anyone within their world need only imagine where they'd like to be and there they'd suddenly appear. But to be able to envision a place, one has to *know* the place. Otherwise the mist kept tight security, their near-sentient camouflage an excellent protector.

However, the laws that governed elemental magick in the angelic realm applied to angels. And the Traveler. Yet idiosyncrasies had clearly manifested with goddess powers at play.

Within seconds, their clean-lined glittering cityscape took shape on the far horizon. The structures, fashioned of microscopic faceted crystals, reflected light in prismatic colors, like an untouched Earth-realm snowfield on a sunny day. All had been erected solely from angelkind's architectural imaginings. Manifested into existence from pure creative thought energized into physical matter.

"You've only ever *seen* our city, correct?" Gut instinct told him she had beheld their world, but hadn't ventured beyond mere peripheral exploration. She'd been a childlike spy tiptoeing into a discovered fantasy world.

Through the connection of their clasped hands, he transported them the rest of the way into angelkind's inner sanctum, directly into their garden courtyards, where his brethren would be gathered.

"Aye," she whispered after they arrived inside. "Skorpius, 'tis...so...verra..." Their inner sanctum rendered her speechless.

No translation necessary.

"Breathtaking." Unable to tear his gaze away from the heady draw of her youthful exuberance, he agreed.

But their private exploration ended, as all good things were doomed to.

Others took notice of their arrival and wandered in their direction.

And within seconds, he and Brigid became the object of harsh, scrutinizing stares. Whispers buzzed ever louder as the curious edged closer.

All around them, a sea of snowy wings arched like the crest of an endless rolling wave. Countless sets of platinum eyes glowed, brightening with offended rage. White hair rippled around pale faces drawn gaunt with their dislike, teeth bared.

Brigid pressed tighter into his side, inexperienced with such blatant unprovoked aggression.

Skorpius growled a low warning at his encroaching brethren. His black wings arched up and spread wide, feathers ruffling with his mightier aggression. Reborn amid the shadows, he'd been infused with the dark emotion. Vibrating with unleashed power, he discharged a measure of his potent magick.

Accustomed to their purist mist, their pristine elitism choked on his brand of cocktail.

Those pale eyes widened. Angels who'd drifted too close halted, subdued. For the moment.

"Pay no attention to them," he rasped, voice roughened by the low growl still lodged in his throat. *The ignorant make spectacles of themselves by deeming something unfamiliar as unworthy. Rise above their negativity. Prove to them what enlightenment is by example.*

What he'd done from the moment his blackened heart had developed.

But it had been one thing to scorn a fallen angel thrust back among them. Darkness had always been an unwelcomed element in the angelic world.

And Skorpius had never blamed any other for reacting in an instinctual manner. Most had been unable to see through his ugly façade to the crushed heart that beat beneath the destruction. The rest had been unwilling. Cass and Orion had proved to be the exceptions. They'd known him too well, cared more than the rest.

But Brigid remained an innocent in the mess of his life—that appeared to be never-ending.

From the periphery, commotion rippled through the hostile crowd. Pairs of white wings snapped down, heads bowed in submission, and the sea parted out of respect to someone of higher rank.

The powerful presence surged the last of the gawking onlookers aside.

Skorpius hooked an arm around Brigid's waist and tucked her behind him, beneath the protection of his wings. And another burst of his dark magick flared out.

One of his own wanted a confrontation? His entire kind threatened a full-frontal assault? They were all in for one hell of an awakening.

Orion stepped through the crowd.

Fierce displeasure marred his alabaster face.

Guard still up, Skorpius gave him a nod. They ranked as equals, no matter their differences. "Brother."

"*Skorpius,*" he hissed on a whisper as he spread his wings, obscuring them from the mob. "*What* have you done?"

A dry laugh escaped Skorpius's tight throat. "*I've* done nothing. My actions, as you well know, don't scratch the surface of our impervious world."

Come forward, all-powerful goddess. Skorpius laced his mental voice with a teasing tone. He bolstered the suggestion to show herself with the gentle nudge of a cool tendril of his magick. Not that a being as powerful as Brigid needed to be hidden. But they also hadn't expected what stood before them. His world, his fight.

"But your actions will affect hers." Orion lowered his voice and wings while he powered down his magick.

A strong calmness that emanated from Brigid washed through Skorpius as she stepped out from the protection of his wings. With sudden determination and clear intent, Skorpius voiced his recent revelation. "I'll no longer…risk…Brigid." Skorpius chose his words with care. Because he still hadn't confessed all to her.

"But…the Authority…" Orion's voice faltered, expression falling blank.

Skorpius leaned toward him, forehead almost touching forehead, and stared into the glittering silver eyes of his lighter twin.

Orion held his ground, his equal in every powerful way.

"*Fuck* the Authority." Skorpius's voice, dropped to a low whisper, might as well have been amplified by a microphone in a concert hall. Collective gasps rippled like a wave, from the stone he'd cast into the frigid pond. When he and Orion glared at them in unison, the fish scattered.

Orion turned back toward him, then sighed. "Watch your insolence, Skorpius. You know I have far more forgiveness than the Authority."

Skorpius eased back, weight shifting toward the heels of his boots. Brigid adjusted as well, the golden currents of her gown brushing against his side, her slim hand sliding into his.

The small gesture reinforced him like a steel support beam.

"The *Authority* has been glaringly silent. I've been thrown into a bonfire and expected to rescue a kitten without singeing a feather. The Authority fails to provide me instructions or guidelines? Fine. I've decided *their* absence of direction has authorized *my* carte blanche."

"I'm *not* a helpless kitten," Brigid purred beside him.

"Merely a metaphor, *goddess.*"

Another raucous of whispers broke out along the court-yard's garden border. Shimmering white mist swirled with the disturbance. Their audience hadn't departed the show after all. They'd simply retreated a healthy distance from a volatile threat.

"That's right, my elitist friends. *Goddess.*" Skorpius wanted that information to sink in with his prejudiced brethren. Untold power changed the game. Perhaps they'd think twice about judging with shallow minds and stubborn hearts. "And this kitten has claws. And teeth." Skorpius couldn't help taunting them. With the undeniable truth. For Brigid had muted her energy when the crowd appeared. Yet in their world, power determined rank.

Relax your restraint on your magick.

On a slow exhale, Brigid did as he asked. The only sounds that followed were loud gasps. Likely from mortification. Swirls of mist eddying in every direction told him they'd been left alone at last.

"The Authority has *never* given carte blanche," Orion argued.

Skorpius huffed out a dry laugh. "*Look at me*, Orion. This is who I am. One of your own who *blackened* your world. And yet here I stand, still in it. I am the same, and yet forever different in all of your eyes. So be it." Skorpius hiked a disdainful chin where the gawkers had hovered. "They *expected* to pick a fight with outcast angel and a human girl, one disgraced, the other undeserving. And our *revered* Authority allows that insidious negativity to fester. They can take their Authority-given rules and shove them where even our glittering light won't shine."

Orion's nostrils flared at the offensive suggestion. But he wisely said nothing.

"Her power grows." Skorpius glanced at Brigid. But she never shifted her calm gaze away from Orion. "And her essence —and the magick she wields—is more *good* than any I've known."

For the first time since arriving, his brother glanced at her. He gave her a respectful nod. "I am Orion, goddess. And I am honored to meet one of the ordained." What angelkind referred to those rare beings gifted with immense power, like the Traveler.

Brigid bowed her head to him, but said nothing. Façade cool, gaze sharp, she remained impassive during the entire encounter. And her magick had even mellowed again to such a degree, another would be hard pressed to detect she possessed any unusual energy at all.

The vibe Brigid radiated? Serene. Humble. Not one fiber of superiority existed in her being.

Unlike the chilly flock of the anti-welcoming committee.

"Where's Cass?" Skorpius just realized her unusual absence.

Orion glanced over his shoulder toward their sparkling city. "The strategy hall, I believe."

Skorpius narrowed his eyes. "Didn't the *two of you* summon Brigid?"

"I did not. And Cass has been preoccupied."

Skorpius frowned. If not Orion or Cass, then who? No other angel would have the kind of power or imagination needed to create a tether on their own.

Which left only two possibilities. Some unknown being who

registered as "good" in Brigid's perception. Or the Authority itself.

When Skorpius turned to guide Brigid from the courtyard, Orion clapped a friendly hand on his shoulder. And a ripple of awareness shimmered into his mind. A mental knock for permission to speak, brother to brother, without Brigid's knowledge.

Skorpius granted his request by relaxing open a mental channel.

She's not the only one who's transformed, evolved. You *have as well*, Orion stated.

What do you mean? Skorpius felt no different. Other than weak and healing after the crash. But he'd since been restored to full strength, in his refuge.

Orion's eyes narrowed, and he pulsed a slight probing magick through Skorpius. *You no longer register to my senses as the same fallen angel. Your darkness appears to have altered.*

Good or bad?

Orion inhaled an assessing breath, drawing in a miniscule amount of Skorpius's energy as if tasting and considering. *Different.*

Great. Plenty of that going around.

Skorpius clapped a hand on Orion's opposite shoulder, then gave his brother a grateful nod.

Orion vanished into the mist in the next instant.

Skorpius glared at the towering heart of the too-bright city, toward his former peers, where the Authority resided. And a heavy shiver quaked through him, like a wild animal ridding itself of excess swamp water.

He stared his whole world down.

Your rules are being rewritten.

CHAPTER 23

When Skorpius turned toward the countless castles that glittered as if frosted in ice crystals, Brigid sensed a growin' volatility from him. Dangerous and powerful. Charged anticipation under the skin of a warrior eager for a long-awaited battle.

But Brigid pressed a hand to his forearm to stay his action.

Black hair ripplin' in the electrostatic air, Skorpius glanced down at her. Those jeweled eyes sparked with energy. But he tilted his head in question.

"'Twould please me to return to the glade." A truth, soft spoken.

Concern etched lines between his dark brows. "Are you all right?"

"Aye." She glanced toward the angels' city. "'Tis beautiful, but bitter, cold. Just like her people." After his justified aggression toward those who'd once considered him family, she withheld no words in her judgment. "I've seen enough. Unless you wish me to meet your...sister?"

"Cass?" His brows lifted slightly, the fondness for her evident in the softenin' of his eyes. "No." He gave a headshake that further ruffled the ends of his hair. "If she's in the strategy hall, she's focused on a mission. Another time, perhaps."

At the mention of his sister, his aggression quieted.

And as his excess energy faded, the air around him began to settle.

Which gave the delightful coolin' mist the courage to flow back in around her. Playful tendrils of iridescent white teased the golden ends of her flowin' dress. Some of the mist peeked around her dress at him. Curiosity at the dark force in their domain instilled bravery, the molecules flowin' around her to brush over his aura.

Skorpius stared at the bolder mist with his own curiosity, expression turnin' puzzled.

She outstretched a hand to him in invitation to lead their way again on the return trip back to their glade. For as wonderful as the welcomin' childlike mist was, she'd experienced enough of the rest of his unkind world.

The warmth of his large hand slid over hers.

A magickal charge ignited between their palms.

And with a bright flash, the white mist vanished.

Pulsin' out another heavy burst of magick, hand gripped tight with his, she arrowed them through the tempest forces between worlds, the dark-matter realm betwixt time. Wiser from the first time-space travel with Skorpius—when she'd been unaware of the necessity of protective magick and a pinpoint destination—she fired out a shieldin' magick bubble around them. The destination? She kept in the forefront of her mind with crisp focus: their glade.

However, *landin'* safely in the next place proved to be tricky. When she'd arrowed them into his world within his lair, she'd visualized them standin' upright the whole time. Even though it seemed they flew through dark-matter space like Skorpius did on Earth: head and feet level.

Upon return to the glade though, even while she imagined

the two of them upright, other images flashed into her brain. The most recent *intimate* images. Of Skorpius stretched upon on the ground, leanin' back on one elbow—with Brigid draped over him.

When Earth's forces tugged harder on their bodies toward solid ground, she banished the thought of them layin' down and forced the image of them standin' up.

Darkness, cool breezes, insect song, and the sweet scent of a recent rain rushed over her senses. Night had fallen over their glade.

Yet with her jumbled image of them standin', then layin', then standin', they touched solid ground with too much momentum; and their feet entangled, they stumbled, and then clinglin' to one another, they tumbled sideways together over the soft grasses.

"*Och!*" Brigid gripped him tight and burst another layer of protective magick around them. After the terrible crash he'd taken last time—while protectin' her from her own folly—she couldn't bear to cause him harm again.

The strength of his body tightened around her as they rolled. But they came to an abrupt stop when Skorpius burst out his own pulse of magick and bent his leg to plant a boot onto the earth.

Both of them sucked in heavy breaths from the exertion. But Skorpius dinna move. He said nothin'.

Then vibration quaked through his chest. Rumblin' low laughter teased into her ears.

A gusted exhalation parted her lips, relief that he'd fared well through her misstep.

Brigid relaxed her cheek against the warmth of his bare chest. "*Nay.* 'Tis *not* humorous," she muttered.

"Ah, but it is."

"Your *apprentice* is still learnin'."

Skorpius adjusted, tipped a finger under her chin, and forced her to look into his eyes. Mirth danced there. "*You* are no one's apprentice. And you well know it."

"Mayhap," she admitted. "'Twould help to practice a wee bit more."

"And not visualize us laying together on the ground."

"Och!" She gave his chest a pound with her fist. "You *saw* that?"

"No." Amusement still sparkled in his eyes. "Suspected."

Skorpius's gaze turned heated as it lowered to her mouth. As hers drifted to his. When his full lips parted, warm air fanned over her face.

Brigid drew in a stuttered breath, charged with anticipation, as her eyes drifted closed. *You're goin' to kiss me.*

I am.

Yet cool air brushed over her lips.

Warmth floated over her nose.

Then his lips pressed to the center of her forehead.

You missed. She opened her eyes.

Strong emotion shone bright in his eyes. "I hit the exact target I aimed for."

Disappointment sank into her chest.

"Soon." He shifted out from under her, then tugged her up from the ground.

"There will be time?"

Unable to stop herself, she stepped forward, closin' the space between them. Her tremblin' fingertips brushed over his bared abdomen, skimmin' over taut muscles that lay beneath skin many tones darker than hers.

Skorpius drew in a loud gasp, chest expandin', as the ropes of hard muscle beneath soft skin twitched at her unexpected touch. Those magnificent black wings arched a wee bit as her cool palms slid up over heated skin. Till her hands rested over his chest, covered his heart.

His wings settled, and he enfolded her within his powerful

arms. Then he pressed a kiss to the top of her head. "We'll *make* the time," he vowed, voice graveled.

But they'd waited when they'd been so close before. The topic of the grave "other" reason had come between them.

Yet since then, another concern had manifested. Of greater import. The primal need to heal a part of Skorpius that her magick would never reach.

"They doona see you like I do." Bein' the target of stares and whispers all her life, they shared common ground. But none of her clan had vibrated with hatred toward her. Sadness and pity, more often than not. For her havin' to endure a brother who'd found it hard to reconcile her birth with two heartbreakin' deaths.

Skorpius stared down into her eyes, searchin', as if for some answer deep within her soul. His eyes shimmered and sparked, alight with intense emotion. "How do you see me, Brigid?"

"You're a brave warrior, a fierce protector." She tightened her fingertips over his chest. "You view yourself as different from the rest. Who I see? The most incredible male created."

Then her gaze tracked over what others had clearly taken note of. "Your midnight wings are more enchantin' to me than the brilliance of a thousand stars."

Brigid slid her fingers up and entwined them with the dark locks that brushed over his collarbones. "And I'm fond of your bonnie raven hair, flowin' wild and free."

Then she searched his gaze in return. "Your eyes, that swirl bluest sapphire and greenest emerald, glitter fiery life from the depths of your soul. Your colorin' and magick may be dark, but all I see is your brightness. The light you try to hide from the world."

His expression darkened. He began to shake his head.

But she slid her fingers along both sides of his jaw, then gently held tight to cease his denial.

Pained eyes pinched shut.

"*Nay*," she argued. "Doona fight your true nature. Skorpius, you are a *great*hearted man."

Those eyes opened back up, doubt swirlin' in their depths.

"Even crushed beneath the weight of somethin' I canna begin to understand, your light *still* shines through all the dark around you. When you're near, I *feel* the goodness within you."

Skorpius's mouth dropped open. Then closed.

Soft lips that she craved to have cover her own hardened into a grim line.

Chest expandin' on a deep breath, his brows furrowed while firm hands cupped her shoulders. "You are wrong. I am not greathearted. Nor a man."

Brigid smiled at his denial and minor detail of their differences, emotion burnin' a hole in her chest. "Weel, then. We're a good match. For I'm no longer a woman."

And mayhap goddesses are not all *greathearted either.*

While she stared up at him with that last statement mentally projected—like he'd been proddin' her to do—his lips softened, then twitched at the corners, as if he'd been pleased she hadn't been deterred. But then a low growl rattled in his throat, as if he'd become irritated at her adoration in spite of his perceived faults.

When he remained rigid, keepin' a firm grip of her shoulders to maintain their distance, she wrenched free and took a step back, breakin' his hold.

Skorpius let her go.

They stared at one another, just out of reach.

The cold air between them grew charged with every silent second that passed.

With a heavy sigh, she crossed her arms. "What do *you* think I see?"

Slow breaths expanded his broad chest.

A muscle tightened in his jaw.

Fists clenched and released at his side, and he let out a more forceful exhale.

"You need to see *what* I truly am, Brigid. One who paid a life-long mortal penance for committing grave sins. Then within an angelic realm meant to foster and protect for the good, I was resurrected, altered, and *allowed to exist* as an example. Forever condemned to battle alongside those who uphold our code and honor, I remain a constant reminder of the heavy price for straying off course. I'm the dragon living alongside innocent villagers. I am their monster."

With compassion burnin' bright in her heart and unshed tears blurin' her vision, she stared up at him without judgment and stepped closer. Liftin' her hands to cup either side of a face at once rugged and bonnie, she smiled. And all the affection she felt for him burst through. The newfound magick within her radiated a golden aura around her, then expanded to embrace both of them together. The energy sparked into the crisp night with wee snaps and crackles.

"*Nay,*" she murmured fiercely, liftin' on tiptoe to press a kiss to one corner of his mouth. "You are *no* monster." She brushed her lips across his, then pressed a soft kiss to the other side. "Within you is a goodness only one truly worthy of receivin' *your grace* could ever see.

"I'm *honored* to know you, Skorpius. I'm forever blessed to have been chosen for your protection. I may have once been your 'mission', as you've called it, but with the strong bond that's grown between us, I've become more. Not a goddess. Not your apprentice. I am your humble servant. I stand here *unharmed by you* and am the better for it. If you're a dragon in your own eyes, know in truth what I behold before me: the most amazin' male. Wings or not, rules or not, sound explanation or utter madness…to me you are a breathtakin'ly bonnie male."

Skorpius's nostrils flared. His shallower breaths rose and fell.

But before he ventured another denial, she laid claim to the fiery emotions churnin' hot within her breast. "And you, Skorpius, are *more* than your sins. You've become more than an angel. More than my guardian. *You*, from your bright soul to your *good* heart—no matter what color it may be—*are mine*."

If her earlier words had failed to move him, the last appeared to shock him immobile.

Even his breaths halted for long seconds.

And a gatherin' of tears glittered over his dark eyes.

Brigid's smile returned, wider. Greater warmth ached in her chest. Another joyful flare of her golden magick radiated out, then sizzled and sparked into the night.

"*Brigid…*" Warnin' glittered in his gaze.

She lifted a single finger to his lips to silence his protest.

Skorpius's eyes drifted shut, a tortured expression washin' over his face.

But she'd allow none of it. "Doona speak of how unalike we are. It matters not how we appear, what we're built from, nor what different worlds we come from. We were brought together by somethin' you said yourself you dinna understand. *Cease tryin' to understand it.*"

His eyes drifted open. Deep emotion sparked in their depths.

"Surrender to what's developin' between us," she murmured.

The ground began to sway under her feet. She snapped her eyes wide open in alarm at the way the world seemed to have… tilted…and dropped her hands from his face to grip his shoulders and steady herself. Then her stomach rumbled like rollin' thunder.

In the next heartbeat, Skorpius waved a cool wave of magick through her. Then he shot her a stern look of disapproval. "You've depleted your energy too far again."

Brigid exhaled in relief, drifted heavy eyelids closed again, then lowered her cheek to rest a wee bit against his chest. "'Twould seem I have."

Skorpius chuckled, the slight movement jostlin' her head. She felt the pressure of his hand stroke down the back of her head as his lips pressed a kiss to her forehead. "You're hungry."

She groaned, buryin' her face against the dip under his shoulder, mortified that she'd failed to account for the energy use, to follow his simplest command. "Aye," she admitted with a sigh.

"Then we will eat." Arms wrappin' around her, he drew her down to the ground.

Mouthwaterin' aromas wafted under her nose upon her next inhale.

And when she opened her eyes, her clan's plaid had stretched beneath them. Fat beeswax candles weighted down each corner. Then the candlelight flickered with a sudden displacement of air as the most delectable foods, hot and cold, appeared on silver platters of all sizes: stewed meats and root vegetables, sliced cheeses and crusty rounds of bread. Shallow baskets held ripe, boldly colored fruits. Crystal bowls over-flowed with crisp fresh vegetables and leafy greens. One platter even displayed half a dozen various baked tarts.

And a large snickerdoodle.

She snatched up the confection first and took a large bite. Once she chewed and swallowed, she arched a brow at him. "*We* will eat? I've yet to see you replenish your energy with food."

Skorpius ran a tongue over his teeth, then gave a shrug. "Figure of speech. I meant you."

She scanned the temptin' bounty in wide-eyed wonder, marvelin' at the appearance of so much food where none had been seconds before. "*Och!*" she whispered. "I canna believe this."

His gaze dropped to hers as he settled his weight back on an elbow, while she finished the wonderfully sweet snickerdoodle. "Really? You've experienced me, time travel, a hoard of hostile angels, what mortals call Heaven…and you're shocked most with food? And I'd manifested you a feast before."

"But"—her gaze wandered over the extravagance—"not to this…'tis so verra much." Enough food for ten of her.

Skorpius grabbed a turkey drumstick and handed it to her. "Here. Eat protein before you pass out." Amusement glittered in his eyes. "I've explained how magick works. You imagine what you want and your thought materializes. Apparently, the feast I manifested for you before wasn't enough to entice you to provide for yourself. And that hard cheese and stale bread you'd appropriated from that castle was a pitiful attempt. You need to think bigger to fuel the enormous amount energy using magick burns. Trust me. Your body will thank you for it."

Brigid took a large bite of the still-hot meat, chewed, swallowed, then devoured more. Magick within her flared warm and bright with each next swallow. And when Skorpius held up a wineskin, she gulped down a good third of a sweet-and-spicy wine.

After lickin' her lips clean, she scanned the food with a slight smile, then stared hard at him. "*Seeeee…?*"

"See what?" he asked. Then in spite of actin' like he dinna need to eat, Skorpius grabbed a handful of plump violet figs, reclined back onto the plaid, and crossed his weathered black boots.

"You *do* have goodness in you." She manifested one of her daggers into her grasp, stabbed a stewed parsnip, then pointed the dagger's tip at him. "Even though you refuse to see it. Your stubborn denial means nothin'." After a satisfied nod, she popped the sweet morsel into her mouth.

One by one, he finished his few figs, starin' at each before tearin' its flesh off the stem. After he finished and tossed the scraps behind him, he stared at her for a few silent moments.

"Goodness has a spectrum like all things do," he finally replied. "Bad would cease to exist without good. Each being is capable of every level along the sliding scale. Ultimately, our actions determine the substance of who we are. Making a cornucopia of food appear, because you need sustenance and it pleases me to have you savor a variety of tastes, comes *nowhere close* to defining my character."

Brigid tilted her head to the side, regardin' him. "Nay. I doona agree. A person's heart dictates their *good*ness or *bad*ness. With every beat, we choose."

She curled down onto the plaid, leanin' against his side, awash with sudden fatigue, but unable to consume another bite of food. Restin' her head into the crook of his shoulder, she skimmed a hand over his chest and splayed her fingers over his thumpin' heart.

"On the verra next beat, we can choose differently. Each echoes good or bad in the outcome. *We* are good or bad, only by our intention behind a choice. And our hearts make that decision."

How profound, he mentally stated, tone heavy with amazement. "Your wisdom belies your age, goddess."

Sleep tugged at her mind, which clouded attempted thought about his accusation. However, with the bit of teasin' in his tone, she let his comment rest. And instead of fightin' her tired body, she adjusted her head against him and let out a weary sigh.

But a low echo of his last word drifted through her relaxed mind, warmin' her heart. For he'd begun to soften her new title of "goddess" with a tone of affection, akin to a lover's caress.

"Often those choice-lines get blurred," he muttered as the warm strength of his hand stroked up her arm before its weight rested upon her shoulder. "Good souls with worthy intentions can become irrevocably bad with one horrendous decision. Some actions are unforgivable."

The land of dreams pulled her down. Her breathin' slowed.

But the substance of his statement still floated into her ears, the tormented self-judgment in his tone registerin' through.

Holdin' to a last bit of awareness while she sank into the calm realm at the bottom of her loch, Brigid pulsed a gentle wave of golden magick his way. "You doona see," she murmured. *"You've already been forgiven."*

CHAPTER 24

With the silent ease of a honed warrior, Skorpius slipped undetected from beneath Brigid while she slumbered deeply. The beautiful creature didn't even twitch at his movement. Whatever inner place she'd tucked herself into had sealed her off from the outer world.

As he stared at her, the powerful words she'd uttered burned in his chest like an iron brand.

And his heart *ached*.

Not total ash, then.

Already forgiven, she'd said.

He didn't know what to think. And in the last few millennia, that had rarely happened.

But how I feel? Fuck *obligation.*

A true and pure connection between two souls rarely happened. He'd lived long enough to attest to that. And the one aberration long ago, when he'd thought he had found a soul mate, had been doomed from the start. And still, he'd taken that risk. Which had taken down a kingdom.

"You'd *think* I'd have learned," he muttered to a brain that had appeared to stop functioning.

But with Brigid, something altogether different had emerged. More profound. Deeper, on an elemental level. A human girl who'd only recently become a woman had further transformed into one of the most powerful beings ever to exist.

Yet she remained humble, understanding, generous. Chose not to be near those who shunned him, yet did not judge them too harshly in return. A bright heart beat within her. And with her acute perceptiveness, she detected some ember of good within him.

Which made him want to stoke that ember into a raging fire of good. For her.

Head still stuck on that unbelievable fact, and certain his heart's fracture had done irreparable harm to his ability to perform his duties impartially, he glanced up at the magick shield that she somehow still maintained without effort or awareness.

Then he dematerialized from the glade, confident the strength of her latest shield would be impenetrable. No one wishing her ill will will be able to detect her, let alone attack her.

Not even Merlin.

As usual, Skorpius returned to the angelic realm into its misted entryway.

Yet the mist appeared more excited than usual. It swirled away from him like it typically did, but then it spun back toward him, brushing over his skin, as if it had never known the true him before. As if Brigid had left some mark of goodness on him that made him new, acceptable...or at least interesting.

Or maybe the mist now saw the ember of good in him, as if Brigid had already fanned it to life.

Orion's observation echoed in his mind: *She's not the only one who's transformed, evolved.* You *have as well.*

Skorpius strode down their pathways, the curious mist chasing and playing in swirls around him, as he puzzled about the totality of events. Brigid had been to their world *twice* before. How many of the baffling occurrences did that pair of anomalies explain? Because beings didn't just "visit" his realm.

Although he could have easily transported into where he wanted to go by visualizing the strategy hall, he enjoyed the brisk walk. Its physicality soothed him and helped clear his head.

And oddly, the amusing behavior of the mist pleased him.

So did forcing his brethren to watch him walk tall among them. After those who'd shunned him had been schooled by their betters about acceptance.

The gardens had refilled with angels, groups of twos and threes on benches, between topiaries and beside statues, walking within the hedge mazes, sprawled on the lawn. All their conversations filtered through his mind at once, fools who twittered on about the uninvited guest brought by their *tolerated* black sheep.

Skorpius ignored them with greater pleasure than usual. For once in the last eight hundred years, it felt liberating to give his brethren something new to buzz about.

He strolled along the crystalline beach that fringed their main river under their brilliant white sky. The tributary sparkled with pure water, infused with the warm effervescent bubbles of angelfire magick that released up from fissures beneath their realm. It meandered from the gardens and flowed uphill into their city. Familiar faces splashed in its swirling rainbow waters. Inquisitive glances strayed his direction. But if any hostility remained, they'd hidden it behind cool masks of open curiosity.

On impulse, he met the gazes of a handful of the onlookers, one by one. Bold. Uncaring.

Not one angel turned away, far different than the norm.

Interesting. He wondered if they sensed the same change Orion had.

Have I become something other *yet again?*

He added that question to the growing mountain of unsolved mysteries. Then he rounded a corner shaped of denser mist, which led to a three-dimensional sparkling latticework made of sharper molecules—the kind that gleamed GO AWAY and sliced any who dared to ignore the natural warning. Yet he strode right through the security barrier, billions of iridescent particles allowing him to pass because he possessed the one thing required to enter their restricted strategy hall: warrior blood.

Only a few dozen angels had warrior blood, the singular qualification to enter the space not enclosed by physical walls and yet contained all the knowledge of every realm in existence. But only warriors on assignment were allowed within, and even then, restricted to the purpose of accomplishing their mission.

The instant he'd been granted access, his vision cleared.

And he'd strolled right in. Apparently just as he'd been expected to. *So still on assignment. And needing to be here.*

One other soul stood in the strategy hall.

A sense of calm washed over him upon seeing her. "Cass."

She glanced up, bright smile already curving wide. "*Skorpius.*"

Ever the focused guardian when it came to her obligations, her attention returned to the image she'd summoned into a three-dimensional viewing space. All aspects of an event as it unfolded at that pinpoint of time flowed through, as if Cass and he had been transported there. In addition to their attaining visual information, sounds and scents expanded through to them too, though on scale to its miniature size. At that moment, heavy machinery trundled along, dust clouding up from its disturbance through a dry roadway.

Skorpius joined his closest friend, black wing nudging against her white in subtle affection, while he took in the scene unfolding before their eyes. United States military tanks rolled through ancient streets. One tank stopped. Its gun turret swiveled to one side. With a mechanical cough, it fired a mortar round into a cave, collapsing it to rubble.

He glanced at Cass. Her favorite two crossed swords were sheathed between the snowy wings on her back. *So deceptive, this one.* Beautiful. Kind. And stone-cold deadly. "Do you think you're armed well enough?"

She glanced back up at him, amusement sparking in her platinum eyes at his joking. A single batt of Cass's eyelash could obliterate a cruise missile into a cloud of harmless dust. "An American military commander was ordered to destroy every cave in his path. His tanks are approaching a sacred place where the waters are blessed, where miracles take place. I'm assigned to give him...pause...with that one. Make certain he sees the abandoned canes, crutches, and wheelchairs *before* his men act."

Skorpius gave her a slow grin. "Entice the human to disobey orders. My favorite kind of mission."

Cass deadpanned him, rolled her eyes, then shook her head with a snort. She returned to surveying her scene, amplifying the discussion between the commander and his soldiers. Her expression sobered while she gathered her intel.

Their missions were no laughing matter. Even with their ability to shift between worlds or dematerialize within one, danger still existed. Warrior-class angels were assigned cases where more hung in the balance than the mere mortal's soul. And when the odds increased that they'd have to take corporeal form with their charges. Because other beings didn't always take the appearance of a weaponized winged creature well—especially humans.

Angels of the more genteel classes served vital needs to lost souls as well, but in a far less do-or-die, *guide-the-right-choice-or-worlds-will-fall-apart* way.

Skorpius's last near-millennium had been occupied with a task which no other warrior angel had ever been assigned—

guiding the very fabric of time itself. Apparently, once he'd fallen dark, his unique magick had garnered the attention of the Authority. And until the prophesied Traveler had appeared, only he could fill the role.

Of course, it was his colossal misstep in becoming mortal that had been the catalyst for his reassignment from human-guardian to time-guardian. Which made him wonder on occasion if he had become little more than a glorified janitor cleaning up his own mess.

His latest assignment? A dual-tethered impossible task, with a temptation to stray off course that seemed tailor-made for him? For the first time in his immortal life had left him in the mental dark. *Twisted irony.*

"World War II?" He focused back on the destruction at the hand of arrogant humans.

Cass nodded. "Patton's Fifth."

He watched on in silence, knowing the gravity of her task. Identifying faces and places only scratched the surface of critical intelligence to be gathered. Countless variations of the same scene layered into her consciousness as she concentrated. And the entirety of the multifaceted information empowered her to be able to complete her assignment successfully.

That same three-dimensional viewing hadn't worked for him with Brigid, however. Either due to the unprecedented dual-tethered mission or that no alternate realities existed. Why he'd consulted the more complex archival map with Orion.

Cass's image disappeared when she straightened with a look of satisfaction. Her body held the confident carriage it always did. Even among warrior-class angels, few had elevated themselves to an elite undefeated status. Orion and Cass were among those revered above all others.

Skorpius had been there with them...once upon a millennium ago.

Cass's firm hand gripped his shoulder. Swirling platinum

eyes with pale blue sparks stared at him. "What troubles you, brother?"

He pinched his eyes closed, scrubbed a hand over his face, and heaved out a relieved sigh. That he could finally decompress. Because the only person in the worlds he dared bare all to, who cared enough to truly help, stood before him.

"I'm lost, Cass. For the very first time in my life, *I have no idea* how to proceed."

The silence stretched wide between them until he opened his eyes.

Cass held his gaze for seconds more before responding. "Give yourself a break, Skorpius. You labor too hard to atone. Let the past die and live in the moment. Your heart is true; it always has been."

True. Good. Females saw unbelievable things in him.

"How can you say that?" He snorted. "Trusting my heart destroyed an entire realm."

Her eyes narrowed. "What makes you so convinced of that? How do you *know* your actions alone triggered the fall of the kingdom?"

Skorpius leveled an incredulous look at her. "Really?" He glanced toward the right and fanned out a black-feathered wing. "I transformed into the opposite of every other angel in existence. I don't recall stumbling into a giant inkwell."

She crossed her arms over her chest, a defiant glint in her eyes. "How would you remember? You were an incoherent mess when you returned. It's a wonder you ever made it back here."

"Wasn't me who made that happen. Trust me. I tried. For decades as a mortal, I suffered the torment of a thousand deaths wishing I could shift again. I languished in a monastery and even prayed to their human God for the ability to remove myself from Earth-realm again." The foul memory of his desperation brought the bitter taste of bile to his mouth.

Cass's enormous patience shone back at him, in her soft

expression, in her relaxed stance. "Regardless of how you arrived back with us, Skorpius, you did and you were a mess. But I've never once thought your current state was forced on you by another. I've always suspected that instead of aging yourself gray like a worrisome human, your destroyed heart darkened you, and colored every hair and feather on your body black in the process."

Her theory held as much merit as any other, yet his mind balked at accepting the premise. Blame and guilt had become a part of his essence to such a degree, all else felt foreign.

Yet Brigid saw in him a goodness he failed to.

Cass insisted he needed to ease up on himself.

A fresh dose of harassment from Isobel would round out the trio of female coddling nicely.

Sarcasm. Great for coping with the unacceptable.

Denial? Even better.

"Thanks, for the pep talk sis, but I'm in need of guidance not cheerleading. I still have no directive with Brigid. But there is no doubt I'm tethered to protect her." He intentionally omitted the opposing task. No point in muddying the waters.

Cass folded her arms. "Which requires you to rely on your instincts."

"Exactly. And I have. However, a variety of new problems have presented themselves." He sighed. "Brigid stumbled into our world through the portal in Brodie Castle. And I'm beginning to wonder if that event alone somehow bonded us together. She's from a dark plane, and I'm the only dark being in ours."

"Then what's the problem? You excel at adapting to new situations."

"That is the exact problem. The *situation*, with Brigid, is not new to me."

Skorpius stared hard at her, willing her to get his meaning. It was embarrassing enough that his heart had fractured. He wasn't sure his mouth would speak the utter ridiculousness.

Understanding gradually washed over Cass, her eyes widening. "No. You *can't* be."

"*Apparently*, I can." He heaved out a weary sigh.

"But you...I hadn't thought you'd *ever* be tempted by another human."

"Neither had I. But she's *no longer* human."

Cass blinked at him. "Immortal?"

"*And then some.* Goddess incarnate."

Cass's mouth fell open. Then it closed. Her expression brightened and she snapped her fingers. "I *thought* I'd sensed a disturbance in the unified field."

When her lighthearted revelation failed to break through his severe mood, her expression sobered and she gave a nod. "Right. Impossible temptation."

"With a *charge*." Goddess or human, it mattered not. Pleasure never mixed well with missions. "I've been refusing to succumb to what's developing between us. But I swear, Cass, the harder I fight reality, the stronger the pull becomes. And I thought the tether was bad." The very thing that bound him to his temptation.

Arms still folded, she drummed her fingers on her elbow while her gaze grew unfocused in thought.

"There's more..." *So* much *more.* But when he considered sharing the added timeline threat—the duality of his mission—the tether that monitored the timeline's status vibrated in dire warning. Therefore Skorpius's lips were sealed on that front.

Cass blinked hard, then glanced back up at him. "What other torment could there be?"

Oh, there was another issue he hadn't addressed. Not even with Brigid.

"Before all this happened, she'd been promised to someone else."

Cass's expression fell. It joined his hopes for coming out of his predicament unscathed.

He'd finally disclosed that critical omission, wide out in the open for someone to understand the impossible circumstance besides him. Humans had an adage that history inevitably repeated itself. But to have a near identical and equally indefensible situation occur twice in history, both involving his wretched self, bordered on gratuitous amusement by the Authority.

Cass squared her shoulders, ready to battle the problem. "Don't doubt yourself. You are clearly not there by choice. Therefore, whatever consequences occur from your actions will be warranted. What is your gut instinct when you're around her?"

"To protect her." Above all else. Even to the detriment of his other task.

"Why does she need protection?"

Above your paygrade, he almost said.

But he'd volleyed that factoid specifically at Brigid, when taunting her to discover her full potential—*before* he'd gotten to know her. Cass didn't deserve the flippant remark. But as the vibrating timeline tether reminded him, yet again, Cass was not approved for full disclosure.

However other, less time-threatening, reasons existed for Brigid's protection. Still served to illustrate his dilemma. "She adventured off on her own, initially without her clan's knowledge, to rescue her missing..." The offensive label got stuck in his throat. *"Betrothed,"* he eventually grumbled out.

Cass's brow furrowed. Then her mouth fell open. "But...I assumed...she *wants* you?"

"She does. Hence one of many dilemmas."

"What are the others?" Her head tilted, eyes narrowing. An inquisitive tracker on a hunt.

Accustomed to her acute perception, he dropped the one

timeline-approved bombshell. "I'm directly responsible for his being 'missing.'"

"You are?" Cass blinked again. "Are you sure?"

"Yes." Skorpius smiled, entertained by her candid disbelief. "I'm fully aware when I pluck a human from one location then shift him to another."

Fingall's disappearance had been a crucial piece in an intricate chain of events surrounding Isobel's initiation and recruitment. As the only guardian of time angelkind had ever had, without any established guidelines, Skorpius had discovered it best to trust gut instinct. And improvise, whenever necessary. As long as the end consequences achieved the desired result, logistical details in the middle had always been inconsequential in his mind.

Until now.

But he hadn't been able to disclose his involvement to Brigid. *Still* wasn't able to do so. If Brigid had discovered that he'd been the sole cause of Fingall's disappearance, she would never have agreed to his protection as her guardian. And due to the great power surges that had initially caused her mood instability, she'd likely have killed his immortal hide out of unchecked anger.

And if he'd survived her discovery of the truth, *he* knew he'd be objective in his guardian role, for it was impossible for him to be any other way. But Brigid would've never believed that.

I'm no longer objective, he argued to himself.

Not with the threat to the timeline.

Could I really end her?

His rebellion against his task, against the Authority, weighed heavy on his *good* heart. Because for the good of all, he'd make the hard call. Not even a choice.

Yes. I'd end her. Difficult as the task would be. Their two tiny lives—immortal but yet still very *endable* if deemed necessary— were inconsequential compared to all life in every realm.

Empathy softened Cass's expression. "I don't even know what to say, Skorpius." She placed a hand on his shoulder and gave a squeeze of solidarity. "You always end up in such impossible situations."

"Tell me something I don't know."

"Okay. Answer me this, Time Guardian. If you had the chance to undo what happened with Guinevere, if you could remove yourself from the situation and let events play out as if you hadn't existed there at all, would you?"

Angelkind never gave merit to any alternate reality *without* their intervention. If an angel had been tethered, then a fracture had already occurred in the structure of the timeline. Their presence alone prevented a greater cascade effect. And if their charge cooperated, the fracture would mend completely.

But Skorpius reflected back to the day he'd stood in the strategy hall almost a millennium ago, absorbing the hundreds of alternate realities had he not succeeded in his mission. Untold horrific atrocities would have transpired *had he not been there* as her guardian—as Arthur's confident. What was a mere fallen kingdom compared to total genocide?

And having Guinevere's trust had been critical. Because Arthur would never have accepted Lancelot's council without Guinevere's influence.

But Cass's true question? Would he undo the grievous mistake he'd made along the way, following a heart that had turned more human on that deep-cover mission?

Would I go back and stop myself from loving Guinevere if I could?

"No." Not even if it would have spared untold heartbroken souls. Not even if it would have saved the entire kingdom. Because the timeline, and all within it, had been realigned.

"Good." Resolute authority shone bright in her eyes. "There's your answer. Don't question your role or overthink the consequences." She smiled and squeezed his shoulder once more. "Love her."

Love Brigid. Simple. Straightforward. Already happening in every other way but physical. And far deeper than he had ever felt before.

"And by the way"—Cass gave his shoulder a gentle smack—"I'd like to meet your goddess."

Orion's introduction with Brigid had been cold. Distant. But necessary. Especially in front of the hostile audience.

But Cass treated beings in a unique fashion. Always had. With far more compassion than any angel he'd ever known. The trait made him wonder if Cass had once been human too.

Skorpius nodded his head, then squeezed Cass's shoulder in return. "Thanks for the blunt advice, sis. And Brigid would like to meet you too."

After they saved the worlds.

INTENT on not disturbing Brigid's crucial sleep, Skorpius dialed his return to the glade forward a handful of hours. He materialized with his back toward a bright sun edging over the mountainous landscape.

But the glade was…empty.

Puzzled, his gaze shot up and around. "No magick shield," he muttered.

No any*thing.*

Preternatural senses instantly attuned, he examined every blade of grass and flower stem, assessed every bird call and insect buzz. No disturbance appeared to have happened. No magick registered. No sign of her existed. Nor any evidence of struggle.

Brigid had vanished.

Yet her tether remained vibrant, held no vibrational urgency. The timeline tether expressed the same tameness.

So, a game, then, he mentally cast out, in hope.

Aye. The softest whisper filtered into his mind.

Hide-and-seek. Relief washed through him as a playful curiosity ramped up.

You…left…me…sleepin'…

Each word floated across his awareness from a different direction. Which meant Brigid either moved swiftly along the edge of an in-between dimension or she'd mastered mental voice throwing—with a complete cloak on her magick.

I had an errand to run. And you *passed out from exhaustion. Your powerful magick had you well protected.*

Nay. Not my magick alone. 'Twas our *magick. Even now, within me, I sense a thread of your power entwined with mine.*

Interesting. He'd been concerned about taking the leap with Brigid. Had even sought counsel with his sister. Then the magick had gone ahead and decided for him. To a point.

Had the same entwined effect happened to him?

Skorpius searched within. Only found his dual mission threads.

Yet Orion had detected some kind of anomaly with him.

Perhaps the blending of their magicks, Brigid's with angelkind's source power and something decidedly other, Skorpius's from their source power and…

Well, there's *the connection.*

He had never known what element or force had resurrected him from mortal death. His brethren had only postulated on what had made him some darker version of his former self.

But maybe he'd been designed to cross paths with Brigid all along.

Because we'd been destined for one another? He had thought they'd been two different species, human and angel. Yet all signs led toward the two of them evolving into something unique unto their own.

Still.

Nothing guaranteed success if he and Brigid moved forward.

He had to be certain. Nothing held back. No secrets. No betrayals. *Not this time.*

Volatile energy sparked in the molecules of air around the glade. Alive, yet unseen to even his preternatural naked eye. But he felt the excited charge, sensed its warm childlike essence. She hadn't hidden within any in-between world. All of her magick and awareness floated around him. Everywhere.

You're wishin' to talk with me? she called, faint echoes floating in from random directions.

Yes. Intrigued by the game, he spread his legs wide, calmed his inner being, and shifted his weight to the balls of his toes. His wings spread with anticipation.

Then catch *me!*

With pleasure.

He dematerialized. *His* way.

A burst of his dark magick fired through every particle of his body as he canted his feathers on end. He became one with the ether, a technique angels had perfected over eons, their feathers more useful than for mere flight. Each angelfire filament was a particle refractor, deflecting light, sound, and scent to obscure their presence.

Och! You vanished!

Perfect. It worked. *Said the spider to the fly.*

A new ripple charged through the air. Emotion. Challenge and joy bundled together. Sparks of energy lit in slow succession all around him.

'Tis perplexin'. How can I still hear you, but not sense you?

The playful unseen sparks of energy continued. Soon a wave pattern emerged.

A part of the same plane, pure energy himself, he chased their tiny discharges. *More energy, less matter.* What she'd become. What he'd taught her. She was a fast learner. Adapt and apply.

Aye. Emotion vibrated in a harder passing wave, as if frustration rippled through the particles. *Are you able to sense me?*

Yes. With a hum of satisfaction, he anticipated where the next spark of energy would fire, then drove all of his magick around it, materializing.

The action plucked her essence right out of thin air. *Caught you.* His hands closed around firmed biceps. And his magick-charged wings enfolded around her.

Surprised, wide silver-sparking eyes stared up at him while she gasped in a breath.

Full peachy-pink lips parted.

Her golden gown shimmered, revealing every perfect curve on her lithe frame.

The *last* thing Skorpius wanted to do at that moment? Talk.

CHAPTER 25

*B*rigid stared up into Skorpius's jeweled blue-green eyes. And *everra* last thought fled her head.

Incredible wings enfolded her body.

Strong hands held her shoulders.

Expression fierce, he glanced down at her lips. And his grip on her arms tightened a wee bit. Then his jaw clenched and his brow furrowed. Like he wanted to kiss her. And fought hard not to.

Somethin' grave troubled him.

Heart achin' for the indecision he suffered for her, she shook her head. "We're needin' to talk," she murmured. To stave off any regret on his part, she placed her hands on his muscular forearms and tugged them from her. "The time has come."

His brows lifted and he sucked in a deep breath, pullin' away. After a step backward, he scrubbed a hand over his face. "Yes." But then he tilted his head and puzzlement washed over his features. "How are you masking your energy? You no longer need the shield to do so."

She curved her lips, repeatin' his directive. "More energy, less matter."

"And yet you stand here in corporeal form."

"I doona understand the whole of it." She stretched out and examined one of her arms from shoulder to fingers. "I'm solid, but now, somehow, my magick alone makes it so."

"Interesting. *Hmmm...*" He scanned her body while his probin' magick shimmered through her. "You've enabled your essence to be light, pure energy waves. No heavier dead matter. Without magick."

"Nay. 'Twas a good bit of magick at the start. While you were gone, some...feelin'...told me to pull down the power shield and pour all of its energy—our entwined magicks—into me. And I'm..." She glanced down, brow furrowed at how to describe the incredible lightness of being.

"*More.*" Fierce pride glittered in his gaze.

"Aye." More goddess. Less human.

Elemental power brimmed within her. Additional skills and talents revealed themselves, one after another, whenever warranted or wished upon. The secrets of the ancients—the knowledge she'd gained by passin' through her castle's wall into his world—unraveled their gifts one at a time, as she'd grown ready to receive them.

Skorpius blew out a hard breath, features tightenin'.

Then he gave a hard nod. "There are two topics. You mentioned you were handfasted to Fingall. And Brigid, you need to know—"

"Nay." She strode forward and placed her fingers to his lips. "*Nay.* We'll not talk of our past. Not yours. Not mine. Not *Guinevere.* Not *Fingall.*"

Long black lashes blinked over wide eyes. Gentle fingers pulled her hand from his mouth. "But...you don't understand."

"Aye. I do." She gave him a stern glare. "My magick has *opened my eyes* to the way of it. I'm no longer asleep. The past no longer exists. All that matters? You and me. Here and now."

He parted his lips, as if to argue.

She intensified her glare. Tiny sparks of energy discharged into the air around her. "We'll *not* speak of it. The past never belongs between us."

After a long stare with conflict brewin' in his eyes, he bowed his head a wee bit toward her. "As you wish."

She exhaled in relief, and the magick-charged air calmed. "And you need not be worrin' about the other reason."

His perceptive eyes narrowed at her. A slow breath expanded his chest. "You know."

"Aye."

But his head turned a bit while his gaze held hers, as if he doubted her claim. "Tell me, then."

"You were sent to kill me." Brigid arched her brows, darin' him to deny it.

But he continued to stare at her, motionless as a stone wall.

She dropped her hands onto her hips. "Doona pretend 'twas not so."

Finally, he gusted out a long sigh. "My blade above your neck gave it away?"

Blade on my neck?

Och! At the start of their journey. When they'd first met. "Sarcasm."

The corners of his lips twitched. "You're learning."

Their violent beginnin' seemed a lifetime ago, yet only a bit more than a sennight had passed. She'd all but forgotten the glint of his sword above her, and her retaliation with an arrow aimed at his eye. In a wild rage of stormin' emotion, unable to contain the immense energy coursin' through her at the time, she'd only sensed the strength of Skorpius's power. And that it had sought to stop her.

But although he had tried to kill her from the start, that wasn't how she'd come to know.

"Why?" She understood that her new magick alone had caused all manner of ilk to hunt her. Yet she dinna understand why an angel *sent to guard her*—why angelkind themselves who'd protected Brodie Castle for generations—would want to harm her.

"The death warrant? Wasn't personal. They determined you a threat."

Sudden defensiveness flared inside. "Another told me *you* were."

"The Traveler?" Skorpius snorted. "Typical."

"Who is 'they'?" Beasts. Druids. Merlin. Unknown others. Brigid wanted to know the identity of all who sought to kill her, regardless of the reason.

"The Authority."

"Authority." She'd not heard of their kind. "They are a people, a clan?"

"In a manner of speaking. More like a collective of consciousness."

Her brow furrowed. "And 'they' feel I will harm them?"

"Harm *all* of us. The consciousness *is* all of us. All races, all species."

Brigid nodded as understandin' seeped in. Pure consciousness. What she'd dissolved into when she'd vanished into nothin'…transformed into everythin'. The unified field.

And yet, the same consciousness had separated her out as foe?

"But I've…become different." Against her will, her lower lip wobbled. A chokin' cramp formed at the base of her throat. Irritatin' moisture blurred her vision.

Skorpius's expression softened. He stepped closer and took her hands in his. "You have."

"Why is *different* a threat?" She slid her fingers over his palms, up his muscular forearms, and grasped a firm hold. The act of touchin' his solidness soothed her.

"It doesn't have to be." He grasped her forearms in return, thumbs caressin' the underside of her arms. "I think that's why I've *also* been sent to protect you. Your fate is still undecided."

"*Och!*" she bit out under her breath. "I *doona* understand. 'Twould be a great thing for a world to exist where 'different' doesn't threaten. Mayhap different can be good."

"Without doubt. That depends greatly, however, on the intention of the one with power."

Brigid remained quiet for several moments while she focused on the problem. And as she did, vibrant thoughts unfurled like blossoms openin' toward the warmth of the sun. "Then I wish peace for all. The different have a right to coexist, as long as they share goodwill toward others, great and small, flora and fauna. And for the powerful, to the better of the great consciousness, that they seek to share the wisdom of the ages, the freedom of the light, secrets of the mysteries."

Slowly noddin', satisfaction shone bright in his eyes. "But what if your idea of 'good' doesn't match theirs?"

"If I'm determined to be a threat?"

Skorpius's gaze hardened. "Yes."

"Weel, then you'd be duty bound to kill me."

The passion in his eyes flattened further, and he sighed. "I would."

She gave a decisive nod. "Then for the safety of all, I would agree."

"That you'd need to be eliminated?" His grasp tightened on her arms.

"Aye. I would command it. Mayhap, I'll stray too far off the path. But would I know it? Does a wanderer who stumbles through the darkness know where they are? Nay. 'Tis up to one wiser to correct the...mistake."

"Me? No. Not wiser. Just older. Responsible for more than one life." Skorpius pulled back a wee bit, clasped her hands, then lifted them to his lips. He pressed a kiss to her knuckles on one hand, then to the other. "And you'll *never* be a mistake."

"More experienced, then. And mistake or not, I agree to forfeit my life for the greater good."

Skorpius shot her a glare full of hot emotion. "You're making me like you more than I already do." His jaw clenched, then released. "It makes the burden of my task all the heavier."

A light laugh bubblin' up from her throat caught her by surprise. "*Aye.* 'Tis all part of my grand plan."

Hands still clasped by his, Brigid stepped closer, till her breasts pressed against his bare chest. Covered by the sheer drape of sparklin' gold magick, 'twas as if their hearts pulsed together, beatin' as one.

Then she swallowed hard, leaned up on tiptoe, and with the touch of a butterfly's wings, brushed her lips over his. "Skorpius. I submit my ultimate death unto your care and judgment. But before I do any of the dyin', I'd like a bit more of the livin'." She let out a wish-filled sigh. "I want to have a glimpse of love."

The softest kiss captured her lips. A slow heat like warmed honey spread down her throat, out toward her fingers and toes. And tingled every scandalous spot between.

But then his mouth left hers. Cool air brushed over her lips and his hands released their hold. Greater fierceness flared in his eyes as his breaths quickened.

Voice lowerin', his question came out gruff. "What do you know of love?"

CHAPTER 26

*S*korpius stared down at who *he* saw Brigid to be, a brave warrior, a hopeful young female.

My female.

One who displayed remarkable fearlessness. Charged headlong into a challenging situation, without hesitation. Pushed until her energy waned long before her will. And woke up after near-exhaustion with a bright spirit and open heart.

She *literally* hugged trees, for Authority's sake.

How could such a vibrant creature be a threat to time?

Without concern for her own safety, she'd drawn a deadly hunter away from her clan, had protected young children against enemy soldiers, faced the most powerful gathering of druids likely ever to assemble—as her duty, with honor and grace.

Brigid's entire way of being eschewed her birthright of nobility within her clan.

Yet millions of seemingly insignificant events shot energy waves through the timeline with every decision made, by each being. No singular soul within its framework could fathom its entirety. Only play their part.

Even if Brigid's role became martyr and his...her executioner.

But no matter how resilient she'd proven herself to be... love? Not for the faint of heart.

All of a sudden, a strange frisson of tension buzzed through him. Different than either dual tether. Almost as if a silent alarm had been tripped. But when he glanced around the glade, all seemed well.

And when he glanced back down at Brigid, she seemed unaware of any intruding energy.

Instead, bright eyes full of innocence gazed up at him, undaunted by his question of love. They softened while she contemplated her answer. "All I've known of love is the horrible pain it brings."

"Pain?" From past personal experience, he knew the fact to be true. He knew, even as they dared fate, it was a fool's errand to imagine the two of them could come out of their difficult situation unscathed.

Brigid's brow furrowed and those luscious peachy-pink lips set into a firm line.

"After my mother died at my birth, Gawain—that bonnie wee one in Da's map room of the past—changed from a sunny lad into a tortured soul.

"And when I'd had to touch the magick wall in that room months ago, when Isobel had vanished? Iain had thought he'd lost her forever. *Och!* the anguish Iain had suffered, 'twas unlike any agony I thought a man could bear. At one point, he'd no longer carried the will to live."

"Definitely a man in love." Because human love and suffering? Went hand in hand.

"Mayhap, we're better off without love. Duty. Honor. Kindness. 'Tis enough." Brigid gave a solemn nod. But then she glanced up at him with an inquiring expression, brows lifting slightly.

"I wouldn't know." Because he'd loved once. And had suffered for it. "Not my department." Hadn't been for a very long time. But the way he felt about Brigid? Perhaps, not even the once. For his emotion toward her eclipsed anything he'd known in his lifetime, immortal or human.

Another frisson of energy tripped through him. Vibrating with greater strength.

A second alarm of warning?

Yet Brigid's penetrating gaze held his, aware of only the poignant moment between them. "You suffered decades in solitude as a mortal. Then died. 'Twas all there in your writin'. You'd chronicled the slow passin' of your endless days. Great sorrow bled across those pages. The only joy you allowed yourself was in the gardens."

She'd brought up his past, but he allowed it. For a brief moment.

Because her sole focus was on who he'd become because of what he'd had to endure, not on the woman in his past. And because part of his focus alerted to something unfolding in the present, a subsonic reverberation that triggered his protective instincts. Mild. But growing stronger.

"I wouldn't call it joy." Skorpius continued their conversation, monitoring in the background, acting as if nothing was wrong. For her sake. And to not dissuade whatever element had begun to surface, to enable him to identify it. "More like forced peace amid wild chaos. Possessing the unparalleled skills of an angel warrior—even stripped of my immortality and magick—made me a ticking time bomb. Serving out a self-imposed penance by sequestering myself away in nature? Was the only thing that kept me sane, therefore the rest of the human world safe."

"What was it like?"

"Dying? Painful."

"*Nay.* Losing a love so great."

"Excruciating." A mortal's truth for a long vulnerable time. And Brigid had just strayed where she had forbidden him to go.

I thought we weren't talking about our pasts.

Her eyes narrowed. *When we were kissin', you asked about love.*

Right. Because he'd needed her to be certain that she understood the stakes if she risked her heart. "Love lost is the greatest pain. Death?" What he'd rather they remained focused on, the final price of what they were up against, for them, for every being. "Not as bad as humans make it out to be. For a mortal, aging is inevitable; bodies in the material realm are fragile and Earth's elements, harsh. But that's all part of human experience. Life is the messy adventure between birth and death. Accepting that illness and death is our destiny makes the suffering a little more bearable."

Brigid eased into his space again and placed gentle hands on his chest. "Which is *why*, if love is not for us, then I'd like to get to the tuppin'."

"Love is not for us?" So resilient. *So* innocent. "Take a close look inside, Brigid. That ship has sailed already."

Her lashes lowered, face tilting down.

With a finger touched under her chin, he lifted, forcing her to meet his gaze. "Be unafraid in this. As you are with all things. Seize the adventure, no matter the consequences."

A tentative smile curved her lips.

"But make no mistake, there *will* be consequences." As there are with all things worthwhile.

"If we tup?"

"There you go with that word again." He snorted at how casual she acted about it. Then his brow furrowed. He had assumed she was an innocent. "What do you know of tupping?"

Shoulders squaring back, she lifted her chin off his finger. Fierceness sparked in her eyes. "I've watched our animals mate. And I *might* have caught one of our warriors and his leman once in the back of the stables."

"Then you understand basic mechanics." Not much else to be gleaned from that sad education.

"Aye."

Another singular frisson of energy pulsed, at a quicker interval. Stronger. And each time the reverberation escalated by a fraction. As if the source of the phenomenon approached nearer. Yet Brigid seemed unfazed, unaware.

"There's more to a coupling than what you've witnessed, goddess." Skorpius drew her closer when another escalating energy pulse tripped through him.

She tensed in his arms at the last word, eyes narrowing. "What 'consequences'?"

Another electrifying pulse. Powerful. Dangerous.

They'd run out of time.

Skorpius needed to wrap things up. But he'd formulated a rough plan. "We'll be bound together." Which was part of the plan, but he needed her to fully understand, commit with full knowledge.

"We're *already* bound together, angel."

"More than we already are." Another pulse boomed. Like base vibrations of a giant's footfalls. Only the giant seemed to be approaching from somewhere in the ether, a parallel realm.

"Aye. More than the slender magick thread that ties us." She touched a finger to her sternum, then pressed her palm to his chest, over his heart.

Shocked, he blinked heavily. "You feel our connection?"

Boom. The foreign pulse vibrated through him again.

"Aye. One thread to tie your heart to mine, not in love, but bound by duty. As guardian." In illustration of not only her awareness but her power, Brigid tugged that delicate thread taut, then sizzled a slight bit of her magick along it.

Skorpius's mouth fell open, but he had no words. Stunned speechless for the first time in his immortal life. No tether had ever been manipulated in such a way. By any being.

Boom.

One of her fingers tapped his chest. "The *second* thread exists to bind us in another manner, not to guide or protect, but to monitor. As executioner."

"You feel them both." He'd been reduced to statements of the obvious. Because the stunners from Brigid kept on coming.

Yet something else kept coming that he could no longer merely just monitor.

Boom.

"I wonder, are you certain 'tis *you* who are the guardian of *me*? Are you certain *I'm* the one who's the threat to time?"

"No." Skorpius wasn't certain of anything anymore.

BOOM!

The last reverberation jarred him so hard, his teeth rattled.

Far behind and high above Brigid, an immense hole tore open into Earth-realm, a black nothingness that blocked out a large portion of the bright blue sky.

Their time had come.

Skorpius crushed his lips to hers. *Close your eyes. And keep them closed.*

Her soft lips molded to his as she obeyed and drifted her eyes shut.

Burst your magick along our tether, as powerful and fast as you can.

When her surge came then blossomed, he exploded his magick outward, hoping to join their two forces along their connection and radiate the combined energy outward.

Because together, they needed to create something greater and more protective than a multilayered dimension.

*a*t Skorpius's direction, Brigid kept her eyes closed. Yet alarm spiked through her at the urgent undertone of his command.

But too many other sensations bombarded her at once for her to care about losin' her sight. The ends of their hair whipped across her face and shoulders, akin to when they'd flown through the air. Radiant heat warmed her backside to such a degree, she dinna dare pull away from his protective embrace. Even the verra ground beneath her feet rolled and swayed.

All because his lips were upon hers, bold, yet soft. Tantalizin'. Invigoratin'.

'Tis always like this? Her lips parted, and the tip of her tongue tentatively touched his.

A growl came from his throat. *Like what?*

Sweet, like honey. And hot, spicy. Breathtakin'. Earth movin'.

Only if we make it so. Skorpius broke their incredible kiss and rested his forehead upon hers. "Open your eyes, my love. See what we've done."

My love. The endearment echoed through her mind.

When she opened her eyes, understandin' flooded in. The wind, heat, and earth-movin' part, at least. For above, below, and all around, a magickal sphere had formed, smaller than the ones she'd erected by half and half again. And thicker, by twice and twice again. In its structure, her golden magick sparked alive within Skorpius's bluish black energy. They'd been wrapped in a cave formed of their woven energy.

But not only the two of them.

The great gnarled yew tree stretched its branches over them. And the ground was littered with its shed needles.

"But..." A new sensation overcame her as she turned within his arms. She focused intently at the pulsin' curtain of their woven energy. And where she concentrated, what remained on the outside revealed itself.

Brigid gasped. She and Skorpius remained in the sphere. As did the yew and the portion of ground with its shed needles. But the sphere *no longer remained in the glade.*

"But..." Words still failed her as she watched. Trees outside of their protective magick bubble flashed in and out. One moment she saw a line of wee saplings, the next a line of wide trunks stood in their stead with their crowns stretchin' toward the sky a hundred feet up.

Day broke.

Night fell.

Full moon.

No moon.

A whiteout of snow.

An explosion of wildflowers.

"I doona..." At the onslaught of images, she gripped Skorpius's hands tight, at once unsettled and amazed.

A tapestry of colorful leaves fluttered by, a swirling column that surrounded their entire sphere, then vanished. Boulders were strewn across a barren frosted glade with no trees at all.

Then no trees, no boulders, nor anythin' but scorched earth. Till wee saplings appeared once again.

Each image existed only for the flash of a lightnin' strike.

The one constant in all? The Highland mountains' silhouette on a distant horizon.

The warmth of Skorpius's face brushed alongside her cheek as he bent forward, watchin' with her. "We made this. Why?"

Close your eyes, goddess. Tell me what we've done.

Delighted with the game, and enchanted by his warm strength and spicy scent wrapped around her, she closed her eyes once again. But this time, she centered herself, dippin' a toe into the depths of her calm loch. Then her awareness rippled out, beyond her inner loch, past the two of them, out into their sphere of magick, into the flashin' realm beyond the energized walls.

"*Och!*" She pinched her eyes shut to hold on to the awareness. "We're travelin' through time. *And so is my favorite part of the glade!* You, me, the tree, a patch of heather." She stamped her toe onto solid ground.

But why? he prodded.

Her brow furrowed as she concentrated, searchin' for another element she'd clearly missed.

Around.

Up.

Behind. *There.* A faint trail of foreign energy pursued *far* behind them, through a blur of scenery changes. It disappeared for many flashes, then reappeared, as if the persistent hound had lost their scent, then retraced its steps. And its signature grew fainter with every flash.

"Our...*hunter.*" She dinna speak the name, refused to give it power by doin' so.

"You failed to sense the danger coming. Before I time-jumped us."

That she hadn't sensed the danger bothered her. Accustomed

to her newfound magick, it had become a second guardian of a sort, an inner herald. She turned in his arms and stared up at him. "Mayhap, I'd become too focused on you."

"Possibly. More likely, because you'd pulled the sphere down and drew it within you."

She'd thought pullin' the magick shield within her had been an improvement. That she'd grown stronger. But clearly her more-experienced angel still served her well. "Are we shielded for a time?"

"We'll have to generate a massive amount of power to keep our private ball rolling through the timeline's energy stream faster than anyone can detect." Wicked amusement glinted in his eyes.

Understandin' took flight within her. And a tendril of excitement heated low in her belly. "Tuppin'?"

On a slow exhale, his eyes sparked brighter. "And *then* some." His bewitchin' lips descended upon hers once more.

A shimmer of energy flowed forth from him, around them. The cool brush of air danced over her skin. High notes of sound along their time-storm's wind tinkled out a faint melody.

As Skorpius began to kiss her senseless, all else faded away. But soon, too soon, he tore his lips away then spun her round within his arms.

And she opened her eyes to wonders anew.

A massive bed spanned in front of the old tree's trunk. Creamy white linens mounded atop it. Hangin' from the branches were dozens of glass vessels, each held a wee candle topped by a golden flickerin' flame. Tendrils of ivy climbed up carved posts at the bed's corners. And sheer white swaths of fabric draped over the top framework of the bed.

"'Tis glorious."

"For you," Skorpius murmured, his lips tracin' the shell of her ear.

A shiver tremored through her from the warmth of his exhalation.

"You keep watching outside," he murmured. "I'll fortify us from inside."

"You will?"

"Yes." He tugged her hair away from her shoulder, and his dangerous mouth trailed lower. Hot kisses dotted down the side of her neck. "The more excited I get you, the faster we'll fly."

"Me?" *Surely, you are affected too.* Because the tone of his voice had lowered, roughened.

"Both of us." *Have no doubt of your power over me.*

Paced by the racin' beats of her heart, each next scene flashed by faster and faster. Until all the points in time began to blur. Then pure energy streamed by, as if they rode the currents of time itself.

A part of her wanted to let go, not worry about the hunter chasin' them.

Let go, Brigid. Surrender to this. To us.

Hot tingles spread through her. From Skorpius's magick? She dinna know.

But how am I to watch and *surrender?* 'Twould be impossible to do both.

But oh, how she wanted to. To steal a wee bit of pleasure in the present moment. All she might ever get.

Skorpius abandoned the spot his lips had been attendin' to at the crook of her neck and came around to face her with a hardened expression. "I've got us protected." He glared at the sphere's wall, toward the blur of light beyond. "Outside and"— he trailed the back of his finger along the shimmer of golden magick that formed the gown above her breast—"within."

A spike of guilt speared through her. *Do I have a right to...this? To us?* When danger threatened to harm not only her, but everyone, in every world.

Yes. "Do you trust me?" His beautiful sparkin' blue-green eyes held hers captive.

Trust. Skorpius himself had warned her to have great care where she placed her belief. Yet, in truth, she knew to her core, that all that Skorpius was...rang true.

Brigid swallowed hard and gave a nod. Skorpius had existed for far longer than she. Had sacrificed much of himself in the protection of worlds, of time itself. And if he could do so, take a wee bit of pleasure on the way to battle for everyone else? So could she.

"*Aye.*" More certain than ever. "I surrender."

CHAPTER 28

*S*korpius sensed the war within Brigid.

Would have been surprised had there not been some conflict.

As a female born to privilege—who had abandoned an easier life to defend a greater good—she accepted nothing less than everything she had to give. To others first. Herself last.

Brigid exhibited determination in venturing so far from home and staying to her course. Wisdom in assessing which battles to fight, when, and how. Bravery in facing down an unknown enemy and prepared to risk everything of herself, or die trying.

And the steely-eyed female warrior, a powerful goddess unlike any the worlds had yet known, had just submitted all she was—to him.

"I've never been more honored."

"Show me." Her chin hiked up a notch. Challenge sparked in those mercurial eyes.

Pride swelled in his chest. That she'd chosen him to share such a sacred part of herself. "With great pleasure."

The outside danger had abated, due to his ingenuity with

their unparalleled woven magicks. A last check of their internal tethers revealed the guardian tie hummed low, constant and stable. The timeline tether, however? Vibrated at a higher frequency since they'd launched their ricocheting sphere into the structure of the timeline.

Skorpius had no idea why. And no diagnostic existed to explain the elevated threat level.

So they'd steal what time they could for themselves. While they were able to take it.

"WEEL..." Brigid's gaze lingered at his waist, then dropped to his boots, eyes narrowing. "Am I to undress...or shall you..." She glanced down at her golden gown, formed of pure energy.

Bold. And right down to business.

Nice.

Yet for her first time? "Lady's choice."

Skorpius stepped back a pace. Then another.

To give her all the space she wanted.

And for him to take all of her wild beauty in, to savor the moment.

A smile curved her lips. *Another game?* "I'm thinkin' we'll both do so." She scanned down from his chest, then paused at the waistband of his leather pants. "I'll take a turn."

With her magick, she cast out a warm glow that penetrated through to his skin.

An instant later, he stood before her in nothing but the boots.

A smirk lifted one corner of her mouth as she stared at their battered leather toes, the half-undone laces. But her amusement faded to curious wonder when her attention floated up, inch by inch, to take a good look at the rest of his body, bared for her.

Then the boots also vanished at her bidding.

"Magnificent," she murmured with unabashed appreciation for his entire physical form.

For you. And no other.

Under the heat of her gaze, he became aroused for the first time in...a very long time.

But he blew out a steadying breath and tempered his excitement.

They had a game to play.

And he intended to take his time.

"My turn." Which to protect her, presented a challenge. For the diaphanous gown that draped her body in fluid golden waves existed as a discharge of her excess magick. How to safely disrobe her when she needed the construct to prevent over-heating?

Divert her energy. At the idea, he burst out a pulse of his magick, which displaced her glittering discharge and cast its energy flow beyond them to further electrify their sphere.

Then he strode forward to close the distance between them. He enfolded her in his arms and kissed her with all the devastating emotion he'd been suppressing.

Brigid clung to him while they explored each other's lips.

Sipped.

Tasted.

Devoured.

The most incredible sounds drifted to his ears: soft sighs and faint whimpers.

A preternatural growl vibrated from his.

Breathing heavy, his head spun. Blood roared through his veins. In his arms stood the one female always meant for him. A fiery spirit. The kindest heart. An unshakable resolve. Unparalleled power. With a beautiful untamed innocence. The combination of her immense power vibrating under such sweet vulnerability proved intoxicating.

Waves of energy radiated out from the excitement they gave

off, following the new pathway for her excess discharge. Subatomic, most of it shimmered as invisible waves. Yet infinitesimal sparks also burst to life, elements around them stirred into excitation. And in their generated sphere that mimicked the gravity of Earth, those tiny sparklers floated from the ground upward.

When Skorpius eventually released her, she gazed up at him with soft eyes, lost in a sensual haze. Until she caught sight of the tiny sparklers as they burst into existence around them.

"*Och!*" she whispered, tightening her arms around him. "'Tis an upside-down snowfall."

He glanced at the phenomenon they'd caused with a nod. "A *magickal* snowfall." No idea what else to call it. Likely the first of its kind.

But not the only first of the moment.

"Brigid?" he murmured as he shifted behind her again. He nipped the delicate top of her ear with his lips. With firm pressure, he coasted his palms over the smooth skin of her hips, then curved them inward, one coming to rest over her belly, the other tucking just below her breasts.

"Hmmm?" She leaned back into his hold, eyes drifting closed.

Bared to his full access, a shiver tremored through her.

"You've not 'tupped' before, correct?" Although she'd alluded to the fact, he had to be certain. How he proceeded depended on accurate information, not guesswork. Slow, not fast. Gentle, not rough. Not at first. About her. Always. For his pleasure would be derived from hers.

"Aye. I've not tupped. Nor had the touch of a man." His hands rose and fell in rhythm with each of her breaths. And they began to slow, deepen, as she fought to maintain control.

Mine. In all ways. Possessiveness spiked through him and his fingertips tensed against her. When a sigh escaped her lips, he splayed his hands wide, sliding them over her skin to soothe.

"Trust me in this. I'll lead, but do whatever feels best. And tell me if you want anything."

"*Anythin'?*"

"Yes." *We belong to each other. I belong to you now. Your desires are mine to fulfill.*

Satisfied she understood, Skorpius wasted no time.

For he had shot their unique protective sphere with great force onto its initial course and had designed it to ricochet nonlinearly through the timeline, never stopping, and gaining speed with the supplemented magick they both discharged.

But the acceleration would only last so long. At some point, the sphere would slow down. Because their energy expending couldn't go on endlessly without rest and refueling.

Yet for next few hours? They'd stolen the private time they both wanted. And had been granted a reprieve that his dual-tethered mission hadn't negated.

Skorpius viewed the moment as a rare gift.

Never had he met someone so attune to him, who saw him for who he was under all the darkness. The remarkable female wanted to share her love with him—even if for the one chance.

And if all they had was the once? They'd make it the experience of their immortal lifetime.

Leading with his fingertips, he glided one hand lower and drifted the other higher, seeking what only his male touch had ever stroked. With hungry lips, he pressed a gentle kiss under her ear, then placed another, a fraction lower. Savoring the soft path, tasting her silken skin, reveling in every sweet shiver and quake, he trailed the sensual kisses down her neck.

Her hitched gasp was music to his ears when his exploring fingers slid up the curve of her breast and delved into her thatch of soft curls. While under his lips, the skin over her shoulder pebbled.

Brigid suddenly grasped his wrists, stilling his hands, then spun within his hold to face him.

A tender blush colored those freckle-dusted cheeks. Lush peachy-pink lips curved into the smile of a temptress. Pressing against him, she skimmed her hands up his front from abs to pecs, then teased him with a succulent kiss.

After several pulse-pounding heartbeats, she drew back. Seductive playfulness sparked in her quicksilver eyes. "Then we'll be *tumblin'* in that romantic bed over there." Her small but powerful hands planted on his chest, then shoved him backward.

Nice. Warrior in all things. Even her first sexual encounter.

"Why I manifested the best." The softest Italian linens. The fluffiest down pillows. The sturdiest mattress bearing optimal spring. Mason jars with the perfect distribution of bubble in their glass and beeswax candles inside to burn clean and long. Even the washstand beside the bed held an ivory porcelain basin and jug, the water within sourced from a pure artesian spring. "Only a bedroom fit for a goddess will do."

Skorpius stepped to the side, then gestured a sweeping arm toward their well-appointed bed. Spreading his wings wide, he held his other hand out toward her in invitation.

Brigid came forward to take his hand, nude yet unashamed, confident in her own skin.

And he swept an appreciative gaze down her body as she moved. She'd grown fit and lithe for battle, yet possessed the gentle curves of the young female she'd become.

Another blush bloomed across her cheeks under his bold attention while she slid her hand over his palm.

His gaze locked with hers. "Beautiful. All of you. Outside, inside, through and through." He lifted her hand to his lips. "*Breathtakingly* beautiful," he murmured over her knuckles.

"Aye." Brigid moved her hand to cup his cheek, searching his eyes. "What you are...to me. Protector of all. Beholden to no one. And yet, you've chosen me."

"And you, me."

A slight smile twitched her lips. "Weel, we've both chosen well, angel mine."

Then with a forceful tug of his hand, she released her hold of him.

The bed's sheer overhead draping multiplied, rippled down, then cascaded forward into an undulating fall of translucent fabric that she slipped behind. After two quick steps, his dreamy nymph crouched, then leapt high before landing face-first onto the center of the bed with a joyful squeal.

With the soft bounce, she rolled over onto her side. Then she patted the white linen covers. "We shall commence with the tuppin' now."

"We *shall commence*? I—" He'd been about to tease her for the formality.

But all words tumbled right out of his head as she further reclined onto the bedding, bending a knee, softening her expression with emotion.

Mouth gone dry, he swallowed hard.

The sight of his female stunned him anew. For under her soft curves and supple strength protected a heart of gold and spine of steel. And for several beats of his fractured heart, he found he couldn't move.

But the glint of mischief in her eyes as she stared back at him —with stark desire for the male she saw in him—sealed the deal.

He forced out a breath. *No holding back. Understood.*

Then he strode forward. Ready to claim what was his by offer and right.

For his heart? Already surrendered.

CHAPTER 29

*T*hrough a billowin' cloud of white fabric hovered the male of her dreams.

The most magnificent warrior.

And within his chest? Beat a kind, noble, and verra good heart. Even if he dinna want any to know. Protected behind an impenetrable coat of armor. Yet offered to her alone. Exposed. Vulnerable.

Doona fear. I'll take care of you. Both her angel and his blackened heart.

But as he stared at her, those faceted eyes hardened and sparked with a brighter bluish green. Then in a flash of movement, he burst through the bed's hazy sheers and pounced onto the bed, crouched above her.

She gasped, breath catchin' with excitement. A rabbit's pulse fluttered in her chest.

Hard muscles caged her body. Sparklin' eyes captured her soul. Wings of starless midnight spread wide above, castin' them into their own secret darkness.

But through her next ragged breaths, his gaze softened and he paused. Arms stiff and locked, he seemed hesitant to proceed.

"I'm *certain*." On a shaky exhale, she hovered her fingers over his ribs, then across his back as she wrapped him in her arms, pullin' his body down onto hers.

But still, concern flickered in his eyes. Doubt, mayhap.

That she dinna understand in full?

Openin' her body and heart to him, she spread her knees and tugged him down until his bared hips touched hers. She slid her feet along his calves and smoothed her hands over his backside, glidin' them to rest over the curve of his buttocks.

He blew out a heavy breath, bracin' his arms to continue to stare into her eyes.

"'Tis my wish," she murmured. "I *accept* the consequences."

His gaze hardened. "To be further bonded."

"Aye."

"To me." A furrow marred his brow.

Her breathin' slowed as she stared up at the proud male who needed to understand his worth. "Aye, angel mine. I'll have no other."

"Come what may?" He finally dipped his head closer to hers and the wild ends of his hair brushed her neck.

Brigid arched up into him, brushed her lips up the hot column of his throat, flicked her tongue out to taste the salt on his skin.

"Aye. Come what may." His mission. Her callin'. The danger they both faced. The unknown that awaited them on the morrow. Or whether or not they'd even have one.

An ache burned hot in her body and soul. To become one with him. To cause his surrender. "We're alone. You in your world. Me in mine." She nipped his earlobe with her lips, spoke the words burstin' from her heart. "We're different from the rest. Yet alike with one another."

Skorpius had stilled in her embrace.

When she relaxed her head down, he drew his head back and searched her eyes once more. "Made for one another."

"Aye." She gave him a wee smile. "Mayhap from the verra start."

Relief washed through his expression as he exhaled.

Sparks fired brighter in his eyes.

And a magickal charge rippled through the air.

Then a primal growl reverberated from Skorpius's throat as he dipped his head down, capturin' her lips with his.

Now we'll commence with the tuppin'? She couldna help but cast the teasin' thought to him.

You tell me. A different kind of tease laced his mental tone.

And the magnificent powerful body enfolded in her arms...shifted.

If Brigid had thought she'd drawn him as close to her as possible, he proved her wrong.

The amazin' heat and hardness of his entire body settled further upon her. Solid muscles pressed her down into the cushions of the giant bed. Another *far more intimate* hardness rubbed along the verra center of her body, sparkin' such great pleasure, she gasped in surprise.

But 'twas the forceful beatin' of his heart against hers—the connection of their hearts that she felt through their magicks—that became her ultimate undoin'.

All the while, a cascade of pleasurable sensations assaulted her from head to toe, catchin' her breath, quickenin' her pulse. Energy from her magick? Discharge from her pent-up arousal? And yet Skorpius gave off a similar frenzied energy. 'Twas as if she'd been a banked fire, he'd been the dried log, and tossed together, they'd not only ignited, they twirled up into snappin' sparks and sizzled into the night air.

On each next breath, the fire stoked with anticipation and ignited all over again.

Soft kisses at first asked, like permission, then firmed till they demanded, took, conquered. Fierce lips molded, pushed, and pulled. Hungry tongues glided, danced, then tangled.

Gentle tugs at the roots of her hair soon intensified. Till he grabbed a fistful of her locks and pulled, causin' a delightful burn at her scalp, and angled her head up, exposin' her neck.

The heat of his breath fogged over the sensitive skin of her throat.

Shivers wracked through her body and her breath caught.

When the weight of his body shifted to her side, a keening whimper escaped her lips. For her entire body throbbed at the loss of him, and the need for connection with him to return.

"Yes?" he murmured against the column of her throat, then placed a coolin' kiss upon her overheated skin.

'Twas another gentled request.

"*Aye.*" She'd no idea to what she'd agreed. All of it. Everra part of her he wanted to take. Everra last thing she needed. "*Yours,*" she murmured, nerves set afire, thoughts incoherent.

Yet instead of takin', Skorpius set a course of slow temptation that stoked her every desire.

In an unhurried pace, he traced circles over her skin with his fingers, skimmin' over and down her breasts. Pebbled to firm points, risin' and fallin' with her ragged breaths, her nipples ached for his touch. But he dinna indulge. Those teasin' fingers trailed ever lower. Splayed wide over the plane of her belly. Clutched firm at the curve of her hip.

Till the heat of his mouth descended upon one strainin' peak.

And his firm fingers slid along the throbbin' cleft between her legs.

An incredible surge of achin' pressure flared from that intimate point, then burst forth in great ripplin' waves of pleasure. A keenin' cry tumbled from her lips at the unexpected intensity.

In the second it took to draw her next breath, Skorpius shifted back over her and spread her legs wider with his hips while he stared down into her eyes. Then he plunged deep inside. A sharp pinch of acute pain preceded a new kind of pleasure that washed through her. They'd become entangled—whole, body and soul.

And her heart swelled with joy from the wonder of it.

Filled completely by him in everra conceivable way, she curved her hips up, seekin' more. She wrapped her arms around him, slid her hands up his back, then stroked her fingers under the soft feathers at the connection of his wings.

A low groan rumbled from his throat as he closed his eyes. He dipped his head down and captured her lips in a searin' kiss. And then their bodies began to move in a rhythmic dance of lovers. At first, slow and sensual. But soon, harder and heated.

All the while, they kissed. Long. Deep. Scorchin' right down into her heart. Burnin' straight through to her soul.

Another storm of pleasure whipped up with speed inside her. Body tight with ache and need, she clutched him, wrappin' her legs around his hips as he thrust deeper, spun her higher.

Clipped whimpers marked her struggle to survive the pressure.

Tightened muscles and heavy breaths revealed his.

Till more intense waves of pleasure broke across her body and washed through her.

Lips locked with his, she screamed into their passionate kiss. While with an echoin' roar, he thrust one last time and attained his own release, his great pulses mixin' with hers.

And with that simultaneous climax, their magicks sparked and flared within them, then exploded through their sphere and out into the streamin' lights of the timeline.

Breaths heavy, bodies slicked with a sheen of sweat, he settled down beside her, but tucked close to her body. The warmth of a black wing covered them both.

After a time, she let out a sigh of satisfaction.

They'd come together, become one, what she'd known had been true for them on some level from the verra start. Mayhap why she'd fought him so hard.

And Skorpius had accomplished his goal of protectin' them. The power of their lovemakin' fueled the sphere.

But not all their magick had been expended, had been cast outward. In truth, she found her deep loch of peaceful power had been replenished. And more. The great depths had expanded into immeasurable darkness. The vast shoreline had widened a hundredfold.

And in a different place within, a bright new black-gold thread had appeared: tied to her heart on one end, connected to his on the other. The energy of it glittered and sparked. Taut and vibrant.

"Skorpius," she murmured. "Do you see?" *The tie within.*

Arm banded over her chest, his fingers had been strokin' along her upper arm. Warm lips pressed a kiss to her shoulder.

But somethin' soft and light landed on her cheek.

Another faint pressure settled onto the back of her hand.

Yes. I see, he replied. Then a radiant warmth burst along their hearts' bond, sizzlin' from his heart to hers.

A third softness alighted onto her thigh.

Curious at the snow-like phenomenon, she fluttered open her eyes, thinkin' their upside-down snowfall had shifted over the bed. And had reversed course to descend after all.

Yet what floated down from above turned out to be a most unexpected sight.

CHAPTER 30

"*S*korpius! Look!"

Brigid startled up, jostling him to tuck back his wing. Then she bolted right off the bed.

Heart pounding, he launched out after her, then tucked her behind him while he scanned out across the energy slipstream. Then he cast probing magick far beyond their sphere, searching for any threat.

But no tension rippled back to him. And the dual tethers remained docile as well.

Pulse calming, he exhaled in relief as she entwined her hand with his.

When he glanced down, he realized she was staring up at the yew tree.

Tiny creamy pink petals fluttered down from above. Flat dark-green needles emerged along the smaller branches. And little red flowerlike bulbs took shape amid the thickening needles.

"Och! The yew's bloomin'. Like we've given it a new spring-time." Brigid released his hand, then walked up to the tree to place a hand against its gnarled trunk. She stared high up into its canopy, then dematerialized and reappeared thirty feet up on a flat section of a wide bough.

Basking in her childlike wonder of the development, Skorpius flashed onto the same branch, only a few feet farther out; he wanted to give her plenty of space to explore.

As a precaution, he scanned even farther out for their enemy. But still no danger registered.

So he perched down on a soft furred section of weathered bark, draped his wings back, then dangled his legs off either side. "Maybe we did give it spring. Our discharge fed the tree pure energy before flaring out into the slipstream."

The tiny flowers continued to float down, many adorning her hair. And those soft copper ringlets had gone wild from their sex play. Only a few coiled down toward the delectable curves of her breasts. The rest sprang outward in every direction.

A beautiful pink flush warmed her ivory skin.

Brightness sparked in her silvery eyes.

And a golden luminosity exuded from her, magick sparking.

In all the worlds, over countless millennia of existence, he'd never seen anything lovelier. "You are"—he swallowed hard —"*beautiful.*" Energy punctuated his meaning, because mere words were inadequate.

Her blush intensified with a radiant smile. "As are you, angel mine."

Unashamed of her nudity, she stalked along the branch toward him. A true goddess of nature, at home in her element.

"What say you we tup again?" His beloved beauty paused before him. And a shy expression softened her features as she tugged her lower lip in. "Here. Up in the tree."

Skorpius flared his wings and held out a hand toward her. "I say: I'm a very lucky male."

She gave a slow headshake, taking his hand as she searched his eyes. "*Nay.* You're a worthy male. The one for me." Then her gaze snagged on his growing arousal. "'Tis quite thick and long…and…curved, like a branch."

He fought a smile and slid his hands across and down her back, helping to guide her onto his lap. "It would seem you nurture all trees."

She placed her hands upon his shoulders, positioned her feet behind his hips, then eased herself down. Halfway there, she crushed her lips against his in a fierce kiss.

Angling his hips, using her slickness to guide him home, he aligned their bodies together.

"Only those I wish to"—she gasped, eyes widening as she slid down, her body straining to accommodate him—"climb."

Pleasure shot through him as she worked herself downward, taking all he had to give. With a measured exhale, he forced himself not to move. Eyes drifting closed, he touched his forehead to hers. "Climb this tree any time you'd like," he murmured.

"So verra hard. So…much…*more…*" Her breaths shortened into pants with her struggle.

"It's the angle." He kissed her long and deep. "The position." He pulled his head back a little, opening his eyes. "Is it too much?"

"Nay." She shook her head, blowing out a slow breath through pursed lips. "'Tis perfect. I wish to have all of you." Pressing her hands onto his shoulders, she lifted a little, then lowered further. Once. Twice. Until she'd snugged all the way down. She tipped her head back and let out a long sigh. "'Tis done. I've taken the whole of you, crown to root."

"Oh, we're not even close to done, goddess." He gripped her hips, tilted his pelvis, then thrust up.

Surprised joy brightened her eyes as she gasped. "*Oh.*"

So he tightened his hold of her hips and repeated the movement. Clutching his shoulders, she curved her hips, rocking them together in the duplicated motion.

And with their renewed sexual excitement, more energy than ever before—far exceeding their consummation on the bed—discharged through their sphere and beyond, propelled them with greater velocity.

Within seconds, a new branch of the tree developed above them. Brigid reached up to grasp the botanical handhold as it thickened and twisted within reach. Had the goddess manifested the aid? Or had the yew provided? Maybe a little of both. The two created a circle of harmony, the tree supporting Brigid to enable her excited energy-discharge to continue.

Up in the tree, hidden from the worlds in their own secret bubble, his goddess rode him. Hard.

And for their second union, Skorpius simply held on, still giving her every angle and thrust he knew she needed while letting her set the pace to take her pleasure.

Soon her pace quickened.

Faint gasps and low moans that came from her grew deeper, louder.

The incredible tightness wrapped around him became slicker and hotter.

His entire world became filled with her: beautiful body, bright soul, generous heart, golden energy.

Then Skorpius's world focused further down into heightened sensation and primal need.

Aching.

Throbbing.

Pleasure.

Pain.

The ragged breaths and low groans? Were torn from him.

Skorpius closed his eyes, gritted his teeth, and held his body as rigid and immobile as possible. But no amount of his restraint held up against the powerful onslaught of her passion.

"*Surrender*," she urged in low murmur, warm breath fogging over his ear. Then her teeth clamped down on his earlobe.

And the sharp bite of pain shot through his nerves, igniting a cascade.

Intense pleasure burst from him, and he growled as the powerful release took hold.

Brigid stiffened, holding him tight as the first pulses fired free. Then she cried out. A flash of heat flared around him, and her waves of climax joined with his.

They clung to each other through the ongoing storm of pleasure.

After blissful seconds, the pulses of their orgasm began to ebb.

Panting breaths started to slow and deepen.

Racing hearts stabilized and strengthened.

After many more seconds dragged forward, once the chaos of their bodies calmed into a tempered peacefulness, Brigid eased back. Soft lips pressed to his.

Skorpius deepened their kiss, overcome by the moment. Astounded by their lovemaking. Astonished by her ferocious innate sexual appetite. Stunned by Brigid in all her extraordinary splendor.

When he opened his eyes, a sparking silvery gaze held his. Immense happiness shone in their depths. Then she glanced around.

The creamy pink petals falling from the yew had thickened. The tree had blossomed again.

And the insatiable and apparently infatigable Brigid pushed up and leapt up from his lap.

"*Och!*" With wonder, she held on to an upper branch and stalked farther out on their wide bough as she scanned their fifty-foot sphere. Then she glanced back over her shoulder, gaze landing on him. "The...*rush*. 'Tis amazin'"

"Indeed." Hard to argue. Similar endorphins elevated him.

"'Twill it always be like this?"

As amazing as their stolen moments, she meant. Could they

hope to have more, she hadn't said. More time. Some kind of future.

Skorpius swallowed hard, unable to break the enchanting spell they'd fallen under. He stood and stalked after her.

But her perceptive gaze held his for a beat. Then her expression sobered and turned to stare out at the streaming lights beyond their protective sphere.

"We tupped in a tree."

"We did."

"Do you think we could...*fly*...within the sphere?"

Her true question lay rooted in physics.

They were passengers inside the sphere, as was everything within it. The forces that propelled the sphere propelled its contents at the same speed. From a physics standpoint, they were one unit. For them to "fly" within the sphere, without breaking through its protective barrier, they'd have to disengage, become something separate. And yet, at the same time, they'd need to propel themselves with matching velocity. As if weightless.

"With magick, anything we want becomes possible."

"While tuppin'?" Mischief sparked in her eyes.

Then she spun, sprinted the last few steps along their branch, and leapt into the air above their bed.

Skorpius launched right as she went airborne. Gaining speed with a heavy flap of his wings, he caught her by the hips. With a burst of his magick, he disentangled their propulsion from the sphere's. Then he spread her thighs with his knees and thrust forward, making them one.

"Oh, yes." Pleasure speared through him. "I *so* want."

For they weren't guaranteed an always. But they definitely had their spectacular now.

CHAPTER 31

*B*efore those amazin' intimate moments—down in the bed, up in the tree, flyin' with the magick energy stream—all within their private sphere, Brigid had never before known such wild excitement, such incredible pleasure.

She'd become a woman.

Nay. More than a woman.

A goddess. But she failed to imagine becomin' so without the one male who'd chosen to be with her. In spite of his obligation. Come what may.

And with the trials to come, which she sensed drew near, if she never had another chance to be with Skorpius again, the wee bit of bliss they'd captured for themselves had been worth it.

Skorpius began to stir beside her.

One silken wing remained draped across her bare body, warm and comfortin'.

Yet on his next breath, he gasped, twisted, then bolted up out of bed.

She remained on the tangled linens and admired his splendid backside.

Those glorious black wings flared, and he ran a hand through his tousled hair. Ever her protector first, he scanned through the wall of their sphere, pacin' the perimeter.

His gaze landed back on her when he returned to the bedside. Concern tightened his features. "I slept."

"Aye."

"For how long?"

She clasped his hand and tugged him back down, cravin' the heat of his body, his touch. "Three hours, mayhap four."

"But—" His brow furrowed, and he stared out at the blur of pure energy streamin' by again. "How are we still moving at such speed?" Then he narrowed his eyes at her, before examinin' her from head to toe. "Are you all right? Did you do this?"

"Aye. *We* did. And I'm fine."

"We?" Puzzlement flickered over his face. "My internal check shows no energy depletion. In fact, I feel energized. But how?"

"I doona know. I awoke and sensed us slowin'. When our old glade began to appear again, I reached out to the energy stream itself and asked it to provide the fuel we needed."

"*Asked.*" His expression slackened.

"Aye."

"The energy stream."

"Aye." She placed a hand to his forehead. "Are you well? You're repeatin' my words."

Muscles stiffenin', he sat up.

She sighed, pushed up from their bed, then sat beside him. She nudged her shoulder into his. "What ails you?"

"That shouldn't be possible. The energy stream, the timeline, has no awareness. Yet you act like it understood you."

"Aye, it did."

Skorpius stared at her, expression hard. "Let's assume the now-sentient timeline agreed and carried out your wish. My body only refuels with darkness, the blackest places in your world, in mine."

"Till now."

He blinked in surprise.

"'Tis the same as with the feast you manifested. And the emerald dress you'd fashioned. And the bed we're lyin' upon. You wished the items into existence. Only, I wished bigger, asked for us to continue to be undetected, and for you to be replenished."

"Simple as that."

"Aye."

Interesting. "It would seem your powers are endless."

She dinna know what the limits of her abilities were. But when she found her peace at the bottom of her private loch and asked with full expectation of what she needed, her magick had granted the few requests she'd made.

Skorpius sucked in a sudden gasp of air. "The timeline thread just snapped taut."

"Because of what I've done?"

"No." He gave a headshake. "If your actions had tripped the tether, its vibration would have woken me the moment you altered the energy stream. Something else just happened."

Brigid leaned up and pressed her lips to his in a soft kiss. "Our time alone is up then."

Eyes driftin' closed, he touched his forehead to hers and sighed. "So it would seem."

A memory flash prompted her to stand from the bed. She stepped forward while drapin' herself in her golden gown of magick, then stopped at the perimeter to gaze at the colorful lights streamin' beyond their protective sphere. And as she stared out into the vastness of the timeline, some thread within her own breast tugged. "I wonder if…"

"Do you see something?" Skorpius's warmth pressed against her, the delightful softness of his wing tucked around her shoulder.

"Aye. A 'vision', akin to what you'd said before." At least, the vibration seemed more real than a mere dream. Closin' her eyes, she chased after the image, which hovered right on the fringe of her awareness. Something important. A heavy feeling of danger. Of destruction.

But as elusive as the wisp of a dream, the fragment vanished. "I canna remember many of the details."

"What *do* you remember?" Warm hands rubbed up her arms, then held her shoulders in firm support.

She leaned back against his wall of strength. "Smoke clouds my eyes, burns my throat. There's a putrid stench. And strongest of all, I feel…heartbreakin' sorrow."

"Emotion registers with greater impact than any other."

"And that draw pulls at me again. I'm to go to the place within the vision."

A wee bit of energy rippled out from him, as if he'd both physically straightened and mentally alerted. "Any idea where?"

"Nay. But I do know *when.*" *Odd, though. 'Twould seem to lead us into the future.*

Not odd at all. We're playing in the timeline. Reason dictates all time-points are fair game.

Fair game? Or a trap. "For our hunter to lure us."

"Which would be his first mistake. We're *not* prey." Skorpius wrapped his arms around her, embracin' her from behind while they stared at the brilliant lights. "We—you and I with our combined powers—are an adversary unlike any he has imagined. And when we choose to encounter him, we will have the upper hand."

She agreed. For her power surged strong, filled her to overflowin'. And still, her magick, the timeline, and the elements themselves offered up more. All she had to do was ask.

And Skorpius's power seemed to have altered as well. Stronger. Darker, mayhap. And yet, akin to her magick, it appeared to be evolvin' into somethin' far greater.

"Into the future," he repeated as he tore his gaze from the lights to stare down at her. "When?"

"Nigh four months forward, whence we'd left the glade."

Skorpius stepped forward and clasped her hand with a firm grip. When she glanced at him, she found he'd already dressed: black leathers over his legs, weathered boots on his feet.

Intensity sparked in his blue-green eyes. "Then, shall we? Seems we've got a date, four months forward." *Your lead.* He gave her a nod to proceed.

As she alone felt the pull of the event, the vision. She alone had the power to pinpoint the "when" of their destination. Unable to sense the actual location, instinct had her direct that choice into someplace familiar: their glade.

Closin' her eyes, she latched on to the powerful emotion and the time of the vision. Then akin to her holdin' the reins of a runaway horse, they vanished from the environs of their protective sphere and flew directly through the ether while she gripped Skorpius's hand tight.

The colorful streams from their energy were replaced by utter blackness, as before.

Harsh forces tugged once again at her senses, but she held her calm and arrowed along her chosen pathway.

Till, with a bright flash of light, they stopped.

Cold ground solidified beneath their feet.

A cloudless blue sky stretched above, the sun hangin' halfway down the western horizon.

The glade encircled them—covered in a blanket of untouched snow.

With her verra next fresh breath of her Highland home, a tight sensation gripped within her chest. The shock of pain had her gaspin' for air as she glanced up at Skorpius in alarm.

Then her whole world blacked out.

CHAPTER 32

*S*korpius dropped to his knees to catch Brigid as she collapsed.

An unexpected pulse of energy had blasted into her the instant they'd arrived. And its percussive force had knocked her unconscious.

Brigid. A gentle mental tap, in the event her psyche had been traumatized.

No response came.

The timeline tether within him snapped taut, then vibrated at higher frequency.

More forceful, then. With a burst of magick, Skorpius shocked her system, shooting enough volts through her to restart an elephant's heart.

Brigid's eyes popped open and her lips parted as she gasped for air.

But responsive? Not so much. An unseeing silvery gaze stared off toward a distant horizon. Then she climbed out of his embrace without any recognition of his existence there, her awareness clearly elsewhere.

No other being nor any energy manifested into the snowy

glade with them. Only a rippling echo of some higher vibration, a communication.

Your vision.

Rapid breaths assaulted her as she faced northwest, stared off toward some distant place. Tears streamed from her eyes. Magick snapped and crackled in an aura that undulated around her, golden and hot.

Instinct warned it inadvisable to interfere with Brigid in her altered state, yet she appeared tortured. And based on the way the timeline thread vibrated in urgency, whatever she currently viewed—possibly what she'd envisioned before but couldn't recall—had vast importance to their mission. Captured in the moment, the information it yielded could give the two of them the upper hand.

So Skorpius reached out to her once more.

Only in a far different manner.

From down in the well of his soul where his dark angelic source-magick flowed, he drew upon its elemental energy. Then he addressed her through the magick, in multilayered voices, words dripping with power.

Ancient Brighid, Bride, Exalted One, goddess of nature, healing, creativity, and justice. What do you see?

His Brigid might not be able to detect Skorpius or any other material-realm constructs, but their magick—each originating from angelfire, unique, and connected from their bonding—recognized like kind.

And in response to his magick words, the golden energy that sparked around her brightened.

But she did not turn to face him.

Nor did she voice a reply.

Instead, a three-dimensional vision appeared between them for Skorpius to see for himself.

Yet the particles that conveyed information to him were more than any mere image. Brigid displayed a full translation of an actual event as it played out, much like Cass had done in his realm's strategy hall. Echoes of the original permeated through into their space and time, not only with sights, but also faint sounds and smells.

And within the small village that Brigid viewed, chaos reigned.

Humans in plain clothes raced in every direction between dozens of thatched huts, eyes wide with terror. Bloodcurdling screams were suddenly cut off, somewhere out of view. The stench of death grazed his nostrils. Their heavy despair clenched at his heart.

Snow covered the rooftops and ground, old-growth forest fringed the community, but no clear landmarks gave any clue as to its locale. Their village could be anywhere.

With a roaring bass rush of sound, a bluish white flame streamed over the scene from above. The magickal flame burned so hot, everything in its path was incinerated in an instant. Only blackened matter remained, leveled to the ground. Small particles of ash drifted up on the breeze.

Silence followed, eerie and absolute.

The scene evolved as their lens pulled up then flew high above the destroyed village.

A beat later, untouched dry earth appeared, a well-traveled road fringed by tall pines to protect from snowfall.

Their view zoomed down to focus on a bright flash over the road. Then scorched earth began to appear, script flowing from left to right, as if a flamethrower had become a pen and the turf, its author's page.

Where one scorched word ended, another flowed forth. Until together, they formed an ominous smoking message: *Become mine. Or the child serves in your stead.*

On the patch of ground beneath the three-dimensional vision, the deep snow vanished.

And the roadway message expanded from the vision into a

life-sized depiction on their own ground.

Brigid's unfocused attention drifted down from the horizon and stared at the copy of the message in their time and place. Her gaze began to sharpen, growing more lucid.

Then the vision dissolved.

Brigid sucked in a quick gasp. She wrapped her arms around her middle, breaths shallowing. Then she shot a distraught glare at Skorpius. "*What* child?"

Two strides forward, and he enfolded her into his embrace. "I don't know, Brigid. But we will find out. Together."

"Aye." Tipping her head to his shoulder, Brigid choked out a ragged sob. Struggled to steady her breathing. Clutched fisted hands to his back with preternatural strength.

Skorpius endured her frustrated venting, becoming her rock amid the turbulent storm. And he clung to Brigid in return, forcing calmness into his shaky breaths. For he'd plunged right to the depths of anguish and fury with her. Because the powerful emotions vibrating through that vision had nearly overcome him.

They had been summoned. The way ahead, clear.

But the horrific message, from the destruction to the scorched earth, had been sent to her. Therefore, the path forward remained hers alone.

His task? To support. Guide, if requested.

And the sedate, but still vibrating, dual tethers agreed.

After a long moment of comfort in each other arms, Brigid straightened, then pulled away. Expression fierce, she stared up at him, then she glanced toward the north-western horizon again. With her full faculties in the here and now.

She clasped his hand and drew him forward. "We've no time to waste. To the ocean."

Skorpius matched stride to hers. "That's where the pull is leading you."

"Mayhap, 'twas all along. But we'd been four months too early."

When they merged with a shadowy game trail, they released their handhold and Skorpius partially dematerialized to stride alongside her. *Or we were right on time. And you needed to evolve; all the events up to this point needed to transpire.*

Indeed. She gave a nod, as if accepting the rightness of the fated theory.

At a fork in the path, she paused.

"Unsure of the direction?"

"Nay. I'll no longer be travelin' by foot."

She closed her eyes, and a peaceful calm washed over her expression.

Skorpius materialized before her, then placed gentle hands on her shoulders. "I'd recommend against wasting your magick to transport there."

Face tilting up, she opened her eyes and her gaze searched his. "We're needin' to be there *now*." She fisted a hand over her heart. "The tether in my breast vibrates with great urgency."

While his pair vibrated no dire threat at all. Which meant all remained as it should with his mission. Regarding her well-being and the timeline's.

Even so, they didn't need her to risk any further energy depletion. The moment they'd stopped generating heat from their sexual encounter—as he'd slept…for hours—she'd begun to expend energy. By sustaining the energy sphere. In transporting them into their future glade. While receiving a vision, then transmuting it into its three-dimensional representation.

"We'll go *another* way." Skorpius stared hard at her. Her lead. His suggestion.

The moment meaning broke through, her eyes brightened. "The *mistin' through trees*."

Exactly. "You've climbed them, hugged them, and passed out against them."

Heat sparked in her silvery eyes. "And tupped in them."

Fighting a smile at her inclination toward humor in the crisis situation, he gave her a tender kiss. "Might as well travel through them."

"While becomin' one with them." *One with trees!*

The childlike joy in her spirit struck him with a heady warmth. Right in that widening fracture of his heart. He stepped back, flaring his wings wide. "If you're ready to learn."

The golden energy of her gown shimmered as she spread her legs shoulder-width apart and balanced on the balls of her feet. "Aye. I've been ready from the start."

"And already you've learned how along the way."

"I have?"

"More energy—"

"—less matter," she murmured.

"You've already mastered the skill. Now incorporate it with travel. Remain half within your realm, and half out."

"But...how does that *not* expend energy? How is that not usin' my magick?"

"When you relax back into pure energy, you're no longer needing power to remain material. All beings' natural state is energy. To become a part of the ether requires less energy, not more."

"*Aye...*" She gave a slow nod, as if searching within and sensing the rightness of it.

Before he thought to suggest the first step, she halfway dematerialized on her own.

A beautiful golden mirage stared back at him. The copper ringlets that framed her face rippled on an unseen energy current, as did the shimmering edges of her gown. Eyes of paler silver sparked joyful with her magick.

Then she faced northwest and stared off into the distance. After a beat, she glanced back at him, brows raised in question.

Her golden aura shimmered upward a fraction, as if she bounced on her toes with anticipation.

Skorpius dematerialized, then floated slowly by her. *Movement is similar to time-jumping. Visualize your destination.*

Where I'm to go. She stared a few feet ahead at an open patch of snowfield, then her body floated over it.

But small segments at a time. You have to have a definite picture of what exists to go there.

With another sightline, she traveled another short distance above the snow.

That's it, he commended, moving beside her.

How do we gain speed? she asked as she veered toward a copse of pines. She paused before a wide trunk, then floated on through it. Then she kept a steady pace, slipped one by one through each next tree.

Concentration. He floated with her, attention both ahead for himself and toward her, to monitor her progress. *Keep your focus on your desired path. The faster you want to go—*

—the farther ahead I'll need to track. Her golden shimmer shot far ahead, then disappeared.

Adrenaline firing hot, he flew after her. *Never lose focus of your path!*

In seconds, he spotted a golden streak streaming through the forest.

I've...got...my...focus. The slow words proved her point.

Good. He gave her a wide berth, but paced slightly ahead of her. *I'm right here if you—*

Race you! Her golden streak flashed out of sight.

Skorpius's chuckle vibrated through the ether. She alone felt the pull, knew their direction.

Silence followed.

But the intense tension of Brigid's focus? Remained.

As Skorpius chased after her, great relief coursed through him.

Because they'd had other options for speedy travel, which he hadn't mentioned. But gut instinct and the calming tethers had directed him to slow her path.

She needed the distraction of a new challenge to calm her emotions, to ready for the fight ahead.

And limited as Brigid's need for him had become—the dual tethers all but going dormant—it soothed his fractured heart to still guide her in any way he could.

For even though no change had taken place with him on the outside—he remained immortal, even though he'd warned himself as much as he'd cautioned her—he *felt* a marked shift within. The evolution Orion had detected? Perhaps. The difference in him that Brigid had sensed? Possibly.

But with a heavy heart, he admitted to himself that something even graver had happened. Impervious dark angel, outcast of his kind, sworn to never become vulnerable again…had fallen.

Absolutely.

Irrevocably.

Terminally.

For no future lay ahead.

Should it be deemed Brigid live? He'd have no place in her world.

If events required her death? He'd be utterly destroyed.

With a resigned sigh—even as he sensed her joy while "mistin' through trees"—he cast out one last directive, toward her, to himself.

Focus on what we have the power to control. Let worry afflict the weak-minded.

CHAPTER 33

*B*rigid drew in a deep breath, burstin' at the seams with unbelievable joy.

I'm mistin'! she called out to Skorpius.

With mastery, he replied.

Pine.

Alder.

Oak. She named each as she identified her target, then became one with the tree, even as she flew right through it.

Pine.

Chestnut.

Yew.

Some...tree I doona know.

Yet all the while, a heavy sense of forebodin' churned in her gut.

Part of it came from her vision, and trepidation of what she'd find once they arrived.

But another part? Vibrated through to her from Skorpius.

He'd insisted that she remained focused? Not to worry?

Focus yourself, angel mine, she arrowed out toward him.

They'd bonded, connected, become one in ways she'd never

imagined a soul could with another. And because of that newly forged tie, she felt a kernel of her male's essence within her. And knew that he'd become troubled.

Deep concern for his well-being vibrated through her.

The solid bark of a pine's trunk loomed.

Her relaxed state faltered.

And she fully solidified.

Och! Arms flailing as she hurtled through the air, she veered wide to fly over open ground.

Focus!

I'm focusin'!

On yourself. *Not me.*

You sensed me worryin' about you? She half-dematerialized again. Then ghosted through another pine. Another alder.

I'm trying *not to worry about you.*

Needing a break from all the focus, she slowed her pace, then solidified and alighted onto her feet in a trot. Then she strode toward a road she'd spotted. Running along the forest edge, protected from the prevailin' winds, and mostly dry from exposure of a full day of sun, it was easily navigable by foot. "How 'bout we walk awhile?"

Once she broke out onto the road, Skorpius materialized beside her. They walked side by side for dozens of yards while she calmed her poundin' heart.

"Talk to me." She needed a distraction only he could provide.

Silent seconds passed before he spoke. "Tell me something I don't know about you."

Warmth at the personal quality of his inquiry made her smile.

The wide roadway broke away from the forest, then veered inland.

But Brigid continued along a steeper rocky footpath, a more direct route toward where her inner pull led her. And she dematerialized again, then raced as fast as she could over the open terrain, no longer at risk to smack into a solid tree trunk.

Some wee thing? Or one of greater import? To challenge herself with her newfound skill, she traced above every bend and curve in the zigzaggin' trail.

Skorpius raced beside her, but over the snowier open meadow. *Both.*

She searched through the memories of her ordinary life. *I doona only have a love for trees. I'm fond of all plants.*

I knew that. You'd zeroed in on dandelions and other weeds to refuel.

Apothecaries have that knowledge, yet doona need a fondness for their craft to master it.

You're no apothecary.

And he'd been more observant of her than she realized.

Hmmm…

Brigid scanned through the events of her life yet again. She'd developed a passion for readin', but with the discovery of his journal—a part of his life she'd no desire to remind him of—he knew that as well.

I love music. And love to dance even more. Ever since she'd been a child. Blood racin', feet stompin', twirlin' about the floor, the delightful moments of revelry had drawn her out of her lonely life and spun her right into the heart of the celebration. Her clan had surrounded her, gaily acceptin' her with them. *'Tis a time when warfare and troubles and grief and loss are—*

—forgotten.

Aye.

She dinna ask how he knew, for she found it hard to imagine angels singin' and dancin'. And again, she refused to broach his past. Vowed to keep him in his present.

I know you, goddess mine. Tone low and gentle, he answered her unspoken question.

Needin' connection with him, even in their half-energy

state, she veered away from the ragged path and flowed over snow turned purplish gray in the gloamin' hour. She brushed her golden magick out to the side, weavin' it together with the glitterin' bluish black edges of his.

And I'm ever blessed for it.

He glanced toward her, blue-green eyes sparkin' in the increasin' darkness. Then he flared out his magick, brushin' her senses with warm affection.

Tell me something else.

Of greater import. Easy. Perhaps the one thing left he dinna know. *I've only one true friend in the world. And she's only just found me.*

Isobel.

She swallowed hard. *Aye. Yet now, I've found another.*

Skorpius brushed up against her with his magick, harder this time, and somehow the force knocked her back into solid form.

She found herself twirlin' upright in the air, wrapped in the solid strength of his arms, enfolded in the dark softness of his wings.

Tantalizin' lips brushed over hers as their feet touched ground at the crest of the footpath. "*More* than a friend," he murmured against her lips.

"Aye." She smiled. "Guardian. Protector. Lover."

He stared down at her, gaze hardenin' further. "More, even than that."

Brigid swallowed, throat crampin' from emotion. About to ask what he'd meant, sounds drifted to her ears. A rhythmic sound. Drums? And strains of a liltin' melody. From a lyre?

A cold north wind blew, carryin' the strains of a celebration, crisp and clear.

She glanced over her shoulder, toward a smudge of tree line due east.

"Have I manifested music?"

AFTER A GOODLY MARCH INLAND, as they followed the clear rhythm into the darkenin' night, they came upon the source of the sound.

With a tinglin' brush of magick, she alighted up onto a wide branch within an old-growth tree to spy on the celebration over a castle's curtain wall. In a thrice, Skorpius pressed against her side, the warm strength of his arm and wing draped around her shoulder.

Mesmerized by the revelry, she stared in silence as she took in the delightful scene.

Barn doors had been thrown wide.

A great bonfire blazed, orange flames lickin' up toward the sky.

Musicians played a tune while lads and lasses twirled.

Nigh two hundred Scots of all ages sprawled over the wide meadow between the barn the stone curtain wall below them. Wee ones toddled as they clutched a parent's hands. Two elder men sat on wooden stools, spinnin' tales to those who'd gathered near and leaned close, eager to hear.

Brigid gazed down at a world that seemed farther away than ever before. She sighed heavily, heart achin'. "Will I ever dance again?"

Skorpius gazed down at her. "Do you want to?"

She stared up into his beautiful eyes. They'd changed a wee bit. Sparklin' their normal blue-green with an inner glow against the darkness, they also appeared to spark with a different hue, like a flamin' sunset. At first, she'd thought it a reflection from the fire. But 'twas more than the orange of a flame. A tiny burst of scarlet flashed, then vanished.

After a heavy blink to clear her eyesight, his eyes shifted back their normal blue-green again. Then she reminded herself that while Skorpius had slept for four hours after their strenuous lovemakin', she had not. She hadn't eaten a bite either.

"Aye. *Someday*, I'd like to."

Not anytime soon, though.

Matters of greater import called her to duty. Begged her attention to defend their land, their verra world, from whatever hunted her power. For their threat sought to destroy all. Over the last days, she'd come to understand just how devastatin' the danger could be.

"Then *we* shall dance." Skorpius's fierce gaze held hers. "I promise you that."

The music ended. And shouts echoed into the night.

All crowded closer toward the open barn.

And in the bright glow of the bonfire, they were able to see the cause of the celebration.

Swaddled in blankets, a wee bairn was lifted high into the air by its proud da for all to see. 'Twas indeed a fine cause for celebration. The reason all her kinfolk toil in the gardens and fight in the forests. Defendin' their lands and protectin' their homes. For the loved ones brought up within'.

A strength rose up her spine.

The quiet depths of her loch warmed, bubblin' magick up.

And a clarity sharpened her mind, steeled her heart.

With the determination of the warrior she'd become, she stared up at her guardian, her protector, her lover—her *more* than a friend.

"Aye, angel mine." Brigid gave him a tender kiss, clasped his hand, then leapt from the tree and burst out into the night as she dematerialized, mistin' off toward the north.

First, we fight. For she felt a battle brewin', straight to her bones. *Then, we'll dance.*

CHAPTER 34

*S*korpius let Brigid lead him away through the night. For the first time in millennia, he relaxed into the ether.

And *enjoyed* himself.

Of course, he still kept an awareness on the dual tethers. Both hummed, but quietly.

He still burst a flare of magick outward, in threat assessment. Yet got no alert back.

Skorpius privately questioned her method of transport. If Brigid had received a strong enough connection through the vision, she'd likely be able to flash directly there, in both time and place.

But with the dual tethers' agreement with her chosen course of action, he didn't even mention the possibility. His interference could be a hindrance.

Her vision? Her call.

And they'd arrive at their destination soon enough. Face the destruction they'd witnessed. Carryout their directives: her calling, his mission.

Instead, for the time being, he marveled at her impressive

skill at "mistin'" through the ether. Even though they'd gone incorporeal, their energies remained connected by their mutual wish. But not just by their wish alone. By the new bond they'd created—heart to heart.

Skorpius had never before been tied to another. Not at an elemental level.

But instead of bucking the unique tie to another being, he welcomed it.

After being outcast by his kind, belonging to another—to his fierce yet kindhearted Brigid—filled him with an unusual warmth.

And as they traveled over the landscape, she flew faster than the leading edge of a storm front. But she kept them close to the ground. And, as she was their guide, he deferred to her preference. Since he'd not had firsthand experience with a deity who received visions, it seemed the wisest course.

Besides, the strength of her magick continued to grow at a remarkable pace. And the tethers of his mission appeared satisfied with the course.

Pine. Alder. Rowan. Soft-spoken mental identifiers from a female who loved her trees.

Chestnut, he added, enjoying their game. And learning something he'd never cared to pay attention to before: tree botany.

Warm amusement glittered from her essence.

They focused on their flight, and the tree-identifying to magnify their focus even further. Away from the direness of the situation.

But after a time, they just flew in companionable silence.

As the sun rose over the mountain peaks in the east, a heavier vibration rippled from her.

What are you thinking about?

What awaits us. She slowed their flight, veered them inland into thicker forest, then hovered over a game trail where she materialized. "We're approachin' the village."

The village from the vision. He solidified beside her. "How does it feel?"

She let out a long sigh, then glanced up at him. "Sadness. Anguish. Fear. And…"—silver sparked in her mercurial gaze —"*death*."

The heavy vibration he'd detected could have come from Brigid, or the filtered emotions from her vision.

Rather than continue on their original course, she wandered toward the edge of a sunny glade, where light swathed a diverse patch of wildflowers and weeds. Miraculously, the blooming plants flourished there in the dead of winter. As if the universe had manifested them just for her. Or she'd conjured them there. Even though he'd sensed no outreach of her magick.

Either she'd become excellent at masking her abilities or her connection with the elements had transcended her newly developed powers, had become second nature.

Yet like the first time when she'd run low on energy, Brigid began scooping up flower heads and plucking leaves, stuffing them into her mouth.

Skorpius fought a smile at her innate actions. Then he snuck out a stealth burst of his own magick to nourish the unusual patch. And the flowering plants multiplied in seconds.

Brigid squealed in delight at the display, then gathered up a wide variety flowers and herbs.

Still, he had to tease her. "What? No feast? No roast pig or stuffed swan?"

Clutching a large bouquet in each fist, she glanced toward him. "Nay. Plants give me greater—" She stared down at her harvest, then at the patch he'd enhanced.

Narrowing her eyes, she strode toward him while she pointed a fistful of flopping blossoms at him. "You…you *knew*! You dinna tell me the whole truth of it."

"If by 'knew' you mean that human food would cease to appeal, then yes. And I won't tell you something that's better learned by firsthand experience. I won't lie to you." Not anymore. Not as long as his mission didn't require an omission or subterfuge.

"Phytonutrients are better fuel." A simple fact.

Her accusing glare continued for a few beats, then she turned toward the center of the glade. She stared up at the sun while soaking its radiant heat into her skin. "As is the sun."

Indeed. A shimmering glow brightened over her skin within seconds. Her diaphanous gown flickered and sparked at the edges.

Skorpius, however, stayed back within the thicker forest, out of the draining light.

But as he stood in the cooling shadows, he detected another change within his body. Like his ability to utilize darkness had altered. Or his need to recharge from it had. Regardless, for the first time, he noticed a clear difference in his makeup. Not *bad* different. But different all the same. Perhaps the anomaly Orion had discovered had grown stronger. Or Skorpius's ability to sense it had.

Brigid spent a few more minutes charging in the direct sunlight, munching her flowers and herbs, then walked toward him.

She pressed her body up against his, skimmed her warmed fingers up his chest, then pressed her lips to his.

Skorpius wrapped his arms around her, kissing her with all the tender emotions his fractured heart had finally allowed him to feel. He had no idea how much time they had left together, but if she wanted to take a moment from her quest to celebrate their union, he would do more than oblige. He'd celebrate with her.

A tug vibrated hard on the timeline tether while they were lost in a sensual kiss.

At that exact moment, Brigid tensed and pulled back. She searched his eyes, brows furrowed.

"You felt that?"

"Aye." She clasped his hand, then began navigating their way along the game trail.

Although the trail was wider than most, likely heavily browsed upon by passing deer and elk, most parts were still too narrow to pass through side by side. Still maintaining physical form, and refusing to let go of his hand, she angled ahead at those narrower points while he followed close behind.

When they broke from thick forest into an open meadow, then walked side by side again, she squeezed his hand and glanced up at him. "Tell me of your birth."

Small talk. Distraction from the weight of the impending moment.

Easy question. But not so simple an answer. "I wasn't born."

That pert freckled nose wrinkled. Her brows twitched down. "You were not born?"

"No. Angels are created."

No point in hiding that fact from her. Very few humans knew of their origins.

But then, Brigid no longer remained human. Not even close. Not any longer.

And yet, much of her raw beauty came from a retained innocence.

Like the slight smile that played at the corner of her peachy-pink lips.

She paused, released his hand, and took two steps back as she stared at him with incredulity. "You came upon the world... fully fashioned?"

Fresh curiosity sent her gaze traveling up along the sweep of his wing from tip up to arch, down his chest, over his abs, the waistline of his leather pants, then lower. But when she reached the end of the line, she stared at his deconstructed military boots.

Skorpius scraped the scuffed toe across the dirt, closer to her.

She gave a heavy blink, scanned back up his body with a noted pause at his groin, then lifted her lovely face until that mesmerizing silvery gaze met his.

Sexual tension charged the air.

Her ivory cheeks flushed a pretty pink.

With a lazy smirk, he let her off the sexual hook. "Not *fully* fashioned." He thumped a thumb against the leather over his thighs. "We *do* get to dress ourselves."

She stepped closer. Rested her hand on his cheek. "Your eyes. The sparks in them?"

"An effect from magick. Windows into our souls."

"Your soul?"

"Yours too." He brushed a loose spiral from her forehead, tucked it behind her ear. "Your eyes swirl like molten silver, spark with the fire of your magick. *More energy* than matter."

She gave a heavy blink, then searched his eyes. "Aye. Yours spark too. With new colors."

"New colors?" More changes in him. All since he'd been exposed to her.

"Aye. At first, sapphire and emerald."

Normal. "And now?"

"Their base color's still blue and green. But the sparks have changed to tiny flashes of sunset: fiery amber and bright scarlet."

Interesting.

Before he had a chance to explore his changes further, Brigid furrowed a brow and turned. "We must go." Then she sprinted down the path. On foot.

Concerned, he brushed scanning magick outward, but detected no other force in the vicinity.

Then with a bead on their inner bond, Skorpius dematerialized. He pursued her, letting their tether guide his way.

In seconds, he caught up to her. But he gave her plenty of space, materializing in the shadows a safe distance behind her.

Brigid had stopped at a clear demarcation line. And what she witnessed visibly upset her, for her golden gown shimmered with greater energy, sparking brighter at its ends, as if a storm brewed inside her.

The ground she stood upon remained a rich brown, covered in the mottled colors of the forest floor. Green pines and leafy shrubs stretched out on either side of her, and backward.

Opposite her? A destroyed world.

A hundred-foot-wide swath of dark ash covered the earth.

Turmoil and anguish still vibrated through the space, time's haunting echo.

Moisture from Highland mists had settled over the scorched remains of where a lively village had once been, congealing the particles of ash into a fine layer of mud. But everything had been flattened. The only way he and Brigid had known what had come before? Her vision.

Skorpius stepped forward to stand beside her. A show of support.

She heaved out a mournful sigh then glanced up at him, tears glittering in her eyes. Pinching them shut, she shook her head. "'Tis my doin'. Were it not for me, *he* would not have struck... this place."

"No." He cupped a gentle hand to her cheek, waited for her to reopen her eyes. She needed to focus on her task, not be distracted by misplaced guilt. "You feel the tethers in me?"

"Aye." She hovered a splayed hand over his heart.

He clasped her hand, pressed it to his chest. "The tethers—for both of my missions—hum low, right and true. This action was meant to happen to align the timeline, to correct its course."

"But..."

Skorpius dipped his head down and silenced her protest with a soft kiss. Emotions running hot from both of them, he flared a dose of magick to channel their feelings into one that would best serve them: fortitude. Because most warriors hated the senseless destruction that happened around them, but they fought on for a noble cause, for a greater good.

"Focus on what we have the power to control," he reminded her. All they could do.

Gaze hardening, she gave a solemn nod. "Let worry afflict the weak-minded," she finished.

Then she straightened her spine, narrowed her eyes, and scanned over the scorched scene once again. She searched for a clue. A next step.

A brush of her golden magick radiated outward.

"*Och!*" She spun toward the north, then darted back through the forest. "Make haste!" she called over her shoulder.

Skorpius dematerialized, then chased after her. *You sense something. A given.*

Aye. Two *somethin's.*

SKORPIUS GHOSTED behind Brigid while she hiked on in her corporeal form. And she stayed within the living forest, pointedly avoiding the scorched dead zone. Even if she had to veer wide, skirting thick bramble.

Instinct appeared to influence her to avoid dematerializing.

Skorpius felt no compunction, the purer energy state as natural as breathing for his kind.

Fifteen minutes into the hike, the ash-covered section ended abruptly.

A crumbled low stone wall curved beyond the end of the destruction. The side facing southward was coated in black soot. A wooden gate had been blown or bent back, ripped off one hinge, and hung cockeyed with its bottom corner buried in mud. Fern fronds that curved over the wall from the north bobbed in the breeze.

Brigid climbed the stone wall, right beyond where the destruction ended. And as before, she kept her footfalls well within the untouched section of land.

Skorpius didn't question her choice. His gut told him *more* than death lay under all that ash. An eerie dread. Something not natural.

Yet if her senses told her to avoid the ashen terrain and press on, they didn't need to investigate the reason.

Skorpius dematerialized to pass through the wall, then followed her, a few paces back.

A wooden hut soon appeared at the edge of a copse of trees. Its small size seemed indicative of a storage structure or a very small abode. Yet it had been neglected and had succumbed to the ravages of time. The thatched roof, covered in moss, had partially caved in. A wooden shutter that had once covered the window had grayed and weathered, the ends falling victim to rot. The doorway stood open, no door in view.

Brigid paused at that dark doorway.

And as she did so, Skorpius detected faint emotion rippling through the space around them. Heavy. Of distress. And terror.

The golden energy of her dress shimmered from the emotional effect, the flowing ends of the gown sparking.

But rather than enter the structure, Brigid scanned overgrown foliage around the hut.

Skorpius, will you materialize, but remain some distance back?

Yes.

The moment he took solid form, he detected a further tense vibration. Then he reflected on what Brigid had said she'd sensed earlier, *"two somethin's."*

But his senses clarified that into two some*ones*. Young. Frightened.

After quiet seconds of staring off at the denser foliage, Brigid backed up a few steps, to stand in front of the decaying structure again. Then her appearance changed, shifting from the golden diaphanous gown into the emerald one he'd fashioned for her and that she'd worn that night into the foreign castle.

She glanced down at her dress, then over her shoulder where her satchel and weapons had been obscured and continued to remain so. And with a satisfied nod, she ventured back out into the open, around the corner from the hut.

Facing the foliage, she called out, voice soft. "Doona be afraid. 'Tis safe. We've come…to protect you."

Silence followed.

When seconds spanned into a minute, then another, she glanced over her shoulder at him. *Mayhap, they might respond to you.*

That could go either way.

My past wee brothers were in awe of you.

Fair point. Skorpius stepped forward to stand beside her. And as he did so, he angled his wings down to indicate the best image of friendliness he could.

"This is a guardian angel I've brought. He's sworn to protect."

Brigid left out a vast amount of details and exclusions to that. But if it served her purpose, Skorpius was not about to contradict her white lie.

Another long span of seconds stretched by.

Then a dense section of bushes began to quiver.

Two young children wrestled free of the foliage. Dirt and soot smudged their faces and hands. Dried leaves and other plant matter speckled their tangled blond hair and torn clothes.

Both stared at Skorpius and Brigid with wide eyes. The smaller of the two clung to the elder's side, then furrowed a tiny brow and pressed that smudged face into the other's tunic.

The elder, a protector, put an arm around the younger's shoulder.

"I'm Connell." The boy squared his shoulder. Lifted his chin.

Brave. Especially in light of all that had happened, the destruction of their village.

Brigid tipped her head toward him. "'Tis verra nice to meet you, Connell."

"My sister, Gunna." He squeezed the little one's shoulder.

"We're honored to meet you, Gunna." *Och! Connell canna be older than five summers. She's mayhap three.*

Shy eyes peeked up at Brigid from the folds of her brother's tunic. Gunna then stared wide-eyed at Skorpius, before eyeing Brigid once again.

"I'm Brigid. This is Skorpius."

"The *goddess*, Brighid?" Connell whispered in awe.

Brigid began to shake her head. "Na—"

"Yes." Skorpius interjected before she had a chance to deny it. "She's Goddess Brighid." Goddess of their homeland. A deity they pray to, honor, and love.

They know. Honesty will hold sway with them. And we need them to cooperate.

Aye.

Don't hide who you are. Be yourself in all things.

Connell's eyes narrowed. "Prove your claim."

When Brigid glanced at Skorpius, he gave an imperceptible nod.

With a whirl of her magick, Brigid's emerald dress shifted back to its natural state, her golden diaphanous gown that shimmered and sparked with her energy. And the copper coils of her hair fluffed into a halo about her face, the ends fluttering softly in an unseen breeze.

The children's eyes widened further. Connell's mouth dropped open.

Brigid knelt before little Gunna, and with slow deliberate movement, plucked a dried leaf from the girl's hair.

At the same time, a shining golden leaf manifested in a lower spiral of Brigid's hair.

Gunna almost smiled when she caught sight of the magick-spun gift.

Brigid cradled the ends of her copper coils in the cup of her hand and lifted the nested treasure toward the little girl in offering.

At first, the girl remained immobile. But then she blinked, took a deep breath, and reached a tiny trembling hand for the golden leaf. With impressive speed, she plucked it from Brigid's hair.

"For you, wee Gunna."

The girl fisted her hand tight around her gift. But said nothing.

Brigid stood, glancing at Skorpius. *I recognize them.*

You do?

Two of the three children from the glade a sennight past. The ones who'd been fleein' English soldiers.

A ripple of panic shot through the ether from Brigid. "Where's your brother?"

Connell frowned, then anger hardened over his expression. "He...*took*...Robert. Yester morn."

At her brother's words and rage, tears welled in Gunna's eyes and her lower lip wobbled. She buried her face into Connell's tunic again.

"Who?" Skorpius asked. "*Who* took Robert?"

"I *doona* know." Tears welled in the boy's eyes as well. His shoulders slumped, the bravery draining from him as he searched his memory, reliving whatever horrific experience they'd had to endure. "Some great flamin' beast we couldna see."

"Flaming?" *The more he can share, the better equipped we'll be.*

"Aye." Connell tightened an arm around Gunna again, doing his best to comfort her. "Fire shot out from…from the *sky*."

"How do you know 'twas a beast?"

"The heavy beat of unseen wings." Connell paused, staring up at the sky above Bridid's shoulder. "The roar right before the fire."

Brigid stood and turned, then surveyed the enormous swath of ash beyond the low stone wall. Her brow furrowed. She glanced at Skorpius, then at Gunna, finally at Connell once again.

How did they survive when the others dinna?

By chance, Skorpius guessed. *Or by design.* More likely, with the threat from her vision.

"Where were you when the flamin' beast came?"

Good. Focus on them. Not the trauma. As much as they could.

"We were playin' hide-and-hunt." Connell glanced back into the forest. "Gunna and me hid up in a tree."

I doona wish to frighten them. But we need to know more.

May I? Skorpius had an idea.

Aye.

With measured steps, Skorpius moved closer to the children, then knelt down on one knee before them. He spread his wings, propped a forearm on his bent knee, then bowed, lowering his head below their height. A position of humble submission, of utmost respect. And the rare sight of his glossy black wings didn't hurt.

After a full breath, he glanced up and stared young Connell straight in the eye. Male to male. "It takes a brave warrior to face down a ferocious beast"—Skorpius leaned in closer, lowering his voice—"Braver still to relive the tale, to aid in the hunt."

Connell swallowed hard, then squared his shoulders, puffing out his chest. "I'm a brave warrior."

"Yes. *Both* of you are." Skorpius glanced at Gunna who shook her head, then buried her face into her brother's tunic again.

"Gunna?" Skorpius softened his voice. "Is there something you wish to say?"

Connell shook his head. "Nay. She'll not speak a word. Hasn't since…" He tightened his arm around his sister. "We'll be huntin'?"

"No." Skorpius stared at the brave Connell again. "*Goddess Brighid and I* are on the hunt."

Brigid stepped forward, "Aye. 'Tis true. And we're here to rescue your brother."

"He's alive?"

"Aye. He is." Brigid didn't offer the details. A hostage for a ransom. The child for her. "Mayhap you can tell us what happened? How did the beast 'take' him?"

Connell huffed out a frustrated exhale. "Gunna and me were up in the tree. Robert leaned upon the woodcutter's cottage, countin' off." He stared out over the village. "We watched the flame come down from the sky. It…they…" His breathing shallowed and his eyes pinched shut.

Skorpius laid a gentle hand on the boy's shoulder. "It's okay, Connell. Focus on your brother. Help us save him."

After several deep breaths, Connell blinked his eyes open. He swiped the back of his hand across his wet lashes, smearing tears through soot across his forehead. "The fire happened so fast. It blazed straight for us. I held my breath, thinkin' we were dead. But Robert had cried, 'Hidden or not, here I—' and the flame stopped, right at the stone wall. Robert flew up from the ground an' started screamin'." Connell rattled off the whole explanation with speed. But now he trembled, breaths shallow, complexion ghostly white.

"And then?" Brigid coaxed with a gentle voice. "What happened to our brave Robert?"

"He vanished," Connell whispered. "Right up in the sky. I thought he got"—he gulped—"eaten."

"Nay." Brigid stepped forward and gave the huddled children a gentle hug, mostly on Connell's side. "I assure you, Robert is still verra much alive."

"Where is he?" Connell asked.

"We doona know yet. The beast is playin' his own game of hide-and-hunt."

Connell frowned. "With Robert?"

"Aye. And with Skorpius and me."

"Will you find him?" Connell looked at Brigid, then stared Skorpius straight in the eye.

Skorpius knew the madman they were dealing with. But the method? The fire? The invisible beast? The vanishing child and a ransom to exchange control of a goddess's powers? All a first in the vast reaches of time. Who knew what odds they faced of finding the boy alive.

Honesty will hold sway with them, Brigid reminded him as she stepped back from them.

Understood.

Reveal only what was necessary.

"Yes, Connell," Skorpius replied. "We will find your brother."

CHAPTER 35

*A*n ache burned in Brigid's chest, heart breakin' for the poor wee ones.

Garb soiled and tattered, hair matted, skin dirt-caked, their eyes were red-rimmed. They'd likely not gotten a wink of sleep.

Takin' care to respect young Gunna's shyness and fear, Brigid touched the hem of Connell's tunic with her finger, then plucked her golden gown wide and glanced down.

"May I use my magick to help you bathe, and mend your clothes?"

Gunna clung harder at her brother's tunic, fists clutched so tight they turned white.

"Will it hurt?" Connell rubbed a hand over his sister's bare arm.

"Nay." Then Brigid thought about the sensation. "A wee bit of a tingle. Warm, mayhap."

Connell gave a short nod. "Me first." He untangled himself from Gunna's clutches, then stepped forward.

Brigid brushed magick over the lad with a shimmer of golden light. Her intention through the energy was to make the lad and his clothes whole again. And while she did so, she also flared out magick into the sky above them to dissipate the mist and let the warmin' sun through.

Connell glanced down as his garb transformed back into a fresh wool tunic and trews, with woolen hose and new leather boots on his feet. Clean blond locks gleamed in the sunlight. Pristine creamy skin radiated health and vitality.

He turned toward his sister. "'Tis fine, Gunna. Doona be afraid."

Puffin' her wee chest out, Gunna furrowed her brow, expression fierce. Hands fisted by her sides, one still clutchin' the golden leaf tight, she took a step forward.

"You're a brave lass," Brigid murmured. "Would you like your tunic?" Her garb appeared to match her brother's. "Or would you like a dress instead?"

After a quick glance at Connell, Gunna stared wide-eyed at Brigid's flowing golden gown. She pointed at the gown.

"Mayhap a simple chemise and day dress." From an impoverished village, the dress would likely be her first.

With a flourish of magick, the wee lass's transformation swirled from head to toe.

Long blond locks took on a bright healthy sheen, twistin' into perfect ringlets. A bonnie yellow day dress settled onto a crisp linen chemise. Woolen hose covered her legs and new leather boots snugged around her feet. Fresh skin glowed, pinkin' at her cheeks when Gunna glanced down and ventured her first wee smile. Brigid even added a front pocket to the day dress, to hold a certain golden leaf, if Gunna chose.

To protect them from the wind and cold, Brigid draped hooded woolen cloaks about each of their shoulders.

Satisfied with their physical state, Brigid's thoughts shifted to the next priority.

"You must be hungry." She gestured an arm toward a grassy spot in the sun, beside the woodcutter's cottage.

With another wave of magick, she snapped a plaid into the

air there. By the time the fabric settled to the ground, every favorite food she'd loved as a child—still loved—manifested upon it. Stuffed goose. Gravied parsnips. Roasted root vegetables. Stewed cherries. Apple tarts with warmed honey. Wineskins filled with artesian water. And she even added a cinnamon-spiced snickerdoodle for each of them.

The wee ones dashed to the feast and dove in with both hands, stuffin' their mouths.

Brigid stepped into Skorpius's arms. "Guess I'll need to clean them once again."

"Worth it." He gave her a brief squeeze, then kissed the top of her head.

She rested a hand over his chest as she watched them eat. "What are we to do with them?"

Skorpius glanced back at the wee ones. "They can't come with us."

Brigid's heart ached so heavily for them, she found it hard to draw breath. And yet she forced the air in, then let out a heavy sigh.

"They've no ma, no da." They'd have a hard time in life. She knew that hardship well.

"They'll survive. Perhaps be stronger for it." He glanced down at her, then kissed her softly. "You are."

Mayhap she'd become the warrior she was because of it.

The pull of her quest tugged at her, a vivid reminder. "But aye, they canna journey with us."

"They'd continue to be at great risk."

As Connell and Gunna feasted, she and Skorpius stood in silence, conteplatin' the matter.

Only one idea surfaced. "You're duty-bound to obey my command."

"To a degree. Yet I'd carry out your request, duty or not."

"Then take them somewhere safe." Brigid couldn't give them

a new ma and da. But she could give them the closest thing, what she'd had. "They need a clan of their own." Scots were Scots. The wee ones were kin to them all.

"*I'm* to deliver them?" Skorpius asked.

"I canna leave; the callin' to my task is urgent. But the danger for them grows."

"You need to follow the clues of your vision."

"Aye. On with the hunt."

Skorpius stared at her, displeasure clear in his expression. "I won't leave you for long."

"Mayhap the castle we'd passed." With the music and dancin'. With the celebration of the new bairn.

Skorpius let out a long sigh, but said naught.

Within minutes, the children had devoured all they could.

Wee Gunna plucked her golden leaf up from the plaid, then dropped it into her dress pocket. She then picked up a snicker-doodle with two hands and tucked the cookie into her pocket as well. Connell offered Gunna his cookie, which was promptly deposited with the first.

"Are you well enough to travel?" Brigid asked, washin' the two children in magick again to clean their food-covered faces and hands.

"Aye." Connell stood and tugged his sister up beside him.

"Very well." Skorpius gave Brigid a chaste kiss, then pinned her with a stern look filled with all manner of unspoken warnin'.

She gave him a nod of understandin'. *I'll take great care.*

Then Skorpius stepped toward the wee ones. "Now it's my turn for some magick. Gunna, hold Connor's hand tight and don't let go. We're about to fly like angels do."

At once, Brigid felt a sense of dread at their imminent departure. "Skorpius!" she called out, hand shot to her breast—over their hearts' bond.

Skorpius stared at her with fierce intensity. Then he placed a hand on Connell's shoulder. And the three of them vanished from sight.

Brigid gasped in sudden panic.

For the strong bond she felt to Skorpius?

Vanished with him.

BRIGID FORCED A CALMIN' breath into her lungs.

"'Tis but a moment's work," she murmured to herself.

Skorpius promised he wouldn't leave for long.

And the inner draw to continue on with her journey intensified. Therefore, she calmed her emotions, emptied her thoughts, and followed where the energy led.

The unusual draw presented as a hot vibration. Nigh an itchin'-ache of sorts. Made her anxious to relieve the sensation. And she'd learned that when she faced the direction true to her course, the uncomfortable tension it caused began to ease. Akin to bein' led by an invisible thread.

After a short walk along a footpath, she emerged from the thicker wood and encountered a road. An open glade stretched beyond it with only a handful of snow patches that still clung to the shade of large rocks. But over the sundrenched road, soot and dust covered the surface.

With Skorpius's warnin' glare firm in her mind, she burst up a shield of protective magick many layers thick, outside of her body. Then she walked along the road, followin' the draw.

Till the hot vibration intensified.

Uncertain what the change meant, she paused at that spot.

Naught but windin' road stretched ahead and behind. Forest sprawled to the east. Glade, forest, then mountains spanned to the west.

A clear blue sky gleamed overhead.

When she broadened her awareness, thousands of heartbeats vibrated back, from birds, small creatures, and insects. She filtered out all of those, searchin' for a distinct human heartbeat. But she found none.

Skorpius's words echoed into her mind: *Follow the clues of your vision.*

A clue. Some sign of where to go next.

But the energy-path ended right there.

She stared down at the sooted dusty road. *The vision's scorched message.*

With a subtle brush of magick that burst as a gustin' wind upon the ground, she lifted the day's worth of buildup, which swept away on the breeze. And there beneath, lay the dire warnin' from her vision still scorched onto the earth: **Become mine. Or the child serves in your stead.**

Hot fury rose within her. But she knew the emotion did her no good, hindered even.

So she centered herself within, found the calm depths of her magick loch.

From that quiet place, she checked that her outer shield still held, kept her obscured from view in the physical realm.

Then she energized the powerful magick within her loch, swirled it forth, examined the message for the any "clues" through the energy of her magick. And the substance of the scorched earth vibrated back to her. A unique energy essence. Other than from Earth-realm. Different than her magick.

Flashin' out from that point in all directions, the conclusion became clear: He'd stolen Robert away...somewhere *verra* far away.

The moment she came to that revelation, the message began to vanish, sinkin' down under the soil till it became indistinguishable. The earth lost all sign of foreign energy, had become ordinary ground again.

Yet one other clue that had been lifted from the message remained with her.

The oily dark scent of the one she hunted: *Merlin.*

CHAPTER 36

Skorpius transported the children to the only place they'd be safe. From any threat.

The realm of angels.

Not exactly the clan Brigid had had in mind.

But the dangerous situation warranted the detour.

Not forever. But for now.

Because none of them could afford to have Brigid distracted.

They paused in the entryway of his realm, to give the children a chance to get acclimated to their surroundings. For to flash from the colorful realm of Earth into the angelic realm's total whiteout took the uninitiated a moment of adjustment.

Both of them gasped in surprise.

"You're safe here," he assured them. "This is my home." A label he hadn't used for the place in ages, but language they'd understand as something comforting.

Eyes widened at the foreign environment, they clung to one another silently.

Skorpius watched them carefully. They'd already suffered enormous shock and loss. Had their home decimated. An entirely new plane of existence pushed their boundaries even further.

Yet he'd not accounted for one particular aspect: No young had ever appeared in his realm.

At first, Connell and Gunna experimented with the cloud-like environment. The ground beneath their feet, though firm, gave a little, bobbing and swaying ever so slightly with movement. And no ceiling existed above. Nor walls around. Only endless amounts of whiteness.

In actuality, all were crystalline particles of varying densities. White in mass, but iridescent when floating or swirling.

"*Mist*," Connell murmured with awe.

Mist. The closest approximation humans could understand.

Connell and Gunna took small steps, learning to walk with the slight movement. Gunna even let go of her brother. Fully absorbed in the wonder around her, she swooshed both hands through the iridescent particles.

And then, to all of their surprise—Skorpius included—the mist reacted to them.

One at a time, playful tendrils unfurled toward them, reaching out to kiss their skin. To begin, at the tip of a finger or the back of a forearm. Others soon brushed across their cheeks, tapped their noses.

Gunna's free laughter at the curious childlike mist tinkled into the muting space.

Connell glanced at his sister, relief evident in his expression, then laughed with her.

The sound of their joy was music to Skorpius's ears. That they'd adapt. Survive.

Not to mention that if the mist that comprised his world accepted the children as friend, the rest of angelkind were bound to. Or so Skorpius hoped.

Skorpius let the children and mist play together for a time.

But once both settled, calming to a degree of acceptance and peace with one another, Skorpius cast a message out into the ether.

Moments later the mist swirled as another approached.

"Cass," Skorpius bowed his head.

"Skorpius!" A warm smile brightened her face. She strode forward, a faint vanilla scenting the air as she moved alongside him. She brushed a wing against his in affectionate greeting.

Gasps from the children drew her attention down.

"Oh, *my*..." Cass stared wide-eyed at the newcomers. Then she blinked and stared at him. "Tell me they are not..."

"Mine?" Skorpius lifted his brows. "Just exactly what do you think I've been up to?"

"Not procreating, then."

He snorted. "Not sure if that's even possible."

"You've evolved into something different than the rest of us." She shrugged. "Who knows?" Cass moved in front of him, then assessed him with narrowed eyes. "You've...transformed...yet again."

"It seems I still am." Once he'd initially detected the change, he'd become able to sense the minute changes. Not that he understood what the new evolution meant. He still hadn't grasped the full extent of what transforming dark had encompassed.

"And so the..." Cass nodded toward the tiny silent but enraptured audience.

"Children," Skorpius supplied. *Human*, he further clarified on the mental plane, beyond sensitive and innocent ears. *Just orphaned.*

They lost their parents?

Not only their parents. Their entire village was destroyed. And they remain in grave danger.

Cass glanced at him. *From the destroyer of said village.*

Exactly.

Her expression hardened. *Otherworldly.*

He gave an imperceptible nod. *Wouldn't be here otherwise.*

"Let me guess. I'm to be their guardian?"

"Do you have another mission?" Skorpius wouldn't impose if she had other duties.

"No." Cass squared her shoulders, then nudged his shoulder with hers. "Consider this mine."

She then strolled toward the little ones with an outstretched hand. "Hello you two, my name is Cassiopeia." Arrowing her wings back, she squatted before them. "But I have a feeling we're going to be very good friends. And my friends call me Cass."

The boy took his sister's hand, then clasped Cass's. "I'm Connell. And this is—"

With hard headshake and furrowed brow, the girl separated from him. Then she held out her own tiny hand. "Gunna," she offered in a lilting voice, soft-spoken but firm.

Cass, that's the first time *the girl has spoken.*

The first of many challenges she will face. They both will.

He had no doubt. *Thank you.* He punched the small words with great depth.

You are welcome. Cass loaded hers with great meaning as well. *But consider yourself indebted.*

Skorpius chuckled as he began to dematerialize. *Already do.*

SKORPIUS FLASHED BACK TO EARTH-REALM, anxious to reunite with Brigid.

Which he found both surprising and invigorating.

After almost a millennium of cynical solitude, his fractured heart had finally caved. With something even greater than love for him. Hope.

Instead of tapping into either of his mission threads, both of which hummed steadily, he grounded himself along their new hearts' tether. And with a touch of magick, he relaxed back into the ether to let their bond lead him to her.

As he ghosted through the Highland forest, gaining speed along their thread, he called tree names out to her with a warm smile.

Pine.

Fir.

Alder.

Amusement glittered through the ether back toward him. *Chestnut.* A pause, then erotic heat radiated through. *Yew.*

Their trees. The first, on business. The second? Pure pleasure.

My favorite.

Mine as well. Another pause stretched, then she rippled out curiosity. *Where are you?*

Skorpius sighted her golden essence up ahead, slowed his speed, then brushed up against her, tugging her out of the slipstream. *Right here.*

Knocked safely over open ground, they solidified into a sensual embrace, arms wrapped around one another.

Damn, I've missed you. He lowered his head, molding his lips to hers in a hungry kiss.

Aye. And I, you. Her hands twisted into his hair at the nape.

Their kiss intensified for long seconds, until she broke away.

Shafts of sunlight speared down through the trees, gleaming off the copper spirals of her hair. A healthy pink colored her freckle-dusted cheeks. Luscious lips, glossed from their kiss, tugged into a flirting smile.

But mercurial silver eyes sparked at him while she caught her breath. "They're safe?"

"They are."

Her slender brows lifted slightly. "A good home?"

"The best home." For now.

But Brigid didn't ask. And he didn't elaborate. Her focus was paramount to all.

"Any clues?"

"Aye. And *nay*." She gave a frustrated headshake. "Robert and..."—her expression hardened as she sucked in a deep breath and refused to speak their enemy's name—"*they* are no longer here. In Earth-realm."

"Yet you found something. You've covered some ground in the short hour I've been gone."

"Aye. 'Tis the pull. When I relax into my magick, I'm drawn toward a place I must go."

Goddess magick. Something Skorpius had no experience with. No angel ever had.

"Well, then. Lead on." He had no other course but to continue his role. To support. And monitor.

She clasped his hand, then picked her way toward a footpath. "We're near."

Skorpius entwined his fingers through hers as she led the way. The path wasn't wide enough to accommodate his wings, but he didn't say anything. Instead, he dematerialized only his wings—an act that took greater energy than even maintaining solid form in bright sunlight—just to keep hold of her hand. Because he enjoyed the simple possessive act.

The pull grows strong. 'Tis beginnin' to vibrate.

Listen. Stretch your hearing outward. An ability he knew she innately possessed, no magick required. She'd exhibited it at their first encounter. But even innate preternatural skills required practice.

Skorpius listened as well.

Through the normal cacophony of noise in a lively forest, other faint sounds filtered through: scrapes of steel over leather, domesticated animal and human breaths, clinks of settling metal, the occasional whispered word.

Brigid squeezed his hand, then paused, drawing him along-side her. *A party of men move ahead.*

Some on foot. Others on horseback, he added.

Aye.

And you're to engage them?

I believe so. After a brief contemplative pause, she nodded. *Aye.*

Skorpius did an internal check as well. The guardian tether? Hummed low. No threat. However, the timeline tether's vibration had not only increased, but grown erratic.

Whatever had to happen with the impending encounter had unpredictable results.

He nearly snorted. Unpredictable? Story of his life.

"Then let's proceed to engage," he murmured, no longer concerned about being detected. He gestured an arm forward. "After you, goddess."

For the outcome apparently depended on her.

Skorpius steeled his heart, preparing to deal with the timeline fallout. One way or another.

CHAPTER 37

*S*korpius didn't attempt to mask their approach.
And neither did Brigid.

Which served two purposes: announced their arrival and identified their quarry.

Because in a wordless instant, the group of men scattered. With near-preternatural stealth. And astonishing coordination.

Only one brand of human warrior possessed such skill—besides Iain's elite guard of Highlanders.

Skorpius said nothing.

Brigid would discover for herself soon enough.

And the timeline's chaotic quivering mandated he remain an observer. For the moment.

"We mean you no harm," Brigid murmured, but with magick brushed through her words to echo them into every ear in attendance.

"M'Lady?" A rustling of leaves preceded a familiar male stepping into view. Blond. Short hair, long beard. Cloaked in black.

"Wilhelm." Brigid tilted her head, as if in contemplation.

Skorpius contemplated with her. *No coincidence*, he offered. *All tied together.* Somehow.

Aye, she agreed. "What brings you here." She glanced around, searching for his brothers.

Wilhelm whistled. Apparently an "all clear" signal, for the surrounding forest came alive with similarly shorn and clad men.

Templars. Skorpius made no secret of their identity to her. Brigid needed to know.

Aye. Confidence strengthened her tone. She'd either figured it out or wholeheartedly agreed.

A dozen men appeared around them at close perimeter. Brigid spun in a slow circle, taking in every face. Skorpius stood beside her and did the same. Unmistakable in his support.

But then, the unthinkable happened.

One face stood apart from the rest.

Skorpius recognized him at the same instant Brigid did.

A soft gasp of shock sounded beside him.

Brigid took two steps forward, then paused on the third.

"Finn?" She frowned, then blinked in disbelief.

Skorpius held fast.

The timeline thread snapped taut, then vibrated.

Whatever transpired between those two had dire consequences. Which required him to stand down. One directive he refused to break—by Brigid's agreement as much as his own—was to not interfere in how events played out, not to imperil the timeline. The realm they stood within, and countless others, depended on what Brigid did with her enormous power when challenged. Good or evil. For others, or for herself.

And the challenge before her? Colossal.

To Skorpius's surprise, when the male took a step forward and pivoted fully to face her, the symbol on his shield revealed from where he now hailed.

After another heavy blink, Brigid's jaw fell open as she stared at the warrior she knew who'd gone missing all those months ago—the Brodie Clan guardsman she'd been betrothed to.

Yet as the blond Viking held her stunned gaze, he winced. Then his expression twisted into one of regret...brewed with a heavy dose of guilt.

Ah, so you'd known, Skorpius thought to himself. *You'd kept a secret from her too.*

That Fingall hadn't returned for a reason. That Clan Brodie no longer held his allegiance. That he'd sworn fealty to a higher power. And no longer had the luxury, nor the inclination, to offer any woman his heart and body.

"*Och,* Brigid." Fingall took two tentative steps forward, halving the ten-foot distance between them, then stopped. "'Twas the only way."

A defeated sigh gusted from the male's lungs.

Then Fingall stared over her shoulder.

His unfocused gaze froze, sharpening as it locked on to Skorpius.

Yeah. Here we go.

The Viking rapidly blinked. Anger shot his bushy brows downward. Tension clenched a pronounced jaw. A quick jerk liberated the warrior's sword from its leather scabbard, whispering its ring into the cool misty air.

The sword's tip aimed at Skorpius's breastbone as Fingall strode forward. "*You!*"

Brigid furrowed her brow at Fingall, then swung her attention toward Skorpius.

Then both men centered their full attention on one another.

"*Thought* we might meet again." Not really. But it sounded like a good conversation starter.

"I *dinna.*" Fingall circled around him, edging ever closer, while he pointed the tip of his blade at various vital parts, outlining the order in which he planned to carve him to pieces.

"'Twas the only way," Skorpius repeated the male's words back to him. That fact seemed relevant to point out.

A hot burst of magick shocked Skorpius's senses.

Fingall gasped, stunned as well. The Viking stumbled back a couple of steps, sword swinging wide before it flew right out of his hand.

Brigid flashed between the two males.

But she narrowed her eyes at Skorpius, accusation in her glare.

Shimmering gold radiated from her skin. Dark pink flushed her cheeks. The ends of her golden gown fluttered, whipping in an unseen wind. Tiny flashes sparked into the air around her, energy that fired out from her core.

Oh, you are furious.

But Skorpius had been waiting for the inevitable to happen. That shoe he'd tossed into the air all those months ago had to drop with a ground-shaking thud at some point. The timeline had a twisted sense of humor. And Skorpius had long been its favorite toy.

"*What* was the only way?" Brigid stared at him for an expectant moment, before shifting her gaze to Fingall.

The Viking's attention strayed back to Brigid. A brief look of longing flashed into his eyes, seconds before the warrior schooled his expression. "My devotion to the order. Protectin' a great treasure, one more precious than any of my earthly wants."

Ah. Well played, Highlander.

Because who's heart doesn't melt when the hero's sacrifice was for the greater good?

Fingall glanced toward his brother Templars. "We've all forsaken family ties, given away worldly possessions."

Brigid stepped closer to him, shoulders rigid, jaw clenched tight, fury banked in those glacial gray eyes. "And you dinna think to send word?"

"Aye. I thought of it. 'Twas no time. And we dinna have a spare man to send."

"Not yourself?"

"Nay. I...*we*...needed..." He ran a hand over his short head of hair, frustration twisting his expression. "Och, Brigid. I had things I needed to learn. Of great import."

"Things."

"The mysteries."

"*Secrets.*"

"Aye." Fingall opened his mouth. Shut it. Then opened it again. Snapped it shut once more. Like he'd become a fish out of water, gasping for oxygen. Myriad emotions flashed across the male's face. It was obvious the Viking wanted to tell her more, but couldn't.

Brigid shot a hot glare Skorpius's way. "And *you?*"

Skorpius opened his mouth. But wisely shut it as well. What could he say: I tried to tell you? Not in a thousand millennia.

Brigid didn't wait for his reply anyway.

Keeping Skorpius targeted in her sights, she strolled toward Fingall, stepped behind him, then around him. Standing shoulder to shoulder with the Viking, she leaned his way and crossed her arms. She narrowed her eyes at Skorpius. "How do you know the dark angel?"

"He'd be the one who attacked me."

"*Reassigned* you," Skorpius corrected.

"While I slept."

Ah, but you'd awakened halfway through. "While you were *docile.*" Because, although Skorpius had dematerialized the warrior from one location and rematerialized him into another, in an instant, the shift had awakened the Viking.

"You *froze* me," he gruffed.

"I *immobilized* you." No subzero temps required.

He'd have knocked the bastard out with his fist, but that would've left a mark. And magick-induced sleep had dangers for the victim. Fingall's risk had multiplied tenfold when adrenaline had spiked enough in his system to enable him to wrap his enormous hands around Skorpius's neck in a chokehold on instinct. Immobilization had been the only way. "Safety first." His own and the Viking's.

Fingall's nostrils flared, a bull seeing red. But the male said nothing further.

Brigid left Fingall's side and took measured steps toward Skorpius in the silence.

"*You* were the cause of Finn vanishin'?"

Skorpius almost argued the point that Fingall hadn't vanished. That the Viking had been exactly where he'd been destined to be all along. But that wasn't what Brigid was zeroing in on. Her pointed unasked question? Was the heartache she'd suffered for months Skorpius's fault? *Possibly.*

"Yes." Up front and center. Cold hard truth.

"And *you* dinna think to tell me?"

"Not my secret to tell." Not as her guardian, not unless she specifically asked. But she hadn't pulled on that personal thread, had actually tied it off, refused to listen to his confession. And definitely not as the protector of time. Back then, he'd done it to preserve the timeline; Isobel's coming as Traveler had demanded the deceptive action.

Brigid inhaled deeply. An aura of magick began to coalesce around her, the palest shimmer in the air taking flight. Probing magick scanned through him as her astute gaze searched his. "Someone *else* has gone missin'."

Skorpius didn't bother playing dumb. But didn't answer either.

Brigid's eyes narrowed. She'd caught scent of the trail, a way to discover what she sought. "Where are the wee ones?"

"Not my secret to tell." Bold truth.

"But you know where."

"Yes. I do." Tucked far of danger's reach, like she'd asked. But banished to another realm, *out of her reach*. Not for just the children's welfare, but because the timeline had decided those children could hold a key to its preservation. As a backup plan. In case Skorpius failed.

The magick Brigid had been gathering flared hotter, vibrated faster. "Safe."

"Of course."

"So, you...lied."

On multiple occasions. "Yes."

"About Fingall."

No point in restating the obvious. Skorpius cast her a *don't-make-me-say-it* look.

"About the children."

His gaze held hers, unwavering. Truth there for her to see. *Don't ask*, he begged. *I won't be able to divulge more.*

"What else have you lied about?"

And you had to ask.

Skorpius sighed. "I'm only able to reveal what's necessary for the mission."

"For the mission."

"Yes."

"What about for me?"

For the warrior. For the goddess. For the female. *His female.*

Skorpius took a tentative step closer, lowering his voice. "Brigid." A subtle plea tinged his tone.

She stood too close to the Viking. The male no longer posed a threat to Brigid; he'd offered his soul to a greater cause. But there were things that remained private.

Between two beings who'd both once been human. Who'd since become other. Who still both retained shreds of their humanity. And had shared those last tender shreds with one another, heart to heart.

Sensing Skorpius's apprehension and suspecting why, Brigid glanced up at Fingall.

Then she powered down her aggression. The magick storm that had begun to churn faded away into swirling wisps, then vanished into nothingness.

After a last stern look at Fingall, she turned her back on the male she'd been betrothed to.

But her unforgiving gaze tracked Skorpius as she stalked off to the side, toward the edge of the forest.

When Brigid reached the edge of the shadows cast by the tree canopy, she shifted her attention away, then stared out across a sunny field of heather.

Skorpius followed at a respectful pace, giving her ample time to process the revelations. Most of which were facts he'd known for a while.

Silent seconds ticked by.

Torn between keeping his distance and comforting her, Skorpius split the difference and stepped close behind her. But he didn't presume to touch. Kept his wings and hands to himself.

"You knew all along," she muttered. The accusation was devoid of emotion. Tone flat and low, she'd only confirmed the fact.

Her gaze remained stuck toward the horizon to the south.

Their secret glade lay somewhere out there.

A place where they'd let down their guard. Where they'd forged delicate bonds of trust. Where they'd connected, had found commonality with another in the vastness of the universe, celebrated who they were together. And accepted their differences. Resigned to their limitations. And their fate.

"Most of it." The time for full confession weighed heavy between them. But as the timeline had mandated his silence before, at her behest now, his duty required the truth. What portions he was permitted to disclose.

"And the rest." Still with the flat words.

"Didn't know he'd *become* Templar." But it made sense, in a way.

"I feel the *fool*." Her voice broke on the last word.

"Don't." He stepped beside her and glanced over, brow furrowing when he caught her pinching her eyes shut, expression pained. "I *never* thought you one. And I do *not* think you one now."

Fuck distance. Skorpius placed a gentle hand on her shoulder. Brigid tensed, but didn't pull away.

His chest ached. "What we had, what we share now between us, it's all still real."

"'Tis based on lies."

"Inconsequential. Only trivial things along our crossed paths, required tasks of my mission. Lefts or rights at unimportant forks in the road. Not what drew us closer on our path."

"But"—she glanced toward him, eyes glistening with unshed tears—"how do we know what matters?"

"Nothing matters in the end. It's the middle that counts the most." Their stolen moments.

You matter. What he felt, but couldn't express. Because it would be another lie. Of course Brigid *did* matter. More than anything he'd ever stood for, believed, or loved, she mattered. But not more than *all things*. No one had that right. Not her. Not him. Not them, together or otherwise.

"Aye." Brigid gave a slow nod. "Life's journey." Her voice had quieted.

Heavy tension between them thickened the air. Made every breath they took a struggle.

Chest aching, lungs burning, he let out a slow exhale. "An amazing journey. Down to the smallest moment," he murmured. *Every one of them. Amazing. Worth it.*

Skorpius felt the sudden warmth of her golden energy. Sensed her envisioning the same.

But everything remained strictly on the emotional plane.

Uplifting energy vibrated all around, but centered strongest from within her.

And she radiated it outward, but focused. A tidal wave of love and adoration. A million lifetimes worth of happiness and pure joy filled him, heart and soul.

But then slowly, as all euphoric things do, the ecstatic feeling faded.

Until no connectedness remained.

To his bone-shaking shock, the dual mission tethers disintegrated. *Both* of them.

Their hearts' bond? A dead filament.

Whatever Brigid had done, whatever challenges they'd faced up until that point, their sudden devastating heartache ended the threat. To her person and to time itself.

Then the obvious conclusion hit him.

It wouldn't have been enough for them to have never met.

They'd had to love. To grow and brighten together. Then accept it as enough, and let it go.

They'd never had a choice.

And Skorpius no longer needed to kill her.

Brigid had already killed them.

CHAPTER 38

*B*rigid dinna know what to do. But she could no longer remain on her path. Not with Skorpius.

Her heart *ached*. The pain of multiple betrayals had gutted her.

"I'm done." *No more hunt. No more magick. No more goddess.*

Skorpius stared at her, his blue-green eyes dulled. "You believe it's that simple?"

"'Tis whatever I wish it to be."

Pride sparked in his gaze. Which told her he knew she spoke the truth.

Then his eyes narrowed a wee bit, and his head tilted. "What of Robert?"

The missing lad. "Do you know for certain he's alive?"

Skorpius exhaled a slow breath, gaze locked to hers. "No."

Her callin', the pull to move forward on her quest, had faded. Nothin' vibrated as "urgent" any longer. All felt hollow, empty…dead.

The magick within had receded down into the depths of her loch, a mere ember.

And if she dinna use it, no threat would remain to Clan

Brodie, nor to the timeline or realms. She understood that now. Her magick had been the cause of everythin'.

"What of us? That was real, Brigid. We are true, and always have been."

She dinna need magick to feel his mirrored pain. The agony vibrated between them, hot and heavy.

"I need to think. I need time."

He coughed out a dry laugh. "Don't we all."

"Without you."

Torment tightened his features. "Well, Brigid. You finally get your wish."

Skorpius vanished.

Her breath caught. The overwhelmin' loss of his powerful presence was immediate.

Brigid pinched her eyes shut, a painful cramp in her throat.

She burned to cry out, to find some release from the anguish.

But the Templars were gathered behind her, out of sight, but there. Because of her.

No matter. Not any longer. They'd have no use for her if she denied her nature.

And so, without explanation, with the use of her powers one last time, Brigid vanished.

The world's better off without a heartbroken goddess in it.

As Brigid dissolved into the ether, she emanated a frigid blast onto the ember of magick.

And the golden flame within…extinguished.

CHAPTER 39

*S*korpius deadened his emotions—a skill he'd mastered over the last eight hundred years—and flashed through the timeline with a singular thought in mind.

Which made him reappear in the distant past.

Brigid may have broken the tethers, ending his official dual mission.

But Skorpius didn't need obligation to bind him into guardianship. Not of time. Nor of her.

Danger still lurked out there.

And he intended to tie up loose ends.

When he materialized into Earth-realm's past, *his* mortal *past*, he skewed his arrival a few hours off and a dozen yards away, to avoid detection. Of his former self. And anyone else.

Lacy ferns masked a cave entrance. Spongy moss covered the ground in all directions.

Tendrils of cool mist writhed along lazy air currents, undisturbed by foreign movement.

Skorpius strode forward, dematerialized through thick foliage, then stepped into the inky darkness of the cave beyond. Intuition pricked at his senses, along with awareness of a unique and powerful presence, one that rang familiar—in two time periods.

A drip echoed into the ancient chamber. Another soon followed.

Cave odors filled his nostrils: musty, moldy, earthy.

Closing his eyes, he allowed his preternatural senses to take in the vastness of the underground symphony of life. Nocturnal creatures slithered and slid. Fungi grew and stretched. Microscopic organisms multiplied on moist clay and in pools of water. Crystalline stalactites hung from the ceiling, and condensation slowly spiraled down from their thick bases to their tips. The mineralized droplets of water then plunged, one by one, into dark pools below.

Movement across the chamber caught his attention.

Skorpius snapped his eyes open, then narrowed them on his expected target.

A deep breath filled his lungs.

Rapid-fire thoughts and images assailed his brain. Past and future funneled together in his mind until only the crisp clarity of the present moment came into view.

"Returned so soon?" The male's voice purred soft. He continued to sort and drop herbs into a crude iron cauldron, not bothering to shift his attention away.

"It seems we have unfinished business."

"I've no further insight to provide you, knight."

A smile played at Skorpius's lips as he remembered the "counsel" he'd requested so long ago as a part of his deep-cover mission. In service to a legendary king, prior to the man's loss of his bride and fall of his kingdom. "I'm not the same knight who sought your help so long ago."

The male paused in his work, weathered fingers hovering over an open vessel, the slender neck of a flask held in his other hand. "You speak of hours as if they passed as decades."

Instinct ruled Skorpius's next actions and words. For if he'd arrived without the timeline balking, then his presence there served a purpose: to learn, acquire, to share. It mattered little which it was, for he'd been trained to flow with his gut and be true to himself.

"Try *centuries*, wizard." Out in the open.

With a long exhale, the male who'd been too busy to deign casting full attention toward Skorpius slid the flask into a slotted-wood holder, then glanced up. A candle that had been partially melted to his granite-slab worktable flickered a flame that danced in the male's eyes.

Skorpius didn't bother to hide his wings. The sorcerer had seen plenty of the fantastical over the course of his life, had likely conjured up most of them. What was one more amid the many?

Still, his opponent's breath caught. Dark eyes widened for an instant, then narrowed.

"What magick is this?" The accusation echoed off the cold stone walls.

"No magick."

"You are not the man who left me hours ago. You are *not* Lancelot."

"I am not." Skorpius ruffled his feathers. "And yet, I am."

The male sneered. "Trickery."

"Says the sorcerer who recklessly commands the elements of his world like a god. Have care what you meddle with, *Merlin*." Skorpius loaded the uttered name with angelic magick, resonated his undeniable power to his foe.

The sorcerer's body turned rigid, expression hardening. "What do you want?"

"Good question." Not to kill the madman at that moment. The timeline wouldn't allow such folly. Events still had to play out.

An unruly dark eyebrow arched at him. "Why have you appeared to me in a different form? Are you not human?"

Skorpius spread his black wings wide, to remove any doubt about what he'd transformed into: *very* not human. "The man you know of in this time is not me." *Well, he is…but he isn't.*

Knowing the power of secrets in Earth-realm, he decided on a particular tact.

"Tell Lancelot nothing of this visit. We shall keep it to ourselves, yes?" Skorpius's conspiratorial whisper caused Merlin to lean forward a fraction. His eyes widened, no doubt along with his ears.

A slow smile curved upon the sorcerer's face.

Oh yes, secrets were a currency greater than gold.

"Do you foretell the future? Do you hail from another world?" Merlin's low voice held a steady, strong tone. It spoke of power and knowledge. He possessed more of both commodities than any other being on Earth, during that time.

Skorpius snorted, unsurprised that he sought more of both. Merlin always tried to get an angle, any edge to help him achieve greater power. A damning fault.

"My story is of no consequence to you, wizard. All you need to know is that you will gain more power. And then you will meet a female who will make you give it all away."

Merlin gasped in outrage.

Romantic history had penned the cause of his demise as a lover he'd grown obsessed with.

Recent events suggested a goddess would bring him down.

Either way, the wizard's advanced knowledge of his fate would make him try to avoid it. Which tended to manifest the outcome with even greater certainty.

"Will it be a witch?" Wide eyes stared at him, seeking, wanting the key to his salvation.

The corners of Skorpius's mouth twisted into a wry smirk.

Merlin didn't need to know further details.

"You will find out soon enough."

Done with the task and satisfied with the outcome—bets

hedged that the wizened sorcerer couldn't grow powerful enough to destroy the fabric of time—Skorpius slipped back into the timeline.

Then a hard tug diverted him toward an unexpected destination.

CHAPTER 40

*B*rigid stirred. Heat surrounded her body.
    Exhaustion tugged her down…
Down…
Utter blackness enveloped her.
Some unknown time later, awareness trickled in once more.
Distant booms echoed.
A fainter bang resonated.
Swordplay rang out.
Yet all seemed muffled.
As if heard through the depths of a great loch.
She fought, kicked, reached, but sank yet again, down…
Down…
A heavy door slammed.
Midday sun shone down, warm and invitin'.
Clouds passed overhead.
Grays of gloamin' darkened.
Then stars glittered across a clear night's sky.
Mists floated in, surroundin' her.
Cool Highland mists, kissed with the promise of life.
Angelic mists, playful, iridescent, rich with the power of magick.

Longin' filled her heart.

Till immense ache burned a gapin' hole there.

With a gasp, she bolted upright.

Awake. Alive.

Disoriented, Brigid took in her surroundin's. She lay in a bed. Damp linen sheets were tangled about her legs.

I'm back at Brodie Castle.

Brigid launched out from the bed. She splashed water on her face—that maids must've freshened when they'd discovered her slumberin'—fastened her hair back with a leather tie, then dressed in a fresh linen chemise and pale blue day dress that had been folded on a chest. All by hand, as she'd done for eighteen summers.

No magick. Never again *magick.*

At the thought of magick, the agonizin' pain set in. The loss of her one true love. And his devastatin' betrayal.

Heart heavy, she left her bedchamber.

But all her cares faded the moment she entered Brodie Castle's bustlin' great hall.

Dozens of people flitted about, hangin' long garlands of pine and fir. Scarlet ribbons were bein' draped along the mantel. Fine silver ornaments glittered in a pile on a trestle table.

Isobel turned toward her, her belly swollen with her bairns.

Four months forward.

"Brigid!" Joy brightened her friend's face. "You're back!"

Brigid dinna know *how* she'd managed to return.

Mayhap a stray thought of her bed within Brodie Castle had sent her there?

Nor did she know for certain how long she'd lain there in those tangled sheets. Hours? Days?

But then, with the vastness of time—and the precious gifts that only lasted for the blink of an eye—Brigid had become painfully aware of how little it mattered.

CHAPTER 41

Following the lead served by the timeline, Skorpius partially materialized into another familiar place.

More than a millennium-and-a-half forward from the cave he'd just visited, into the future.

A different musty scent filled his nostrils.

Undertones of the rich spice of leather teased his brain.

Formidable bookcases stretched up toward a coffered ceiling trimmed in crown molding.

A vehicle horn honked in the distance.

Skorpius spun around to confirm. *Maclaren's office.* He'd reappeared in the office of Isobel's professor and mentor. *In the twenty-first century.*

His gaze snapped to the desk. *The magickal box.*

The artifact still stood there—unmoved.

Hidden power snapped from beneath its surface, begging every cell in his body to touch. The object, a servant that recognized its master.

"Why?" The word hung in the air, the riddle of his journey gaining complexity. Because his inner chronometer registered a date *after* he'd pointedly removed that particular box from that desk—when attending to his mission to usher in the Traveler so many months ago. And yet, there the artifact sat. Which meant someone, at some point, had repositioned it there. *But who?*

Accustomed to a clear itinerary on missions, the mysterious labyrinth he traversed continued to bring challenge he hadn't faced in centuries.

Excitement thrummed through his veins at the facets of the game.

Then another inexplicable pull snapped his attention to a large paned-glass window. A human female stood some forty feet beyond, her hand grasped by another female attempting to pull her forward.

The female, tall for a human female, with straight hair of dark ebony, dug the stiletto heels of thigh-high boots into manicured grass. She slowly lifted her gaze toward the window. Toward Skorpius.

The female's blue eyes locked on to his.

Her ability to see him was unmistakable.

Even though he had not taken full corporeal form.

Skorpius expanded his senses toward her.

"Chelsea, *come on.* We're late already," her friend pleaded.

But the female ignored her and wrenched her hand free from the unwanted grasp.

Chelsea lowered her face but never took her gaze from Skorpius. Instead, she narrowed her eyes and took a measured step toward the window. Then another.

Curious, he shifted his focused awareness away from the artifact, then ghosted into the shadow of the drapery.

Chelsea's gaze followed for those few brief seconds. When he stopped, she held his position. She'd conveyed that his movement and current location had been detected and noted.

Then her gaze traveled to the box. Her lungs inflated with a quick inhalation. A slow smile curved her lips.

Skorpius's jaw dropped.

The force that had brought him there wanted him to witness that female *see him*. And the box. Perhaps the timeline wanted Skorpius to understand that Chelsea recognized what both of them were.

"*Chelsea Morgana Smith.*" Her companion dropped her hands to her hips. "If you don't come with me this instant, *as you promised*, I will completely disown you as a friend."

Chelsea licked her lips. Hunger glittered in her covetous gaze. She scanned the side of the building. Counting windows, noting the location of the office, he guessed.

Her gaze flicked back, holding his in clear message: *I see you. I know you see me too.*

Skorpius gave an imperceptible nod in reply: *Game on.*

Understanding washed through him when Chelsea finally allowed her friend to drag her into the adjacent building. Of why he'd been diverted there: A greater timeline scheme unfolded.

Chelsea was unique among humankind. And her friend had no idea.

Likely no one of her world did.

And Chelsea's existence proved what angelkind had long suspected would happen, given enough centuries.

Accomplished what Merlin had been trying to create his entire life.

That humans—born as physically weak but intelligent creatures—could harness energy.

And evolve into something...*more than human.*

Skorpius sighed and pinched his eyes closed. His fractured heart ached at the devastating reminder of a spectacular female that had become *so much* more *than human.*

One who had become *everything* to him.

CHAPTER 42

*N*igh a sennight had passed since Brigid had awakened in her bedchamber.

The first handful of days had dragged by, helped by a buzz of activity in decoratin' the castle to prepare for what Isobel called "Christmas."

A second handful of days had passed a wee bit quicker, before and after the arrival of the kind lass Susanna. *An* English *lass!* And their clearly smitten-with-Susanna commander, Robert.

Brigid had done her best to ease Iain's concern over her whereabouts over those past months, skirtin' the topic and avoidin' him as best she could. And her dear friend Isobel had done her best to aid her cause.

But one afternoon, Brigid had tossed in her sleep durin' a nap fraught with nightmares—mixed with sensual dreams of all that she'd lost. And she'd thundered down the stairs shoutin' into their great hall. Evidently half out of her mind, all care tossed to the wind.

"I am done with that damned angel!" Brigid stormed up and barged in between an arguin' Isobel and Iain, arms crossed over her chest.

Iain's gaze snapped to Brigid. "What did you say?" He stepped closer, glaring at her.

Unafraid of her brother, Brigid shot him a frosty glare. "Done."

"The rest of it." Iain's voice iced over as he towered over her.

Her voice lowered, vibratin' hot with banked emotion. "With. That. Damned. Angel." Brigid arched a brow at him.

"I hadn't been aware you'd been with that damned angel." Iain raised his brows.

Seconds crawled by as he waited, a laird and older brother expectin' an explanation.

Brigid relented on a sigh. "Aye, Iain, you have. You know Skorpius had been bound to protect me. Weel, I've been gone a while, you've been busy with the clan, and 'tis a verra long story." She arched a defiant brow at him. "I'll share it when I'm ready."

And then, the celebration of Christmas had begun in their great hall one night.

Brigid had been handin' out tankards of a spiced apple cider that Isobel had insisted upon. When a sudden pulse of energy had flared hot in her breast, straight to her heart.

And as she'd glanced up toward the source, there he had stood, magnificent as ever. *Skorpius.*

His gaze had shot her way at that same instant.

Agonizin' pain had shredded her heart anew at the sight of him. "What is *he* doin' here?" she'd shouted, after he'd dangled a green bundle with a red ribbon from a hook over his head. Somethin' about *mistletoe*, Robert had remarked. Then the whole room had faded away.

Skorpius's chest had risen and fallen deeply as he stared at her.

A great sense of affection had emanated from him.

It had *infuriated* her.

The night had passed in a blur of anger and avoidance.

Till she'd collapsed into her bed, utterly spent. Then had sunk down into a deep slumber.

Down...

Down...

*D*ARKNESS PREVAILED.

Drips echoed.

Crystalline surfaces glittered.

Stagnant moldy air filled Brigid's lungs.

Nay. Not her *lungs. Another's.*

Small. Frightened. The boy? Robert?

But...'twas as if she *were* he.

Confusion reigned. Am I *aware in a dream? Or was it a vision?*

Regardless, her senses were as if through the boy's body.

A choked-off whimper lodged in her throat.

The beast must not sense my fear.

Shivers of cold.

Brigid came to her own awareness again and searched, but she couldna see. Where am I? She wondered.

Starin' into the darkest spaces, then glancin' around, she began to make out the features of what seemed like a cave. But not enough to know where the place was located. Which she'd need to do to transport there.

Och! No magick. Never again *magick.*

Mayhap, just the once. 'Twould be worth it for the boy.

But would it? Or would all the realms be endangered?

A hot angry vibration rippled forth.

Arms banded around thin legs, huddled into a ball on the wet cold stone, she held her breath and hoped the beast wouldna notice her.

Putrid stench filled her nostrils when she finally gasped for air.

Then a tarlike scent followed.

A metallic taste lingered on her tongue.

Faint clicking moved from right to left.

The scrape of a heavy, long object dragged by.

She tucked her feet back, pressed herself against the wall.

Prickles tingled. The sensation of bein' watched.

Forever there. Forever watchin'.

Forever waitin'.

Forever... there.

Brigid startled awake, gaspin' for air. Tears sprang to her eyes, heart achin' for poor Robert. She'd felt his fright, was certain that she'd had a vision of his whereabouts in her dream.

Or had it been a trick?

Merlin had done so before.

Usin' only her human senses, she scanned through the shadows of her bedchamber.

Moonlight streamed in from the narrow windows, their tapestries pulled back. Dyin' embers glowed from the stone hearth.

But only cold silence filled the space.

No presence appeared to be there. None but her own.

Reason made her believe all she'd had was a bad dream, darkened by her worries.

Then her mind traveled where she'd forbidden it to go, to the wise advice of a guardian: *Focus on what we have the power to control. Let worry afflict the weak-minded.*

And then her heart ached at the memory of the dark angel standin' proudly in their castle's great hall. Mere hours ago.

"*Och!*" Brigid yanked the linen covers back over her head. She forced herself down into the deep calm of her motionless loch, then willed herself into a *dream*less *vision*less sleep.

CHAPTER 43

Skorpius had known that he'd likely encounter Brigid at the castle.

When Isobel had sent him on the mission to obtain mistletoe for her Christmas celebration?

He had made a sarcastic remark, as per usual.

Had told Isobel nothing, as per usual.

But not one thing within Skorpius remained remotely usual.

Anticipation of returning to Brodie Castle thrummed through his veins.

Because he'd actually hoped to run into Brigid.

Hoped.

Like some lovesick human adolescent.

And at the sound of Brigid's angered reactionary outburst, his pulse had accelerated.

With excitement.

And joy.

All *feelings* no self-respecting warrior angel ever embraced.

Yet the sight of Brigid, eyes blazing with fury, tempestuous emotions running hotter than ever, at the sight of him?

Worth it.

After too many days of trying to occupy himself without any new mission, popping into various timeline points as a casual watcher, monitoring the progress of Cass with Connell and Gunna—from afar, so as not to interfere with their adjustment —he came alive with a true purpose again.

Gain back Brigid's trust.

Except...*now what?*

Skorpius had no plan. No clue as to how to proceed.

Other than a strong desire to get under her skin again.

Brigid had told him she needed time to think.

Skorpius had given her almost a week.

Ages, as far as he was concerned.

SKORPIUS HAD DECIDED to give Brigid another full day to recover.

Or stew.

Either worked in his favor.

But he refused to waste one more night.

The festive excitement at the castle had elevated to a fever pitch. Based on the chaos in the kitchen, the priest located in the great hall, and the palpable level of anticipation in the air— to do with their commander, Robert, dragging newcomer, Susanna, under the mistletoe the evening prior?—Skorpius would swear a Highland wedding was about to take place.

Angels didn't partake in such vow-filled nonsense.

But then, Skorpius had apparently evolved beyond mere angel. Twice over.

And he had an entirely different kind of bond to secure.

When guests began appearing through the hall's front door, Skorpius floated his shadowed energy through the darkened hall upstairs, down the way from the bedchambers. Right as Brigid and Isobel stepped out from one of the doors.

Brigid slid flattened hands down the bodice of an emerald gown while Isobel adjusted an unruly copper ringlet that had fallen loose from Brigid's hairpin. Once the curl had been secured, Isobel clasped Brigid's hand and began leading her down the hall toward the stairs.

Until Skorpius fully materialized.

Both females paused and turned toward him, peering into the shadows.

Angelic power had that effect.

Brigid scowled.

Skorpius engendered that effect.

She sighed heavily, then turned toward Isobel. "Go on without me."

The Traveler glanced down the hall then turned back toward Brigid, casting her a concerned look. "Are you certain?"

"Aye. I hold my own with him." Brigid turned back toward him after Isobel nodded then departed out of sight. "I'll deal with... *Cupcake.*"

At the condescending nickname, an instinctual growl reverberated from his throat.

But then the corners of Brigid's mouth twitched, as if she fought a smile at his reaction.

Oh, yeah? She liked him riled?

Right back at you, goddess, he cast out to her. *I love how you hold your own with me.*

CHAPTER 44

*B*rigid stalked down the hall, the silken skirt of her favorite emerald gown rustlin'. As she neared the darkest alcove at the end, she heard the door to Susanna's bedchamber softly thud as the Englishwoman closed it to join those gathered in celebration downstairs.

"*Why* are you hoverin' here, Skorpius? I *warned* you to stay away from me." Her blood nearly boiled over as his spectacular form came into view from the shadows. No amount of fury at him lightened the impact he always had on her—a fact that angered her all the more.

He gave her a cool smirk. "Why *ever* would I want to stay away from you? You wear pissed-the-*fuck*-off so very well."

Accustomed to modern-speak profanity from Isobel and Iain, Brigid rolled her eyes.

"*Niiice*," he purred, drawin' closer.

Brigid backed up a large step, not that one fiber of her Highlander self would ever back down from a fight or challenge—especially with *him*—but...she found she couldn't breathe. Skorpius had stolen all the air.

His immense power washed through her.

Dark.

Erotic.

Undeniable.

In sudden panic, she turned.

But Skorpius flashed from feet away to *against* her, pinnin' her body to the cold stone wall.

Brigid froze, immobilized.

Those glossy black wings arched high over his head, then curled around her body. The soft warm feathers brushed over her bare arms. He towered over her, then bent his head down. Strands of his wild hair tickled across her cheeks.

Brigid turned her face away, did her best not to inhale, and pinched her eyes closed. "Go. Away." The words got growled out between clenched teeth.

Her traitorous heart fluttered a rapid beat.

And unable to hold her breath any longer, lungs burnin', she finally inhaled deeply.

When his musky cinnamon scent filled her nostrils, she well-nigh sobbed as a flood of tender memories crashed through her.

Skorpius's voice softened, a deep raspy purr that misted heat over the skin of her neck. *"No."*

Brigid wanted to punch him, wished she could knee him in the groin...*needed* to make him feel some fraction of the pain she felt—the all-consumin', torn-to-pieces, scorchin'-veins-with-*everra*-heartbeat torture she'd been endurin'. Yet their closeness and his massive strength prevented her from causin' him physical harm. Though she knew if she delivered it...he would take it.

"Please." The whispered plea that fell from her own lips both surprised and irritated her.

Skorpius eased back. His blue-green eyes seemed to flash

their own tortured pain at her. "I'll do as you wish...for now. But you know it's impossible for us to part. You've seen to that."

And then, to her amazement, a hot flare seared into her breast. Their hearts' bond vibrated anew, from a surge of magick from him. The thread glittered bluish black, golden white, and a third flamin' scarlet color.

Brigid set her jaw, anger firin' hot. "*Doona* make this my fault," she growled, advancin'. "'Tis true, *I've* made choices. But *you* made them first."

Skorpius edged back while she pressed forward. But his unexpected yieldin' only bolstered her aggression.

Brigid pushed into his space until he'd backed against the opposite stone wall. She glared up at him, her nostrils flarin'. "*Mine* were selfless. Yours...were not. Touch that good heart I *know* you have down deep in that chest of yours and give me the space I need. Do somethin' for another, for once."

A dangerous low growl came from his throat, vibratin' so powerful, it rattled her teeth. The beast within him flared and his eyes *did* flash at her, brightly, their blue-green color swirlin'.

Skorpius bent low into her face, forehead nigh touchin' hers as he stared at her, heated gaze penetratin' her verra soul.

Brigid held her ground, refusin' to move.

"*Every damn thing I've done since I've met you...has been* for *you*." Pain radiated from him.

Agony burned in her heart. From havin' injured him. From bein' destroyed by him.

Expression tortured, his eyes drifted closed. He inhaled deeply, as if capturin' her scent.

Then he abruptly vanished.

Brigid stumbled forward into the cold stones of the wall, where he'd stood a second prior.

Tears sprang to her eyes, heart feelin' as if he'd ripped it straight from her chest and taken it with him.

But she stifled her sob. Choked down her emotions. Pinched back her tears.

Then Brigid squared her shoulders, turned on her heel, and strode down the hall toward the celebration downstairs, toward her clan. To be among family: those who'd never betray her.

CHAPTER 45

*L*ess than an hour later, Robert and Susanna's nuptial proceedings had concluded.

The celebratory feast had commenced.

Musicians played a lively tune.

Revelers danced with unbridled gaiety.

And diners ate and drank…and laughed.

Skorpius materialized in the kitchen and leaned a hip against the corner of a sturdy worktable.

The cook and four servers stared wide-eyed at him.

"Hungry?" A server angled a silver platter with a roasted goose toward him.

"No, thank you." Polite decline. Human custom. Helped pass the seconds until the next part.

Three.

Two.

One.

Brigid stormed into the kitchen, from the back entrance.

Skorpius glanced at her, unhidden warmth in his gaze. "Hello, love."

"You."

"Yes. Me." Skorpius shoved off the table, spread his legs shoulder width apart, and squared his shoulders, preparing for battle. "And you."

No doubt in his mind.

The trouble would be getting Brigid to admit it.

Brigid swept a cutting gaze at her serving staff.

But in their paralyzed shock, no one moved a muscle.

Chest huffing with unspent energy, she lifted an empty crystal bowl from a wooden buffet and hoisted it high, as if to throw it at him. But she clenched her jaw and replaced it back down.

"*Out*," Brigid growled, glaring at him.

"You want to throw something at me."

"Aye."

"But you don't wish to *actually* destroy a prized object." Crystal and glass were still rare at that Earth-realm time. Rarer still, sought after, and incredibly expensive in the Highlands.

Her eyes narrowed at him. "Out," she commanded again.

"Magick would come in handy." An innate nature that she struggled to keep a lid on. "Create a bowl. Destroy a bowl."

The kitchen staff either didn't take the hint or didn't think Brigid had been addressing them. But with their rigid stances and glazed-over eyes, Skorpius suspected they'd been shocked into inaction. One way to solve that.

On the worktable between them, he manifested a lineup of fist-sized launching items: crystal bowls, silver platters, glass stemware.

Brigid grabbed a silver platter and beamed it at him.

He dematerialized long enough for it to pass right through him.

The platter crashed against the stone wall.

A golden goblet followed. Then a bejeweled tankard. Followed by a crystal wine decanter.

Each time Skorpius went incorporeal for the split second required. Satisfying explosions followed.

The staff blanched, white as ghosts. At Brigid's throwing. At his disappearing.

Then Skorpoius glared at them, flashed his eyes, and snapped his wings wide. *Out!* he bellowed into their feeble minds as his primary feathers scraped pots and platters off the tables to launch them crashing to the ground.

The gawkers scattered in an instant.

Skorpius folded his wings back, rounded the worktable, and stalked Brigid with measured steps.

She edged back, keeping the distance between them. "You lied!"

"Withheld *mission-required* information." Not much of a defense, but the truth.

Magick simmered just under the surface of her anger. A shimmer of golden aura flared out, but then vanished when she drew in a deep breath. Her struggle to contain her massive power was evident. To find release, she fisted her hands, let out a hearty growl, then screamed in frustration.

Breaths labored, eyes wild with fury, she reached for another item to throw.

Skorpius manifested a fist-sized crystal ball onto the worktable.

Brigid pitched it at his face.

When he shifted incorporeal, the ball sailed right through him, out the kitchen doorway, then collided with satisfying smash on a stone wall out in the great hall.

"I never directly lied to you. Not about anything that mattered. *Never* about us."

She grabbed a crystal platter from the table, then whizzed it with the flick of her wrist. "There is no 'us.'"

After the platter sailed right through him, he materialized once again as it shattered in the other room.

He held her gaze, took more slow steps forward. "Now who's lying?"

Brigid backed farther away. And moved dangerously close to flaming ovens.

Skorpius stopped his advance, not wishing her to be harmed.

"You're twistin' things." She advanced a step toward him, face reddening. "I trusted you!"

When she reached for a plate filled with food, Skorpius manifested a half dozen expendable metal items in a row.

Brigid plowed through the lineup, launching each item at his body. All the while, she growled and shouted unintelligible words that vibrated with the pain of her emotions.

Yet for each one of those missiles, Skorpius decided to remain solid. He took the beating she wanted to dish out. Each item bounced off his muscular frame, then ricocheted in various directions around him: crashing against a kitchen wall, banging across wooden shelving, clattering to the floor.

Tears welled in her eyes as the last was thrown. Her lower lip quivered, but she bit it into submission. "Where are the wee ones?"

"The children? Safe." All he'd been able to divulge at that moment.

Brigid pinched her eyes shut and shook her head. She wrapped her arms around her middle, an effort to console herself.

Skorpius longed to pull her into his arms, wanted to ease her suffering. Yet he'd been the cause of it. And she needed the fight between them, all part of the healing process.

"I canna stay here. I doona belong," she muttered. "Not any longer."

Wearying of the fight, she drew in a shaky breath, then exhaled, shoulders slumping.

"You belong with me." To prove it, he pulsed another burst of magick along the thread between their hearts. And the bond vibrated with warmth.

Brigid gasped in surprise. "Doona…"

But Skorpius didn't stop. Couldn't even if he'd wanted to.

He took another step closer. "It takes courage to be true to ourselves."

"Doona touch me."

"To accept who we are takes bravery."

"And what of bein' true to another?"

Skorpius held her mercurial gaze. "Trust without proof takes the greatest strength of all."

Tears sprang to her eyes again. Deepening breaths grew ragged. Trembling lips parted, but no words came forth.

With a tortured groan, she lunged forward, punched her fists forward to knock him out of her way, then fled into the castle's great hall.

Skorpius scowled, displeased that she still denied the truth beneath it all, and stormed after her. Nothing in any realm would stop him. Not even her doubts.

When he entered the great hall, he caught a glimpse of her copper tresses flying behind her before she disappeared down a dark corridor on the opposite side of the hall. The wedding celebration in the middle of it had ground to a silent gawking halt.

Onlookers stood motionless on the dance floor, stared at him from the trestle tables.

Father John, the clan's priest, stepped forward, as if to intervene. Yet the male gaped at him and crossed himself. Twice.

Skorpius glared at the brave but foolish male as he passed and arched his wings high. "Not. One. Word. *Priest.*"

Then he shot a scathing look toward the clan's commander, Robert. A warning.

But Skorpius never broke stride and crossed the large room in a handful of seconds.

As soon as he penetrated the deeper shadows of the corridor, Brigid burst out from an alcove. *"Doona follow me!"*

"You've said that before." Before they'd come to know one another. Before they'd realized they were different. And made for each other.

"I mean what I say." Silver eyes sparked at him, full of passion.

Finally taking the liberty he'd been longing to, denying himself no further, he enveloped her in his embrace and brushed his lips across hers.

A gasp feathered across his mouth.

Their hearts' bond surged with renewed strength, glittering bluish black, golden white, and a novel burnished scarlet.

And they both joined into the kiss, tender, slow, filled with love, pain, and a fragile glimpse of hope.

Until someone approached, about to enter the corridor from the great hall. The Traveler, by the energy signature. A friend Brigid would need for support.

Skorpius drew back, holding Brigid's gaze with ferocity.

"Take great care." He tucked a stray hair behind her ear. Wide entranced eyes stared up at him. "You're leaking magick again, *goddess*."

The glittering aura she'd been unable to contain seconds ago —as she'd surrendered to their kiss—snapped back inside her.

Skorpius fought a smile as he licked the sweet taste of her from his lips.

Not only had he gotten under her skin, he'd proven that she needed to take a good *truthful* look there herself.

Then he vanished. To give her the last amount of time any of them could afford.

CHAPTER 46

*B*rigid wandered the keep the followin' day, lost inside the tumblin' thoughts in her head, confused by the jumbled emotions of her achin' heart.

Isobel and Susanna had consoled her the night before.

When Skorpius had vanished—again.

After he'd kissed her. And…she'd kissed him.

Oh, how she longed to believe him. Trust in the two of them.

When she ventured back through the great hall for the hundredth time, her brother Gawain stood at the far end, facin' the Christmas tree they'd decorated as a clan two nights prior under Isobel's direction.

Brigid dinna need to see what had captured his attention.

For she knew of the great treasure he'd hung there from a branch.

"Forgive me," she murmured, then turned to leave him be.

"Nay." Gawain glanced over his shoulder at her. "Stay a moment."

"Verra weel." Her heart went out to the brother she'd inadvertently wronged. To the child who'd hated her, that had struggled to embrace her existence all her life. To the warrior who'd only recently begun to come around and warm to her. In his own way.

She came up beside him.

He eased closer, till their shoulders nigh touched.

For long seconds of silence, they stood side by side before the tree.

And they stared up together at an ornate silver-and-gold pendant that hung from a high branch by a delicate silver chain. The necklace had belonged to their mother.

His shoulder nudged against hers. "I *do* forgive you."

Her eyes pinched shut, holdin' back tears. She swallowed past a cramp in her throat.

Then she exhaled a lifetime of relief. "I'm grateful for it."

"Follow your heart," he murmured.

"What?" Brigid stared at him, confused.

Gawain turned toward her, dark green eyes starin' into hers. "The angel."

"Skorpius." She felt it important that her brother knew the angel's name.

He gave her a nod. "Don't waste your time here."

"But...how do you..."

He snorted. "Everyone knows."

"*Oh.*" The thunderous fight from the night before.

His hardened gaze searched hers. And a flash of recognition brightened his expression.

Then he repeated words spoken years ago to a wee lad and days ago from a protective sister, "Death and life, 'tis but a thin veil betwixt the two. *Cherish those ye still have, whilst ye have them. Hold them dear.*"

And love yer wee sister, Brigid remembered the hopeful advice she'd given. Tears welled in her eyes all over again.

"I *do* love you, wee sister."

"Gawain, I..." A weight fell heavy upon her chest, and she found it difficult to draw breath.

Strong arms pulled her into a warm hug.

And the tears fell. Sobs wracked her body.

But Gawain dinna let her go. He only tightened his hold. Let her fall into the release she'd desperately needed.

Long seconds later, the torrent subsided. After a sniffle and a hiccup, she pulled back. Then she rested her head under his shoulder and stared back up at their mother's glitterin' pendant.

"Gawain? How did you find it in your heart to forgive me?"

"Nay." He squeezed her shoulder. "Speak no more of forgiveness. 'Tis been long granted. You'd done nothin' but fight to survive. And you've lived with great happiness. You've brought joy to this clan."

"But..." Brigid recalled a far different childhood. "You'd always shunned me, been cold."

"Aye." He sighed heavily. "A young lad's pride and anger. But I'm older now. No longer the fool."

She thought of her anger with Skorpius. About things that he'd felt he'd had no control over. "Mayhap fools are slow to forgive."

But Brigid dinna want to be the fool. Not with another's heart at risk.

"Aye." Wise and older Gawain glanced down at her again. *"Follow your heart."*

CHAPTER 47

$\mathcal{T}$he night after their kitchen blowout, a jarring pulse of power vibrated along the hearts' bond that connected Skorpius to Brigid.

But when he flashed to her location, darkness filled the space.

Brigid slumbered in her bedchamber.

Yet in the next passing seconds, her brow furrowed, she whimpered, tossed to one side, turned to the other. Linens tangled around her legs in what was clearly a disturbed sleep.

The golden magick she'd been keeping a lid on in her waking hours had drifted outward. The shimmering fabric of her diaphanous gown fluttered away from her prone body in an unseen energy breeze that she discharged.

Brigid. He cast her a gentle call on the mental plane.

Seconds ticked by. Another restless turn followed. Breathing shallowed. Lips parted.

But no reply.

"*Brigid.*" He punched her name with power.

She gasped, then startled upright.

He remained right where he'd arrived, standing at the foot of her bed.

Copper spirals of hair tumbled about her shoulders. Silver eyes sparked with magick.

"Skorpius?" Doubt tinged her tone as she furrowed her brow.

"You…" He began an explanation, but a sudden flash of uncertainty gave him pause.

Would she welcome him?

Or were they in for another spectacular fight?

Sarcasm felt wrong. After what they'd been through, she deserved more: a softer approach.

And the truth. "Our hearts' bond burst out to me. And I'd thought…it seemed…you'd needed…assistance."

Awkwardness had never been a trait he'd possessed before.

Skorpius blamed the fractures in his heart.

And whatever "evolution" he'd succumbed to.

"Nay," Brigid murmured, stepping from the bed. "I dinna need 'assistance.'" Holding his gaze, she took measured steps toward him. "I need *you*."

Brigid made no attempt to hide her shimmering magick. Instead, she flared her energy out, broadcasting to all the realms that the goddess was back. And more powerful than ever.

When he opened his mouth to speak, she placed a finger over his lips.

And they instantly transported to another realm.

Into the total darkness of his lair.

Then Brigid leaned up and pressed her lips to his.

The kiss began soft, tender. But soon ignited into a passionate storm, breaths shallowing, pulses quickening.

Their clothes disintegrated as the heat between them electrified.

Skin to skin, they crushed together in a tight embrace.

An eager whimper flared from her throat.

A primal growl tore from his.

And in the hidden dark corner of a realm that had created them both, two powerful beings cast different from their own worlds, found solace in one another's arms.

When Skorpius wrapped the warmth of his arms and wings around her, Brigid shoved him against the cold stone wall.

And as she closed her eyes and tilted her head back, he trailed frenzied kisses down the column of her neck.

While he got lost in her sweet exotic scent across her shoulder, then down between her breasts, she roved her hands across his abdomen, then down between his legs.

She gripped his arousal, then pulled hard.

He spun them around and hoisted her high.

And as they clung to one another in his private enclave of darkness, she fell, he thrust, and they crashed together in an explosive burst of energy.

But their simultaneous orgasm was only the beginning.

Magick burst forth from them, then circled back around and surged through them again, heightening their excitement, fueling their need. A glittering bluish black glow flared out from the surrounding rare-element stone surfaces: floor, walls, ceiling.

And as the angelic realm's elemental magick wove together with her unique magick and his, unusual colors sizzled into existence. Rooted from a darker spectrum, blended hues of rich warm gold, deepest black blue, exotic burnished orange, and fiery scarlet sparked into their atmosphere.

Their movements slowed as the ecstasy heightened.

Skorpius backed off the wall, holding her tight, plunging so deep they were seared into one.

Brigid clutched and clung, arched and curved, wrapped tighter and rode harder, as she surged ever-increasing intoxicating power from her heart's center to his.

The two of them climaxed again and again.

Their coupling was primitive and aggressive, beautiful and brilliant.

Magnificent. Skorpius kissed her tenderly, as they floated down from an extraordinary high, bodies calming, hearts warming. *Just like you.*

Brigid smiled against his lips. *Magnificent like you.*

Like us.

Aye. Perfect. Together. Us.

They collapsed down—onto a soft mass of black satin pillows and sheets manifested from their entwined imaginings —becoming a lazy satisfied heap of tangled arms and legs.

And for a silent span of moments, there they laid, basking in the bliss of their reunion.

Their sparking newly created magick drifted down, back into them, renewing their powers.

After a time, once breathing deepened and pulses steadied, Brigid splayed an open hand over his chest, nuzzled her face against his neck.

She placed a gentle kiss there, then exhaled. "I forgive you."

Skorpius closed his eyes and exhaled a great sigh of relief. "Thank you."

Then he made a private vow. Never again would anything come between them.

They were one in their quest. And if that meant the destruction of Brigid to save time?

Then they'd tumble into that abyss together as well.

CHAPTER 48

*T*otally spent and thoroughly charged all at once, Brigid pushed up from a mountain of shiny black pillows.

Skorpius leaned up on an elbow, starin' at her with banked heat in his gaze.

She smiled at him. "What?"

"You look happy."

"Aye." For Brigid finally belonged. To Skorpius. And to the world. It had taken her to fully accept who she was—who'd she become—to arrive there. But in that moment, naught felt truer.

"Well, then. Get dressed." He stood and manifested his leathers and boots back on. "We've got two errands to run."

With a tinglin' exhale, her golden gown flowed about her body. "Errands?"

"Would you like to meet Cass?" Skorpius offered her his hand.

Nervousness spiked through her. But then, she banished the feelin' and slid her hand over his palm.

And they transported from the darkness of his lair into the brightness of the outer world.

Angelic mist swirled about in playful tendrils, flashin' with tiny rainbows as the particles twirled. A great sparklin' river meandered through white sandy banks. And on the rise through hills of fluff, stood an enormous crystalline tree with a massive clear trunk and a sprawlin' chandelier of branches.

But as amazin' at the incredible tree was, what had been suspended within it made her gasp.

Amidst faceted crystal leaves, perched on a wide bough that flattened toward the trunk, was a spectacular open-air tree-house. Glitterin' latticework stretched up two sides. A solid wall of mist closed in the back. And the front stretched open to over-look their sparklin' river.

Squeals of joy and tinklin' laughter pierced the quiet space as two familiar wee ones charged off the front edge and leapt high into the air. Thick ropes of mist instantly formed within their reach. And as the children caught the misty vines, tendrils of mist wrapped around them and swung them safely to the ground.

"Connell! Gunna!" Brigid burst with happiness at the sight of them, hale and whole.

The children ran up to greet them, barefoot and in gauzy white linen tunics. Long blond locks bouncin', cheeks pinked, smiles wide.

But wee Gunna paused before her, then curtsied. "Lady Brigid."

Connell bowed low, then glanced at his sister. "*Goddess Brighid.*"

Brigid bent down and swept them both into her arms in a hug. Then she kissed each of their temples. "*Brigid,*" she corrected, "if you please."

The children tore off toward the crystal tree's trunk, then began climbing with unseen foot and handholds. "Watch us again, Brigid!" Connell called out.

Skorpius gestured an arm wide. "And this is my sister, Cass."

A glorious angel with snowy white wings and pale blond hair stepped forward from the base of the tree. An imposin' figure, to be certain. But Brigid felt no animosity from her.

Cass gave her a welcomin' smile. "You must be the female who captured my brother's heart."

"Aye." Brigid glanced at Skorpius, warmin' at the truth of it. "And he mine."

The white angel strode forward and tugged Brigid into a strong embrace. "Cherish him. *None* compare," she murmured into her ear.

Brigid drew back, confident in that fact. "Agreed. And I do, and will, with all that I am."

Cass gave her a hard nod. "Splendid."

He stared at them both with an incredulous expression. "You know I can hear you."

Brigid hardened her features. "If you prefer, we can reenact smashin' kitchen fights."

Skorpius enfolded Brigid into his arms. "Let's save our fight for the real battles." He gave a quick nod to Cass. "Speaking of, on to the next errand."

"Well done, children!" Brigid called out as the two wee ones flew through the air to catch their thick misty ropes.

Then Skorpius and Brigid vanished.

CHAPTER 49

*S*korpius brought Brigid straight to the archival map in the angelic realm.

Clasping her hand in his, he bent down and gave her a tender kiss. Then he touched his forehead to hers and closed his eyes.

Their time had ended.

The battleground awaited them.

"When your magick reached out to me—"

"Our hearts' bond."

"Yes. You were tossing in your sleep. A vision, perhaps?" He'd had a hunch.

She frowned. "Aye." *The same nightmare I've had everra night. Over and over.*

"Did you see a place? Identify where to go?"

Her brow furrowed deeper. "Nay. And I've tried. I can feel the boy, Robert. He trembles. He's cold. Hungry. Thirsty. And terrified."

Skorpius turned her toward the inert wall of mist that hung before her. "Try now. This is a very special map. If you think of a place, stare, and visualize hard enough, the location you seek will appear and grow larger."

"In truth?"

"Yes. If you concentrate hard enough. And if your envisioning supplies enough details."

Brigid stared intently at the misty wall. *There's darkness*, she thought toward him as she recalled the vision. *Wet stones. A musty odor. And crystalline spires hangin' from the ceiling.*

No change manifested on the map. The mist remained placid.

Brigid sighed in frustration. "'Tis not obeyin'."

Skorpius shifted to stand behind her. Strong hands rested upon her shoulders, slid down her arms, then folded over her belly to tuck her against his solid strength. The warmth of his breath fogged over her ear. "Close your eyes. Go back to your vision. Find your calm and *become* Robert."

Slowing her breath, Brigid drifted her eyes closed. Seconds dragged on into minutes. But soon, the map began to respond. Skorpius waited until landmarks populated, rivers and lochs appeared, mountains stretched forth and shorelines expanded.

Open your eyes, Brigid.

"*Och!*" She pointed toward the expanding image of a cliff on the northwestern edge of the Highlands, above the ocean. "There! 'Tis the cave from my visions. Robert's there!"

Skorpius stepped beside her. "Then, so is Merlin."

Brigid shot him a hard look, passion and determination in her gaze. *All or naught.*

Do, or die trying, he added. *Together.*

Till the verra end.

Pride fired hot in his chest, sizzled across the hearts' bond they shared.

That's my warrior goddess.

That's my darkest angel.

With a last glance at her target point, and no doubt the

vision firmly in her mind, Brigid held out her hand to him, prepared to take the lead.

More than ready to follow her anywhere, he clasped her hand.

And they vanished.

Skorpius and Brigid materialized into the center of an enormous cavern.

Crystalline stalactites and stalagmites stretched from the floor and ceiling, connecting into glistening columns—eerie sentries to an underground realm.

Stagnant air hovered, moldy and oppressive.

Through the surrounding rock, moisture percolated in slow measure from the unseen world above. One drop at a time eventually fell in various shadowed recesses, their occasional pings echoing along the hard surfaces.

Brigid released his hand and strode forward, undaunted by the dark unknown.

While her attention drifted upward, she emanated a brighter golden light. The aura surrounded her, then expanded outward. And as particles of stale air began to glitter with the warmth of her essence, a freshness began to swirl through.

Skorpius coughed out a dry laugh. "Of course. You're ionizing the air."

She frowned. *I canna feel Robert.*

He's here. He had to be. *Search with me. Something's bound to be familiar.*

"What're those markin's?" She nodded up the farthest wall as she approached it.

Giant vertical lines scarred the rock walls. One after another appeared, all in a clearly human-created line. Or *other-than-human* created.

"Ah. I'd wondered where it was." Skorpius spoke aloud, hoping to incite their hunter out into the open.

"Where *what* was?" Brigid's gaze lingered on the long row of uniform indentations.

"Merlin's secret source." Oh, yeah. Skorpius laid it on thick and loud. Perfect sorcerer bait. Speak to the egomaniac.

"Secret source?"

"The sarsens. For Stonehenge. Legend says Merlin himself placed the rocks. But they were quarried from an unidentified cave. I believe we're standing in it."

"Why lead us here, then?"

"Reach out with your magick." *Follow along, my love. Trust me.*

With a surge of energy from Brigid along their hearts' bond and a brief nod, she closed her eyes. Her expression relaxed into sweet serenity.

Then in a gentle wave, particles illuminated. The number increased by tenfold, then tenfold again. Until trillions of tiny atoms sparkled with her silvery gold hue. And each particle became an extension of her senses as she probed through dark, analyzed their surroundings.

After a time, she expanded the particles outward, *through* the stone surfaces, and beyond.

A slow gasp escaped her lips.

Brigid's eyes opened and she pegged him with an awestruck stare. "'Tis an incredible power, vaster than—" she stopped short.

Understood. They treaded lightly with words or thoughts and energy, to avoid manifesting that negative thing. "Likely the source of Merlin's power. Why meet us on Earth-realm turf? He probably thinks he has some home-court advantage here."

"Nay." Brigid shook her head. "The source is elemental. Available to all."

"Who have the ability." Skorpius gave a slow nod, volleying the trap-baiting back to her.

"Weel, Merlin doesna know that."

"Apparently not."

A percussive surge of power detonated through the air.

The ground shook beneath their feet.

Dust rained down from the rock ceiling overhead, fissures splitting open from the stress of the sudden quake.

"'Tis inconsssssenqential," a booming voice ricocheted through the cavern.

"'Bout time you showed." Skorpius stretched his awareness outward, but detected nothing. "We were just discussing your downfall."

"Yoursss…" The location of the voice shifted, ghostlike.

"Nah." Skorpius shrugged, not bothering to track the wizard. "I just checked my schedule. Not my time yet." *Baiting? You bet.*

"You'll ssssee." Additional sounds emerged as the source of the voice moved around them: gravel scraping, minute clicking. "The time for heroesss hassss passssssed."

"So has lispssss," Skorpius taunted.

Yet in spite of the calm Skorpius endeavored to embody, an ancient dark magick rippled through the cave, ruffling his feathers.

Skorpius shook the slight agitation off and exhaled his own brew of ancient and dark. A spark of his blackish blue energy ignited, then glowed around him. He arched his wings, readying to fly. "Your disembodied voice doesn't spook us."

Brigid's golden magick began to draw back toward her, each glittering particle sharpening in vibration as its density increased. An instinctive protective shield.

Skorpius gave her an approving nod. His warrior could take care of herself.

Then he rolled his eyes toward the ceiling. "Face it, old man. You're *has-been* news."

"Not in thissss form."

A moving shape began to grow solid around them, cell by cell, piece by piece—gleaming metallic scale by metallic scale.

A claw the size of one of those Stonehenge sarsens took shape, attached to a reptilian foot the length of a bus.

Myriad clicks sounded as an enormous barbed tail manifested into existence and curved around them, gravel crunching and scraping as its weight dragged over the ground.

"Looks slow. Cumbersome."

"Aye." Brigid backed farther away from it as she scanned over the length of the legendary beast from its deadly tail up the hump of its back, as scale by scale, more of the creature revealed itself. "All the power you've drawn to sustain your form. 'Twill be your undoin'."

"Basssslesssss," the voice boomed. And an unearthly crimson illumination spread forth as the image revealed more and more: the glowing breadth of a chest, a thick serpentine neck, hooded eyes smoldering with ruby fire, an elongated snout tipped in smoking nostrils, sabered ivory teeth. "You've not yet *ssss*een all the glory of this*sss* form."

Nope. And they didn't need to.

If they were comparing physicality, the hollow bones in Skorpius's wings made for nimble flight. He'd take that any day over being a creaky cumbersome giant. "Looks uncomfortable."

Have you sensed the boy yet?

Nay, Brigid replied from afar. She'd moved along the perimeter, while Skorpius kept Merlin distracted.

"Feels*sss* invincible."

Keep searching, he urged Brigid. They had only a small window before things got ugly.

Skorpius stared straight into the fiery eyes of the dragon. "Only a fool would think so."

However, something disconcerting began to happen.

Brigid and Skorpius possessed an immeasurable amount of unique and powerful magick combined. Yet their energy started to swirl away from them—to coalesce around the creature.

And the power that clung to Merlin like a shadowy aura behaved far differently than most. Like each particle had become infinitesimal black holes, sucking every bit of the surrounding energy into themselves. The wizard had clearly tapped into some primordial source that Skorpius had no knowledge of.

Yet at the same moment of incongruity, a new ability manifested within Skorpius. He could directly detect the health of the timeline. And *what* threatened it. No tether required.

And he detected an enormous threat.

It felt as if a magnetic needle had formed within the well of his magick, pointing toward a threat, urgently seeking to strike it down.

And the targeting needle shot erratically back and forth.

Between Brigid and Merlin.

His timeline-protecting magick couldn't decide the greater threat: goddess or wizard.

Brigid had never been the sole threat to time. Her developing magick had only ignited its possibility. And Merlin's greed for power? Attracted him like a kamikaze moth to her newly fanned flame. The potentiality of their alliance—voluntary on Brigid's part or not—proved the greatest threat. A reality that Skorpius and his magick existed to prevent. No matter the cost.

"Come to me, goddess*ssss*." The dragon's ruby eyes glittered toward her, and a beam of the deep red particles burned a path through her golden energy, aiming to entrance her.

Brigid's magick surged outward, but then lost traction when Merlin's ruby beam blazed right through, a destroying flame to delicate snow.

Skorpius tensed to move, but found his entire being frozen in place.

Brigid appeared to be similarly immobilized.

Skorpius dug deep, finding faint sparks of his magick, but he lost his hold on amplifying the energy. *What kind of foul magick did you find, wizard?* Never had Skorpius encountered a power that could dampen angelfire.

Brigid's muscles shook with effort. The golden shield she'd erected did the same, particles vibrating. "*Nay.* I'll not go *anywhere* near you."

"Oh, but you will." Tendrils of heat swirled through the cave, snapping and sizzling every molecule of moisture in their wake. "For the sssssake of thosssse you love, you will."

A low growl reverberated out. From Brigid. "*Nay!* Doona dare be threatin' my people."

"Your people? Imagine the power *for them*. What would you do to ensssssure they never starve?" The dragon taunted.

Brigid's magick swelled, flooding the cavern with glowing light. But she didn't move toward the beast. And neither did her newfound magick.

Instead, with deep breaths, she began to calm.

Skorpius did the same, drew within, grounded himself into the origin of his magick. And his angelfire magick flared bright, growing in mass as his composed focus fanned its flame.

Merlin's beady dragon eyes flashed at the denial. "The child will serve well in your sssstead!"

Now! Skorpius broke free of the foreign enchantment, then blasted magick into Brigid as he launched into flight.

Found him! With a powerful blast of her own, Brigid broke free of her stasis. At the same instant that the dragon blazed an unearthly stream of fire at her.

An instant later, nothing remained on that stone floor but a scorch mark.

Brigid?

A muted energy vibrated back toward him. Not anything

that translated with meaning. But Brigid's energy signature all the same.

Stay alive. They hadn't discussed any plan. Hadn't made contingencies if they got separated.

Because threat to time or not, he and Brigid needed to figure that next part out together. After the battle. *Survive!*

CHAPTER 50

The instant Merlin had given thought to the stolen child, Brigid had arrowed a pulse of magick on to that image and captured the boy's location straight from his mind.

But she'd also had to fortify her essence, protect the part of her within her magick.

For the hungry turmoil inside the sorcerer's brain had roiled like a ragin' thunderstorm, hellish and destructive.

Then her energy had shot back from the dragon on the fiery flame it had surged forth. Brigid's awareness had ridden the dragon's fire as it had blasted over her fragile body.

Heat like none she'd ever imagined scoured at her essence.

And then she'd disappeared.

Chillin' blackness pressed in, suffocatin'.

Till her inner flame of magick reignited. And her golden glow filled a stone cavity no wider than a trestle table. With her layin' prone on its hard surface.

She pushed into a seated position, but still had to duck her head to keep from knockin' it against the low ceilin'.

Brigid then radiated some energy outward, similar to when she'd constructed her shield, to analyze where she'd gone.

Och! The clever Merlin had buried the boy into a tight chamber within the solid stone of the earth. No air moved in the space. The only water was scant condensation on the cold hard surface. Light ceased to exist in the sealed tomb.

A sudden faint whimper sounded low and to her right.

When she turned, she caught sight of a huddled form.

Brigid flared a probe of magick over him and pushed over to his side.

The poor lad had his head dropped between bent legs. Despair emanated from his soul. The pulse of his frail body had grown thready. Robert was wet, filthy, and wracked with shivers.

When he tried to lift his head, she had to touch a finger under his chin to help lift the weight. But that one small touch of his skin set her fingertip afire. The lad burned with fever. An unseeing gaze stared through her.

"Doona worry, Robert. You're safe." As can be.

And through that single touch to his chin and a burst of her magick, she transported him the only place she knew where Merlin could never reach him.

The total darkness of the tomb flashed into the bright whiteness of another realm.

And a crystalline tree house enveloped them, with latticework walls made of mist and the air vibratin' with the hopes of two other wee ones.

But Brigid dinna search for the others. She couldna stay.

Instead, she infused the feverish boy with a powerful healin' dose of her magick, eased him onto soft ivory pillows that she'd manifested for him, then called out into the ether. *Cass?*

Brigid.

The children have a surprise waitin' in their tree house. She shot the angel an image of the slumbering lad. *I must go.*

Understood. Well done.

BRIGID TRANSPORTED BACK into the cavern, but she'd intentionally positioned her return into a cramped low-ceilinged corner, a goodly distance from where the dragon had been located.

The instant she materialized, she powered down her energy. She sought the calmness of her loch while stokin' the inner flame of her magick to prepare.

And with all she had, she focused to calm herself. Kept up her strength. While she searched the cavern for Skorpius.

Glossy black wings soared overhead, then dove low. Skorpius flashed a burst of soothin' magick toward her. *Stay right where you are. Promise me.*

Aye. Brigid dinna understand why she couldna help, but refused to ask and distract him. For she dinna wish to cause Skorpius harm. *I promise.*

The enormous dragon slithered and curved through the massive cavern. Hints of movement flashed. The gleam of articulatin' scales appeared. Then disappeared.

Skorpius banked along the curve of the cavern, swung around as he arced high, and burst out a massive amount of energy. Then a bluish black ball of fire—the size of a cottage—blasted forth from his chest, roared through the cavern, and detonated along the spined back of the mighty beast.

The dragon never stopped his movements, appeared wholly unfazed.

However, Skorpius's wings flapped in slower rhythm as he circled about. His energy appeared to be fadin'.

Glee sparked in the dragon's ruby eyes. "Your magick is waning, angel. My form is*sss ssssuperior.*"

"Go ahead and think that, wizard."

Skorpius! Allow me to assist.

No! Stay where you are. He swung around, wingbeats draggin' as he tried to gain altitude. *Trust me.* A great amount of energy began to vibrate from him as he neared the cavern's peak then banked once again. *No matter what happens.*

Brigid swallowed hard, not likin' the dire sound of that. In any manner. On a shaky exhale, she sought the soothin' calm of her inner loch. *I trust you.* Whole truth. All she could offer.

Skorpius folded his wings back, anglin' down toward the dragon, then dove straight for him. A vibratin' energy burst forth from his body in a bright flare of blue light. And as his winged body descended alongside the dragon, an incredible ball of his blue fire exploded against the belly of the beast.

Brigid snapped her eyes shut from the blindin' glare.

But she reached out with her magick, attemptin' to sense what happened.

Skorpius landed on both feet, but stumbled forward, barely remainin' upright. He shook his head, then wobbled to the side. He appeared dazed. Weakened.

From behind Skorpius's strugglin' form, the dragon rose. Up and up the mighty beast stretched, great chest expandin' as it drew in breath.

Brigid opened her eyes and lunged from the space where she'd promised to remain. *Skorpius!* He couldna mean to ask her to stand by and watch him suffer. Surely, that hadn't been what he'd meant.

Those sparkin' blue-green eyes locked on to hers. "It must be done." He exhaled, shoulders slumpin'. "To save time." His wings drooped, the primary feathers crumplin' against the stone floor. "To protect them all."

A great wind funneled toward the inhalin' beast. Red-hot fire glowed from within its swellin' chest.

Skorpius swallowed hard, then pinched his eyes shut. *Know that I love you, goddess mine. Sacrifice. To protect them. Above all.*

Heart breakin', Brigid closed her eyes. *Know that I love you, angel mine. Always. Forever.*

The roar of flame was deafenin'.

The fire of a thousand suns blasted across her senses, even with the shield of her magick.

A cloud of chokin' smoke besieged her, burnin' her lungs, nose, and eyes.

Cold darkness then prevailed.

An eerie silence reigned.

The cloud began to dissipate with her tormented exhalation.

Unable to stop herself, Brigid rushed forward. Anguish burned hot in her heart as she stopped short of a pile of ash on the stone floor.

The dragon loomed over her, delight vibratin' in the air. "Victorioussss."

Brigid snapped out her magick into a multilayered shield to protect her, her magick, and what remained of Skorpius.

"Nay!" She crumpled to the ground where her bonnie angel had stood mere seconds ago. *"Nay!"* An achin' cramp choked at her throat. Agony burned in her breast.

Tears fell freely as she mourned the instant loss.

Sacrifice? The devastatin' pain was too great. They hadn't enough time.

I doona understand! She dropped her head into her hands and sobbed, stricken by her emotions.

"Oh, yessss." Merlin slithered around her, pennin' her in. "You ssssaved the child. Your lover fought valiantly for you. A true knight of old."

Brigid blocked the vile creature out. Extended her magick outward, searchin' for some sign.

The oily essence of the hunter seeped over her senses, coated her golden light with a sticky putrescence. "Submit, fair goddesssss. You, *and* your delicioussss magick, are now *mine.*"

"Nay!" Utterly destroyed at the finality of it all, Brigid

allowed fury overtake her. *"Never!* You will *never* attain me. *Never* my magick."

Tears streamin' down her face, she stoked the great well of magick within her.

Then she punched all of her power straight into the ground.

White hot, golden flamin' energy blasted out. And kept blastin'.

Silvery tears with salty sparks of magick flowed into the energy stream, flashin' and sizzlin'.

On and on, Brigid blasted all she had, everra last particle.

When the last of it flowed out, when all that remained in her loch was cold emptiness, she collapsed onto Skorpius's ash.

Tears continued to stream down her face.

But her magick? Ceased to exist. She'd willed it straight into the earth.

At the distant reaches of her awareness, Brigid thought she'd heard a dragon scream.

But no energy remained within her. Her power had been fully expended.

And barely able to draw breath, Brigid closed her eyes and waited to die. She dinna struggle, simply drifted downward. She wished to join her Skorpius in the afterlife, wherever he'd gone.

Into a strange place, she floated.

Time slowed.

Elements expanded.

Tiny embers of magick sparked within her fallin' tears as they dropped into the ash, one by one.

Power on a subatomic level began to gather.

Vibrations rippled forth.

At first, the slightest quiver.

Then a greater tremor.

Soon dust danced across the stone.

Brigid gasped as an odd surge of energy shocked over her senses.

The dragon reared back, beady eyes narrowin' at her.

Particles of ash floated up and began to swirl about.

Brigid backed away, wishin' and hopin'. *Skorpius!* she willed toward the strange outburst of energy. *Come back to me. Finish this battle with me!*

A great quake followed. The entire cavern bucked and moaned from the pressure of it.

All of a sudden, the pile of ash ignited into a roarin' fire of magick. Flames of darkest midnight, brightest white, brilliant gold, burnished orange, and fiery scarlet licked higher and higher.

Then in a great burst, a birdlike creature soared up from the ash in the brilliant rich colors of the flames, darkest at the core and glitterin' at the edges. Great wings of fire blazed. Twinklin' black eyes sparked with a flash of blue-green.

With an unearthly screech, the magnificent birdlike creature soared through the cavern with unbelievable speed, the darkest shootin' star.

The dragon swelled its great chest, flarin' up to breathe that deadly fire once again.

But right as Merlin opened his long reptilian snout, the shootin' star arrowed straight into its gapin' maw. And the flame the beast expelled ignited with the furious magick flames of the dark bird.

An immense explosion detonated through the cavern, then blasted down through the earth.

Brigid was thrown back by its percussive force.

She tried to snap out a magick shield. But only a fizzle sparked within her loch, then died.

So she instinctively curled into a ball.

Dust rained down from above.

The crystalline pillars shattered.

Deafenin' roars rumbled forth all around, the roof collapsin' into piles of rubble around her. But its sound distorted through her ringin' ears.

Till all the sound faded away.

Only her ragged breaths and thumpin' heart remained after the ringin' subsided.

After a time, even the dust cleared.

But then, she detected another sound.

The rasp of another breath.

Adrenaline shot through her and she bolted up, knockin' shards of stone off of her body. Filled with new hope, she shoved piles of rocks away from a large pile. Till she made out the shape of somethin' dull and black.

Dusty black *feathers*.

Skorpius? She collapsed beside the still form. *"Skorpius!"*

CHAPTER 51

*O*ne slow-firing synapse after another, Skorpius came to awareness.

The sound of his name echoed, somewhere off in the distance.

In Brigid's voice.

Concern laced her tone.

Fear, even.

I'm here, Brigid.

Och! A hard tug jarred up his arm. *You scared me nigh to death!*

I'm fairly certain I actually *died.* With concentration, he pushed himself up out of a pile of rubble.

Brigid grabbed his hands, helping to free him.

Then she drew him into her arms, and her soft lips covered his.

Relief cascaded through him as he lost himself into the sensuality of her kiss.

After their excitement calmed, he broke away. Then he glanced around, scanning across the darkness of the cavern. "What happened?" All he remembered was flying toward the dragon, and Merlin's furious mental cry at him: *I'll have my vengeance!*

Brigid's attention shifted down to stare at the stone floor. "Over the last hour, I've been gainin' magick back, bit by bit. Till I could finally detect some amount of his foreign energy."

"He's not dead?"

"Nay. I doona think so. But he is entombed. *Far* down into the earth."

"He's become part of the rock he'd mined." Vengeance thwarted. Perhaps permanently.

"Aye."

Weakened by the effort of their battle and the drain of their magick to end it, they leaned upon one another.

But then, Brigid stepped back, blinked hard, and scanned his body from head to toe. She stared over his shoulder. Then her gaze snapped to his eyes. "Your eyes are still the same, glitterin' blue-green with their sparks of flame and red."

"But I'm no longer the same, am I?"

"Nay. You've lost your wings. Are you no longer an angel?"

Skorpius glanced behind him, then arched his shoulders up and flared out a burst of magick.

Dark enormous wings shimmered into existence, far larger than before. Yet instead of pure black, the filaments of every feather reflected a dusting of gold. When he spread them wide, they reflected every color.

"Like ripplin' firelight," she murmured. "And your hair."

"What of it?" He shook it, catching a flash of color at the tips.

"It remains inky black at the crown"—she sifted her fingers through it—"but your temples and under-strands shimmer with gold, silver, and many fiery reds, from bright copper to deep burgundy.

"I've become *more* than an angel, I think."

"Aye." Brigid gave a slow nod, then glanced at the rubble-strewn floor again. "When you burst up from the ground, from nothin' but dust, you appeared as a great bird set aflame. Your wings blazed."

"I'd been evolving. But couldn't make the full transformation without that flaming death." Skorpius had instinctively sensed what was needed at that last moment. Every cell in his body had shut down to prepare for the resurrection. "A phoenix, from the ashes."

"You're a *phoenix*. Born again." She smiled then kissed him softly. "Like me."

"Like you." Born again. Both given a fresh start, to live an entirely new chapter—together.

Brigid slid her hand into his. "*And* a worthy male." Her gaze lifted, and she stared into his eyes. "*My* male."

The calming warmth of gratitude coursed through him, and a heavy sigh parted his lips. He closed his eyes and lowered his head. "You humble me."

She pressed a gentle kiss to his temple, then hovered her lips over his ear. "'Tis *I* who've been humbled. Just doona die. Never again. My heart canna bear it."

"Agreed." His new ability to monitor the timeline agreed as well. The sacrifice had been made. "I am yours. For every moment, of whatever life we've been granted."

"*All* the moments. I want them all."

"Greedy goddess."

"*Your* goddess."

Skorpius stepped back, clasping her hands as he took a good look her.

He had never seen any creature so beautiful, wanted anything more in his eternal existence.

But he wasn't the only one who'd transformed from the magickal explosions of their battle.

Hair that had once shined a coppery red had burnished into a darker golden yellow. Creamy skin now radiated a rose-gold flush. And those silvery eyes swirled and sparked nonstop, mercurial, molten. But her spirit of kindness and generosity shone through the brightest.

"*My* female." Mate of his. Whatever they'd evolved into. Whatever the future held.

Not that any of the details mattered.

Skorpius no longer had a duty to protect her. He'd done so with his last dying breath by choice. And he'd make that same decision all over again.

For her. For everyone in every realm.

And the rift in time? Had healed.

By their bold action, together willing to die for the good of all, they'd created an explosion of magick that had resonated through the ether, sealed the wound, strengthened its foundation.

"*The world's* goddess." Brigid belonged to them all.

Leaning against one another, arm in arm, they worked their way out from the rubble. Soon, fresh mineral scents ionized the air, leading them out.

After a dozen steps through a large gallery that led toward daylight, they paused.

The high vibration of powerful energy signatures spiked across their awareness. Additional souls had gathered, somewhere out there, beyond the outer threshold of the ancient cave.

Then they both glanced down. For the first time since the battle, they noted their nakedness.

With a crooked smile, Brigid manifested his black leathers and worn military boots, frayed laces and all.

Skorpius gave her a knowing look, then manifested a regal outfit for her, a goddess of nature. Across her shoulders draped a downy white cloak, fashioned from every naturally shed snowy owl feather along countless timelines. Beneath, her original deerskin hunting outfit appeared. Daggers weighted into their sheaths. A curving bow and quiver of arrows settled along her back.

Then, hand in hand, they emerged from the cave.

And they were definitely not alone.

The twelve Templars, including Fingall, stood on twin long-boats in the channel.

Additional knights stood watch from various cliff-side positions.

And fanning out from left to right, down the rocky shore-lines and perched along the cliff tops, stood the druid masters who had challenged Brigid in the field, staffs held high, hoods drawn forward.

But one by one, in a slow wave, each individual showed respect to their mistress. Every Templar planted his sword, took a knee and bowed his head, genuflecting in a great honoring succession. Each druid drew back his hood, bowed his head, and vibrated out a low tone.

Then the druids' toning grew in strength.

The genuflecting Templars stood upright in unison, then joined the druids' intonations.

Great slabs of stone from that far rocky shoreline, once sliced from the sheer cliff face by erosion and time, floated high into the air.

Then Brigid began to intone beside him.

Her magick flared, growing in strength, and the stone slabs soared higher. With a sudden flash of immense power from her, the massive stones launched out like a starburst, scattering over the globe.

Wherever the sarsens landed, and whatever else had tran-spired every step of the way along their journey, his new connection to the timeline hummed low in quiet approval.

And Brigid's garb had transformed yet again. Back into the shimmering golden gown that suited her best.

The druids and Templars continued to watch her from afar.

"'Twould seem that I'm called to serve them."

"At some point," he agreed.

"But not now." She let out a heavy exhale. "Not anytime soon."

Because that chapter of her journey had yet to unfold.

She glanced at him. "And the threat to time?"

"Gone." *Thank Authority.* "Ready to go home?"

"Aye." She held out a hand toward him. "Mayhap, we'll rest a while."

"But…*after*. Right?" He hovered his hand over hers.

Mischief sparked in those stunning silvery eyes. Then she clasped her hand to his and flashed them back to the private darkness of his lair. *Their* lair.

"*Aye*." Brigid shoved him against the wall. Then she obliterated their clothes and proceeded to kiss him senseless. "We'll rest a good long while. *After.*"

EPILOGUE

Grab the rope! Skorpius mentally shouted as they arrowed through the midnight sky high above a foreign Earth-realm land.

Race you! Brigid called back. A game they'd been playin' over the past days.

Both of them misted through the frosty air. So that she could fly as easily as he.

They raced toward a massive silvery cloth structure that floated perilously high over open ocean. Its fabric glowed for a few seconds as she dove toward one of the dozen golden cords that dangled from atop it.

She regained solid form and grabbed hold of the fat silk rope with both hands and entwined legs, swingin' forward from her impact.

An instant later, his incredible heat wrapped around her, arms banded tight around hers.

"Grab your *own* rope."

"We'll slide down together," he murmured, lips pressed to the shell of her ear. "Loosen your hands."

Instead, Brigid let go and grabbed hold of his muscular arms.

When he loosened his grip, they plunged toward a craft that hung below the inflated fabric.

Skorpius heaved outward toward the end, then swung inward to land them upon a polished wooden deck.

"'Tis a ship in the sky!" Twirlin' about, she marveled at the details. Benches along the side. Rails spannin' the edges. Colorful silk pillows were strewn about the floor, both fore and aft. Low tables offered food and drink.

"A balloon dirigible. An *airship.*" *Manifested just for you.*

From your imaginin'. Like he'd done with the sumptuous bed in their private sphere. Only their airship hung in the real world. Over a black ocean.

Fresh air swirled about them.

A loud blast of fire flared heat up into the balloon.

"What land is that?" She stepped in front of him alongside the rail and slid her right hand over his while she stared out through the darkness. Countless towers glittered on the horizon. "*When* are we?"

"That's Hong Kong." He gave a nod to their left as he wove their fingers together and wrapped his other arm around her. "We're here for Chinese New Year. Twenty-first century."

They'd experienced many adventures in the days over the past fortnight. Some within Earth-realm, as they explored crowded cities and wide-open spaces all throughout time. Others spent in alternate realms, in wonderment over strange landscapes and unbelievable life forms.

On Christmas morn, Skorpius had surprised her by deliverin' Connell and Gunna to become a part of Clan Brodie. But he'd flashed right back out to spend the day trainin' Robert. Apparently, exposure to the dragon's magick and time spent in the angelic realm had instilled powers in the lad the Authority found promisin'. And Robert wished to become a warrior angel.

When she'd asked, *An angel without wings?* Skorpius had replied, *Robert's transformation is yet to come.*

And durin' those days, there had been several missions Skorpius had to depart on, alone.

She'd even had a first duty of her own as goddess, a guidin' appearance with the Templars. In a cave secret to humankind. An introduction of sorts. To the vast powers of the mysteries.

But for the quiet moments to themselves? Like the one where they hovered high above a future Earth in one another's arms? Worth all the seconds they had to spend apart.

All of a sudden, flashes of color erupted into the sky near the towers.

"*Och! 'Tis lightnin'!*" She pressed back into his warm strength and glanced upward, right as another bright explosion happened, a glitterin' flower that blossomed over the water. "*Nay.* 'Tis not natural."

"It's fireworks."

"'Tis magick."

"*Hmmm...* Let's see if it is." Skorpius drew her to the other side of the airship. He stared out into the darkness, over open ocean. Then he surged forth a burst of energy and a bright explosion lit the sky with the fiery colors of his dark energy.

She clapped her hands. "Let's do one togeth—"

His lips pressed to hers. And energy flared along their hearts' bond.

Sensual and overwhelmin', she melted into the incredible kiss.

After a boom, then softer crackles, they glanced up to catch their newly created brilliance. A whole bouquet of magick blossoms exploded, some blackish blue, some flamin' orange, some deepest scarlet—all fringed with sparks of her silvery gold.

"The night"—she sighed, then stared up into his glitterin' blue-green eyes—"'tis perfect."

"*Almost.*" He kissed her softly, then broke away to stare down at her. "Close your eyes."

She did as he asked, tryin' not to smile. *You've spoiled me with surprises this last fortnight.*

Keep them closed. He shifted her hands: positioned her left upon his shoulder, slid his left beneath her right.

Her lips twitched. *Skorpius, are we about to* dance?

Another loud burst sounded, the airship's fire flarin' heat up into the balloon. Then total silence followed as they floated through the night-chilled sky.

No peeking.

In the next instant, she dinna have to.

Lively music exploded into her ears. Laughter echoed and feet stomped. Warmth brushed across her skin. And the scents of her clan's great hall washed over her: lavender rushes, cracklin' logs, cooked foods, pine boughs from Christmas.

Skorpius swung her about. "*Annnd* open!"

With glances left and right, she spotted faces at the edge of the floor before all continued on with their dancin'. Iain and a verra pregnant Isobel, slow dancin' in the corner. Robert and Susanna twirlin' much faster. And most of their warriors stompin' about with lasses held tight in their arms.

But Brigid's lovin' gaze landed back on her magnificent phoenix.

His wings blazed above: inky black to midnight blue to burnished flame to darkest scarlet.

Her golden gown shimmered and sparked, vibrant with her energy.

After all they'd been through, they were finally able to become their true selves. Who they'd always been destined to be. Surrounded by their clan. A family they together belonged to.

"Another Christmas celebration?"

"New Year's Eve." He glanced at Isobel. "I convinced someone to throw a party tonight."

For us?

For you. *And for them all.* "Do you like my surprises?"

"Aye." She laughed as he spun her. "Verra much."

"Good." Skorpius slowed their turn, then stopped altogether. Great intensity sparked in his blue-green eyes as he stared down at her. "Get used to being spoiled. Because a fortnight is the blink of an eye."

Filled nigh to burstin' with unbelievable happiness, Brigid sighed, leaned up on tiptoe, and kissed him softly. *Such romance.*

Power sizzled along their hearts' bond, bristlin' with a flash of irritation, then warmed with lighthearted amusement. *Tell* no one. *But this fractured heart and I are loving you into eternity.*

Thank You!

Thank you for experiencing Isobel's adventure with us in *Born of Mist and Legend*.

If you enjoyed the story, please express your love for *Born of Mist and Legend* by recommending it to friends in person, by email, on Goodreads, and through book clubs and reader groups.

And if you value reviews to help guide you into your next book, as we do, please help other readers by sharing your review of *Born of Mist and Legend* on your favorite retailer and book community sites.

Incredible thanks to everyone for extending your love of *Born of Mist and Legend*.

Reviews are cherished love notes to authors
and tantalizing invitations to readers.
Appreciated by all. ♥

Want to read more?

～

Escape to where it all began in the
the novels of the **Highland Legends** series…

Forged in Dreams and Magick
Bound by Wish and Mistletoe
Born of Mist and Legend
Found in Flame and Moonlight

～

Isobel's time-travels occur in the short stories
of **THE TRAVELER: Initiate Years** series…

Veil of Realms
Secrets of Alexandria
Panther Rising
Stones of Power
Highland Magick

～

ALSO BY KAT & STONE BASTION

THE TRAVELER: Initiate Years

Veil of Realms · Secrets of Alexandria · Panther Rising

Stones of Power · Highland Magick

Highland Legends Series

Forged in Dreams and Magick · Bound by Wish and Mistletoe

Born of Mist and Legend · Found in Flame and Moonlight

Unbreakable Series

Heartbreaker · Rule Breaker · Lawbreaker

Forthcoming: *Ball Breaker · Icebreaker*

No Weddings Series

No Weddings · One Funeral

Two Bar Mitzvahs · Three Christmases

For Valentine's

Standalone Novels · Novelettes · Collections

Brand New Year · The Espionage Effect

Braving Soteria: The Quantanauts Collection

Romantic Poetry for Charity

Utterly Loved

ABOUT THE AUTHORS

Kat Bastion won several awards for her bestselling debut novel *Forged in Dreams and Magick*.

Kat & Stone Bastion's bestselling first novel *No Weddings* and the No Weddings series were named Best of 2014 by multiple romance review blogs.

When not defining love and redemption through scribed words, they enjoy hiking in vivid wildflower deserts, ancient tropical forests, and historic urban jungles.

Join our Bastion Family Adventurers!

Be in the know with preorder alerts, exclusive bonus gifts, and occasional free stories:

https://www.katbastion.com/email-subscription/

Let's be social…

facebook.com/KatANDStoneBastion
twitter.com/KatBastion
goodreads.com/KatBastion
bookbub.com/authors/kat-bastion

CHARITY SUPPORT & AWARENESS

Your purchase of *Born of Mist and Legend* helps the victims of human trafficking because a portion of the net proceeds of all Kat & Stone Bastion's books are donated to charities who support them. These charities are creating legislation and prosecuting criminals, rescuing and restoring victims, and raising awareness in the effort to eradicate the tragedy of human trafficking.

"A single act of kindness is the foundation of many miracles."

— KAT BASTION, UTTERLY LOVED.